THE WILD INSIDE

THE
WILD
INSIDE

A NOVEL OF SUSPENSE

CHRISTINE CARBO

ATRIA PAPERBACK
New York • London • Toronto • Sydney • New Delhi

ATRIA PAPERBACK

A Division of Simon & Schuster, Inc.
1230 Avenue of the Americas
New York, NY 10020

First Atria Paperback edition June 2015

ATRIA PAPERBACK and colophon are trademarks of Simon & Schuster, Inc.

For information about special discounts for bulk purchases, please contact Simon & Schuster Special Sales at 1-866-506-1949 or business@simonandschuster.com.

The Simon & Schuster Speakers Bureau can bring authors to your live event. For more information or to book an event contact the Simon & Schuster Speakers Bureau at 1-866-248-3049 or visit our website at www.simonspeakers.com.

Interior design by Dana Sloan

Manufactured in the United States of America

10   9   8   7   6   5

Library of Congress Cataloging-in-Publication Data

Carbo, Christine, author.
    The Wild Inside / by Christine Carbo. — First Atria Paperback edition.
        pages cm
    1. Government investigators—Fiction. 2. United States. Department of the Interior—Fiction. 3. Wilderness areas—Fiction. 4. Glacier National Park (Mont.)—Fiction. I. Title.
    PS3603.A726W55 2015
    813'6—dc23   2014018897

ISBN 978-1-4767-7545-6
ISBN 978-1-4767-7546-3 (ebook)

For my mother, Françoise (Jeanine) Schimpff,
and my father, Robert Schimpff

Every death even the cruelest death

drowns in the total indifference of Nature

Nature herself would watch unmoved

if we destroyed the entire human race

I hate Nature

this passionless spectator this unbreakable iceberg-face

that can bear everything

this goads us to greater and greater acts . . .

—PETER WEISS,
The Persecution and Assassination of Jean-Paul Marat . . .

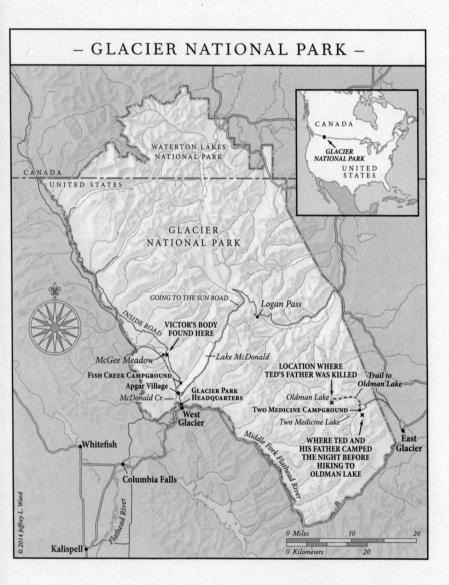

– GLACIER NATIONAL PARK –

WATERTON LAKES
NATIONAL PARK

CANADA
UNITED STATES

GLACIER
NATIONAL PARK

CANADA

*GLACIER
NATIONAL PARK*

UNITED
STATES

GOING TO THE SUN ROAD · Logan Pass

INSIDE ROAD

**VICTOR'S BODY
FOUND HERE**

McGee Meadow

— Lake McDonald

FISH CREEK CAMPGROUND

Apgar Village

McDonald Cr.

**GLACIER PARK
HEADQUARTERS**

**West
Glacier**

**LOCATION WHERE
TED'S FATHER WAS KILLED**

*Trail to
Oldman Lake*

Oldman Lake

TWO MEDICINE CAMPGROUND

Two Medicine Lake

**WHERE TED AND
HIS FATHER CAMPED
THE NIGHT BEFORE
HIKING TO
OLDMAN LAKE**

**East
Glacier**

Middle Fork Flathead River

Whitefish

Columbia Falls

Flathead River

Kalispell

© 2014 Jeffrey L. Ward

0 Miles · 10 · 20

0 Kilometers · 20

Fall 1987

PALENESS SLIPPED INTO the dark sky and erased the stars as gracefully and peacefully as if nothing had happened. I struggled for breath, my chest shuddering violently each time I pulled in the bitter air. My teeth clattered noisily, and I couldn't feel my legs. I knew my jeans had been wet earlier, and they were frozen and hard as cement now that the fire had faded.

I continued to stare in the direction he'd been dragged. All the noises had ceased except the sound of the gusting wind and the water lapping on the shore. But all the others—the screams, the grunts, the scuffling sound of the underbrush . . . Even the small animals I'd heard scampering for cover . . . had not resumed their activity. And the fire— its crackles and pops had stilled as it died to a pile of white ashes with small embers. I couldn't remember starting it. Couldn't remember feeding it and keeping it stoked. A gust of cold wind slapped the smoldering smoke into my face. I flinched and tried to stand, my numb legs not wanting to work. I clenched a long stick and stared at it as if my arm had morphed into an alien appendage.

I quickly looked back to the opening in the brush that I'd been watching for several hours, even when the light was syrupy dark and I'd waited for amber eyes to come for me. The branches of bushes and small, stunted spruce were broken, the skunkweed and bear grass flat-

1

tened and smeared with a trail of blood. I squeezed my eyes shut and pictured my ma and my sisters at home in their warm beds. I ached for my mom, for her arms around me. Then I heard the screaming again in my head. Right between my ears, expanding and pushing against my skull. I started to run, first stumbling, then full force. I ran and ran, faltering and tumbling over the hard, lumpy ground, over the edges of buried rocks and exposed roots on the well-maintained trail. I ran until it all went black.

1

Fall 2010

IF I COULD reveal one particular thing about my way of thinking it would be this: I was a fourteen-year-old boy when that feral, panic-filled night ruined my ability to see the glass as half full. It's still hard to talk about, but in terms of self-definition, nothing comes close to that crucial three-hour span of hellish time when the emotional freedom that comes from trusting the foundation one stands on would wither like a late-fall leaf. Up until then, my mom, Mary Systead, with her hazel eyes and dimples, a hospital pharmacist and a lover of self-help and pop-psychology books, had always ridden me about being a positive thinker, telling me that I had a bad habit of seeing the glass as half empty and that if I didn't learn to overcome it, it would have a bad effect on my life. At the time, I had no idea what she was talking about. And later, I couldn't imagine what could be more negative than what ended up happening: losing my dad and lying in the hospital for weeks like a heavy bag of sand, listening to the orderlies telling me how lucky I was not to have died.

But that desolate late-summer night all those years ago at Oldman Lake, the stuff of great sensationalism and freaky campfire stories, isn't what's interesting to me now. What *is* notable is my knack for glimpsing the dark intersection of good and evil in people and seeing how it can be traced back to that fateful period. Because, although this can be taken as positive thinking itself—and I'll admit that traces of it creep in—my critical nature has made me fairly decent at what I do, which is working as a special agent—we call it Series Eighteen-Eleven—for the Department of the Interior's National Park Service.

Most people think of me as a glorified ranger because nobody ever imagines that crime occurs in the nation's parks. But it does: drug manufacturing, cultivation and trafficking, illegal game trading, theft, arson, archeological vandalism, senseless violence, and, of course, homicide. Not to mention that the woods happen to be a great place to dump bodies. The United States has fifty-eight national parks with about eighty million acres of unpaved, unpopulated land. I and two guys from the department are trained to undertake homicide investigations and are stationed in the western region, which means our offices are in Denver so that we can cover numerous sites: Yosemite, Yellowstone, the Grand Tetons, Bryce Canyon, Glacier, Joshua Tree, Mesa Verde, Death Valley, the Great Sand Dunes, the Olympic Peninsula. . . .

Mostly, we work solo on cases, even homicides, since we have so much help from Park Police—they're Series Double-O-Eight-Three. Sometimes, being assisted by Park Police is helpful, but sometimes it's a pain in the ass since we're not in the habit of working together and we often clash in the way we go about the little things. It's the nuances, like knowing when to stay quiet, when to offer a small compliment, when to put on the unimpressed, bored look or to take the lead or to follow.

The other thing that can be traced to that night is my obsession with the grizzly. *Ursus arctos horribilis.* The grizzly was listed in 1975 as a threatened species in the lower forty-eight after being trapped and hunted to near extermination in the last century. One would think I'd be terrified of them, and here's the deal: I am. In fact, I became a policeman after college, because even though I double-majored in criminology and forestry, I felt this fairly significant panic at the base of my sternum at the thought of being alone in the woods.

There's a catch for me, though: when I read or know about one of them getting shot by a hunter (always accidentally they claim) or getting euthanized for becoming too dependent on human garbage, I'm conflicted. I can't tell if I'm pleased, sad, or pissed off. It's as if each time one of these specimens, with their scooped, broad noses, cinnamon and silver-tipped coarse hair, eyes like amethysts, and the infamous hump protruding like a warning, is killed, either another piece of my father dies with them or he is given a small slice of justice. Over the years, I've become more and more intrigued, as if they've taken on some godly status. I've studied them from afar—reading everything I could get my hands on: mostly journals and published graduate theses on behavior, habitat use, and demography. After all, knowledge is power, and power helps alleviate fear.

So one could say that for a detective-slash-quasi-grizzly aficionado, I was heading into a perfect storm with this next case. And I could say this about the case as well: my torn recipe for positive thinking, with its already unpatchable shreds, would turn to jagged teeth, biting me even deeper than I thought possible.

2

THE WAY I see it, negative thinking can have positive outcomes. Take my habit of rolling a quarter across my fingers, just under the knuckles where you teach kids how to track the number of days in the months. I'm a lefty, so I can only do it on that hand. When I was about fifteen I saw a guy rolling one behind the checkout desk at the County Library where my sisters and I would go after school until Ma finished work. I figured that since you could even get attached to the inanimate, to a particular object, you stood to lose that object. And even if careful, you could still misplace it, like when I lost the one-inch-long shark tooth I had found in the woods behind our house in Florida. I had religiously carried it with me everywhere for good luck.

But a habit or a behavior was different; you couldn't lose a habit, not one that you intended to keep. It could stay with you for the rest of your life if you chose it. So instead of getting attached to *a* particular quarter, like the 1964 all-silver quarter my father gave me when I was ten, if I could learn how to roll one instead, it would be the action I loved, not the object. If I lost the coin, it could always be replaced.

So rolling a quarter (this one happened to be a Vermont, with a man collecting sap from two maple trees) on a late-October early morning in our department offices in Denver is exactly how Jeff La-Matto found me. The coin's new shininess flickered as it flipped and slid down and out of each crevasse between my fingers, hid under my palm, then reappeared by my thumb to begin its journey again. My

7

coffee mug was full and the *Denver Post* spread before me. Being a Saturday, we were only teed up to work until noon.

"Well, Teddy boy." LaMatto caught me off guard and almost made me drop the damn quarter. "Looks like you're heading out in an hour and a half to your hometown. Better pack your undies." He threw the file he was holding onto the side of his desk. "Lucky me. I get to stay here on the Thompson case."

"What's happened?" I resumed my rolling.

"Didn't get the details, but it sounds like it might be a strange one. Boss definitely wants you 'cause of your expert*ise*." He hissed the *s* on the last syllable.

"Expertise?"

"Your neck of the woods, right?" Jeff knew that Kalispell, Montana, was where I went to high school and worked after college for the local police force for three years after getting my degrees at the University of Montana in Missoula. Three whole distressing years of feeling like I was going to suffocate in the town that my family moved to so my parents could find their mountain paradise: forty minutes from Glacier Park, twenty to the nearest ski resort, and fifteen to Flathead Lake, the largest natural freshwater lake west of the Mississippi. By that third year, in spite of the "big sky" and the open fields, everything felt too close: the streets, grocery stores, movie theaters, schools, barns, trees, and alfalfa and hay fields. Every time I'd get in my unit vehicle to work, I felt like I couldn't sit still and that my skin wanted to itch. Each pothole I'd hit on the shabby roads made my jaw clench. Each time I'd have to pull over to drag a bloated and bloody dead deer off a city road, I got more and more irritated. I shouldn't even mention the shotgun marriage to Shelly, the miscarriage, and our divorce eighteen months later.

I knew I had to get out, so I applied to the DOI Special Agent Series Eighteen-Eleven. I was perfect for the position because of my officer training and my dual degrees. After getting in, I did about fifteen months as a background analyst, another eighteen in trafficking, then worked my way into homicide. "Somebody dump a body in Glacier?" I asked.

"Not sure. Said something about a griz."

"Oh." I stopped rolling and wrapped my hand around the coin. I felt that tiny clench, like a small imaginary fist gripping right above my stomach. Nothing that surprised me; I've learned to live with it, like a person with an ulcer endures the knife twist of pain up high in their gut. "Has one fed on a carcass?" I pressed the serrated edge of the quarter into the point of my chin.

He shrugged. "Not sure. He was vague, but that's my guess. Said there'd been a mauling."

"A mauling?" I felt like I was being toyed with and eyed Jeff. His close-cropped strawberry-blond hair picked up the first strokes of dawn fingering through the large windows by our desks. A coworker and sometimes partner on more severe cases, Jeff loved to be secretive, feeding bits and pieces at a time like I was a dog begging for a biscuit. Plus he thought he was funny, like when he imitated Arnold Schwarzenegger or John Wayne. There's nothing more irritating than having to dredge up a fake smile or laugh for a partner. For a witness, no problem, for a partner, big problem.

"I guess you could call it that." He punched some keys on his cell, talking to me with the distant interest of a parent trying to complete a task while a child asks too many questions.

"What do you mean—you could *call* it that?" Feeding on a stiff is far different from a mauling, and if it was a mauling, it didn't have anything to do with us. The rangers handle maulings; we handle crime. "Either a bear attacks or it doesn't. They find drugs on the body?"

"Don't know." Jeff held his cell to his ear and stacked some files neatly to the side with his free hand. He'd been acting particularly superior for the past month and a half because he had solved a case in the Tetons involving a hitchhiker who went missing. If you asked me, he'd gotten lucky, getting a dead-on clue from a tourist who came forward with a picture he happened to take showing the missing guy right next to the Jenny Lake trailhead sign. What are the chances? When I mentioned it to Jeff, he gave me some tight-assed comment about luck being where "opportunity and preparation intersect."

For me, opportunity and preparation hadn't intersected for some time, and I happened to be on our supervisor's shit list and three-strikes-you're-demoted-back-to-trafficking policy. On my last case, I irritated some higher-ups in the FBI because my experience in background analysis came in a little too handy, and I ended up discovering some unsavory ties between the coal industry and a Virginia politician teed up to be appointed secretary of the interior. Sean told me I was getting older, losing my edge, and should know better than to poke around where I don't belong.

"He just said something 'bout a potential homicide victim and a mauling. Wants you in his office in five to fill you in."

"Why didn't you say so earlier?" My chair squeaked as I stood and slid the Vermont quarter into my pocket.

. . .

I caught the next flight out from Denver, leaving by 9:20 a.m. and arriving in Glacier Park International Airport an hour and a half later. It was 11:30 when a park ranger pilot named Moran, who didn't look more than twelve with chubby, pink cheeks like a baby, fetched me at the airport in a park helicopter used for backcountry searches.

By car, we were thirty minutes away from the West Glacier entrance, by helicopter, five, and since local crime scene investigations had already been on scene for a few hours, every minute counted. My supervisor, Sean Dewey, had informed me earlier that one of the two local FBI guys stationed in Kalispell had been called in to meet the chief of the Park Police and the county sheriff, but had deferred the case to us since the local FBI guys were knee-deep in some type of militia-band drama. Not to mention that they rarely dealt with homicide anyway.

I know it's confusing, but the way it works is this: when there's a life-threatening incident or a possible homicide in a national park, the National Park Police, which is federal, comes in and preserves life if there are survivors; then the scene. But to preserve the scene, they typically need help, so they call the county sheriff's office, which has concurrent jurisdiction with the part of the park it contains. Ultimately though, the feds have preeminent jurisdiction, so if the FBI or DOI think they need us, we come.

I threw my bags in the side storage panel of the copter, let the pilot lock it up, and hopped in. Just like in Denver, there wasn't a cloud in the sky in the Flathead Valley, just a dim haze from the locals burning their fall slash piles that paled the azure sky. Smoke—house fire, campfire, slash burning, chimney—it didn't matter. The smell of it would forever trigger something inside me. And campfires—I would never enjoy them the way most do. I shooed the pinprick of agitation away like an annoying fly. An eerie sense of calm lingered in the air, like this was just some fall day in which I was going fishing with some buddies, the tall peaks of Glacier looming in the distance, marking the presence of some ominous and separate world.

"Ready, sir?" The pilot looked at me after I slammed the door. He placed his headset over his navy cap, tentacles of fiery orange hair curling out from under, then handed me a pair.

"You new?" I asked as he finished his preflight.

"Been here two years." He smiled. "In my thirties," he offered as if he read my mind. "Been flying since I was twenty-one. For the Army. Finally got out after serving my last tour in Afghanistan and got lucky enough to end up here."

"Busy summer with the centennial year?" I changed the subject, not wanting to talk about anything on the personal side.

"Yeah, hugely busy. Over one-point-eight million. Absolutely nuts."

He flipped a few more switches and a high-pitched whine rang out as the rotors started. "Felt like I was working for friggin' Walmart. Thank goodness the place died right after Labor Day."

"Yeah, population growth—it's a bitch," I said into my mouthpiece against the escalating roar. "Happening even out in proposed wilderness."

Moran didn't respond, and we both sat for an instant before he began working the panel before him, as if he were pausing to think the same thing as me—that things *dying* for the fall meant the place was quiet and still enough for a crime like this one to go undetected. I peered across the airfields toward the highway while the rotors swung into full power. I knew the place too well: the highway billboards, the storage-unit business with the gimmicky windmill in front, the marble and tile store just past it, the feed and farm place where we'd buy deworming medicine for our dogs and cats because Ma thought it too expensive at the vet's and would do it herself. And, of course, the gateway to the park to the north. The Columbia Range to the southeast and the Whitefish Range to the west subsided into lower-elevation hills framing the park's luminous mountain caps. Their greenish-blue, tree-covered ridges contrasted with Glacier's treeless jutting peaks. People describe them as beckoning, like jewels, but, really, they don't beckon. If anything, they guard. They warn.

"The ranger that came across it," Moran said as we ascended. "She's pretty shaken."

I nodded. "Where's she from?"

"Pennsylvania. Been here for years, but has never seen anything like it before." He let out a small nervous laugh that I couldn't really hear but could see by the slight shake of his shoulders. "Not like these anyway."

"Sounds like it's a new twist for all of us." From my chest pocket, I pulled out my notepad, where I'd scrawled details down during my meeting with Sean and found the ranger's name along with the chief of Park Police, Joe Smith. "So, this ranger? Karen, Karen Fortenson—experienced?"

"Oh yeah. Probably mid- to late forties. Nice gal. Came to work Swift Current Lodge as a teenager. I think she's been here as a ranger since her early twenties."

"How soon did Park Police get it sealed off after she reported it?"

"Within thirty, thirty-five minutes."

"So no one else got near the scene besides this Karen and Joe Smith?"

"Not that I know of."

"How soon was the county forensics office called in?"

"As soon as your boss gave Smith the go-ahead." Moran flipped a switch on his panel. "Around eight thirty. They arrived 'bout forty minutes later."

I nodded. Working regionally, of course, meant we came in late and irritated everyone with our usurpation of the case. But the beauty of it was that there was less waiting for the details since much of the analysis was taking shape and much of the evidence would be getting photographed, logged, and bagged. In the park, where every raccoon, mountain lion, coyote, raven, and eagle wanted to get the remains when mama or papa griz was done with his or her share, the quicker an expert got on it, the better.

"We're touching down in West Glacier, and we'll drive from there." He banked sharply so that we could land a few miles south of West Glacier. As we descended near a group of tall cottonwoods, the vicious wind rattled the branches so thoroughly that yellow leaves filled the air like confetti, and I have no idea why, but for some reason, perhaps because of the frenetic energy the helicopter created, I thought of the televised New Year's Eve ball-drop in Times Square. We were a long way from the swirl of energy created by New York City's population, DC's, or even Denver's, and I found myself remembering the overpowering need I had felt after my marriage fell apart to leave this area—to go to a city where I could become anonymous, as if my life was a child's

Etch A Sketch toy and I could shake the slate clean, the drawing dissipating into a creamy fog of filament, and start over again.

. . .

Before we moved to Montana, we lived in Gainesville, Florida, and my father, Dr. Jonathan Systead, worked for the University of Florida as a pathologist. He came home every night smelling of formaldehyde and the mysterious tang of other important laboratory smells that the humid Gainesville air seemed to intensify in his clothes. One Saturday, a sunny fall day in late November—I remember it because it was the day after my twelfth birthday—my father took me to work with him.

The laboratory was smaller and more cluttered than I recalled. The last time I had been to work with him was when I was five. But it didn't matter, it still felt like a place where only intellectual and important things happened, even though I couldn't fathom what those would be. I only knew, as most young boys believe, that my father was the most important piece of the puzzle to whatever discoveries were being made.

In my memory, the room takes on a chiaroscuro effect—a narrow space filled with black microscopes, white rows of shelves with tall textbooks, old petrified bones, and joints on display, stained coffee cups on Formica countertops left from other students working under my dad's tutelage. A yellowing model skeleton dangled in the corner, and dark refrigerators hummed quietly in the background. My father sat me down on a black vinyl swivel stool, and I began spinning around and around until he said, "Ted, stop that. Not in here." I stopped and rested my bony elbows on my lanky thighs.

My dad turned the knob on a microscope and looked intently into the eyepiece. "I'm looking at what's called a frozen section," he said. "It's a very thin slice off of a brain."

"A human brain?"

"Yes. But I don't have a good sample here, so I'm going to need to get some more."

I hopped up from the stool and went and peered over his shoulder. "Who did you get the brain from?" My dad wore a white lab coat and thin latex gloves. He slid open the lid of the cold, glass machine that he called a cryogram. From the large blade in the center, he scraped a minuscule portion of white matter off a section of brain—frozen to a white cauliflower color.

"Someone was killed," he said. "Usually, we put the organ in formalin to preserve and study it. But with this one, the police were in a hurry to understand the pathologies associated with it, so when we did the autopsy, we cut a portion of the brain out and froze it in liquid nitrogen so we could study it immediately." We went back to his microscope with his sample on a thin glass slide, and I watched him grab another to prepare the specimen. When he was ready, he dimmed the lights.

"Why such tiny scrapes of it?"

"To learn about the body. Smaller segments teach about larger systems. I study these shavings to learn about pathologies, diseases— things that go wrong in the brain. *Mortui vivos docent.*"

"What?"

"*Mortui vivos docent.* The dead teach the living."

"Oh." I could tell he was going to that place in his mind where things got mysterious and too complicated for me. I figured he'd be silent now, lost in thought, when he surprised me. "School going okay?" he asked.

"Yeah." I looked at the shelf of textbooks, most of them with the words *neuro* and *anatomy* in the titles. Not that I needed to avoid his gaze; he was intently staring at his samples. I was no good in science. In fact, I had just gotten a slip from my teacher that day saying that I'd gotten a string of Cs and needed a parent's signature confirming they were aware of my grades. I still had the folded note burning a hole in my pocket. I began to swing again, side to side this time instead of all the way around.

"Good, well, I need to tell you something. Your mother and I have made a big decision." He glanced at me for a second, then back to his work. "We've decided to move."

"Move?" I said. "Where?"

"Montana."

"Montana? Isn't that really far away?"

"Yes. In fact, where we'll be going is less than an hour from the Canadian border."

"You're kidding, right?" I began to swing faster and farther to each side, my hands tucked under my thighs. My dad wrote something in a notebook beside his work, then placed the pencil back on the page and looked back at me. "I'm not kidding." He rubbed the bridge of his nose between his thumb and forefinger and placed his forehead back against the eyepiece. The little bulb under the slide projected upward, illuminating his forehead like a sliver of moon. "It'll be great. There's skiing, sledding, ice-fishing, snowball fights with your sisters . . ."

"But why?" I blurted.

"Many reasons. But mainly, we've always wanted to live near the mountains."

"But," I said again.

He lifted his head, his mouth lax and partly open, his eyes wide, filled already with other thoughts about his work. I didn't finish. I wanted to tell him that I couldn't leave my friends. How I was finally getting a little cool in sixth-grade middle school and that I didn't want to leave the beaches, swimming, and surfing. I wanted to yell at him, but I knew there was no use. Arguing with him was pointless when he sat that way, speaking slowly in his white lab coat, his eyes buzzing with curiosity and showing flashes of how his brain tick-tocked with all the important mysteries of the human body. I took my hands out from under my legs and began using my arms to swing, pushing off the counter next to me and splaying my feet wide.

He didn't look up. I swung faster, not knowing what to do with his news until my right foot hit the cabinet under the counter so hard that he startled and banged his nose against the eyepiece. "Ted," he barked. "How many times do I have to tell you not to do that?"

I looked down at the white floor, sulking about having to leave my buddies and the heat—the smell of Coppertone still thick in my olfactory memory bank. I was unaware that moving would bring consequences far more complex than the trade-off of beaches for mountains, surfing for skiing, and suntan lotion for long johns.

. . .

It shouldn't have surprised me that Eugene Ford was there when we landed in West Glacier, because it's business as usual for me to talk to the park superintendent whenever I enter their arena. But for some reason, it felt absurd that I should meet him not two minutes after having my feet on Glacier Park's soil. Moran introduced me to Ford and a Park Police officer, both looking stiff in standard gray-and-green Park Service garb. I already knew they called him Gene, even though in my fourteen years of service for the department, I'd never met him. In fact, Glacier was one of those parks that had the least amount of homicides of all the parks in the Northwest, so I'd only been needed on some small-time poaching issues early in my career, but his name loomed large in my family's history. In those days, I'd caught earfuls from my mother on him—how he'd lied to the press and blamed my father for being careless, that it all could have been avoided with more careful camping habits.

What I later tried to get my ma to understand was this: parks, ships, and prisons are tightly controlled places, and the super is the guy feeding the public relations officer and decides what goes out to the rest of the world. He may have made my father look careless, but he was only buffering the park, protecting the tourism trade, no matter the perfidy. I told her these things as if I had no hand in the game—a lie I would keep telling myself as I reentered Glacier.

"This is Officer Monty Harris," Ford said after we shook. He would have no reason to remember me other than the Systead name, and I'd be lying if I didn't wonder if he had any recollection of it after all these years. Suddenly, I became aware of every aspect of my appearance, every flaw: my disheveled hair, my slouching shoulders, my boyish face. "Officer Harris is going to tail you."

"Tail me?" I stood taller, pulling my shoulders back wide. With the officer's briefcase, glasses, and prim mouth, he looked like he belonged in a library running card catalogues.

"Help you out. Show you around." Ford's features were angular and sloped downward. Even the outside corners of his narrow gray eyes seemed to point toward the sides of his shoulders.

"Not sure I need it." I wasn't certain why I was put off by the suggestion. It's not like we didn't frequently get help from the uniforms.

"Oh, that's right." Ford squinted. "Smith told me you're from here. That you used to work for the Kalispell force. Well, the park's not the Flathead Valley. We think it would be good for you to have some assistance."

"Nothing like familiarity." I shrugged nonchalantly as if I had no care in the world, and I ignored the uneasy pit forming in my gut. "Let's get going, then." I held my hand out for Monty to lead the way.

• • •

We drove from the West Glacier helicopter pad to the scene in Monty's SUV, up a twenty-seven-mile washboard dirt road called the Inside North Fork Road that leads to a ranger station on the north fork of the Flathead River. Few tourists drive it because not many know about it, and if they do, they soon turn back because it's too dusty and bumpy. I had the urge to grab my quarter, but I knew I wouldn't be able to roll it effectively.

Other than some small talk, I was glad Monty didn't chat while he drove. I took in the forest and was struck at how much it had changed since I'd seen it over twelve years ago. The Roberts fire of 2003 had lashed through and decimated it. Skinny ashen trees like old bones crossed over one another on the forest floor, while hundreds of char-coaled trees managed to continue standing. Thick reddish bark peeked out between black strips, revealing the sturdier ones as the old ponderosas trying to survive like great-grandparents of the forest.

I was relieved when we began to emerge from the burn area just about five miles into the Inside Road, where green trees and mostly lodgepole pines and tamaracks with needles like yellow felt lined the dirt road. Flathead County's Crime Scene Services van was parked behind a park ranger's car and beside a line of caution tape. We pulled in behind two white county sheriff vehicles. A Park Police officer who'd been sitting in his car with the door ajar stepped out to greet us. "Hey, Benton," Monty called. "This is Agent Ted Systead. I say that right?" He had pronounced the "stead" as "steed."

"Close enough." I shook the officer's hand. Usually, people missed the first syllable and pronounced the Sys part as *sise* instead of the short *i* sound, like *sis*. But people usually got the "stead" right. I didn't correct him because I'm not one of those people who care if my last name gets butchered. What's a name really, other than another signifier? So many are attached to them as if they bring immortality, and in a way, they do. But I can say that there have been many criminals caught because they were simply too proud or ego-driven to quit dropping them around. *Yeah, Johnson, met him in the bar; he was drunk and mentioned that he stole that Buick. Oh yeah, Briggs, I've heard of him. My girlfriend used to date him before he took up with that neo-Nazi gang.*

"He's from the Northwest Regional Division Homicide Unit," Monty added. "Came in from Denver." He said this as if I'd come across the border illegally.

I gave a curt nod. "And you guys were happy that you finally had some quiet after your crazy summer?" Officer Benton tried to smile, but his face had that whitish-green tint like he'd been battling nausea. "Up for showing us the way? If not, I'm sure we can find it." I gave him my laziest grin possible to try to ease any anxiety. I was known for that—for an easygoing smile that calmed people's nerves, even when nervousness or pessimism brewed beneath my own veneer. It was this incongruous thing about me—my skeptical nature paired with a childlike grin that made you think I didn't have a malignant bone in my body. I've also been blessed with my mother's thick, dark wavy hair, so that at forty, I still have youthfulness about me, not entirely unlike the pilot Moran, which throws people off and has come in handy more than once when I enter the interrogation room.

"No, I'm good," he said. "It's just in there a ways." He pointed toward McGee Meadow.

I took a deep breath and could smell the pine and the pungent decaying fall skunkweed. I knew the trail, if you could call it that. During snowy months, it's not maintained and the underbrush and fallen logs claim it. From the road, you wouldn't even know where it was if it weren't for a little worn red, cross-country ski marker set high up on one of the ponderosas.

"The trail to McGee Meadow." Monty lowered his voice for an official effect. "In the winter, the locals ski in from Fish Creek, then cut over to McGee Meadow and out to Camas Creek Road and loop back. With all the snow, they have to find these markers." He pointed behind me to the small tin flag nailed to the tree.

"Yeah, I know."

"You've done it?"

"Several times." I thought of my ex, Shelly, and me with our cheap cotton long johns getting soaked to the bone with sweat even in the cold of February as we trekked up the ol' snow-covered Robert Frost–looking road. Even all these years later, I could recall the smell of her cheap, overly sweet perfume made pungent by her perspiration, while we stood peering down and arguing over whether the large tracks in the snow were moose or elk.

"One of the CS guys said we can't come in on the path," Benton said, almost in a whisper.

I gave the officer a quick pat on the shoulder to lead the way, and just as he stepped ahead, a raven let loose a piercing caw that made him pause. A cool breeze rattled the trees and a few small-diameter lodgepoles rubbed against one another and made an eerie groaning sound.

We stayed left of the trail, trekking through vibrant red-and-yellow brush. A few stray spider filaments touched my face. The autumn light, although bright, felt slanted and oblique. Mostly, it felt quiet, as if it were waiting for something to happen. Unlike direct summer sunshine that had something specific to say and shouted it, this light held mysteries and patiently whispered its secrets. I was aware of our noisy, rustling movement through the foliage, as if we were disturbing such secrets. The fist at the base of my sternum clenched tighter, and I thought, only for an instant—like a shutter opening and closing—of the raw, wild solitary desperation I felt at Oldman Lake after I got the fire going and sat in my own wet pants, waiting in shock for enough light to make it down the trail so I could run for help.

. . .

We reached the spot a quarter of a mile in and about fifty yards off the path, where several huge old-growth ponderosas stood more vibrant, like sentries for that particular patch of forest. To our left, only one line of yellow caution tape draped from tree to bush to tree. Out in the woods, there was no telling how large a circle to mark, so there was simply no point in doing it. One line to block the area from the trail was sufficient.

Two CSS techs in tan coveralls busied themselves. One inspected foliage, peering at branches of a small spruce, his gloved hands pulling down a limb and tweezing something from the bark and bagging it. The other snapped photos and carried the evidence log.

A county sheriff spoke to Joe Smith, chief of the Park Police in West Glacier. Wispy tips of fine white hair shot out from under his cap against his still-tanned neck. His sizable but sinewy frame reminded me of some lean animal on the savannas of Africa. Monty and I waited for his wave to cross the tape. The officer who'd walked us out had stayed back and just stood on the trail.

"Thanks, Officer." Smith followed a line of small orange flags that delineated where he could walk without angering the lead crime scene investigator. "Go ahead and just head back to the road," he yelled over us to him, "and continue making sure no one without clearance tries to wander back here, will ya?"

I had worked with Joe not only in DC for seminars we were all forced to attend, but several times when I was on the local force and needed to collaborate with park officials. Actually, I considered him a friend. We had gone out to shoot the shit a time or two when we needed an off-duty beer in DC. As far as I could see, he never let ego interfere with his work or his friendships, and in this line of work that was certainly refreshing.

"Systead." Joe refocused on me and smiled. He held out his hand to me.

"Good to see you, Chief." We shook, grabbing each other's shoulders with our free hands. He then greeted Monty and introduced us to Sheriff Walsh, using my full title, Special Agent Ted Systead from the Northwest Homicide Division of the Department of the Interior.

Walsh looked me up and down, not a hint of anything but confidence in his icy blue stare. He obviously could care less about titles—special agent this and that division—and I have to say I respected him for it. "Heard you used to work for the Kalispell force in the midnineties. That so?"

"That's correct," I said.

"Oh." He shrugged, still unimpressed. "Well, not sure how this one'll break down, but the victim might be local."

I could sense Joe tensing a bit. And so, the usual pissing contest had begun on some level. I couldn't blame Walsh if he was irritated. I mean, the Park Police had called his forensics unit first. From his perspective, there was no need for our intrusion, and I wasn't convinced yet that there was a need for us either other than that we were federal and Glacier Park was federal.

"From Martin City," Walsh continued. "*Outside* the park. Before that, he lived in Trego, that's t'ward the Canadian border."

I shrugged, knowing that where the victim came from made no difference. The crime was clearly in Glacier, but again, I could understand where he was coming from. He and his boys, being from the area, would have an easier time investigating a local. "Yeah, Trego, right past Fortine." I couldn't help but remind him that I knew the area well. I caught a glance from Monty out of the corner of my eye and could sense Smith subtly let out a pent-up breath, relieved that I was *local* enough for at least some credibility with Walsh.

I looked around to take it all in. Blood smattered the dirt and bushes around the tall ponderosa. Layer upon layer of duct tape circled the victim's chest under his armpits, around his hips, and all the way around the tree. What was left of his upper body hung limply like a broken and solitary puppet someone had raided for parts. Blood soaked what was left of a barely recognizable strip of shirt draping from one shoulder toward the hip on the same side. I caught my breath and held it until my pulse began to race.

Some equally shredded and bloody jeans still hung from a belt around his waist, but his entire thigh had been ripped cleanly off as if a butcher had sliced it off with a knife. Huge chunks had been bitten off the other leg as well, and one arm from the shoulder down had been ripped clean away. His head dangled so that I couldn't see his face straight on, but could tell that a large flap from his skull and the side of his face had been bitten away.

My throat began to tighten, and I began to feel as if my feet were barely touching the ground. I swallowed hard. "Who's lead tech?" I turned away, found Walsh's steely gaze first.

Walsh pointed to a woman whom I'd not spotted when we first came. She was walking to join the other techs in the woods farther past where the taped line ended. "Gretchen Larson. I'll introduce you in a minute."

I turned back to the body and the smell of earth, decaying flesh slowly warming in the October sun and a hint of that overly pungent skunky bear smell seemed to grow stronger. Flies buzzed everywhere, and I could feel the fingers of that imaginary fist in my sternum spread out as if trying to reach my stomach and my throat, where the beginning of either fear or nausea built. A tech snapped photos somewhere off to my side, and the smooth clicking of the camera in the distance pulled me away from the chill rapidly spreading inside me.

"Have you ID'd him yet?" I asked.

"We think so. A Victor Lance."

"He have ID on him?"

"No, our guys found a first initial and last name on the inside of his belt and we have someone in the system who matches the name and what we've determined of his build. Won't be sure about prints until the remains get to the lab; his remaining hand has been chewed on."

My father's gold wedding band flashed in my mind and I wasn't sure why. He rarely even wore it because, as he always told my ma, it interfered with scrubbing and putting on and taking off his gloves.

"From the pinkie and ring fingers that are left," Walsh continued, "we think we can get a match. So far, we can't tell from the face, but if it is him, turns out he was charged 'bout four years ago with threatening to beat up the attendant of a Town Pump quick stop if she didn't hand over a couple cans of chewin' tobacco and some cigarettes."

I stayed quiet, and Monty seemed to have enough sense to follow my lead, perhaps because he was starting to look a little faint. I wondered if he'd been around a stiff before.

"We might have to look at his teeth if we can't get it from his prints. If there's family around, we're leaning against having them ID'ing him for obvious reasons." Walsh adjusted his belt, hiking his pants up a notch. "Tape is thickly layered and tight under the armpits and around the hips. Arms were not bound. Like some goddamned freak show."

Monty whistled a low note to express his utter understanding that it *was* weird.

I said nothing and slowly walked closer to the victim, my head tilted to the side as if from curiosity, when really I was trying not to allow that internal fist from getting a straight shot up the back of my neck and into the back of my skull. It wasn't like I hadn't seen numerous dead bodies, some of them downright gruesome, like the time some guy took an ax to his wife in his backyard not far outside Kalispell. Or the victims from that serial-killer case in the Grand Canyon that got so much press. LaMatto and I almost didn't nail that scrawny Uncle Lasko—not until he had slit three women's throats, raped, and dismembered them.

And it's not like I hadn't seen bodies picked at or chewed on by wild animals before either; there was no way to avoid that when you worked with murder in the woods. No, the deep-reaching queasiness was nothing new, but the sensation I was getting with this one was: I felt as if my legs had suddenly detached from under me and my torso was simply hovering slightly off to one side, as if my body had been transposed into an out-of-focus holograph.

I put on my gloves. "Mind if I have a look?" I yelled over to the crime scene tech, crouched at the base of a tree outside the taped area with another tech. This was my subtle cue to Walsh that I would now be taking the investigative lead; I had no intention of waiting for him to introduce us *later*. The county crime scene group would, of course, stay on the scene.

She stood and came to us and before she caught up, Monty whispered, "Know her?"

"No. You?"

Monty shook his head.

She was stout and no more than five foot five. Very blond with fair skin and pale blue eyes. "I'm Gretchen Larson." She spoke with an accent that explained her name, her eyes, and her blond hair. I figured she was either Norwegian or Swedish. Possibly Danish or maybe German, but I doubted it. The consonants were not so hard.

I introduced myself and Monty, who seemed to stand up taller as I did. "What've we got?"

"White male, late twenties to midthirties. Dark hair from what's left of his scalp. Part of it from his forehead back was peeled off. Canines, not claws. But we really need to get this to the lab." She glanced at her coworkers as if she were a bit hurried and annoyed that we were on the scene so late, even though we all knew that she and her crew would be at it all day and possibly tomorrow. She wiped her forehead with her sleeve.

I nodded and noticed perspiration still catching on her wide brow, the shimmering white blond at her hairline giving way to a honey color farther out, her hair tied into a tidy, short ponytail. She wore thick, black-rimmed glasses that clashed with her fair complexion and seemed like they belonged on a brunette instead. An interesting contrast, I thought, but I didn't understand why she seemed a bit irritated with us. It's not like they were holding the body here for me. Crime Scene Services does what needs to be done to preserve and investigate the scene and keep things intact for as long as possible. Once the body is removed, it can take an entire day, or even two, to get it all checked out and with the blue sky, we had lucked out in terms of weather. If rain or snow were encroaching, they'd be setting up tents and tarps and frantically trying to get the body out of here, and it wouldn't matter if we'd gotten a peek or not.

"Not a big guy, maybe five foot eight. Medium build." She pushed her glasses farther up on the bridge of her nose with a cocked wrist.

"Can we have a look?" I held up my gloved hands.

"Sorry, only a look. Too fragile to prod around—like shredded beef at this point." She pronounced the *sh* sound so that *shredded* sounded like *sredded*.

"I can see that." I could also see flies on the thick, coagulated blood that hadn't fully dried and yellow jackets—no maggots yet—on the patches that were on the ground and had fully dried. It's as if they had already come to some agreement on who got what. The type of bugs, among other things like the blood's degree of coagulation, would help Gretchen and the pathologist determine how long the body had been dead.

Monty, paler by the minute, pointed at the victim's side, under his rib cage, where a gaping hole exposed his intestines, almost as if a great white shark instead of a bear had taken a bite. Grizzlies could go one of two ways: they could behave almost civilized and take clean, neat slices of meat as if they had used a carving knife, or they could rip everything to shreds like wild coyotes. These remains had the look of the knife around the thigh and stomach cavity, which—to our benefit—left the bloody duct tape in place, but had the coyote look on the one arm and the leg from the knee down on the same side.

"Nice." Monty swallowed hard, looking as though he might faint. "Teeth." He was barely audible. It was more of a statement than a question, but Gretchen answered.

"For sure. The punctures are from canines here"—she delicately pointed one white, gloved index finger—"definitely not curved claws."

"Do we know yet whether he was alive or dead when this happened?" I felt something move on the back of my neck and for an instant thought it was a yellow jacket, until I realized it was a bead of sweat sliding down my back.

"Don't know yet for sure." Smith's voice came over my shoulder, sounding closer than I thought. I was starting to feel like my senses were off—like the slanted light was transporting me into some twilight zone where at any minute a grizzly would charge me from behind with the ghost of my father riding him. "All we know is that someone bound him and gagged him here."

"Wouldn't make sense to tie up a dead guy, now would it?" Walsh added, his voice sharp in the woods.

"No," I admitted, shaking my head slowly. "It wouldn't."

Monty chuckled. Good for you, I thought, that you're getting your game face back on. "Footprints?" I looked at Gretchen.

"Bear and deer prints that are much older. I think we have some boot tracks that have been messed up by our bear shuffling around. Victim had boots on."

"You find 'em?" I asked. Gretchen threw her head in the direction from which she had come. "Found more remains over there. Buried."

"Did you get some prints from the trail?"

"We have a few and possibly some from the road too, but they could be the ranger who found them. We won't know until we get the plaster from them and compare."

"How about nails from the fingers that are left?"

"We'll be checking those for DNA to see if he fought whoever put him here or the bear."

"Any prints on the tape?"

"No, there's blood on it, and on the other side of the tree, which has less blood, we've so far just found smudges, possibly from gloves. Quite a bit of the tape by the hips has been decimated by the bear. We'll see what we can get for fibers in the lab. But as I said"—she pointed to the tree again, where a tech still crouching snapped pictures of what lay at his feet—"we've found some buried clothing scraps and remains over by that tree.

"Typical grizzly behavior," she added, "to bury remains, just like a dog or a lion." She directed this to Walsh, as if she figured she didn't need to explain to me, with my slightly prissy and shiny gold badge attached to the pocket of my navy coat that read Department of the Interior, National Park Service, what was typical bear behavior and what wasn't.

"Gee, didn't know that," Walsh said sarcastically. Being local, he was obviously just as familiar with bear activity as any of us.

Gretchen's face was stone-still, as if to let Walsh and the rest of us know that she had no time or patience for sarcasm, ego, or turf wars at a crime scene. I liked her for this, but I wondered what could possibly possess a forensic specialist with a foreign accent to take a job in the narrow atmosphere of the Flathead Valley, where about every tenth car had a huge decal of the Ten Commandments on the back window. I knew, however, that the valley's beauty was a draw for quite a few high-level professionals wanting to live in the mountains. Not to mention my father.

She began to shuffle away toward the buried remains and all four of us—Walsh, Smith, Monty, and I—followed, knowing better than to step out of the line she cut. She kneeled down by the other techs and pointed to part of the victim's leg that still had scraps of jeans on it and his foot clad in a bloody and dirt-caked cowboy boot.

"Good, then," I said. "We've got his tracks and prints off of these, I'm presuming. And we can see if we can find tracks that aren't from this boot print around here and see if any additional fingerprints might be on it."

"Long shot on more prints than just his, but you never know. At the very least, if he's in the system, as the name on the belt suggests, we should be able to make a match." She looked around at the ground. "We've got a lot of grizzly tracks around."

"Let's keep looking for boot tracks that don't belong to this boot," I added.

Gretchen shot me an I-know-how-to-do-my-job look, but her tone did not betray her professionalism. "Sure thing," she said. "I'm going to have the guys wrap what's left of the body and get it out of here in the next fifteen to twenty to the refrigerator and off to Wilson in Missoula. So if you need to look at it some more, have at it. Just don't touch anything and follow the path I've designated."

I turned back at the victim, lifeless and torn to shreds, then at the dirt around me and saw the track. The elongated shape with toe pads close together and claw points a good two and a half to three inches away from the tip of the pad. A black bear's prints are easily distinguishable from a grizzly's since the black bear's pad has a wider spread and the claw points lie closer in. I glanced up and noticed Monty observing me curiously. I wondered if I was pale, then I looked back to the ground that no longer looked firm and hard but soft and shifting, as if it might open up and swallow me.

That print, innocent and natural in the dirt, haunts me still.

3

___

FROM THE MOMENT I set foot back into Glacier, that clench at the base of my chest had become more pronounced, and I wish I could say that I was professional enough to wonder if I should mention something to Sean: that a grizzly-mauling-combined homicide might be a bit tricky for a guy with my history. But to be honest, I never even thought of it. Why would I have? The mauling was secondary—a fairly obvious occurrence when you've got bait tied to a tree.

When I entered the agency, none of the guys on the force, including Sean Dewey, our managing supervisor, inquired about my dad's death, even though we had to go through extensive background checks. I can't describe how thankful I am for that, because for months I lost sleep (even had a nightmare or two—the angst-filled exposure type where you show up for an interview late and nude) over whether or not they'd look into it. I never lied about anything; that bit of history just never came up after I passed my psych eval.

In general, I don't talk much about the attack at Oldman Lake, which is on the east side of Glacier Park, because it's like an old injury that has thick scar tissue covering it. Talking about it only rips bits of that scar away, which seems like a useless thing to do to a wound.

I did do some counseling for a few months right after the incident, but it turned out to be a waste of time. The counselor didn't know what to do with me and my puffy adolescent cheeks, oily skin, and my too-long wavy hair shading my eyes as if to give a constant finger to the world. I think she thought that if she sat silently and patiently in front of me, I would get so uncomfortable that I'd begin to talk or she'd eventually ask the key question and I'd ignite, emotions flying from me like a Fourth of July sparkler.

Only I wasn't ready to talk, especially to her—this overly thin, birdlike woman who made the hour go on forever by only asking two or three questions throughout the session. *How is concentrating on your schoolwork going? How is it dealing with your friends now that you are grieving? How are your sisters handling things?* Most of the time, I'd just shrug or give one-word answers: fine. I was at least thankful that she didn't make me look at Rorschach inkblots or play games in the small box of sand filled with plastic dinosaurs, soldiers, and other creatures that she had in her office for little kids.

I begged my mom to let me skip it altogether, and in her own grief, her shoulders slumped, and her eyes weighted with dark circles, she didn't have the energy to fight me. But eventually, I sought out help when I was in my early twenties because my temper was becoming a problem, along with too much drinking. Both Shelly and my mom begged me to try counseling. So I found some psychiatrist trained in post-traumatic stress disorder, who had been treating Vietnam vets in Missoula. I found him to be quite likable in an interesting professorial way, like I was learning about dreams and psychology rather than about myself.

He loved the Jungian model, and he'd begin every session asking me about my dreams. One time I told him that I dreamt that I had been under the water scuba diving around an old yellow school bus, inspecting it, trying desperately to get in. But I couldn't make the door or the windows budge. He got a huge kick out this, saying how wonderful the mind was to put *scuba* and *school bus* together. He repeated it several times like a child: *scuba, school bus; scuba, school bus; scuba, school bus.*

Then, as more of a side note than the main theme, he leaned back in his chair, his stomach popping out and stretching the white fabric between his shirt buttons, and added with a brief flick of the hand and a softening of his low voice, almost a whisper, that he thought the grizzly had stolen my youth along with my dad. He said that I most definitely had angst about the loss of my childhood, which the school bus represented, at a most critical time during puberty.

Even though I felt a shiver crawl up my spine when he softened his voice like that, it seemed like an okay thing to have a semi-overweight, teddy bear–looking guy solve my dreams like puzzles and present them to me like neatly wrapped gifts for my psyche. Only they didn't really do anything other than make me say, "Ah, yes, I see," as if I was finally getting a math equation.

He told me, still as if only a no-big-deal afterthought, that my anger was the part of me that became the perpetrator, and in this instance, that meant the bear, and that in those moments, I could disown myself and would suffer no consequences for my actions. In essence, he told me I had to let go of the perpetrator inside me—to let go of the grizzly.

Ah, yes, I see.

. . .

On the way to Glacier's headquarters in Monty's park SUV, I called Monica in Denver, our information analyst who is our main link to the FBI's National Crime Information Center and to the National Law Enforcement Telecommunications System. She would tap into Montana's state automated fingerprint ID system, which checks fingerprints against a database containing millions in order to link a body to a name. I wanted to see if they'd gotten a secure ID yet and was semipleased to find that they had: the victim was the man from Martin City.

Monty opened a window and took a loud breath of fresh air. "Mountain air." He sighed. "It's why we work for the nation's parks, huh?"

I laughed.

"That funny?"

"It is if you knew how much time I spend in a cubicle in smog-filled Denver."

"Oh, so what did that gal you called say?"

"That our victim is this Victor Lance."

Monty nodded. "And they know this because . . . ?"

"The prints on the ring finger match the prints in the system," I said. "Gretchen used her laptop to get the print from his ring finger into the system before the body even made it to Missoula."

. . .

With its community dormitory-type structures, various single-story, rectangular houses, and offices trimmed in a government pea-green shade, West Glacier resembles a small military base. The houses are designed for summer park personnel and host various offices like USGS Global Change Science Center and the Glacier Field Station. We parked in front of the main headquarters, a tan 1960s-looking Arizona brick structure in need of some remodeling. We met Joe in the reception area, where a teardrop-shaped wooden desk sat quiet and empty. The receptionist was home for the weekend.

Joe showed Monty and me the room for us to use, and I caught his eye and asked right in front of Monty if I could have a word alone with him. I followed Joe back to his office without even looking at Monty, leaving him in the room that had been set up with a table, chairs, pens, paper, and a long white dry-erase board. "No offense," I said after Joe shut the door. "But this Officer Harris, well, I think it might be best if—

Joe held up his palm. "Sorry, we've got no choice in the matter. Ford was adamant that he tag along."

I had gotten that unyielding vibe from the get-go, which I suppose is why I was having a hard time accepting the guy, even though he hadn't been much of a problem, and I had no good reason not to want to work with him. Yet. "Look, I'm not sure he has a good feel for this. He obviously spends more time as Ford's right-hand man than in the field. If they want someone with me, I'd rather have one of your other guys, someone closer to you than Ford, maybe that Benton."

"Benton?" Joe squinted. "Benton's even greener. Seeing that scene was about all he could take for one morning."

"And Harris isn't green?"

"Not as green as Benton. He was pretty good in the field before moving into Ford's office. Look, I feel your pain, but Harris isn't bad. Give him a try."

"We could use him for something else, to man the tip line or something."

Joe sighed. "I'm sorry, but Ford has already spoken to Sean. It's a done deal. Sean concurred that you needed an assist on this one. I think we can all agree that this case is just a little weird, huh?"

I sensed that this was more about Ford keeping tabs on the situation than it was about helping us solve the case. But if Sean Dewey had spoken, then I had little choice until I could get a chance to talk to him myself. "Okay." I held up my hand. "We'll see how she goes."

"Come on. I'll show you around."

I nodded, trying to decide whether to take it up with Sean or let it lie. Given my status lately, I knew taking anything up with him was not a great option. I'd make do, and maybe Monty would turn out better than I'd given him credit for. Maybe it was all in my head, and he wouldn't be Ford's spy and would have more skills than I was expecting.

. . .

"So"—I grabbed my Vermont quarter and began rolling it when we went back into the room where Monty was—"we'll start with Ranger Fortenson, then we'll speak to whomever she spoke to first and whoever else went to the scene with her before getting the Park Police involved."

"That's easy. She radioed me first." Joe leaned against the long, green counter in the room and crossed his arms. "I asked her if there was anyone else in the immediate area that she could see—anyone injured—and when she said she couldn't see anyone, I told her to get her pepper spray ready in case the bear returned but to get back to the road immediately and wait for assistance.

"I was out at the West Glacier Café having my Saturday breakfast." He rubbed the back of his neck. "So I called Ken Greeley, who I knew was supposed to be out checking on some folks who were reported for camping out at Fish Creek Campground when they weren't supposed to be. Plus, there'd been some bear trouble there about five days ago."

"Ahhh," Monty said, as if we just got some great clue that would solve the case. "Same bear?"

"Might be. Probably. But won't know unless we find the one we think it is and get its DNA. Or worst-case scenario—euthanize it and inspect its stomach contents. And I don't know if we'll allow that to happen until there's proof that it was a grizzly that did this guy in and not the perp. If the guy was already dead, then the bear didn't do anything out of the ordinary, other than go for a carcass that happened to be human."

"Yeah, there's been a lot of bear activity this fall," Monty added.

"I'll say." Joe sighed. "It's been a very cool and wet summer, and the berries came out very late. They're all scrounging for what they can get. We've had problem bears all over the Flathead Valley this fall and several around the campsites here."

I didn't say anything. Through the door, down a corridor leading to a back entrance, I could see a female ranger come in who appeared to be our Karen: medium height, average weight, and a tail of no-nonsense dark, slightly graying hair tied back. For some reason I didn't want to discuss the grizzly and felt a strong, childish urge to yell at both Monty and Joe, *Forget the goddamned bear.* But I shoved the urge down, knowing that it would be out of character for me.

And it *would* be out of character for me; usually, I loved to discuss in detail what would be typical behavior for a grizzly, that they don't characteristically attack and eat human flesh, that a bear usually bluff-charges or hurts someone only because they get between a mama and her cubs. I cleared my throat instead and pointed down the hall to Karen, where she stood talking to the officer she came in with.

Monty and Joe looked.

"That's her with Officer Greeley." Joe nodded. "I'll get her, and she can tell you the rest."

. . .

After we got set up Karen came in with her head held high and strength in her dark brown, liquid eyes. I greeted her first, and she already knew Monty. She didn't seem as shaken as Moran had mentioned in the helicopter, but I used my boyish smile and calm voice with her anyway. I could see Monty out of the corner of my eye take out his notebook and a pen.

"Would you like some coffee or tea?" I asked.

This brought a laugh from her. "I already made the coffee before you arrived. Maybe *you'd* like a cup?"

"Maybe I would." I smiled. My mom and sisters, Shelly too, always told me that I had a one-dimpled grin, another slightly boyish feature that came in handy with a female or two, but I was sort of glad that I didn't have a dimple on each side like my mother, because the cute-guy role only went so far and sometimes pissed more people off than you'd expect. As far as I was concerned, I was glad to be over six feet with long, lanky, sinewy arms that counteracted my face and made me again, seem like a contradiction of sorts.

Karen had that unimpressed-with-my-type-or-any-man's-type quality that women over forty sometimes possess—that they've lived enough lives to know what we're all about and that it might not actually be worth even a smile, much less a flirt.

"I'd love some." Monty ran a hand through what there was of his military-cut hair. "If you don't mind."

"No, no, sit." I held out my palm to her. "Tell me where and I'll grab us a couple of cups."

"Don't be silly," she said. "Been working here for over twenty years. I'll get the coffee."

It was when she returned with two white ceramic cups—one in each hand—that I noticed she was shaking. Monty and I thanked her, and we all took a seat at the sturdy cream-colored rectangular table. "Okay," I said even more soothingly than I originally thought I needed to after observing her unsteady hands, "we know you've had quite the shock, not that you haven't been around plenty of grizzlies around here, but this, well, this . . ."

She held out her palm, still quivering, to signal, *Say no more.*

"Let's just begin with what you were doing this morning before you came across it."

Karen bit her lower lip. "Well, it's weird. So coincidental, but this year, I thought I'd get a jump on the cross-country markers and make sure they were all in place. I'd been talking to Joe, Joe Smith," she reminded us, "'bout putting new ones up because the old ones are so rusted. They used to be bright red and easy to see, but now they're difficult to spot."

Monty leaned back and took a sip of his coffee.

I stayed leaning in, one elbow on my knee. "Makes sense."

"So I drove up the Inside North Fork Road and parked."

"Which side of the road?"

"Right side, following traffic, not that there is any on that road."

"And what time was that?"

"Around 7:30. Us rangers, we're up early. Sun hadn't been up long and everything was still on the dark side in the shadow of the mountains."

Monty scribbled in his notepad and she glanced over at him.

"And then . . . ?"

She drew in a deep breath so that it hissed, as if she were taking in air through a cocktail straw. "I found the marker and the trail, pretty covered this time of the year, but game keeps it somewhat recognizable before the skiers cut the trail."

I nodded.

"I decided to walk in a ways to see if any of the other markers were visible farther down the trail. And as I got in just a little ways, I smelled bear—that strong, earthy, skunky smell, and got out my capsaicin bear spray. I was about to turn around and leave, but then something off to my left caught my eye." She massaged her hands nervously together.

I gripped the quarter in my palm. "What was that?" I spoke gently to nudge her on, as if she were fragile, but knew it was unnecessary. This woman had more guts than half the guys I'd ever worked with in DC or Denver—including myself—being out in the woods of Glacier Park alone at dawn in the fall.

"The, you know, the tree where he was . . ." Her voice was escalating. "Just, just horrible . . ." She stared at me, her eyes concentrating as if she were trying to make the image vanish. Her brow wrinkled, and I noticed age spots on her forehead near her hairline, revealing that she'd been out in high-elevation sun for many years. I knew she must have many wildlife stories to tell. I suddenly had an urge to take her to a nice coffee shop and sit and tell stories that had nothing to do with this situation.

I let out a deep breath before speaking, "Okay, so when you noticed the body, what did you do?"

"Well, I stood there shocked for a few seconds and tried to understand, I mean, you have to understand, these weren't ordinary remains, I mean, Christ Almighty, bound to a tree like that?" She shook her head rhythmically.

I waited and was thankful Monty also assumed the silent role.

"But it came fairly quickly to me that the body had been mauled by a bear, so I looked around afraid the bear might still be there. I—I . . ." She looked down at her hands.

"Take your time," I offered.

"You have to understand that this was upsetting."

I snatched a quick glance at Monty again, fairly certain he would continue to keep quiet, but with someone you've never worked with, it's hard to know. Plus I could be wrong, but he seemed to be getting an impatient, glib no-kidding look on his face. I reined in her attention by nodding and speaking more softly. "I very much understand that."

"So I know this wasn't professional of me, but I . . ." she said. "I ran. I ran back to the road. I was afraid, and I've seen plenty of grizzly in my time, and have definitely not run away, but this, this . . ."

"Is that when you called Smith?"

"Yes. When I got to my car. He told me to look for others and then to get to the road for safety. I don't think I told him that I was already *at* the road. I—" She looked down at her lap. "I just said, 'Yes, sir,' and waited until Park Police got there. Ken. Officer Ken Greeley."

"Again. Completely understandable, but I need you to think hard now, was there anything at all in the woods surrounding the area or maybe near the road that seemed strange, any noises or people when you first drove out or were out walking that caught your eye? Any tourists? Any cars that you remember?"

"No, it was completely quiet except for the birds and a slight breeze, enough to make the trees creak. Just as I'd expect in October on the Inside Road. There aren't that many people on the Inside Road in the heart of the season, much less in October. And the burn has made it even less desirable for people to go that way. Sometimes we see a researcher or others interested in seeing wolves heading out toward Logging Lake trailhead, which is known for frequent sightings of the North Fork wolf pack. But I hadn't seen anyone for over a week."

"Any little things that come to mind?" I continued. "Tire tracks on the road? Footprints on the path? Did you smell anything besides the bear? Maybe cigarette smoke or a cologne scent? The smell of a campfire?"

Karen sat still, her eyes narrowed, her brow still crinkled. "No," she said after a pause. "There was nothing except what I saw at that spot."

"So when did Ken arrive?" I asked.

She shrugged. "Within five to ten minutes. It felt like forever, waiting there on the road, but he was only at Fish Creek, so it couldn't have been more than ten minutes."

. . .

Ken greeted Monty first when he walked in, and it was obvious they also knew each other. Ken was tall with thickly muscled shoulders and arms like a football player, and when he sat down, the office chair suddenly seemed to shrink, like it might not support him.

"You probably know this, but there's been a bear around Fish Creek for the past few weeks," he announced.

"Yeah," Monty said. "We've heard." Monty isn't over five-nine, thin-necked, and pointy-shouldered, the opposite of Ken, and the two of them seemed to fit like two different-size pieces of a puzzle. "Smith told us that. Want some coffee or something?"

"No, I'm fine." Ken chewed a piece of gum, his jaws working it with purpose, a little mangled dirty-white shred popping in and out of view as he turned it in his mouth. He was definitely revved up and under different circumstances, I'd have to wonder if he was on something, but people exhibit different responses around a death. There are those that get shaken and almost afraid to speak, those that spike an adrenaline rush and become hyperhelpful, and most often, those who clam up. I suppose it's a defense to not let death too near.

"Let's start from the beginning," I said. "What time did you get the call to go assist Karen?"

"I'd say it was about quarter to eight. It's not that far from where I was."

"And when you drove out to her, did you notice anything suspicious?"

"No. Just dirt road and forest. You could tell it was going to be a beauty. A great beautiful, peaceful morning, really. The kind of day we live for out here."

Monty nodded in agreement. I knew it well also, that the area had very few sunny days, and its residents had a saying that in the Flathead, there were four seasons: almost winter, winter, still winter, and road construction. "Were there campers at Fish Creek or, wait—" I held up my pen. "It's not even open for camping, right? You were out there to check on some campers who weren't supposed to be there?"

"That's right. This particular campsite closed on September sixth even though most of the others stay open until October thirteenth."

"Why's that? I just assumed it was closed because of bear trouble." I leaned back, planting my feet firmly apart. They felt heavy. "Not true?"

"No, we've had bear trouble at Fish Creek all right. But only because people sneak in and camp because the gate's been open for some construction this fall. It closes on the sixth every year, though, because of the type of water system it has. The pipes aren't in very deep, and they freeze too easily, so we have to drain them early."

"I see. Did you find the campers?"

"I did and I ticketed them. I have all their information if you want it." He looked at me, and I nodded that I would. "I told them to pack their belongings and leave and was on my way out when I got Smith's call."

"What did you do when you reached Karen?"

"I had orders to tape off the trailhead and wait for reinforcements."

"Which came how quickly?"

"Five, ten minutes." He bobbed his knee up and down and shook his head in small, quick movements. "Smith and two more Park Police, one a bit later since she was ordered to stop and seal off the Inside Road from anyone who might happen to drive out that way."

"And then Smith and who else walked in?"

"*Me.* Smith and me." He glanced at Monty, then me, incredulously, astonished that we didn't know he was one of the first Park Police on the grisly—no pun intended—scene.

"And . . . "

"Well, we went out there and—" He quit bouncing his knee as if the image in his mind sobered him. "Smith made me wait back at the game trail so we didn't disrupt the site, and he walked close enough to get a better look. Then he radioed for the main office and instructed them to call the county in."

Monty glanced at me to make sure I was getting it all down, which I was, and then we let Ken go after he gave us all the information he could on the Fish Creek campers.

. . .

Gretchen and her techs were still working, circling farther out, photographing and logging every bush or piece of ground that looked disturbed. I have deep respect for those methodical and patient enough to work an outdoor crime scene. Working an indoor scene is no rodeo; it's a slow, strategic, and tedious process but add the outdoors and it gets twice as complex.

"Anything new?" I inquired.

"Found some poor-resolution boot prints in the brush next to the trail, and it doesn't match the victim's print, so whoever else was out here might have walked out next to him beside the trail. I doubt we'll be able to get plaster. They're too faint, and we mostly have only identified them because of broken brush and disturbed foliage. We only got a partial toe print in some dirt, and that's how we know it doesn't match the victim's."

I turned to Monty. "Deliberate and smart enough to *not* use the trail."

"Yeah, but it's not that obvious of a trail."

"True, but perhaps more obvious than walking through the thicker brush to the side of it. Any scraps of clothing or blood near the print?" I turned back to Gretchen.

"Not yet." She wiped her forehead with her forearm. She was sweating even more than earlier in spite of the crisp fall air. "We'll keep you posted."

. . .

Monty and I drove to park headquarters, where I made a list of all the people we needed to talk to while we waited for more information on the victim: who and where his family was and what kind of trouble he might have been in, based on the fact that he had a record.

While we were there, we grabbed Joe and headed out to get a bite to eat at a small restaurant still open outside the entrance to the park. Everything in West Glacier had been boarded up for the season, including the West Glacier Mercantile, the restaurant, and the Canadian Visitor Center. The only reason the Glacier Café and a bar in a small chalet were open was because they sat outside the park, directly facing the trestle used for the Burlington Northern Santa Fe Railway trains that cut through the Hi-Line and run along the border of the park. White letters against a beige panel on the railway overpass read: Gateway—Glacier National Park.

I hadn't eaten anything except some anemic biscotti cookie thing on the flight over, so when we got to the café, I figured I better put something down even though the nature of the case had made me lose my appetite.

"What are you guys thinking?" Joe asked after getting our coffee from a dull-complexioned waitress with a nose covered in pimples. She had to have been directly out of high school, if not a dropout, which wasn't unusual for the area. She told us in an unanimated voice that the bison burgers were decent and that the soup was beef barley.

"We're thinking," I said when she left, "that we need to talk to that couple that were illegally at Fish Creek last night. Greeley gave us the information. A Kaylynn Lowden and a Jarred Mercord from Spokane, Washington. Greeley believes they're heading east toward the Sweet

Grass Hills, so they shouldn't be difficult to pick up. We've got Highway Patrol on it."

"Depending on what kind of time they're making, they shouldn't be much farther than Cut Bank or Shelby, unless they're running," Joe said in a monotone voice between sips of coffee. "What about the bear?"

"What about it?" I asked.

"You need it for evidence?"

"Not until Wilson reports. I suppose from your perspective it's important to know whether the victim was alive or not when the bear went after him for public safety purposes."

"Even if he was alive"—Joe shook his head—"I'm not sure I'm interested in putting this grizzly down. Not when the damn body was bait for him, dead or alive. Not to mention that he might still be in hyperphagia, eating everything in his sight for hibernation."

"Have you discussed it with your guy Bowman?" Joe, who'd acted as lead ranger for the park longer than as chief of Park Police, and one other guy, Kurtis Bowman, were considered the bear specialists. They usually led the committee in charge of making the recommendation on whether to take a bear's life. I'd never met him, but it was just one of those things I knew from the reading I'd done. I had seen Bowman's thesis on how the drought and warming trend of the past decades increased beetle bug infestation of the whitebark pines because the beetle bug was rarely eradicated in the winter without sustained freezing temperatures. Blister rust, a fungal disease, also killed the trees. This affects the grizzlies in Yellowstone, who depend on the caches of white pine nuts stashed across the forest by red squirrels to fatten up for winter hibernation. Grizzlies entering the den for the winter with less fat bear fewer cubs. And if their body fat is too low when they go into hibernation, they will often abort their pregnancies. Luckily, the grizzlies in Glacier rely more on huckleberries to fatten up than on the whitebark pine nuts.

"I have." Joe nodded and pursed his lips like he was deep in thought. "Know him?"

I shook my head. "Just heard about him."

"I know him," Monty added.

I glanced at Monty and resisted the urge to say to him, *Great, want your Boy Scout points now or later?* "Look," I said to Joe, "are you not worried . . ." and had to pause midsentence until a loud train passed. "About the bear now being habituated to human flesh?" I felt that clench again, and a subtle shortening of my breath, just enough to make me shift in my seat and straighten my back to open up my shoulders. It's not like I necessarily wanted this animal put down either, but I was curious as to what Joe, Bowman, and Ford were thinking. I couldn't shake the feeling that somehow this bear's fate was significant, interwoven into mine, although I knew I was just being superstitious.

"Oh, we're worried, all right. Especially if the guy was alive; that makes it worse. If the guy was dead, we're not thinking it's grounds to put it down. But even if he was alive, we're just not sure it's enough to put a federal bear down, especially when he's in a prehibernation state."

"Do you know which one it is?" Monty asked.

"We have a pretty good idea. It's most likely our Fish Creek bear. He's been around the area for some time. Doesn't cause much trouble, other than pound on the garbage cans. But I'm guessing it wouldn't be too hard to trap him."

"How old?"

"About four. Big for his age. Strong specimen. The committee will take that into consideration. Males can be sacrificed more readily than females, but the gene pool for males is getting watered down because of inbreeding since the patches of forest available are shrinking, and that prevents them from breeding with bears great distances away. This guy"—Joe took a small sip of his coffee—"he's only been away from mama for about a year and a half now."

"You make it sound like he's so cuddly." Monty gave a half smile.

"Not cuddly, just a normal grizzly," Joe said.

"We'll have more information after we get the time and sequence of death figured out," I added. "Unless there's an absolute reason for why we need to cut this bear open, I agree that there's no point in euthanizing him."

. . .

It was a fact that humans were each other's worst enemies in the woods. For example, in the last two centuries only about a dozen Montana hunters have been killed in bear attacks, and none by wolves or mountain lions. More hunters have been killed in plane crashes or even murdered by hunting buddies. And many, many more have been killed accidentally, where they've been mistaken for game by other hunters or been the recipient of an accidental firearm discharge while taking the gun out of a car, a boat, a tent, crossing a fence, or even tripping and falling on it.

In Glacier Park alone, that number is eleven for grizzly bear attacks (resulting in fatalities) in the last one hundred years, my father being one of those unlucky statistics. And here's the deal: it's not like I want anyone to think that my life isn't normal because of it. Other than the fact that I'm a detective and see a few mind-blowing and evil things that reveal the utter baseness of humans now and again; for the most part, my existence in Denver is fairly routine and uneventful, full of a little too much tedious paperwork and a fair amount of traveling to the nation's Northwest parks for criminal activity that isn't always so interesting.

Obviously, such a traumatic event at a young age can be life-altering, but because I was young, I'd like to think I was resilient. Change didn't leave much time for grief as other influences soon swept me away in the wave puberty brings.

I'd have to admit that I've been largely unsuccessful at relationships. There had been other girlfriends since Shelly that didn't work out well, but I live my life calmly and in control, and this case should have been no different for me, only something felt off-kilter. Just a small reeling sense, like I was sitting in a rowboat safely at the shore of some high mountain lake and somebody just gave me a nudge out to the middle of the lake without a paddle. But the lake was calm, and there was no storm, so it was kind of enjoyable in a strange way—as if I'd simply drift back to shore.

Of course, there was the obvious, that I was working a case involving a quasi-grizzly mauling in the very park that took my father. But his death was something I'd lived with my entire life, and I couldn't see how it could have any bearing in this instance and why it would make me feel that something was on the verge of snapping in or out of place. But it was there, and the only thing to do was shoo it away and get back to work.

So after I looked over my notes, Monty and I spoke to three out of five more rangers who had been in the area over the past four days, all of whom noticed nothing out of the ordinary.

Then we got three calls in ten minutes: one from Gretchen—the body was at the lab in Missoula, which actually has a state-of-the-art crime lab and a noteworthy pathologist, Reeve Wilson, whom I'd dealt with before. We would be able to talk to Wilson by the next day. Wilson had agreed to come in on a Saturday evening because a federal bear was involved and apparently, Gene Ford, the park's superintendent, threw his weight around, adamant that this thing needed to be handled in a timely fashion.

The second came from Monica. The victim's mother, fifty-three-year-old Penny Lance, lived and worked outside Kalispell in an area or township called Evergreen. She had divorced Victor's father, a Philip Lance, in 1985, when Victor was only two. She never remarried and worked for an auto repair shop called Travis Auto on LaSalle Road. We were no more than half an hour to her office or home, but since it was Saturday, going on four p.m., I knew we had a good chance of catching her at her place.

The third came from Walsh—a Glacier County deputy had found

the couple that had been camping at Fish Creek at a convenience store gassing up in Browning and insisted they return to West Glacier for more questioning. Apparently, they were very helpful and, although irritated at having to backtrack, they didn't seem like they had anything to hide. They would be in by early evening.

4

P‌ENNY LANCE LIVED in a neighborhood of about twenty small, brightly colored houses: light blue, yellow, red, green, even a pink one, making the neighborhood seem like one overgrown Easter basket. Small, surprisingly lush, and slightly overgrown and weedy lawns with very few trees lay before each home. I could tell that these lawns normally would be dried out and brown any other year with less rainfall.

Penny's one-story house was a light eggshell-blue color. A Russian olive tree with silvery slender leaves caressed the side of the house, and a Buick the color of a dark plum sat in her driveway. I took a deep breath. I was relieved that I didn't have to track her down, but it never got any easier: delivering such news to a parent not expecting it. It almost always hit hard enough that it felt like a physical punch.

I rang the bell as Monty shifted his weight back and forth. I had asked him on the way over if he'd done this before, knowing he probably hadn't. I was right. He had every reason to be anxious.

"Well, at least it looks like it might be just her for now. No big family to address." I shrugged. "That might make it a bit easier."

Monty nodded as a woman looking older than fifty-three opened the door. She was small, no more than five-three, and I could smell cigarette smoke instantly. She had that superannuated blond look, her overdyed, brassy hair hanging to her shoulders with about two inches of dark gray springing from her roots. That's where my eye went first until I quickly refocused on her narrow blue eyes framed by deep crow's-feet.

I wanted to tell her to go ahead and grab a cigarette, anything she wanted at all while she could still do it in the comfort of everyday normalcy before we ripped it away. It didn't matter that Victor had some criminal tendencies or could have been mixed up in something dangerous; this woman would still love her boy no matter what hardships her family might have seen.

"Ms. Lance?" I said. "I'm Ted Systead. I'm a detective for the Department of the Interior. We handle crime in the US national parks. This is Monty Harris with Glacier Park's police."

"Hello, ma'am." Monty tipped his head.

Her eyes narrowed, and she crossed her arms over her chest. "What's happened now?" She looked irritated. This was a woman familiar with difficulties.

"May we come in?"

"What?" She crossed her arms and gave a heavy-lidded stare. "Is he in some kind of trouble?"

"He?" I asked.

She shifted into a one-hip stance, getting ready to go onto the defensive.

"I'm sorry, ma'am. Do you mean Victor?"

She shrugged and shifted to her other hip. She was not going to say any more.

I sighed. This was no time for games. "Ms. Lance, may we please just come in for a moment?"

She gave a surrendering little shrug, opened the door wider, and held out a hand. She was wearing jeans and a purple, somewhat ratty sweater. No shoes. No socks. I couldn't tell if she was cold, but the effect of her small, bony feet on off-white linoleum in October made her look fragile. She followed us in and closed the door. "Can I get you something?"

"No, no, thank you."

"What it is then?"

The living room was small, with a beige couch and a deep green La-Z-Boy recliner. I made a mental note that if she got unsteady it would be easy to help her into the recliner. The television played some college football game, and I decided not to ask her to turn it off because it wasn't on very loud. "Ms. Lance," I said softly. "We have very bad news for you. We very much regret to inform you that your son was found in Glacier Park this morning. I'm afraid it looks as if he's been killed."

Penny stood frozen for a moment, her mouth slightly open and slack, as if the words had not yet registered. Then she let out a small squeaky moan and slowly put her palm to her mouth.

"We're very sorry."

"What?" She shook her head. "Why are you telling me this?"

I could see a mixture of anger and fear flood into her eyes. I couldn't answer her question with the obvious: *because you need to know since you're his mother, because he's never coming back.* "We've identified his prints, which are in the system."

"But—" She began to lose her balance. I grabbed her arm and helped her into the La-Z-Boy. She shook her head back and forth, then looked up to me, then Monty for answers, her face now racked with confusion with deep lines creasing her brow. "But how, what happened?"

"I'm sorry, but it looks as though he was mauled by a bear."

"What?" Her voice was loud and she pulled her head back, a turtle-like move. "A bear?"

"It's very complicated, Ms. Lance. We have some work to do to figure this out. But it looks as if your boy was forced into the woods by someone. Then, coincidentally, he was mauled."

Penny began to shake her head violently, her brow still deeply furrowed. "What on God's earth are you talking about? Jesus Christ, what are telling me?" She sprung out of her chair, her eyes darting from me to Monty and back, her hands by her sides clenched in fists as if she could fight away the truth. "What in the hell is going on here? Why are you saying these crazy things? Is this a prank?"

"No, ma'am. It's not. I know it's strange and we don't have all the details. But it looks as if your son, one way or another, was murdered."

"By a damn bear?" Her frantic voice sliced the air. She was still unable to grasp it. I asked myself why anyone would.

"No, by the person who kidnapped him. The grizzly is coincidental. The person who left him there is responsible, and that means murder whether the person who put him there meant it to be or not."

She wrapped her arms around her waist and stood in silence. Monty and I stared at her. I could see Monty's jaw muscles clenching.

"Where is he?" Her voice was small now, like a little girl's.

"He's with our state forensics lab. With good doctors."

There was no way she could see him, not now, not ever. There were only remains—a bundle of horror that only a pathologist might be able to make sense of. Penny began looking around the room for something, perhaps her cigarettes, her lighter, a glass of water . . .

"Can we get you some water, Ms. Lance?" I motioned to Monty to go to the kitchen to grab some.

"Where do I go?" Her eyes filled with tears. "Where is he?"

"No, I'm sorry, you can't see him right now. Please, Ms. Lance, please sit down." I gestured to the chair.

"But—I, this can't be right." She kept shaking her head, her mouth agape. "But why?"

"We don't know that yet. But we promise to find out." I could hear Monty closing a cabinet and running some tap water.

"Someone kidnapped him?"

"He was bound to a tree. Someone or perhaps more than one bound him to a tree."

"Jesus." Her watery eyes widened and a tear slid down one cheek. "But why? Who?"

Monty came back in and tried to hand Penny the glass of water, but she didn't pay any attention to his outstretched hand. She stared at me with wide eyes.

"I'm sorry that we don't have many answers for you. If anything, we're hoping that you might have some information that might help us figure out who's responsible for this." More tears began to slide down her cheeks. She slumped back down into the recliner and let her face fall into her hands. A TV commercial selling cell phone services with privileged, childish teenagers came on, its playful silliness mocking the seriousness of this mother's situation and far too trivial for the tragedy spreading before her. I grabbed the water from Monty and went to kneel before her. "Ms. Lance, I'm going to need to ask you a series of questions to help us find who's responsible for this. Would you like us to leave you alone for a bit and come back later, or would you like to talk now?"

She shook her head, her face still buried in her hands. She was sobbing harder, almost choking. "No," she blurted. "Don't leave." She said this as if our company could possibly add some comfort to the situation.

I set the water next to her on a side table and looked at Monty standing by the kitchen door. He held out his hands to say, *What do I do now?* I held up my palm for him to stay put. "We're not going anywhere," I said. "Take your time. Can I get you some tissues?" I nodded to Monty to find some in the bathroom. In the meantime, I walked over to a narrow table with framed pictures dominating a lacy runner to give Penny a moment to rein in her sobs.

There were several photos of two small brown-haired children, a boy and girl who I presumed were Victor and his sister. In one, they were in bulky winter jackets, the boy missing several front teeth in his big grin, the girl patting snow onto a snowman they were building.

In another, they were in colorful bathing suits on a small bright yellow raft, giggling and splashing around in a sparkling mountain lake. The camera caught the water spraying up around the kids, the sunlight illuminating the droplets into strings of bright, clear gems.

"Okay," Penny finally said after blowing her nose and wiping her eyes again. "I'll try."

• • •

I made sure she had a few sips of water and led her through it. She had not seen Victor for over two months, which would have been early August. She had seen him at a family get-together, but he was jittery and asked for money.

That's what he always wanted, she told us. She said that Megan, Victor's sister, would often tell her that if she'd just taken the time to add it all up over the years, she'd find that she'd probably given him over forty thousand dollars. But Penny refused to let herself believe that. Over the past three years, she said she'd gotten better at not enabling him and giving him so much. But every now and again, she slipped and couldn't help but slide him a hundred here and there for food.

Megan wouldn't speak to her mother if she found out she gave him money because she always said that Victor just used it on drugs, not food. Penny wasn't sure if she believed that or not. There were times when she really believed Victor was turning things around.

"Did you give him money in August?"

Penny nodded. "Only a hundred. That's all I had. Things have been tight with the economy the way it is. I've taken a cut in pay to keep my job."

"What did he seem like then?"

"Like usual. Skinny, jittery, pale, but I couldn't tell whether or not he was using. You have to understand that he's been this way for so long."

"For how long?"

"He started drinking when he was around eleven. Pot followed soon after. I didn't find out until he was about fourteen when he started not coming home at night. When he did come home, he'd be drunk and stoned, and Megan told me she'd heard that he was getting into harder stuff like heroin. I talked to all the school counselors, but nothing helped."

I nodded. "And heroin's been his drug of choice ever since?"

"I'm not sure." Penny sighed, then swallowed hard. "Well, actually—" Tears filled her eyes again, her face strained. "He got into meth about three or four years ago, when he was twenty-four or so. I spent every cent I had in retirement to get him into rehab in Kalispell. He went for ninety days, and it seemed to help for a while."

"How long is 'a while'?"

"I think a year or so. Even had a decent girlfriend for a while."

"What was her name?" Monty was taking notes. I had my notepad out as well and was getting it all down.

"Leslie."

"Last name?"

"I, I think it was Boone. She had a little boy named Lewis. Cute boy. Leslie seemed to really like Victor. From what Megan has told me, Leslie had gotten into meth too, but had recently cleaned her act up for her son's sake."

"And?"

"And nothing. Nothing came of it. I had hopes that he'd stay straight for them. But then he just started disappearing for longer periods without visiting, and when he did show, he'd need money, he always claimed, for food or rent. When I asked about Leslie, he'd say that was over, done. Never said why."

"How long ago was that?" Monty asked from his spot on the couch. His voice seemed to surprise Penny because she looked at him wide-eyed. In fact, his voice surprised me. He had not spoken a word since we'd come, and normally I tell whoever is assigned to me to let me do the talking, but it had seemed unnecessary with Monty since he was a guy of so few words.

I decided to let him ask away while I continued to take notes. And I must say, I felt superior, vaguely proud, like a mentor watching his subject learn as he branches out. And since Monty was so close to Ford, it gave me some satisfaction that Monty might actually like to learn investigative work, might actually be good at it, and want to leave Ford hanging at some point in his career. I nodded to Monty to continue and leaned back in the chair I'd brought in from the kitchen earlier so that I could sit across from Penny.

"About six months ago. She hasn't been in the picture since some-time last May."

Monty wrote this down, then glanced at me. I lifted my chin to nudge him on.

"Has he had any other girlfriends besides her?"

"Not that I've met. Megan said that his old girlfriend, Mindy, was with him now and again and . . ." Penny sighed. "Mindy was bad news. A real druggie."

"What's Mindy's last name?"

"Winters."

There was a pause. Monty looked at me.

"Did Victor have any other friends who might know his where-abouts over the past few days?" I asked.

Penny shrugged. "Nobody worth mentioning. Always different stragglers here and there. I don't even know the names of half of them. I would just beg him to not hang out with such people."

"Such people?"

"You know, druggies. You could tell because they looked skinny and unkempt, just like Victor was starting to look all over again. You might talk to Daniel. Daniel Nelson's been a buddy of his for some time."

"Can you think of anyone in particular that would want to harm Victor? Did any of his friends catch your attention for any reason at all?"

A look I couldn't quite pinpoint, something even sadder than her present grief, swam across Penny's eyes like a dark shadow of a fish. She looked down. "No." She shook her head, then put her tissue to her eyes again. "No, nobody in particular, but there have been a lot of bad people in my son's life because of all the drugs."

"I understand, but, Ms. Lance, it's important that you tell us everything and anything that might be pertinent."

"I will," she said robotically, her eyes vague and her attention slipping away into deeper grief. "I think, I think I really need to go to my room now." Her entire body sagged, her frame like a small wounded animal lost in the big recliner as she hunched forward. She folded her arms between her chest and her knees as if she had a stomachache. Her small feet lay pale on the floor with her toes curled under. I thought of a bird perching on a wire.

. . .

"Wow," Monty said when we got back in his SUV. "Intense."

"Yeah. Usually is. She took it better than most, though. She's a tough one."

"I guess so." Monty shook his head and made the same low whistle he had made at the crime scene. "Dealing with a druggie son like that, I guess it would thicken your skin."

"Yeah, but she thought of something near the end there. Not sure if it was important, but something crossed her mind that she either didn't want to share or simply saddened her even more. Made her fade."

"I was writing and didn't see her expression."

"I could be wrong, but we'll be talking to her again."

"I noticed you didn't ask about the father." Monty kept his eyes on the highway.

"Next time," I said. "We got more than usual under the circumstances. Often they're too distraught to even undergo questioning."

Monty nodded.

I thought about our victim, Victor Lance, as I looked to the Whitefish Range, the bare runs of the ski resort cutting down Big Mountain like prominent veins on the underside of a wrist.

5

THE ILLEGAL CAMPING couple seemed like they were out of a sit-com. They were young and constantly bickering. Kaylynn Lowden had crazy, curly, haywire reddish-brown hair, a big smile, and an unrelent-ing giggle, and Jarred Mercord had a dark, brooding, sulky look that neutralized his girl's enormous energy and filled up the makeshift in-terrogation room at park headquarters, making it seem too small for the three of us. All her remarks teetered on the naïve, and it didn't take long to realize she knew very little.

When we brought Jarred in, it also didn't take long to realize he didn't know much either, although it seemed like some kind of a game to him. His comments desperately worked toward sophistication and headiness but fell short primarily because of his youth. When we asked him to try to recall anything strange occurring during the time they were camping at Fish Creek, he said in a deeper voice that *"all cred-ibility, all good conscience, all evidence of truth come from the senses."* Then he added: "That was Nietzsche," as he flipped his head to get his long hair out of his face.

I rolled my eyes.

I have to give it to Monty. He was learning quickly, and he had more patience than I did with this kid. Just when I started to feel like I was going to shove him against the wall and tell him to stuff the so-phistication bit, he gave a scrap of information that was at least a tad bit useful when Monty asked if he'd seen any cars driving by.

"I saw several out all day. It was so nice, so people were coming and going, mostly driving up the Camas Creek area," Jarred said. "But I did see one vehicle more than once, and it was later in the evening than the others."

"What kind of vehicle?" I asked.

"A dark truck. Black or dark green maybe."

"The make?

"I don't know, maybe a Chevy or a Ford."

"Size? Small pickup or standard?"

"Standard."

"Why did it catch your attention?"

"I don't know." He shrugged. "Guess 'cause I saw it twice. And it was close to dark and I was out walking."

Jarred had first seen the truck sometime around five p.m. It went past him when he drove out of Apgar Village and was turning north on Camas Creek Road to head back to the campsite. Then while walking on Fish Creek Road to take some pictures of McDonald Lake with the sun going down at around quarter to seven, the truck had been heading away from Fish Creek Campground and away from the Old North Fork Road. He didn't recall who was driving or if there were passengers, and he certainly didn't notice a license plate.

We got Jarred's address and phone number. I gave him my card and told him to call if anything else came to mind.

"Right on," he mumbled, then added, "you know, as Tolstoy said, *All violence consists in some people forcing others, under threat of suffering or death, to do what they do not want to do.*"

"I'll keep that in mind," I said and sent him back out to Kaylynn.

. . .

Twilight fell upon us, and a bitter breeze soughed outside. The leaves of a maple tree rattled against one of our office windows. Late October and early November comprise the edgy heart of the Montana fall, pregnant with constant weather variations: sunny calm days, endless changes in wind, heavy black clouds refusing to rain for days, then finally releasing angry downpours for weeks. Then, just as easily—unexpected sleet, fog, snow. The entire atmosphere echoed my own restlessness. There was an anticipatory feeling I was carrying, but un-identifiable and out of reach like a word on the tip of my tongue. A sense that things were on the brink of change, perhaps only because Glacier Park carried this constant crepuscular quality that came with the long, overly enormous mountain shadows, the changing light, the cold ground, and a restless urge to keep moving while the varying shades of yellow-and-red leaves quivered and the squirrels and chip-munks busily gathered food at a frantic pace.

"Sharp kid," Monty announced.

"Yeah," I said dryly. "If I ever need to solve a case involving clues with quotes from German philosophers or Russian authors, I'll give him a jingle."

Monty chuckled.

I had to admit that Monty had been more helpful than I'd initially expected. He knew several of the rangers, and although he didn't seem as friendly with them as one would think he'd be for working in the same park, nobody appeared bothered by the fact that he was around.

"Hungry?" Monty arched his brow.

"Not really. You?"

"Getting there."

We both sat silently. It was that moment where I knew I was at the muddy trailhead of the case, barely taking the first steps. We had peo-ple to talk to, and I was hopeful answers would come quickly based on the fact that the victim was mixed up in drugs and was in the system.

"What are you thinking?"

"'Bout dinner or the case?" I asked, knowing very well he meant the case.

"The case?" he said.

I sighed. "I think"—I stood and leaned against the counter—"that

Walsh could be right and that we can pretty much assume that the guy was alive when the bear got him. There would be no reason to bind an already dead body to a tree. What would be the point?"

"There would be no point. If he were already dead, you would just toss him out there if you wanted the corpse eaten."

"Or bury him. You wouldn't bind him, unless you tortured him first and then killed him."

"So whoever taped him," Monty said, "must have wanted to torture him either way, whether they wanted him alive or dead. Then the bear came along."

I nodded. "Torture him, hold him, make an example of him. But what a risk to leave someone alive out in the woods. If someone discovered the victim before he was attacked, the guy would be completely exposed."

"So whoever did this, *if* they left Victor Lance out there alive, took a huge risk—actually went out of his way—to leave his victim alive like that."

"If that's the way it went," I said. "It could be to torture or to stage. It could also be a lesson or display of some sort. Maybe to make a point to other druggies who don't pay up?"

Monty shrugged.

"At any rate, either way, our guy got lucky. The bear did get Victor Lance."

"Yeah, and that makes me wonder . . ." Monty drifted off.

"Wonder what?" I asked.

"The burn area. It's my understanding that not many bears or other predators go through that area much, so if the killer knows anything about animal behavior, he must have known he was taking an even bigger risk that the guy would not be attacked by an animal. Maybe he didn't want him attacked and just wanted to hold him there, like you said."

"But that's not true about burn areas. Fresh vegetation and new roots popping up attract all sorts of animals. I'll double-check with Bowman, but I'm pretty sure about it."

"Then again"—Monty raised a shoulder—"we're probably giving the killer way too much credit. He probably doesn't know a damn thing about animal behavior or burn areas."

"That's right."

"He could just be some psychopath," Monty said.

"If that's the case, once we start digging in, he shouldn't be too difficult to track." I looked at Monty, his short dark hair, pale skin, and wire-rimmed glasses perched on his pointy nose, and wondered what would make a guy like him become Park Police, then end up tagging along behind the super, probably picking up the guy's dry cleaning, and sitting on his ass before a computer all day writing reports.

Most Park Police and rangers I know take the jobs because they want to be outdoors. Joe Smith was the perfect example. Some are jacks-of-all-trades and can still pack a horse and handle a chain saw and some are educators, historians, and naturalists. But most of them understand that without warning, their job can turn from the leisure pace of helping a tourist who's lost their keys, warning people that their dogs aren't allowed on the trail, and clearing out bear traffic jams to the high stress of dangling thousands of feet in the air to rescue overzealous hikers or sightseers who find themselves in dangerous crevasses.

Most want the job because they know that on a clear summer day, it can be the kind of job where they almost feel guilty for getting paid for it. And on a bad day, they find a frozen body in one of the fast-running streams: an old grandpa who slipped backward off a rock while taking pictures of his wife and was washed downstream.

Monty didn't look like any of the above. He had an obsessive-compulsive-accountant look with what appeared to be premature gray hairs beginning in his sideburns and begging the question of his age. "So, Monty." I cocked my head. "How come you wanted to work for the Park Service?"

"What?" He seemed surprised I asked.

"Why did you become a park officer?"

"Uh, the usual reasons."

"Which are?"

He pushed his glasses higher on the bridge of his nose. "Which are none of your business." He stood up and grabbed his coat.

I smiled and slowly my grin turned to a laugh. "Right answer, Officer Harris." I grabbed my coat as well. "Right answer."

. . .

The cabin assigned to me by either Joe or Ford had two bedrooms, a bathroom, a small kitchen, and a main room with a river-rock fireplace, deeply scarred wide-planked wooden floors, and several west-facing windows darned with old red-and-blue-plaid curtains.

The wind had picked up from bubbling, playful tousles to forceful shoves, and the cabin creaked with each gust. I was tired but wired. I felt small in a cabin in a place like Glacier, cold and deserted this time of year with the gusty weather, the mountains, and the icy waters a reminder of my insignificance—my thread-thin presence in the great fabric of nature around me.

I knew I wouldn't sleep well. I never did on the first night of a case. There were too many images, details, and questions darting through my mind. And, of course, there was the lingering rawness that at first drapes over you after breaking bad news to a victim's family, but by bedtime, presses into you, squeezes into you like shrink-wrap. I kept picturing Penny Lance's frail frame curled up as she hugged her stomach.

Monty and I had gotten some dinner at the Glacier Café, the same place we had lunch because of the lack of dining options in West Glacier. I knew I'd have to hit Hungry Horse, the closest town with a decent grocery store, and stock up on some things as soon as I had a moment. In the meantime, I went next door to the café and grabbed a six-pack, some beef jerky, and some OJ for the morning.

After dinner Monty drove me back to headquarters to meet Joe, who had a park vehicle gassed up and ready for me. He had finished the paperwork, making it legit for me to use it while I was on the case. We said good night to Monty, and I followed Joe down the road to my new home away from home, which really wasn't so bad. Aside from the damp cold and the musty smell, the cabin was homey enough.

One good fire would push out the chill. I made one with some leftover logs and some paper I had ripped out of an old *Trout Magazine*, grabbed a beer, and sat in an old-oak Adirondack-style chair to go over my notes. I took out a quarter and was surprised to see that it was still the Vermont. I'd used change at the convenience store but apparently managed to hang on to it. I began rubbing the quarter between my thumb and forefinger, its surface quickly made smooth by the natural oils from my fingers.

Victor Lance, drug problem. Penny Lance, the enabling mother. Father—absent, but I had Monica on it. She would come up with his whereabouts and access divorce papers to see what kind of role he played in Victor's life, at least financially. The rest I would find out from his sister and Penny. As far as girlfriends—one decent, one not so decent. Probably a host of others that Mom didn't know about. This was just the beginning. Tomorrow would have to bring more, much more. The old adage about forty-eight hours was sort of a cliché but not entirely; the first forty-eight are the most important. Cases can go cold quickly if strong leads are not established within a two-day time frame. Often, you could get a suspect and a strong lead if you did your homework, canvassed correctly, did extensive background checks and copious interviews. Over the years, though, forensic science and information technology had dovetailed in a way that both complicated things and made them easier. What you found in forty-eight often needed to wait for days or weeks anyway for testing and lab results. And in other ways, tests and computer technology sped things along drastically, shoved you in directions you might not have considered otherwise.

The fire popped and grabbed my attention. It never failed to make me uneasy. The orange flames fingered around the logs, waving and flickering. I thought of my mother. I would call her and see her when I came across some time. I would have to visit my middle sister, Natalie, as well. She lived in Whitefish, a small town north of Kalispell at the base of the ski resort with her husband, Luke, and their two boys, Ian and Ryan.

My oldest sister, Kathryn, lived in Minneapolis and worked for Merck Sharpe & Dome. She'd been divorced for over five years after finding out that her husband had cheated on her more than once over the years. Their divorce, long and ugly, ended up with a fifty-fifty split of their kids. I hadn't seen Kathryn in about three years, but I'd seen Ma and Natalie last year for Thanksgiving. They'd be happy to know I was working within driving distance less than a year after my last visit. Although, any mention of Glacier Park usually set my mother on edge. I never discussed that actual night much with either my mother or my sisters. By the time I got out of the hospital, everyone walked on eggshells around me.

I peeked outside. The temperature had dropped considerably. I brushed my teeth and found an extra blanket in a closet in the bedroom and went to bed. I tossed and turned until thoughts of my father pushed into my mind. I was investigating a case involving a grizzly in the park he so desperately wanted to get to know, to grow old near. He had told us on our drive to Montana in the dead of winter (we moved from Florida in time to start school in January after Christmas break) that he wanted to hike an average of sixty to seventy miles per summer, about five or six ten-mile hikes, so that by the time he was sixty-five, he would have logged over thirteen hundred miles of Glacier's terrain under his feet. Very doable, if only he had lived past his second summer of residing in Montana. I pushed the thought away; it was no use going there.

After his death, I never stepped foot into Glacier until I became a junior in high school, when heading to Glacier to hike became the hip thing to do. At first it was just picnics, playing Frisbee and drinking beer and whatever else we could get our hands on in out-of-the-way places, but then I began dating a girl named Kendra, whose father loved the park and insisted every Saturday that she join him for hiking.

If I wanted to spend time with her, I had no choice but to go along. And they were hiking machines. I ended up hiking Gunsight Pass with them, twenty-three miles in one day. I could barely walk up steps the following morning. Then Siyeh Pass, Huckleberry Mountain, the High Line Trail, Mount Brown Lookout, Piegan Pass, Snyder Lakes, and more. I was terrified of grizzlies, but we never camped and were always out of the woods by dark. I walked with my hand on the shiny black plastic safety of my bear spray attached to my belt.

I came to appreciate the beauty of the park, and after getting in shape, the way my body felt after a long hike—the lactic acid buildup in my thigh muscles. The way the summer high-elevation sun felt on my face and the mountain air in my lungs. I felt empowered that I could jump back on the horse, overcome my fear to be in the place at all. After two summers of extensive hiking, I came to realize that the woods were a part of me. I liked to learn the names and identify the wildflowers: Indian paintbrush, fireweed, bear grass, arnica, glacier lilies, purple-and-gold alpine daisies, monkey flowers, and pasque blossoms. I enjoyed seeing the striped chipmunks, the marmots we call whistle pigs, the moose, the scruffy spring sheep and goats, the golden eagles, the elusive elk. I saw several pine martins, black bears, and even the extremely rare family of wolverines running across a snowfield. I didn't see a grizzly during either of those summers, not even far away on a hillside or from a car in a bear jam. I considered myself protected, as if I'd done my time. I would be spared from coming across a grizzly ever again, even if I played in their backyard.

But even more than the beauty of it all, I felt the pull of the park in the way an extreme athlete feels the rush that comes from heading headfirst into fear, topping the next highest peak, the largest ocean wave, or the triple aerial off the tallest outcropping. Only I didn't need to go climb the world's highest peaks. This was a different kind of purpose, something more subtle, yet just as potent. I suppose it was my youth, my aggression, my desire to tackle something and win. Glacier Park had taken my father from me, and it became my private battlefield. If I could nudge just close enough without getting hurt as I did before, I could enter the pastoral, be that woodsman. It would be what my father wanted.

Taking forestry was also my attempt to nudge up to the half-ass woodsman in myself. I could study the forest in a safe setting, among students and professors. But reality hit when getting a job in the field stared me right in my naïve face. The clenched fist of fear settled in as I discovered that being a loner in the woods was not an option for me. Ultimately, human crime, with all its unpredictability and craziness, was nothing in comparison to the predictable, pitiless austerity and order of nature, its definitive underlying pattern that would fundamentally always mock the human call for world peace.

I listened to the wind still picking up outside, breathing through the trees like heavy sighs of a death angel. Whether I wanted to believe it or not, this place, with all the horror it held in my heart, was somehow home. Even with its rarity, power, and ominous vibrations making me want to pull the covers up over my head and kick and scream like a child, I felt its arms enfold me in an embrace of history and familiarity. I did not know what I expected from it. Obviously not to see my dad, with his unruly hair and Sonny Bono mustache, striding up like the Ghost of Christmas Past. No, I didn't know. Not safety. Perhaps familiarity, beauty, rhythm, truth, even danger. And something unidentifiable—something for the dark threads that ran through me to spool onto.

6

I WOKE READY TO tackle a busy day ahead. When I peeked outside to check the weather, I saw the wind had ceased, the sky had completely clouded over to a milky gray, which hung low and oppressive, dissolving halfway down the lower mountains into the blue-green pines. I hoped it wouldn't rain because it was best if it stayed dry as long as possible. Even if Crime Scene Services was done, the longer you could hold a scene close to its original state, the better.

I drank some OJ, took some stray Tylenol I found at the bottom of my toiletry bag for the pounding I felt in my left temple, and called Dr. Wilson in Missoula to see if he was ready to give me a rundown on his results. It was only quarter after seven, but I thought he might be in early. Sean had also called Wilson to back Gene Ford and gotten the case pushed higher on the priority list due to its strange nature and the fact that we had a federal bear situation potentially involving public safety.

In fact, it had become high enough of a priority that as soon as I hung up from leaving a message for Wilson, Sean called to inform me that he'd requested Nicholas Moran to fly me to Missoula to meet with Wilson, rather than talking to him on the phone as we normally would. It was always best to get the information from the pathologist firsthand, but I wasn't thrilled about leaving when I had a lot to accomplish. In addition, Gene Ford showed up at the hangar to come along.

I had spotted him at the hangar with his coffee-colored leather briefcase, his full-on ranger garb, including army-green olive pants and matching jacket heavily pocketed with shiny badges. I had thought, here we go again. He wore a round-brimmed hat the color of hay, which made his downward angling face look even longer in contrast.

As a greeting, he simply said, "Too bad we don't have yesterday's sunshine for today's flight."

We, I had thought. "I take it you're heading to Missoula?"

"Thought I'd join you. See what the pathologist has to say. Besides I've got business at your old stompin' grounds at the College of Forestry to give a talk on invasive water species. So I'll be staying on."

The trip took no more than twenty-five minutes. I sat in the back of the helicopter with my earphones on low, feeling lucky that the noise deprived Ford of the privilege to press me for information. I couldn't exactly pinpoint why he rubbed me the wrong way other than I knew he was keeping close tabs on me by assigning Monty, who was practically his personal secretary, to me, and now coming along to Missoula. I wondered if he'd be joining me to view the remains. Part of me hoped so, because I didn't think this man was up for it. Not many people are up for the slicing, poking, and prodding of the stone-white flesh, as if the victim is some random meat being prepared by a butcher for later use. So by the time we were in Missoula in the Forensics Science Division of the Montana Department of Justice's State Crime Lab on 11th Avenue, and Wilson came out to greet us, I was secretly dying to see Ford hit the door running with his palm covering his green mouth.

"Hello, gentlemen." I turned to see Dr. Wilson in a white lab coat approach us. Ford introduced himself and they shook hands. "And Detective Systead."

"Pleasure to see you again." I shook his hand as well.

With his olive skin, broad nose, and slightly red-rimmed and watery eyes from probably working most of the night under fluorescents, Dr. Wilson wasn't more than thirty. He looked as if you saw him at the grocery store, his tennis shoes would be untied, his hair gelled into a faux hawk, and he'd be buying chocolate milk for himself. Again, I was forced to register that, at forty, I was actually considered old in my field. The younger pathologists knew the latest and greatest in technology, the older ones had the experience. Usually experience won, but because Wilson was extremely bright, he was known as one of the best in the Northwest. The University of Washington wanted to keep him, but he apparently liked the idea of living in Montana more. "You both all right with seeing my work?"

"I'm good," I offered, then glanced at Ford, lifting my brow and making it obvious to Wilson that Ford was the one who ought to concern him.

Wilson followed my cue and studied Ford. "Have you been to a postmortem viewing before?"

"No, but I've seen all sorts of remains in the woods. I'll be fine."

"Okay then." Wilson waved for us to follow.

We went through double-swinging hospital-type doors, the smell of formaldehyde pushing through my nostrils. We walked down a long, wide hallway and into a large windowless, clinical white room with five autopsy tables, sparkling stainless-steel sinks along a sidewall, four square stainless freezers, and two taller refrigerators, the kind that looked like they might hold groceries.

The entire room spoke of sanitation and sterility, as it should. But the stark austerity—the remains splayed on the cold table—would remind anyone of the dark, primal dysfunctions, and instincts that bring such pale and bloody flesh—such broken life—to the table. My routine encompassed this reality too, but when I did my job well, I saw the whole spectrum: the motive, the circumstances, the personalities surrounding the victims, the other crimes adjoining the homicide. The pathologist sees only the dead body, the disease, the rape-victim samples, piecing together a context to put it all in.

What was left of Victor Lance lay pathetically under the bright lights, a pitiful combination of ripped, sagging flesh, exposed bones, and innards arranged to look as put together as possible. Ford was actually lucky because the bear's violation had already been so brutally thorough that Wilson's necessary incisions were minimal, more of a stitch-up job, a salvaging of puzzle pieces. It was more difficult to see intact, pure skin sliced open, the *Y* incision making the skin fold to the side, exposing the unfathomable parts of our bodies that we carry daily but never glimpse.

Wilson motioned for us to approach the table as he put on his plastic gloves. I walked right up, but Ford hesitated. I thought I heard him swallow hard. Wilson did too and said kindly, "You sure you're up for this?"

Ford nodded, his face much paler than minutes ago, and shuffled closer to the table.

"So what we have here is an adult male, twenty-seven according to your records." He glanced at me. "Height and weight both on the very lower end of normal for an adult male, but I don't think from disease. I see no evidence of any obvious pathology other than his teeth." Wilson pointed to the victim's gum line set against bone since half of his face had been peeled away by the bear. His cheekbone, jaw, and teeth, too long and yellow—sinister as any teeth without a mouth enclosing them tend to appear—were exposed. "His teeth show past decay along the gum and the classic collapsing jawline of a meth user. Meth dries out the gum, a condition called xerostomia, and leads to excessive bruxism, or grinding of the teeth and the inward cave of the jaw. And even though the bear has cracked the skull and made this indentation"—he pointed at the right side of his skull—"we can still see that his jaw is inwardly caving from wear and tear and not the bear's crack."

"His mother," I added, "has verified that he was a user."

Wilson nodded. "When the toxicology report comes in, we'll know if he was using within approximately seventy-two hours of the time of death. My bets are on some type of ephedrine or pseudoephedrine, all chemicals frequently used to make methamphetamine."

"And time of death?" I asked.

"Well, there are some interesting time-of-death issues. First—" Wilson poked at the dark gaping cavities around the rib cage and stomach. Out of the corner of my eye, I saw Ford take a step back and look away. Wilson glanced at him. "Okay there?" he questioned again with a kind voice.

Ford nodded. He was tougher than I thought. I was waiting for him to bolt at any minute, but he was putting up a good fight.

Wilson cleared his throat. "The arterial bleeding is interesting because, though from your perspective it doesn't seem so, the volume is less than you would normally see with a bear attack victim. The arteries produced less blood than would have been typical."

"Wait." I held up my hand. "So are you saying that he was or wasn't alive when the bear attacked?"

"I'm afraid, alive. But usually victims of animal attacks bleed more excessively since their panic level is so high and the heart is pounding furiously. With this guy, it's almost as if he was in a state of shock already. Or was only semiconscious since his arterial bleeding indicates that he was not in a state of panic."

"So, the bear," Ford finally spoke, but his voice sounded thin in the large room. He covered his mouth, turned away, and coughed, letting a retching sound escape. The sound pierced the cold room and seemed to echo. Suddenly the air felt difficult for me to breathe. "Excuse me." Ford gulped. "The bear," he tried again, "so the bear was attacking someone limp and weak, maybe unconscious, almost dead? Dead to the bear?"

"There was enough arterial bleeding at the time of the attack to show that he was antemortem—" He glanced at Ford. "Alive," he added. "But like I said, when the bear attacked, he was not struggling or moving vigorously. In essence, he probably would not appear to be a threat to the bear like a healthy person might."

"Tracks showed a grizzly." I felt the clench, remembering the track with the claw track measuring around three and a half inches. I knew a black bear's claw usually measured about one and a half inches long. "Is that consistent with your findings?"

"Absolutely. Canine marks are consistent with the measurements of grizzly teeth, jaw angle, and claw depth." I knew that the fang of a grizzly could measure up to four and half to five inches, while a large black bear's fang was closer to three to three and a half inches.

"Any possibility of human DNA on the body?" I asked.

"There's very little blood, skin, or hair beneath the fingernails of the remaining arm, indicating not much of a struggle with the bear, consistent with the fact that he was not panicking when the bear came at him. We haven't completed the tests yet, but I don't think there will be human DNA samples available. Unless we luck out on some of the duct tape, but I wouldn't get your hopes up. I'm not seeing much to indicate that we'll get anything."

I sighed, shaking my head grimly at the thought of no DNA.

"But, ah." Wilson held up a finger, a faint delight emanating from his eyes. Of course. There had to be some enjoyment for him, or how would he come to work each day? Just because the dead bodies were the visible reality (not the campfire stories one heard) that violence dwells in the cracks between our safe, small worlds didn't mean the bodies were finished telling their tales. Wilson might even listen to them with compassion. I remembered the Latin cliché, *mortui vivos docent*, mumbled by my father when he took me to the university with him and told me that we'd be moving three thousand miles away—how he whispered it softly. *The dead teach the living*.

"I found"—Wilson pointed a white-gloved finger to the right shoulder of the victim— "something interesting. As you can see by the canine marks here, the right pectoral has been ripped clean away to and under the rib cage." He pointed to the dark cavity below the ribs. "The grizzly has also cleanly ripped away the spleen and the ascending colon. But if you remember, part of the victim's shirt was draped over the right shoulder. We're still running tests, but the part of the shirt hanging over the rib cage, although soaked with coagulated blood, shows a small amount of granular residue in a shape that looks as if it were part of a saucer or small plate-size circle that I think is a stippling pattern."

"Really?" My voice must have sounded excited enough for Ford to pipe up.

"Stippling?" Ford asked, his mouth completely green now.

Wilson nodded. "Stippling is the pattern the firing of a gun leaves on a victim if fired at close range. We've run those tests, and there's just enough residue to see that it is part of a larger pattern emanating outward from the abdominal area that was eaten by the bear."

"And the bullet?"

"Gone. Most likely in the gut of your grizzly."

I made a low whistling similar to Monty's. "Okay then. So victim was chained to a tree, then shot. From what distance?"

"Having any pattern at all suggests a proximity of six to twelve inches. If farther away, stippling wouldn't appear. Plus I've found some interesting marks on the lowest rib that appear to be made from the bullet, which, if I'm correct, the trajectory of the bullet would have been downward." He delineated a path from the right pectoral to the medial side of lowest rib.

"So the shot would have been fired from high to low and at an angle?"

"That's what I'm thinking so far."

"Hmm," I mumbled.

"Yeah, the trajectory angle of the bullet is a little weird. I'll let you know if I come up with a different read after more analysis."

"Any signs of sexual abuse?"

Wilson tilted his head for a moment, as if to consider the question. "No. From all I'm seeing on the remains, which isn't that much, but enough to make some solid deductions, is that this man was not sexually abused. We have found no bodily fluids on him. He was chained, shot, and eaten by a grizzly. And he was eaten within a short time frame before dying from the gunshot wound—close to being in shock or unconscious."

"Do you know the time of death?"

"Just a window. He died between one and eight p.m. on Friday, but"—he held up his finger— "from the remaining skin, the enlarged pores, the frostbite on his fingers, and the state of dehydration in the liver, it looks like the victim was exposed for a long time before he was even shot. His level of dehydration and the abrasion marks on his ASIS and under his armpits from the tape suggest he was chafing against those for a number of hours."

"Can you say how many?"

"I'd say he was out there for at least eighteen to twenty-four."

"So he was out there Thursday night too?"

"That's right."

"How long would you say passed between the bullet entering the victim and the bear attacking?"

"About sixty to ninety minutes."

"So the bullet could have been fired as early as eleven thirty and as late as six thirty on Friday?"

Wilson nodded. "Give or take. Yes."

• • •

On our way out of the building, Ford excused himself and went into the men's room. I had to use the restroom myself, but decided I would give him his privacy. I had no desire to hear someone retching in a stall next to me.

He returned with a damp look around the edges of his thinning hairline, as though he'd splashed water over his face, and I figured he had, indeed, lost his breakfast. I found myself vacillating between having contempt for the old man for having worked for the Park Service for over thirty years and still unable to keep his cookies down to having a strange sympathy when I considered my own troubled breathing back in the lab. His face looked deathly and deeply etched with thousands of small lines. I considered that in a few years he'd be replaced by some experienced ranger who would run circles around him.

He recovered from his pallor by the time we made it back to the car and said he would give me a ride to the helicopter. While he drove, he reminded me that he planned on staying in Missoula for the night, said his wife was coming to meet him for the evening, and they'd both drive back to the Flathead the next day. He even offered the fact that the wife put Missy, a two-year-old golden retriever, in the kennel for the night to join him. He didn't tell me his wife's name. I don't know why he gave me any details at all, but I sensed he needed the small talk to try to shuffle the images he now forever held in his psyche to some other place not so present.

After he pulled up to the aviation office, killed the engine, suddenly everything seemed to get too quiet, and I thought I smelled expensive cologne. I was certain he wasn't wearing it when I stood next to him during Wilson's presentation, so I figured he had a bottle in his briefcase and had put it on in the bathroom to get the smell of formaldehyde out of his nostrils. Again, I felt an odd sympathy I wasn't expecting. "Look, Systead." He turned to me. "The park's just seen its best attendance in years, even with it being the rainiest summer in a long time."

I didn't say anything.

"So there're a few obvious things here that I don't feel like I need to spell out to you but will anyway, just for the sake of being direct."

"Fair enough," I offered. "Shoot."

"The most obvious is that this should be very much downplayed with the press, which I would think works to your investigative advantage as well."

I nodded. "It does."

"Okay then. We're on the same page."

"Sounds like we are." I opened the car door, ready to get out and be on my way. The cologne was making me slightly nauseous. Plus I had a lot of interviews to conduct upon my return, and whatever modicum of sympathy I was feeling was quickly vanishing with the haughty tone of Ford's voice. "Thank you for the ride." I placed one foot out the door.

"Additionally—" He wasn't finished. "We're in a bit of a pickle with this grizzly situation mixed up in it. I don't want this smeared all over the nation like some major grizzly mauling because it's not. It's simply an issue of remains. You heard him, the guy didn't even put up a fight. He was half-dead already."

I nodded.

"But I also don't want this going down as some hyped-up park murder either. I don't know what freaky thing happened out there, but I can tell you it was just some weird fluke. Nothing's as scary as it first seems."

I shrugged. "That's what I'm here to try to find out, sir."

"I understand that, but you need to know where I'm coming from."

"I do understand."

"Good then. You're welcome."

It took me a second to recall that he was responding to my earlier thank you for the ride. He smiled a stretched smile, a little too tight, toothy, and coffee stained, and the corpse's skeletal Halloween smile stabbed into my mind. "You know," he continued, "one of my top priorities this year is to strengthen communication between the four hundred and fifty employees and fifteen hundred volunteers the park has."

I grabbed the door handle to signal my departure. "Sounds like a solid plan."

"It *is* a good plan. And teamwork—we're looking for teamwork when it comes to Glacier, between all its factions. Canada and us, the tribes and us, DC and us."

"I can see that that would be good too." I stayed put in my seat, my hand still reaching out to the handle.

"And with this particular investigation, I'm thinking a little team-work is important as well."

I shrugged. "Most certainly, sir. It's been a teamwork situation since the get-go with the county sheriff and their forensics lab, your rangers, Park Police, the Department of the Interior, the state crime lab." I gestured in the direction of the university nestled against the brown, eastern hills of Missoula. "A lot of chefs in the kitchen already. But by nature, certain things in an investigation need to be kept under wraps."

"I understand that, but I need to be kept apprised of all developments."

I gave him a single nod, not feeling like making a verbal affirmation. I thought of saying, *Isn't that what Monty is for?* Instead, silence dropped heavy into the space between us.

"So"—he wrapped his hand around the keys in the ignition, ready to turn the car back on— "that's why I've been keeping in close touch with Walsh, Smith, Bowman, and Sean Dewey."

I climbed out of the car and looked back in, resting my elbow on the door. I decided I needed to play nice. "Look, whatever I've got is yours unless it somehow jeopardizes something in the investigation, which I can't see why it would. So no worries." I forced a smile.

"Good, then you also shouldn't have a problem with the fact that I've spoken to your boss and we've come to an agreement that my office will handle anything to do with the press."

This didn't necessarily bother me; dealing with the press was a pain in the ass, but it was crucial that it was done right. I knew, of course, that reporters had been in to check the activity logs with both the city and the county, as they do every day, and that they knew about the dispatch to Glacier. And I knew, from Sean, that Walsh and he had agreed that the feds would handle all releases. What I didn't know was that Ford had talked Sean into deferring to Ford's department for all releases.

I thought of how Ford and his gang handled my father's mauling.

The saved clippings I saw only once before I left for college. My mother kept them in the top drawer of a bedside table in her room, the thin paper now slightly yellow with age and smelling like the oak of the drawer. A strong urge to walk away without saying a thing overcame me. I fought it. Told myself that he would do all he could to protect the park, and this was a plus for me to not have to deal with reporters.

"So," he said, "I'll need you to defer all questions from the press to my department." He stared at me, his brow up.

I nodded. "Just make sure you give them enough so that they keep their noses out of my work."

"All right then." Ford held out his hand, smiling.

I shook it and forced a smile. "Hope you and your wife enjoy Missoula." I shut the door and walked away, needing to take a bigger, deeper breath than I expected. I definitely needed some coffee.

7

W‍HEN I RETURNED to West Glacier, I ran into Joe Smith and a younger blond gal, a good inch taller than him, who turned out to be one of his daughters. Although I felt a kinship with Joe, I didn't know much about his family. I remembered that he had, in the past, mentioned a thing or two about his wife and kids, who were off living their own lives. He introduced her as Heather, his oldest, and said they were heading out to lunch.

"I'd invite you along, but Monty's in there waiting for you. He's been diligently working." Before I had left for Missoula, I had left orders for Monty to see if Victor had a cell phone and if so, to get the records, to check with the border patrol in Eureka and St. Mary, the train stations in Whitefish and Essex, and to contact the airport for anyone suspicious who either came in or tried to leave in the last week. None had anything strange or out of the ordinary to report. Additionally, I had asked him to contact Walsh for information on known meth dealers in the area and to make sure he had tracked down the addresses of all the individuals we planned to question when I returned.

"Glad to hear that," I said. "I'm sorry, but I need to speak to you." Heather had her father's almond-shaped eyes, but they were green, not blue. "I'm sorry to interrupt, but you wouldn't mind if I stole your dad for a few minutes?"

"No." She fidgeted, shuffling her feet a bit and glancing to her father, then back to me. "Of course not. Take your time," she said with a tentative, but pleasant, smile.

Joe put an arm around her. "Hon, you go ahead in your car. I'll meet you there in ten."

. . .

"The bear," I said immediately to Joe as soon as his daughter was out of earshot. "The damn thing most probably has a slug in his gut."

"What?"

"Wilson's found a stippling pattern on the victim."

"You're kidding?"

I told him about the autopsy, about the victim being out all Thursday night and Friday during the day, about the timing of the death, and the fact that the victim was alive but not responsive when the bear attacked.

"So except for possible evidence in the bear's belly," Joe said, "from the park's perspective, there's no reason to put him down. To that bear, the guy was as good as dead."

"I suppose so," I said. "But the bullet, as you know, is always an important piece of evidence."

Joe nodded. "Talk to Sean. I'll talk to Kurt Bowman. Ultimately, it's going to be the super's call. All we do is make a strong recommendation. Even though it's your investigation, you know that he makes the final call. But he'll listen to your department's recommendation"— he shrugged as if he didn't completely believe his own words—"if it's going to obstruct justice in some way."

"Yeah, I know." I sighed. "Look, I have no desire to put this beast down, especially if we don't even find the bullet. He could have crapped it out by now."

"It's a possibility but unlikely if he's near the end of his hyperphagia when his digestive system slows down to gear up for dormancy. We probably still have time," Joe said.

From what I'd read, prior to hibernation, grizzlies go into hyperphagia—an excessive eating and drinking period to fatten up for hibernation—and can gain up to four hundred pounds. During this time, they eliminate large amounts of nitrogenous waste. But right after this stage, just before hibernation, grizzly metabolism slows to a snail's pace, and they don't go very much until right before they den up.

"And the corridor of water near McGee?" I switched focus to the gun. "If I recall my geography of the area, there are four bridges, maybe five, but two are smaller streams and easy to search. Can we get some metal detectors on the smaller streams today?"

"Absolutely." Joe nodded.

"And given the high likelihood of disposing a gun in deeper water, there are three main rivers with bridges."

"McDonald Creek, the Middle Fork in West Glacier, and the South Fork, past Hungry Horse," Joe offered.

"Yep, plus there's the Flathead in Columbia Falls, but that's a pretty populated area. I'm more interested in the two in the park. Can we get Walsh to agree to some divers?"

Joe tilted his head and rubbed the back of his neck. "Yeah, I think I can talk him into it, especially given the fact that Walsh's department has actually solved several crimes around the Flathead that way." He grabbed his keys from his pocket and looked at his watch. "Let me catch up with my daughter. I'll be back in ten to deal with this. We should at least trap the bear as soon as we can."

• • •

Kurtis Bowman, the bear guy, came in as soon as I had hung up from speaking with Sean, who is stereotypically crabby enough of a boss to say that he didn't give a rat's ass whether I ordered the bear down or not—that he simply wanted me to do my job in whichever way I saw fit.

"So you're recommending that we put this bear down over a bullet?" Bowman tried to ask nicely, but I could hear the edge in his voice.

"Ted Systead." I set my coffee down on the local newspaper I'd been reading before Sean returned my call, stood up, and held out my hand. I had finally checked out the Sunday news and seen that Ford had given very little information, just that the sheriff's office was called in to investigate a death of a twenty-seven-year-old male named Victor Lance early on Saturday morning. No bear was mentioned, no foul play, no use of the kidnapping or the murder word, not much other than the victim's name had been mentioned. Monty had joined me, and we were planning to question Lance's sister as soon as we figured out the bear situation.

"Kurt Bowman." He briefly shook my hand, then looked at Monty. "Hey, Monty." He tipped his head.

"Good to see you, Kurt." Monty smiled.

"Look," I said. "I haven't made a recommendation yet. I didn't say I wanted to put him down. However, Wilson believes it's in the bear's digestive track, and I'm sure you know that ballistics are important to investigations. It potentially tells us what kind of a gun was used and sometimes we can come up with a computerized match in the FBI or ATF database if there's been another crime committed with the same gun in which a slug was identified. Not to mention, if we find a suspect with the gun in their possession, we can get a match."

"Yeah, I get that, but grizzly bears are important to ecosystems. And this one did nothing wrong."

Dealing with a federally protected park bear was a tricky situation. We needed to weigh and balance all factors: the importance of locating evidence vital to any investigation and the bear's danger to other humans now that it had fed on human flesh versus the need of the grizzly species to keep a healthy young male alive. When it came to the investigation, we needed to figure out the best way to get the bullet because it could be essential for the conviction of the criminal, if not the solution to the crime. Short of euthanizing the bear and cutting it open to search its intestines, the next best step was to wait for it to defecate.

It was reasonable to suspect that it would pass the bullet eventually, at which time it would go into hibernation and form its fecal plug, which prevents it from defecating in its den while hibernating. Giving the bear a laxative would upset this delicate process, and though it might not kill him outright, the change in gut metabolism, intestinal flora, and hormonal balance would likely mean the bear would die during the hibernation process.

I agreed with what Bowman was saying—that the bear had done nothing overtly dangerous to humans, and I'd decided not to push putting the bear down because of that. Instead, I thought we should capture it and go from there. But Bowman coming in with his guns loaded made me want to play the devil's advocate, because I was in the same mood I'd been in since I'd stepped foot in Glacier. In a crazy, completely nonsensical way, I felt it was my job to somehow subdue Glacier's wild energy so we could solve the crime. "No, but he's fed on human flesh. Do you not see that as a problem?"

"We do." Bowman sighed. "We do, but under the circumstances, we would not put a bear down for this. He is not actually a conditioned bear or even habituated." I knew that he was trying to label the bear, making the distinction between conditioned and habituated, because earlier in the year, a review board in Glacier had tinkered around with definitions to help the park's Bear Management program after they had to put down an old sow who had never been aggressive to people, but instead had gotten a little too curious and slobbered on tents, checked out a few backpacks, and held trails when people approached. Many of the locals who'd enjoyed seeing her around got enraged that park officials decided to kill her and made numerous angry calls to headquarters and wrote letter after letter to the small local papers nearby.

From what I remember reading, a conditioned bear referred to one who had stolen food, damaged property, or displayed aggressive behavior toward people. A habituated bear only meant that a bear had become *tolerant* of human presence. The definitions apparently matter because how a bear is classified helps cast its fate.

"He doesn't approach people or tents, backpacks, or food storage containers when people are present," Bowman continued. "Only banged on a few containers when the campgrounds were empty. He hasn't bluff-charged innocent people walking down a trail, or even held a trail. He smelled blood and acted appropriately. As far as the bear is concerned, those remains could have been elk."

"Yeah, an elk looking exactly like a human." I leaned my hip against the counter and crossed my arms, baiting him further. "Come on." I narrowed my eyes at Bowman. "I don't have to tell you that grizzlies are intelligent." And they are. It's common lore that a grizzly's intelligence compared to a black bear's is like comparing a dog's brain to a mouse's.

"Listen, other than banging on a garbage container or two," he repeated, "he's not a conditioned bear. He's not aggressive. We have no reports of him being hostile to anyone, ever."

I caught my lower lip with my front teeth, then let it pop out, my teeth scraping the flesh underneath harder than I intended. I sensed I was in some weird zone, like I was on thin ice with conflicting emotions about a *Glacier Park* bear. I actually surprised myself that I was doing less than advocating for the bear like everyone else seemed to be doing. "I know this is a shitty situation." I sighed. "But if this investigation goes unsolved because we didn't get the evidence from this bear, which, quite frankly, could potentially end up doing damage to someone else in the future, we'll all be in a heap of trouble."

Bowman looked at the white linoleum floor for a moment. Monty watched us both. "Really now"—Bowman lowered his voice—"what are the chances that getting the bullet will help you solve this case?"

"You'd be surprised." A moment of silence enveloped us until Bowman took in a deep breath.

"Agent Systead," he said, "do you know what the population of grizzlies is in the Northern Continental Divide?"

"Actually, I do, around seven fifty, eight hundred." I knew that the Northern Continental Divide Ecosystem, called NCDE, in western Montana had the largest population of grizzlies in the lower forty-eight. This included Glacier, the Bob Marshall Wilderness, and the Rocky Mountain front. But still, even with it being the largest, the population of grizzlies in the lower forty-eight was only two percent of what it once was when grizzlies inhabited a range from the prairie lands to California and from central Mexico on up to Alaska. "And numbers are up in Yellowstone, in spite of it being a bad year for them there," I added. I knew that deaths there this year neared record levels, but still, numbers had risen to six hundred for the first time since recovery efforts began in the seventies.

"So?" Bowman said, one lip curled in disgust. "You think those numbers are high? An estimated seventy-five of them were killed or removed from the wild, do you know what that means?"

I didn't answer, just folded my arms in front of me.

"It means that one grizzly has been taken out for every eight counted this year in Yellowstone. Not to mention that since that ecosystem is fairly isolated, the limited variety in breeding practices is hurting the viability of the population. And I won't even go into the effects of their dwindling supply of whitebark pine nuts as a food source."

"But that has no bearing on the situation here. Safety is safety, on more levels than just one—in terms of finding the person who committed this crime and in terms of grizzly management in the park. Risk management is risk management." I was ready to end this conversation. "Look," I said with some finality, "first and foremost, we're searching for the weapon, and if and when that turns up, we will need the slug. I told you when you first came in that I did not want to put this bear down and for now, I don't intend to pressure you or Ford to do that. But I need that slug."

Bowman widened his eyes.

"So at the very least, we need to capture it and see if he purges soon and we can find it in his scat."

Bowman nodded vehemently. "We can definitely do that."

Silence enveloped us, and I could feel my heart palpitate faster at the thought of capturing the bear, at the thought of euthanizing and cutting him open if he didn't eliminate the bullet. I don't know why I cared. Evidence was in the bear's belly, and if I screwed up another case because I had too much compassion for a damned grizzly and didn't push the right course of action, Sean would not be happy. "Good." I nodded firmly. "Put the culvert traps out immediately and have someone inform me when you get him. I'll also need someone extensively checking his scat. Don't lose an ounce of it, and make sure Gretchen and her team are called in to check the surrounding area where you trap him for all the piles within a five-mile radius."

Bowman shook his head, a hopeful look on his face. He really cared about sparing this bear. "I can have some of my men checking even farther out than that."

"Great, just make sure they don't touch the bullet if they come across it."

"All right, thanks. We'll do our best," Bowman said and left the room.

Monty stared at me. I'd forgotten he was even in the room.

"You ready to go?" I asked.

"Yep, I'm ready." He held up his notepad.

I grabbed for the car keys in my pocket, my palms slippery with sweat and my jaw clenched. "I'm driving," I said, pulling out the keys.

. . .

I didn't exactly want to be around when they went grizzly trapping. And I was already way behind in my questioning because of my trip to Missoula and this bear dilemma, which was not helping me get rid of the morning's headache.

Monty and I headed first to Victor's sister's apartment in Columbia Falls, no more than ten to fifteen miles from West Glacier, a town that lies before the entrance to the canyon leading to Glacier. An old aluminum plant sits at the base of Teakettle Mountain and was one of the biggest employers in the valley for years, but died a slow death as global demand for aluminum shrank and cast hundreds of locals out of work. Luckily, a mill called Plum Creek, an international timber provider, still supplied a number of jobs, but with the recession had to lay off large numbers. Houses suddenly became hard to sell, and banks began foreclosing on people while they looked for jobs that weren't there. Meanwhile, in Whitefish, just fifteen miles to the west at the base of Big Mountain on Whitefish Lake, houses still sold to wealthy Californians, Texans, and mostly Canadians rich on oil money who were taking advantage of the low market.

As we drove through the canyon, through the succession of poverty-ridden, two-gas-station, three-church, and three-bar towns—Coram, Martin City, Hungry Horse—Monty ran me through his discoveries. They were meager. Lance did have a cell phone but didn't pay the bill. It was shut off the month before. Records from the prior months were being emailed to me as we spoke.

Then my phone rang twice as we continued through the canyon by the Flathead River past the confluence of the middle and south forks. Monica called to confirm that Victor and Megan Lance's father, Philip Lance, failed to make the paltry support payment of two-fifty per month that the court assigned him back in the eighties. The second call was from Ford, which I silenced. Of course, not a minute after I killed the ring, Monty's phone rang and he, being the good little boy he was, answered it promptly. I pulled out my quarter and began rolling it over my knuckles, my right hand on the wheel.

After a string of "Yes, sirs," and an evil glance from me, Monty said good-bye.

"Your boss angry?" I asked.

Monty shrugged. "I don't mean to tell you how to do things, but shouldn't you have called him right away about your decision to trap the bear?"

"Why? It's not his investigation. Usually the super's not that involved in law enforcement efforts anyway. I'm just wondering why this guy is so gung ho to be involved."

"He's always been very hands-on," Monty offered. "It's his park, and he has the ultimate say."

"Really? US National Parks don't belong to the citizens of the United States?"

"You know what I mean." Monty stuck his phone back into his jacket pocket. "The bear's a big deal, and if the press gets ahold of it, this thing's going to get complicated for the park, and that's Ford's deal."

"Um hmm," I grunted. "Well, it won't be the first time a grizzly needs to be captured. Usually, the public's thankful for keeping 'em safe when it comes to bears."

"Not this summer. People were outraged over the Lake Ellen Wilson bear they put down."

I didn't reply. I'd had enough of talking about bears. "Anyway," I said dismissively, "I knew Ford would find out faster than I could even pull up his number."

Monty glanced disapprovingly at my quarter rolling, then stared out the window silently until we reached Megan's apartment above a small soup café on the main drag in Columbia Falls. She actually worked in the café but had taken the day off under the circumstances. Megan's mother had given us her cell phone number, and we had called to make sure she would be home and available for us to stop by.

. . .

Megan answered the door smoking a cigarette. She had apparently showered before we came, her long dark hair sleek and dripping wet patches onto on her mauve T-shirt on the mound of each breast. Thick eyeliner and mascara attempted to hide the puffiness in her eyes. She had invited us in and showed us to a small, round kitchen table and plopped herself down in front of a window next to her kitchen sink.

Monty and I sat without an invite. The wet patches, like badges of help-lessness, made her look slightly pathetic and made me pause before I found my words. When I did find them, I gave my condolences, Monty following suit.

Megan sat, framed by the gray sky, still dismal at two thirty in the afternoon. Her shoulders slumped downward as if her arms were weighted. Her eyelids draped heavy with grief and perhaps caution, even skepticism. Past the mascara, she had the type of eyes that could change from dark brown to tan to hazel with the slightest shift in light. I began to think my initial impression of her vulnerability was wrong, and in the partially shaded hardness of her eyes, I thought I saw a flicker of contempt. She might not be as helpful as I thought the little sister would be. "Smoke?" she offered.

"No, thanks," I said.

She looked at Monty as if weighing him. "You?" She stretched out the pack of Camels to him.

"Uh, no, thanks." He sat up straight, poised.

She shrugged and took a few draws of her own and held it in her lungs with her chin lifted.

"Ms. Lance." I sighed. "Finding who did this to your brother in-volves us trying to dig up as much information as possible about him, especially the days leading up to when this awful thing occurred."

"I haven't the faintest idea of what he's been up to for months now." The edge in her voice didn't match my initial impression either.

"And why is that?"

"In case you haven't figured it out yet, my brother wasn't exactly a pillar of the community."

"Your mother told us about his addictions, and we know he was charged with theft at a local convenience store."

Megan pursed her lips together and tapped her cigarette into a glass ashtray spotted with dirty black spots. "I didn't much approve of his lifestyle, so we stayed clear of each other."

"When was the last time you saw your brother?"

"I believe it was this summer. In Aug—" She caught on the word, suddenly betraying her sorrow or perhaps guilt for not seeing him sooner before his life was taken. I waited, the silence not going anywhere, providing enough space for her eyes to well up. I could hear the cars driving below on Nucleus Avenue. She peered out the window toward a flattop roof across the street, but she looked as if she weren't seeing the things in front of her, only working the task to push back tears. "In August," she said firmly and crushed her cigarette into the tray. "I saw my mom give him some money and it pissed me off. We were at a barbecue for my uncle Lou's birthday out at the cabin. And you know, even at a fucking family barbecue, he had the one-track mind going, like a dog sniffin' out a bone." She shook her head angrily. "After my mom gave him some money, he left, and then I had some words with her about it. I ended up leaving early and angry."

"So August—what was this barbecue?"

"Eighteenth. Uncle Lou's birthday."

"And where's the cabin?"

"In Glacier. My mom's family is one of those that, somewhere along the line, got grandfathered into being able to keep property in the park, near Apgar."

Surprised, I glanced at Monty. I made a note that I needed Monica to run a full background check on the mother's family. I hadn't expected Victor to have a connection to the park. There are a number of people who still have cabins and even a few who reside year-round in Glacier. "Near Apgar on Lake McDonald?"

"Yeah, near Fish Creek, you know, up that dirt road from McDonald Creek, near those other cabins."

"The north Apgar Road?"

"Yeah, that's it."

"And someone stays there year-round?"

"My uncle Lou does. My grandparents have both passed on. They wanted Lou to have it. He loved it the most and spent a lot of time there in his life. He takes good care of the place. Plus Lou works in Hungry Horse, closest to the cabin."

"So your uncle, his last name?"

"Shelton." She took out another cigarette with a limp hand, lit it with a blue lighter, and folded one leg up under her. The picture of her with her brother on the raft came to my mind, and I imagined her lazily dangling her toes in cold Lake McDonald, enjoying her brother's company in happier times. "My mother's maiden name."

"Were they close?"

She blew smoke out of the corner of her mouth so that it plumed before the window. "My mom and Lou?"

"No, Victor and your uncle?"

"I doubt it, but you'd have to ask Lou."

I glanced at my notebook, the black stripes across the yellow paper, my chicken scrawl tilting backward like most lefties' writing does. I lifted my gaze back to her with intensity to stake claim to the idea we needed to get down to business. "Help us out here, Megan." I lowered my voice. "What's the deal with your brother? What trouble was he mixed up in?"

Megan took another drag. "I don't know what he's been into lately. I honestly don't." She looked tired, caught between grief and anger like a semicolon between sentences, resigned to the loss, but pissed about the waste of her brother's life. We knew she was two years younger than Victor, twenty-five, but her eyes held hardness the way shells hold the ocean, as if on some level, she considered that Victor chucking his life away perhaps made no difference—that perhaps it didn't matter if he tossed his life into a Dumpster at age eleven or lived an entirely different life—nurturing it with care until it took root and blossomed, then withered into old age.

But perhaps I was being overly dramatic because of the bear growling at me from the corner of my mind. "Somewhere along the line"—

she sighed heavily—"things just went wrong. They say some people are just born bad apples, and I've wondered if my own brother was one of them because even though he could be really sweet at times, he just always seemed to make bad choices. That day at the cabin, when my mom gave him money, I wasn't upset because he was using again. I'd long since surrendered to the idea that he was a fuckup, and ain't never going to change that. But my mom, see, she's a good apple, and I didn't want to see her pissing any more money away on him."

"Understandable." I leaned in closer, my full interest on her. I could sense Monty shifting slightly closer too. "And why a bad apple? Why not just someone troubled or someone hurting with a nasty addiction?"

Megan shook her head, her lips tightening again as if she might clam up. I sat back again to give her space. She didn't speak.

"I mean," I tried again, "there's the obvious—the meth. Was there something about that or any other bad-apple stuff you can think of that could get him killed?"

"Honestly, mister, I wouldn't know. It's just an expression. Basically, my brother could piss off a lot of people." She lifted her chin, anger now full in her eyes, the grief going somewhere else for the moment, as if it had gotten a nibble of relief and scurried back to its hiding place.

"Do you know any names? Who his dealer was?"

"No, they were always changing. Last one I knew was a guy called Stimpy. I think 'cause his name was Stimpson. Don't know his first name and this was at least a year ago."

I saw Monty write it down. "Do you remember any others?"

She shook her head.

"What about girlfriends?"

"Oh Jesus, he had all sorts of winners in that department. Some girl named Tara for a while, don't know her last name. And someone named Rita. Don't remember hers either. And Mindy. Mindy Winters. And Leslie Boone. And there were lots of others here and there."

"Would any of them have any reason to hurt him?"

She shrugged. "My brother could be pretty mean, verbally and physically, but he could also be a charmer. If he set his eyes on you, he could make you feel like the most special person in the world."

"He hit any of them?"

"Not sure, but I saw a black eye once on Mindy, if I remember correctly. Not to mention . . ." She trailed off, looked out again. A group of chickadees flew perfectly in unison, zigzagged before the window, then all landed together on a wire linking to a roof across the street. I could tell she saw them because her eyes darted as she tracked them.

"Not to mention . . ." I nudged her on.

She cradled her cigarette in the ashtray and stood up, leaving the smoke to rise in a cloudy, borderless bundle between Monty and me. "Look, can I get you some water or something?" She shuffled to the kitchen, her slippers scuffing across the floor.

"No, thanks." I reached over and nonchalantly put the cigarette out. Monty had already backed his chair a few inches away from the table, and I could tell by the slightly strained look, the tightening between his nose and his upper lip, that he was trying to avoid inhaling too deeply. I figured not many park employees were used to cigarette smoke. "You were saying?"

"Nothing." Megan opened a pumpkin-orange cabinet, the paint chipping along the edges and exposing a darker wood underneath. "Not really sure." She had the type of body where, from the waist up, she was very thin, but her hips were round and curvy, her jean-clad thighs rubbing against each other when she walked. She closed the cabinet door a little too loud and brusque, her anger definitely outweighing her sorrow.

Monty and I stayed seated. "Look, Megan, I know your brother wasn't a good brother, but good or bad, he was your brother, and he still deserves a thorough investigation of this crime. Were you about to say *not to mention that he hit me*?"

"Oh Jesus." She laughed a cold laugh, moved her wet hair behind her shoulders, and shook it out while raking her fingers through it. "Are you fucking kidding? Plenty. But it's not like I didn't hit him back. We weren't exactly your average Disney family. But, you know, I eventually learned to stay clear of him. But that's not what I was going to say." She wiped the back of her hand across her cheek as if there was a leftover tear there, although I didn't see one, perhaps a trail of salt. "What I was going to say was, not to mention his more recent craziness. Just something I heard"—she waved her hand in the air and looked at the floor—"maybe involving animals." She leaned against her Formica counter the color of dirty river runoff and crossed one leg over the other.

"Animals?" Monty asked surprised. "You mean incidents of animal cruelty?"

Megan shrugged. "Possibly."

"Since he was young?" Monty asked again and this time, unlike when we questioned Penny Lance and he chimed in, I was slightly taken back and irritated to hear him questioning Megan—to know he was somewhat of a participant, a poacher in the waters into which I was casting. Instead of feeling like a productive mentor, I felt a stitch of resentment rise inside of me, and the only possible explanation I could conjure was that Monty had defended Ford in the car. Not obnoxiously, just enough to add some edge, just a tiny minnow of an intrusion in already crowded waters. I shoved the twinge down because I knew I was being irrational. I refocused on Monty's question, which also irritated me, especially since Megan was about to tell us about a particular incident, and Monty was leading her to the more general—away from the specifics, a no-no in police inquiry. But still, I was curious. His question was pertinent to understanding Victor Lance. If he was abusive to animals as a youngster, it could indicate that he was a potential sociopath.

"No." She shook her head. "Nothing like that. It's, it's just something I heard lately. You have to understand that Victor was an angry and confused kid, especially after our dad left."

I nodded. "Your father split when you were pretty young?"

"Yeah, he moved to Washington when I was about eight or nine." She came over and sat back down. "We stayed with him some when we were little. After he moved, we rarely saw him after that. Victor was pretty hurt when he left, went into a sort of depression for a long time. I remember when he was little, he used to be really good at spelling. Loved to study the dictionary even and always used to win the school spelling bees, but after our dad left, he quit trying in school completely and my mom couldn't get him to spell a word for her, even for fun, after that."

"Victor and your father were close?" I asked, giving in to the line Monty had taken us down.

"I guess." Megan shrugged indifferently, but her eyes showed something akin to fervor. "As close as you could get to a guy like my father." Now that we'd gotten her going I sensed that she could go on, resentment now eclipsing the fond memory that had risen. "I guess that would explain Victor's mean gene. My dad was no picnic either. Hot-tempered and hated certain groups of people. Catholics, Jews, Arabs, black people, liberals, you name it." She laughed bitterly. "Christ, he'd never even met an Arab or a Jew, and you could count the number of blacks on one hand who live in this town, so I have no idea what there was to hate. As it is, the whole friggin' area's an advertisement to the Aryan Nation."

"So, Megan"—I needed to rein this in—"what was it that you heard involving animals?"

"Well, that's what I was getting to when you brought my father into it." She sounded like an upset child, irritated by my question. She relit the cigarette I had snuffed out, sat back, and held it to her young lips, plump and now pouty. "Last spring, there was an incident with a dog at the mouth of the canyon, near Columbia Mountain turnoff." She pointed her cigarette out the window, in the direction of the canyon, where the Flathead River cuts through. "It was written up in the local paper. Someone had tied the poor thing, a Lab or something, by its leash to a fence post, then beat the shit out of it with a bat. I remember being disgusted, but not thinking anything more of it."

"Uh huh." I gestured for her to continue.

"Then in July, I ran into my brother's longtime buddy, Daniel. They've been friends since elementary school."

"Your mom mentioned him."

"Anyway, we had a few beers together and he brought Vic up. Said he was worried about him using again. I had said, 'What's new,' but he said he heard something strange. Said he'd heard from another mutual friend of theirs, Rick Pyles, that my brother and another guy were the ones that beat this poor dog. That they'd been trippin' out of their minds."

"Do you remember who the owner of the dog was?"

"No, but it was in the paper, so you could look it up."

"Did the dog die?"

"Eventually. The article said he was taken to a vet, and they put him out of his misery."

"How did you leave it with Daniel?"

"Nothing really. What was there for us to do?"

"Did you talk of doing something about it, going to the cops or talking to your brother?"

"Yeah, we discussed it. But we weren't positive it was Vic. Just hearsay, you know. And going to him would only piss him off. I did tell my mom about it, but she said that it was just talk and that she knew he would never do something like that. She begged me not to spread such lies."

I remembered Penny Lance's look when we were done talking and actually, I had a pretty good idea that she at least suspected her son had changed enough, perhaps because of the meth, to possess the potential to do something like that.

"Thank you, Megan, we've taken up enough of your time and you've been a great help."

"What's next?" she asked.

"We just keep plodding along, asking questions. We may need to ask you more, but for today, that's enough." I stood up.

She crushed her cigarette out, stood, and walked us to the door. She seemed stronger than when we had come in, as if our questions, or rather her answers, were some form of sustenance.

8

"Beat the shit out of a black Lab." Monty winced, then made his signature whistle when we returned to the car. The whistle didn't bother me; I was sort of expecting it now, like the regular chime of a clock.

"Sounds like our victim definitely pissed some people off."

"I'd say so," Monty said dryly. "I think I remember reading about that in the paper. Nice guy, huh?"

"A real love bug." We learn early that it's best to never sympathize with the victim, to never get emotionally drawn in over any factor at all, even if the victim was a child. But honestly, when the victim was a creep, staying neutral was definitely much easier. The danger of going too far the other way, not caring at all and even feeling contempt, was equally ill advised. Both extremes invited miscalculations and misjudgments. "I'll get Monica on the news article, and we'll pay a visit to the treating vet and the owner of the dog. Right now, I want to speak to Lou. With his cabin being closest to the crime scene, there might be something there." I looked at my watch. I'd definitely be working very late.

"And what do you think about the animal thing?"

"Could be something there. It's hard to say. If the owner of the dog found out who did it, I mean, it fits with the teaching-him-a-lesson thing. Sweet revenge. Tying him to a tree for any wild animal to give him what he deserves?"

"But what about the gunshot? If you were going to let him get tortured by wild animals, why kill him?"

"Yeah, it doesn't quite square. Unless you went back to check, saw

103

that no animal had gotten him yet, so you shot him. Then as luck would have it, that animal comes along anyway."

"It fits," Monty said. "I know people love their animals, but would anyone go to such lengths and kill someone over it?"

"People kill over much less. I worked on a case where the guy killed his buddy over a motorcycle that they'd both worked on. And it wasn't even a Harley, some piece-of-shit Honda. But, thing is, it's always best to stick with the most straightforward explanation."

Monty looked at me with an eyebrow raised.

"This meth business, right?"

He nodded.

"It's the most obvious thing, and no denying that the meth world is one messed-up place. 'Course you know that excessive users are prone to paranoia, violence . . . schizophrenia. Yeah." I nodded. "Twisting this into some kind of animal cruelty situation would probably be a mistake, but that doesn't mean we won't check it out." I looked out the window at the pines interspersed with the bright golden tamaracks on the hillsides against a milky, fading sky that scattered a dull, pointless light, one that suggested a lack of grace, meaning, or purpose. It was the thing I hated most about Montana, the endless gray throughout so many months of the year, as if it were mocking my inability to stay buoyant and content. "Whoever got him out there must have used the gun to do it, and trying to secure tape while holding a gun to someone's head would be tough. It's definitely plausible that this was more than a one-man job."

"But doable for one."

I couldn't tell if it was a question or a statement. I answered anyway, "I suppose," I said. "Doable."

. . .

Monty looked up Lou's address on his laptop, and on the way to the Shelton cabin we made a quick stop at headquarters to get a printout from Monica on the dealer, an Andrew Stimpson, which she rounded up from the Bureau of Alcohol, Tobacco, Firearms and Explosives.

Two years before, the ATF sent in an undercover agent to work the area because there'd been a major methamphetamine ring running between Spokane, Washington, and the Flathead Valley. At its height, about twenty-five people were involved in trafficking the drug. Eventually, twelve residents, five from the Flathead Valley in Kalispell and seven from the Hungry Horse and Coram area, were convicted and are still serving anywhere from sixty to two hundred months in prison. That left the newbies in the area, like Stimpy, to play around with developing their own connections, and the police didn't fully have a good feel for which way the newbies might swing. Whether they'd be bringing it in from Washington again or setting up shop and manufacturing more from small-time homegrown operations. Monica found Stimpson in the regional drug-task-force intelligence database with only one offense: he'd been busted for disturbing the peace outside a bar and had dope on him. He was suspected of dealing within the Spokane importation ring, but they had no proof, so he was free as a bird.

When I walked in, Joe came out to greet me, a serious expression on his face, and with no apparent reason, an undertow of anxiety tugged at me. "What's up?" I asked.

"We've got the bear."

I nodded, felt my stomach grip, my breathing quicken, and even my palms felt immediately slippery. "You're kidding? So soon?"

"He was hanging around the McGee area. Maybe thought someone else would turn up dead. Went right to the concoction—a savory little mixture of fermented cow's blood and rotten fish."

"Has anyone found any of his scat?"

"Not yet. We're hopeful, though. No one wants to cut this guy open. He's a beauty, very healthy. He's put on his hyperphagic weight, probably close to seven hundred pounds. We're checking his DNA with the saliva found on the victim to be absolutely positive that he's the right one."

I took a deep breath, felt the incoming air fight to expand laterally against my tightly bound ribs. It was such a simple thing—the bear crapping the bullet out—that it seemed too easy. I hoped that's all it would take. I didn't want to be in a position to ask the park's bear committee to have him cut open. Besides the outside chance that we might find other pieces of clothing belonging to the victim in the bear's gut, plucking the bullet out of a pile of scat with some tweezers certainly was the simplest solution. And looking at Joe, with his experience and fatherly advice flickering in his dark eyes, it all seemed like it could work out. "I don't want to euthanize him either, Joe. But it still doesn't solve the problem that he's fed on human remains."

"I know, but hopefully we get the bullet without drastic measures. Bears drink tons of water as they near hibernation to help with elimination, so we'll make sure he's got more than enough."

I nodded but could see a tenseness in Joe's face. "Something else?" I asked.

"Actually, yes," he said. "Can you come into my office?"

I glanced at my watch. I didn't want to be rude, but time seemed to be flying away from me at warp speed.

"It'll only take a moment."

I followed him, in some ways relieved to have a plan in place with the bear, but still felt a strong undercurrent tugging at me. When I entered, I saw Joe's daughter sitting in one of his desk chairs. Joe motioned for me to take a seat. "Remember Heather?"

"Of course." I held out my hand to her before sitting, hoping my palms were less moist now. She was wearing a lightweight tan coat and had on a dark green scarf knotted around her neck. She gave me a closed-lip smile that seemed genuine. "Nice to see you again."

"Likewise." She shook my hand, her grip light.

"So what's going on?"

"It's in this morning's paper. You seen it?" He nodded to the copy of the local daily news on his desk.

"Yeah." I picked up the copy and quickly glanced at the small article. "Exactly as I'd expect Ford to handle it." I set the paper down and flicked it with my finger. "Hardly gave any information at all."

Joe nodded, still looking tense, the muscles in his jaw tight.

"So, what's the problem, then?" I looked from daughter to father, took in their similarities—pale eyes and fair, weathered skin.

"Well." His gaze stayed on Heather as he began. "When you met us earlier on our way to lunch, Heather had wanted to meet with me for a reason."

I sat still.

"Turns out when she read the victim's name in the paper, she was shocked because she knew the guy. In fact . . ." He looked down, picked up a pencil, and began rolling it between his thumb and forefinger. "This is sort of hard for me." His voice sounded small, vulnerable, something I'd not witnessed before. Jack-of-all-trades, always-in-control ranger, who becomes chief of Park Police didn't get weak. "I have another daughter."

"Uh huh." I nodded, glanced at my watch again; it was almost four p.m., and I wanted to get to Lou Shelton's place.

"She's been in and out of trouble with drugs since she was a teenager." He rubbed his forehead. "She was even screwed up on meth for some time. Anyway, long story short, Heather came to tell me that she had dated this guy for over a year. I had no clue." Joe shook his head.

Now Joe's tenseness made sense. Leave it to family matters, the one thing that can drop a person to their knees. I looked at Heather, then back to Joe. "Your daughter's name?"

"Leslie," Joe said.

"Still last name Smith?"

Joe shook his head. "No, she's been married and divorced, but never took our name back. It's Boone now."

"The victim's mother mentioned her. Liked her, in fact."

"How sweet," Joe said with sarcasm, then his face seemed to suddenly droop and he looked down. I could see that there were demons in this closet.

"Leslie's been difficult for my mom and dad." Heather's voice was soft but matter-of-fact, as if she had only said, *the bathroom's down the hall*.

"She's, she's just"—Joe picked it up again—"been a very frustrating kid, and now . . ." He trailed off. He looked down again and the room became silent.

"She has a boy?" I asked.

Joe nodded. "I hate to say it, but I've had no contact with her for some time. Call me stubborn, but I got fed up. Tough love, whatever you want to call it." He brushed his hand in the air as if swatting a fly away. "I'd have no clue who's in her life. It's better that way. But, yes, I have a grandson, and Heather's nice enough to make a habit of bringing him by to see me at times."

"And his name?"

"Lewis," Heather offered. "Lewis Boone."

"Where is Leslie now?"

"Around, at home, with Lewis. She's moved on, seeing some other guy named Paul Tyler, but I figured Dad better know that his daughter had a relationship with, you know"—she paused, her head twitching to the side as if searching for the right term for the victim—"this guy. I knew he didn't know who she was involved with these days." She looked at her father, now less confident, checking in to see if she was saying something wrong. He nodded her on. "We don't talk a lot about her, it just upsets everyone."

"Did you meet Victor?"

Heather nodded. "I saw him numerous times over the course of their relationship. I think they were together for about eight months or so."

"How did it end?"

Heather shrugged. "He treated her poorly. But so do all her boyfriends. She makes less than optimal choices in that department." Again, she glanced at her father.

"So she broke it off?" I asked.

"I'm not sure. Maybe. We're not talking about high levels of monogamy with this guy or my sister. He could've just as easily started seeing someone else."

"Your sister doesn't talk to you about these things?"

"Not really. A little but she's, well, she's fairly private."

"How was Victor with Lewis?"

Heather shrugged again, her eyes flickering to her father, then back to me. "I guess I couldn't fully say, but I don't think Lewis particularly cared for him."

"How much time do you spend with Lewis?"

"Just a bit here and there," Joe broke in. "He's a pretty decent kid considering what he's grown up around."

"And you?" I turned back to Heather.

"I help my sister out with him now and then, when she's busy. He comes and helps me with my horses. And sometimes I pay him to ride my mower in the summer. I taught him how this year when he turned eleven."

"Do you know how they met?"

Heather shook her head.

"Aren't these questions for Leslie?" Joe broke in.

"Yeah, sure." I reached in my pocket for my notebook. Joe shifted in his seat as if he couldn't get comfortable. "I've already got Leslie's address because we planned on questioning anyone involved with him, but"—I fingered through my notepad—"let me double-check that I've got the right place. Lodge Avenue in Coram?"

Heather nodded.

"Does she work?"

"Cleans for small businesses. Mostly in Hungry Horse and Coram. Hungry Horse Grocery is one of 'em."

"Anyway . . . " Joe got up, his features flat, as if he'd had enough of a boring school lecture. "I just thought you ought to know, but I've got a bear to attend to."

I stood too.

"Want to come see him?"

His question took me off guard, as if I were a little kid who wanted to check out a grizzly in a zoo. "Ah." I cleared my throat. "No, thanks. Got too much work to do. Too many people to visit yet."

"Suit yourself." He shrugged. "But he's a beauty."

"I'm sure he is." I couldn't help but feel like I was being toyed with, the butt of a joke. I'd never told Joe about my history, and I was pretty sure he wouldn't connect the dots even if he had heard about it down in Yellowstone. Back in the eighties, he was stationed as a ranger there. As far as I knew, he didn't come to Glacier until about '87 or '89. There was the slight chance that Ford had remembered and clued him in, but even if he had, it wasn't Joe's style to toy with anyone.

"By the way," I said, "what do you know about a Lou Shelton who lives by Fish Creek?"

"Nice enough guy. Keeps to himself and his family. Why?"

"He has a family?"

"I think so, a wife or a lady friend. And a son, a teenager, I believe. Might be hers, and he's the stepdad 'cause I think he's been divorced and his children are adults now."

I nodded. "Any chance you know what he drives?"

"Sure," he said. "Black Chevy four-by-four. See him coming and going all the time around here. It's a small world in Glacier when the tourists are gone. Do you have something on Lou?"

"I'm guessing you didn't know that he was Victor's uncle?"

Joe looked at me, wide-eyed. "Ah, shit—you've got to be kidding?"

I shook my head. "We'll talk to him, just as we'll talk to your daughter and everyone else."

"I reckon you will." Joe sighed and walked out the door.

9

We FOUND LOU'S place without difficulty. Just as Joe said, a black Chevy with an extended cab sat in the narrow gravel driveway beside a gray-planked cabin with burgundy shutters.

I had an intuition about this guy, and my feeling was sharpening. Although I had considered the spotting of the truck by Jarred a long shot since the guy lived in the area, the idea that this case could be quickly put to rest by discovering evidence in a truck was a pretty juicy carrot before me. In fact, I felt strongly enough about him that I told Monty on the way over that there was a good chance we might need to go for the oldest trick in the book: good cop, bad cop. Just to see if we could make him nervous enough to slip if he had something to feel guilty about. I briefed him, telling him that it was his job to be nice and courteous, which he is anyway, but more outgoing and talkative than usual, helpful when I'm not, so that the guy would feel he had someone he could relate to and not completely clam up.

Monty had smiled and said that he'd taken some acting classes in high school and had been in a few plays, including *Julius Caesar* and *Comedy of Errors* as the servant twin. I couldn't imagine Monty acting on a stage, and it made me chuckle, but I quickly stopped myself and just said, "All the world's a stage."

"Yes, it is."

When we pulled up the narrow drive, I saw who I assumed was Lou raking dried and withered leaves that had fallen from a maple beside his cabin. He had on a brown denim jacket, faded yellow gloves, and a

111

baseball cap. He peered over to us with an impenetrable squint, even though the day was not bright. He leaned on his rake like some tried-and-true but tired mountain man, and I couldn't help but think of Jeremiah Johnson. He was medium height and fit, not in the gym-workout way with bulky muscles and smooth skin, but in the consistently outdoors way—sturdy and weathered. I recalled Gretchen's description of Victor, how he had a small frame. Lou set his rake against the cabin and came toward us.

It was a stroke of bad luck that he wasn't inside so that Monty and I would have more time to look around his truck—check for anything suspicious and maybe even measure the width of the tires in case Gretchen had come up with anything more on the tracks from the Inside Road.

"Mr. Shelton?" I avoided looking too closely at the truck so that he wouldn't get the idea that we were curious about it and then clean it just in case we came up with enough cause to get a search warrant.

"That'd be me."

I introduced ourselves, told him we'd like a word with him, and I noticed Monty following my instruction beautifully, smiling fully with bright white teeth, shaking Lou's hand vigorously, saying, "What a nice spot you have here."

Lou nodded, his eyes still narrow, inspecting us. "Been in the family for generations."

"Yeah, as Agent Systead mentioned," Monty said, "I work for the park, so I'm fairly familiar with a few of these homesteads." He looked around, up the gravel driveway we came in on, toward the lake and the mountains. "You know. How the park owns about twenty-some cabins on the lake, but that there are a number of other ones that are privately owned and are not part of the EA."

I knew Monty was referring to the Environmental Assessment Program that was exploring alternatives for the management of its cabins owned by the National Park Service.

"That why you're here?" Lou looked like he could spit.

"No, sir," Monty said. "Not at all." Monty explained the reason for our visit and Lou sighed, scratched his close-cropped beard with the side of his glove, then nodded that he understood. He had heard about Victor from his sister. He took off his dirt-stained gloves and set them on a woodpile, then led us to his front porch, where two old Adirondack-style chairs sat. I looked around to see if any neighboring cabins had people around when Lou caught my glance.

"Nobody 'round here," he said. "We can sit out."

I followed Monty and took a seat. "Nobody home here either?" I pointed my thumb to Lou's cabin.

"My wife's at our boy's soccer practice in Columbia Falls."

I nodded, then glanced at Monty, hoping he'd go ahead and make a little more small talk, ease us into this one.

"How old's your son?" Monty followed on cue.

"Fifteen. Ninth grade. He's my stepson."

I whipped out my notebook from my pocket and leaned forward, dug my elbows onto my knees, and fixed my gaze on Lou. "I'm sorry for your loss, but I need to ask you some questions about your relationship with your nephew."

"That's fine." He still held his squint, deep crow's-feet fanning out from the corner of each eye. "I might just ask you some questions too—like what the hell happened out there? My sister's a wreck."

"That's exactly why we're here, Mr. Shelton." I leaned back into my chair as if I was in it for a long, good story. "Let's begin with you telling us how your relationship with Victor was."

He scoffed. "Could hardly call it a relationship. Let me just say from the get-go that I'm real sorry this happened. I feel sick about it. It's . . ." He shook his head and fully opened his eyes for the first time since we'd arrived. "It's horrible, what happened, but I don't spend a lot of time with my nephew. Never have."

"And when was the last time you saw him?"

"August. Here. At a birthday party Becky threw for me."

"Was that the last time you spoke to him?"

Lou nodded, almost imperceptibly. "Listen, I'm not gonna lie to ya. I didn't much care for Victor, for the way he treated my sister. She always breakin' her back to give him money for his trash habits."

"As long as we're being honest here, Mr. Shelton." I leaned forward again. "I need to ask you what you were doing Friday afternoon and evening."

"What the hell." He pressed his palm to his chest. "Are you implying I had something to do with this?"

"Not necessarily." I kept my gaze steady. "But could you please answer the question."

"I . . . I was, I don't know. Let me think." He removed his cap and rubbed his forehead, then replaced it. "I worked around the house most of the day. Then"—he sighed—"I had a fight with Becky, so I stormed out. It was afternoon. I guess it was around four or so. I went to the store in West Glacier and got some smokes."

"And after that?"

"I started to go home, but then I couldn't go back. I was pretty upset, so I drove out toward Fish Creek to that little parking lot off to the side there and sat and gathered my wits."

"And how long did you stay there?"

"I sat for a while. Smoked a cigarette. Then I got out and went for a walk to the lake and hiked the trail around it for some time. Beautiful night, deep-blue sky, and the tamaracks all yellow. I walked maybe a good hour. I got back to my truck before seven. I know because I only watched the beginning of the sunset, and it was just starting to get dark when I returned."

"And then?"

"I went home, and Becky and I had a talk. We had dinner and we were in for the rest of the night."

"And the boy?"

"He was with us too. He went to a movie with a friend. Came home around nine. His buddy dropped him off."

"So let me see if I've got this straight," I said. "From sometime after four to just before seven p.m., you were alone at the entrance to the old Inside Road to the North Fork, the very same road that leads to McGee Meadow, where your nephew, who you don't have fond feelings for, was left to die?"

"That's right." Lou's jaw tightened and he glared at me. "Bad coincidence, I guess."

"Guess so." I lifted my brow. "Hmm," I mumbled and held my palm up as if to say, *what I am to think about all this*?

"Look"—Lou leaned toward me—"you're absolutely fucking nuts if you think I had anything to do with my own nephew's death."

"I'm not accusing you of anything here, just trying to understand the situation. Let's back up a little, shall we?"

Lou glared at me.

"What were you and Becky fighting about?"

"None of your goddamned business is what."

"So I take it that whatever you were fighting about just happened to make you feel like you needed to go to the Inside Road?"

Suddenly Lou stood. His squint had returned full-on and he pointed a finger at me. "Listen, who the hell do you think you are, strolling onto my property like this and accusing me of doing something that horrible to my nephew?"

I held up my palm to calm him because I knew I had definitely set him off, which I intended to a bit, but not to set him on fire. "Mr. Shelton, I'm not—"

"The hell you aren't. Let me ask you this—why the hell do you think I live here? Have you looked around or are you too busy putting on that shiny badge of yours to notice what we've got here?" He sneered at my chest, and I could see that he was a man who had utter disdain for authority. Perhaps specifically for the Department of the Interior. It was no secret that a love-hate relationship existed between the inholders of property in Glacier and the Park Service. Many of these people grew up in the park, met their wives and husbands on romantic, full-moon summer nights, loved their places with a vengeance, but felt hobbled by the Park Service and its long list of do's and don'ts.

"I'm a simple guy," he said. "Don't care much about church. I stay out of other people's business, including my sister's. This here"—he gestured to the lake, its turquoise water from glacier silt near the shoreline giving way to sapphire-blue farther out, and the mountains surrounding us like some pastoral setting in a vivid Bierstadt or Moran painting—"is my church. If I don't have enough sense to go find some peace . . . calm down among the likes of this place after a fight with my wife, then I'm an idiot." His eyes were narrow, on fire, eyes that had seen intense things, and I wondered if he'd been in Vietnam since he looked about that age. Or if he dodged, headed to Canada to seek the beauty of the mountains, his modus operandi all along. He continued to glare at me, standing above me until I fidgeted in my chair and it creaked. I heard a raven caw and a cold breeze touched my nose. Then he sat back down and folded his arms.

I waited a second to see if Monty would add a little good-cop flavoring to the mix, but he didn't. He sat, more stunned than poised. "So am I to take it that your love of this oh-so-special place is meant to be some kind of alibi?" My voice dripped with sarcasm. I couldn't help myself. My anger at Glacier Park and all it held, including this man who loved the woods unabashedly with no hang-ups like mine, leaked into my voice in spite of myself. "An automatic given," I added, "that you had nothing to do with your nephew's murder even though you were at the entrance to the area around the same time of the incident?"

"Listen, Lou," Monty broke in and glanced at me nervously, holding his hand up like he was a second-grader asking permission to speak. "I know how you feel. I feel the same about this place. If I had a fight with my wife, I would chill out near Lake McDonald too, especially if I lived where you do." He looked around to take in the view: the white-capped peaks with dark-gray clouds hanging above and beginning to crack open to show patches of blue above. Monty whistled to show how impressed he was with Lou's spot in the Crown of the Continent.

This was the first I'd known that Monty had a wife, provided he wasn't making it up for Lou's benefit. If he *was* making it up, he was good and catching on way quicker than some of the guys from the Denver office. Lou gave Monty a long stare as well, not moving a muscle, his arms rigid before his chest. "But," Monty added, "you need to understand that we have to account for everyone's whereabouts during this time frame."

"Correct," I chimed in. "It's a process of elimination is all. So we can eliminate you from the investigation."

"Well, I don't have witnesses other than the chipmunks and the ravens." He unfolded his arms and gestured to the woods. "If you want me to take some kind of lie-detector test, I will. You still use them things?"

"Polygraphs? Sometimes, but that's not necessary for now, Mr. Shelton," I said.

Lou nodded, calmer. I asked him if he had any information or knowledge about Victor's dealer or dealers, knew of the Columbia Falls black Lab incident and if there was any relation to Victor, and if he knew anyone who would want to harm his nephew. He gave us nothing useful on any of these fronts, except to confirm that his nephew was, indeed, a druggie and had a temper problem. Lou said he had very little contact with Victor and liked to keep it that way for obvious reasons.

"Okay, then." I finally closed my notebook. Other than the guy having no alibi and whatever hunch I was having, I had nothing specific enough to claim probable cause, which I needed in order to get a search warrant for his truck. Not having an alibi wasn't enough. I'd have to wait to see if Gretchen came up with any tire-track prints that would give reason to bring us back.

· · ·

The sun's rays suddenly sneaked under the layer of clouds that had blanketed the mountains the entire day. It lit up the lower hills and trees with a golden hue as we drove away from Lou's place toward park headquarters. We hadn't eaten all day, and Monty mentioned that he was starving and wanted to get home, so I took the opportunity to ask him, "That true what you said to him about your wife?"

"Yep," Monty said. "Only, we're not together right now. Separated."

"I'm sorry to hear that." I looked ahead at the glowing ridge before me. There was an exquisite beauty in the rich light that reminded me of the way I usually feel when I listen to an intricate piece of classical music, like Dvořák or Chopin, how I float to some ineffable place of bittersweet and raw human emotion. For some reason, Lou had gotten to me. I had expected that he might get uptight, but I hadn't expected my own agitation, and I felt a little guilty and slightly bare; as if Lou had unwittingly and indirectly peeled some thin, but essential top layer off of me. "Kids?"

Monty shook his head.

"How long you been separated?"

"Only about two months."

"So there's still hope?"

Monty looked out to the side of the road without answering. A strong sadness seemed to drape over him, his head tilting toward his shoulder as if it had suddenly grown heavy. It made me wish I hadn't asked. We drove the rest of the way in silence, and eventually the golden light disappeared and the temperature dropped rapidly.

When we got out of the SUV at headquarters, a bitter rawness in the chilly fall evening enveloped us and made the mentioning of hope entirely insignificant—a mere faded, dried leaf lost in a pile to be raked and bagged like the ones beside Lou's cabin.

· · ·

The next morning I woke with my stomach growling. The night before, I ended up grabbing some microwavable sandwich wrapped in plastic at a convenience store in Hungry Horse. I decided I needed a real breakfast with some protein. I grabbed my coat and headed out into the early crisp morning with a clear, cerulean sky framing the mountains. I was surprised to see the peaks shed the weighty clouds of the day before so quickly because once they settled in, they often stayed trapped in by mountains for days. The blueness brought a sense of order, making me feel instantly lighter, like I was set to make some real headway in the case.

I drove to the café in West Glacier, half-expecting to find Joe or Monty there. In fact, I found both: Monty with a pile of pancakes two inches high and some bacon; and Joe with a bowl of oatmeal, I suspected his morning usual.

"How's it going?" Joe asked.

"Good and hungry," I said.

"It's the Glacier air." Joe held his spoon in one hand and pointed at a chair with it. "Sit."

"You've come to the right place, then," Monty said.

"I can see that." I nodded to his stack of pancakes coated with a bluish-purple syrup, then grabbed a nearby chair and pulled it up to the head of the table. "Huckleberry?" I asked.

Monty nodded. "Delicious. You should try some."

During the height of the season, along with Flathead Lake cherries, all the tourist spots on the highway through the canyon were known for selling anything that could be made with wild huckleberries: ice cream, syrup, jam, scones, fudge, pies. Suddenly I felt nostalgic, and thought of my family picking huckleberries near the Hungry Horse Reservoir the first summer we moved to Montana. An image of Natalie with a blue-stained smile popped into my mind, and I remembered my dad telling her that she'd never get any in her jar if she continued to eat five to each one she saved. "You're here early," I said to Monty. "You even go home?"

"Of course, got a great night's sleep too."

"Excellent," I said. "So, where's home? C' Falls?" It's actually *Columbia* Falls, but the locals abbreviate it.

Monty pointed toward the direction I'd just come. "Dorm thirty-six, next to the community building."

"Oh, so we're practically neighbors?"

"That's right." He shoveled a wad of pancakes in his mouth and chewed vigorously. It seemed out of character for him. "Sorry I haven't swung by with a huckleberry pie."

"You've still got time." I caught Joe looking at us. A thin smile played across his lips, and I could tell he was relieved to see Monty and me bantering a bit—as if the slight friendship we'd accomplished made Joe feel better about backing Ford. "How's the bear?" I said to Joe.

"On my way to check on him after this."

"No bullet yet?"

"On my way to find out. Want to join me?" Joe turned to me.

This was the second time he'd asked me, and I still wondered if there was something up—as if I were Sheriff Brody from *Jaws*, utterly afraid of water, yet still being asked to go for a boat ride. But Joe's eyes were wide and clear—free of mischief or ill intent. "Maybe." I gave a one-shouldered shrug. "Right now I need to eat. And," I said to Monty, "I'm meeting Gretchen at seven thirty to check out Victor's lovely home."

"In need of some interior decorating tips, are ya?" Joe asked dryly.

I smiled. "Absolutely. See if he's got any new color combos I just can't live without." I peered over my shoulder just in time to see the waitress come over with a menu for me. This one was middle-aged and pleasant-looking, with a soft smile and a bad perm, the ends of her dishwater-blond hair seeming to dissolve into nothing. I wondered if she was the mother of the girl who served us when we came for lunch the other day. Joe introduced her as Carol, and she welcomed me to the area. I ordered some eggs, hash browns, and toast and asked as politely as I could for her to make it snappy. "Then I'm off to . . ." I momentarily paused because I felt awkward mentioning Joe's daughter as someone I needed to question while on a murder case. And I had to think for a second whether it would bother him that Monty was in the know-how about Leslie.

Joe looked at me with patience.

"To talk to your daughter," I said after weighing in my mind that he would not care that Monty knew. After all, Joe had backed Ford in assigning Monty to me.

Joe lowered his pointy chin and said nothing. He grabbed his coffee and sipped it, then cleared his throat.

"Anything from the creeks?"

Joe shook his head. "Nothing."

That didn't surprise me. It was the deeper water that I knew needed to be searched. That is where a gun would be thrown. "Any word from Walsh on getting the divers out?"

"They're on a job right now on Flathead Lake. Getting some car out that went in last night. Some intoxicated guy forced the oncoming vehicle to cross the center line, forcing two teenagers to swerve and go into the lake."

"I'm sorry to hear that. Survivors?"

Joe shook his head.

"Then they've got some other job to do on Tuesday—he didn't say what, but said he might be able to get them on McDonald by Wednesday or Thursday."

"I guess that'll have to do."

"You find what you were looking for with Lou yesterday?"

"Yes and no. Nothing conclusive, but he doesn't have an alibi."

"It's hard for loners to have alibis."

"You think he's a loner? He's got a wife and a stepson."

"Yeah, but that doesn't mean he's not a loner," Joe said. "Some people are the world's best at being alone in the company of others."

He could have been quoting Shelly. She used to tell me those exact words. "But I don't know . . ." I bit my lower lip.

"Know what?" Monty asked.

"About him. I mean, I can tell that he's definitely got his own code of ethics, that guy. But that doesn't mean his code doesn't include taking care of a nasty nephew."

Joe shook his head. "I don't see it, but what do I know? I'm just used to traffic violations, petty theft, and snorting deer 'round here."

"Why don't you see it? How long have you known him?"

"Lou? He's been here since before I came in the early nineties. Never been a problem. Keeps to himself, except for one time he got pretty ornery at a forum the park held to invite the public to comment on the management of NPS-owned Lake McDonald cabins."

"What was the problem?"

"Can't really remember what bone he had to pick. Probably just getting people riled up over the idea of the Park Service poking into the inholders' business."

"Are there many problems between the inholders and the park?"

"Nah." Joe wiped his mouth with his napkin. "Just the usual. Somebody getting bent out of shape over being told what they can and can't do. Last lawsuit was over someone getting angry because the park was restricting the use of an ATV even though they were only using it to access their own property."

"And was Lou involved in this?"

"Not that I recall." Joe looked out the window, his gaze faraway. I could tell, deep down, he was bothered about his daughter being involved with Victor Lance.

Monty moved his plate an inch or two away from himself to signal he was finished eating just as Carol brought my eggs. She set everything down on the table quickly, but carefully, all the while looking out the window, just as Joe was doing. I could tell she'd been waiting tables a very long time.

. . .

Victor didn't really have much in the way of neighbors in Martin City—just a double-wide about a tenth of a mile to his west and a small log cabin about a half a mile to his north. Victor also lived in a trailer—a run-down dirty peach-colored one propped up on gray cinder blocks at each corner. Gretchen met us at the front door, pushing up her dark-rimmed glasses with her wrist. She held out her hand for us to come in. "Please do not touch anything," she said.

I nodded. "Happy not to. And how's your morning in this peachy place?"

"Cute," she said without smiling. "I've gone over it with a fine-tooth comb yesterday." Again, she had trouble with the "th" at the end of tooth, so that it sounded more like "toot." "Obviously, this place is a pit." She gestured around the dingy room scattered with dirty clothes, empty cigarette packets, beer cans, whiskey bottles, old pizza boxes, and plastic wrappers from all sorts of junk food. Unwashed pots and pans towered in the sink, cabinet doors gaped open, and no food was in the fridge. "But there's no sign of struggle or foul play. No unusual fibers. Prints are mostly his. It's just poor living conditions for a guy who didn't care how he lived."

"No meth lab?" I asked.

"Nope, no chemicals or apparatus along those lines."

We looked around the place. Monty almost tripped over an old rusted hubcap lying on the floor. "Jeez, this is depressing."

"Makes you want to volunteer for the DARE program, huh?"

"That or slit my wrists," Monty said dryly.

"Yeah." I nodded. "This place is definitely a target-rich environment."

"Target rich?"

"Never mind."

"I gotcha," Monty said. "The whole area."

"Yeah." I was referring to the entire canyon. I took another look around. The way Victor had lived was nothing out of the ordinary for many people involved with meth in the area. Over the years, the canyon had become a haven for meth makers and users with its own culture of distraught individuals hooked on the horrible stuff, seeking each other out and, perhaps unintentionally, making drug and criminal activity the norm. In my high school in Kalispell, everyone referred to the canyon as "the Line." Back then, it was known for housing the dealers of marijuana, crack and heroin, and anything else that could get you toasted. If you wanted to be a little crazy, go get drunk and high on a Saturday afternoon with your buddies and be let into all the bars underage, you'd head *up the Line*.

My ma used to warn me: *water seeks its own level*. She said that the people often continued the cycle of their own hell, collecting welfare and getting high to find some kind of escape from impoverished circumstances. She used to say that when an area got known for its drug use, it meant that was only part of the story—that it was always about much, much more: economic troubles and the loss of a way of life. I figured she was being overly dramatic for my sake, but if she were here with us at Victor's trailer, she'd be saying, "I told you," with her arms folded before her chest, her chin held high. Later, by the mid- to late nineties, after new ways to cook methamphetamine began to spread to inland America, making it became the fastest way to make some money in an area where jobs were hard to come by and cycles were uneasily broken.

"I found the cell phone." Gretchen held up a plastic bag. "Batteries dead, but I'll let you know if there's anything interesting on it as soon as possible."

"Thanks." I nodded. "He didn't pay his bill. Surprise, surprise. But we've got records from the past year up until September."

"And there's something else," she said.

I looked at her.

"The traces found on the duct tape," she said, leaning into one hip. "The analysis on the chemical makeup of the tape came in and was confirmed to be a type of capsaicin."

"Capsaicin?"

"Yep," Gretchen said. "But in much lower amounts than used in bear spray."

"So what are you thinking?" I asked. "That the blood on the tape diluted the spray? Are you thinking that someone sprayed Victor or gave him spray to use and it accidentally got on him?"

"No, I'm not saying that at all." She leaned over to put the bag with the phone in her bag. "We have no evidence that he was sprayed or sprayed toward something else and got it blown back into him. The element is only on the tape and had to have gotten on the tape prior to being wrapped around the victim. It was stronger on one edge than the other, as if the entire roll had simply been next to or was sitting in something that had leaked, perhaps an earlier leak of bear spray in a pack from some time ago. There's no trace of it anywhere on the victim at all, not the scrap of shirt that was left, not his scalp or hair that's left . . ."

"Curious," Monty said.

I nodded and instantly thought of Lou's home and that I needed to get inside to see if I noticed anything suspicious lying around, like duct tape, bear spray, or firearms. Although, even if I did, everyone in this neck of the woods has bear spray and duct tape. I thought again of how finding the slug could potentially give us a better reason to search Lou's home, and if we could get a match on some tape fibers and a pistol, we'd have the case.

. . .

We left Victor's by eight a.m. and spent the next half hour checking with the two neighboring residences to see if anyone had noticed anything out of the ordinary before Victor was taken. When I asked them, both laughed and said that everything the guy did was out of the ordinary: loud parties, cars coming and going at all hours of the night, fights with high-pitched female voices.

The neighbor who lived farther east of Victor said he couldn't hear much from his place and didn't notice much one way or the other. He said that Victor did flip him off a time or two over the summer when he had yelled at him to slow down because he was driving on the dirt road too fast and kicking up dust.

"What kind of vehicle?"

"Some old truck. An old Toyota. One of those small ones. Dark blue, I think. Looked like it was on its last leg. But I've also seen him on a motorcycle a time or two."

When I asked when the last time they'd seen him was, the neighbor to the west in the double-wide, a graying wiry-haired guy with overly shaded glasses—the kind that make you wonder what's being hidden—said that he'd seen him drive by on a motorcycle sometime before dark on Wednesday. I told him I appreciated his time, and Monty and I left, half thankful for rural Montana—for being spared the tedious job of going door to door in neighborhood-dense urban areas.

10

In a homicide investigation, someone inevitably brings God into the mix, because when you're dealing with human beings unstable enough to commit murder, questions on the order of things, of evil, and whether or not the devil played some role often pop up.

My father didn't believe in God or some overriding and predetermining entity. My mother, raised Catholic, did. In spite of my mother's prodding for me to go to church with her and my sisters after my father died, I refused. I felt I had received a get-out-of-religion-free card and was born into a completely neutral zone. I couldn't understand why my sisters didn't choose to play the card too. Fortunately, staying neutral has worked fairly well in my line of work.

In one of my college criminology classes, I remember reading about an incident involving Ted Bundy when he was only three years old. The serial killer's aunt had told the account and had claimed that while in the household of the grandparents who actually raised him, she had fallen asleep one afternoon on the floor. When she woke, the little Bundy had completely surrounded her with knives and was standing over her with a wicked smile.

If this incident was accurately told, it begged the question of whether little Teddy boy could have learned or acquired the tendency to do harm through his environment so early or if he had been born with it. A girl in one of my study groups had insisted that the devil had decided to do his work through the boy. Some other guy in the group had scoffed at this, saying it was utter nonsense. Everyone in the group fell into a raging discussion about religion.

"Then explain to me why a three-year-old would be compelled to surround someone with knives?" I remember the gal had placed her hands on her hips, her chin lifted in defiance.

"There are such things as psychiatric disorders," he had replied.

She ended up so angry that she left early. I stayed neutral because I had very little to offer on the subject, and eventually everyone decided that my evasiveness was a problem, that I was weak for not taking a stance. I had shrugged and said, "Why in the hell would I fight over something I have no understanding about?"

"Being agnostic is a cop-out." Another guy from Lake Placid with smooth shoulder-length blond hair and faded jeans with large holes, just the right worn-in leather boots and a perfectly soft flannel shirt (we used to call it the affordable-poor look) had glared at me.

"I don't care whether it's a cop-out or not," I had replied calmly even though I had to admit that the guy had gotten under my nose, and what I really wanted to say was, *I don't give a flying fuck what you think*. It wasn't that I hadn't thought about it; because I had. Copiously. As a teen, I went over ad nauseam whether it was written in some divine plan or not that my father be taken. Whether that grizzly was just a bad apple or different than the others, who wanted nothing to do with campers or hikers. Whether, in the end, it was simply the wrong weekend to go camping, bad timing, and unfortunate circumstances, or something much more predetermined and mysterious. If we had not gone camping that weekend, would the heavy-leaden foot of fate slammed down on cue anyway, taken him in a car accident, a house fire, an early heart attack?

At any rate, it was Leslie Boone who brought God into the mix first. She said that Victor Lance's death was God's doing when I told her that Monty and I were visiting to speak to her about her ex-lover. We went on Monday morning, and she had let us into her white mobile home with mauve trim on Lodge Avenue off of Gladys Glen Road in the small town of Coram, north of Martin City and Hungry Horse.

Her mobile sat nestled among pine trees not far off US Highway 2 outside of Glacier Park. We waited until her son, Lewis, had taken the bus to school, then found Leslie putting away breakfast dishes. She let us in and showed us to a small living room with a lavender carpet and flowery wallpaper blistering at the edges and peeling away from the wall near the top. A ceiling fan hovered too close to my head. It was off, but I felt like I had to sit down as soon as possible to get away from it in case some unexplained force turned it on.

Leslie, still in her black terry-cloth robe, excused herself momentarily to walk back to one of the bedrooms and came out holding a Bible. She sat down with it in her lap, stroking the cover like it was a kitten. I wanted to ask, *What's with the Bible?* But I knew better. I could tell that she had struck some fragile balance with whichever concept she was clinging to, and it was literally saving her life, keeping her from all too voluntarily diving back into a black sea of bad habits and overpowering needs. I shuddered at the amount of mental and physical strain it must take to abstain from a crank addiction.

"God finally taught him a lesson," she offered.

The smell of burned toast pervaded the room, begging for the windows to be cracked open. Now that I was sitting out of the fan's way, with the smell sharp and the mobile stuffy, I wished she would turn it on. "That's certainly one way to look at it," I said nicely, not snotty and with a sweet smile. I wanted to be encouraging with this woman because I didn't know how easily she might break. The bouts of paranoia for a recovering meth addict take a long time to beat.

"There's *no* other way to see it." She sucked on her bottom lip and made a kissing sound. Her face seemed to want to fold in on itself. "What goes around comes around."

"Well, I suppose I should thank him for keeping me employed then." I smiled closed-lipped, holding back the desire to tell her that she was mixing up religions with the karma thing. Or maybe not, depending on how you looked at it. That was the thing about them; you could always dice 'em up and serve them any way you wanted. I pulled out my notebook and looked as pleasantly as I could at her, at her pallid complexion, slight build, and the dark circles discoloring the milky translucent skin below her eyes. They held a haunting quality, as if her troubled life had lent them pathos, if not wisdom. I tried to see her father's features in her and could only see some similarity in her thin nose and wide-set eyes. She was much smaller than her sister, Heather, and she reminded me of someone, perhaps an actress, not because she was exotic or particularly beautiful, but because of the anxiousness in her expression. "When did you last see Victor?"

"I don't know. It's been a while."

"How long's a while? Weeks, months, several days?"

She sighed. "I guess a couple weeks. He'd come by—it might've been a weekend, but Lewis wasn't here, so maybe it wasn't a weekend and he was at school." She shrugged. "Or maybe he was with my sister. Anyway, he was just looking for a fight."

"A fight?"

Leslie set her Bible on the floor by her chair, went to the kitchen, and returned with a pack of cigarettes and a lighter. "Yeah," she said through the corner of her mouth as she lit it. "He had heard that I'd been seeing someone and wanted to know who it was. I suppose you know we used to see each other; otherwise, you wouldn't be here."

"When did it end?"

"Summer. August."

"You tell him you're seeing someone else?"

She shook her head, then looked out the window, one elbow resting on her other arm hugging her waist, the cigarette dangling in her fingers as if it might fall. She had that elusive quality, as if she belonged on some overly anorexic photo shoot of drugged-out, hollow-looking young women who might blow away with the next strong wind. Or that she might fade away like a ghost at any moment, wisps of white matter left in her place. I felt for Joe—could almost feel his pain pinging somewhere inside me. I glanced at Monty sitting on the other easy chair jotting information down, quiet and poised as usual. "Why not?" I asked her.

"Because he had a temper." She began pacing. "That's why."

"And you were protecting him?"

"Pretty much."

"His name?"

"Paul. Paul Tyler. Nicer than Victor ever was." She stood still for a moment and shook her head, her eyes distant.

"Do they know each other?"

"No. Thank the Lord." She bit her lower lip, then sucked on it. "He's watching out for me and Paul now. And Lewis."

"Who is?"

"The good Lord." She turned to me, her eyes irritated.

"Oh, yeah, sorry." I held up my palm. "So the last time you saw Victor, which was about two weeks ago—"

"Maybe three." She sat down.

"You said he was angry?"

"Yeah, the usual. Started yelling at me for seeing someone else. Calling me a slut." Still holding her cigarette, she picked up her Bible again and hugged it to her chest and began rocking back and forth. I noticed it had a sticker of crossbones on its underside. It was the local Bones Church, I thought, the latest craze in the area, that had helped save her, offered the young and the unmoored salvation with its message wrapped in cool, skateboarder imagery. "Threw the usual fit. Said I'd regret it."

"Did he threaten you or Paul? Or your son?"

"I don't know. I guess. He was always spewing out threats. Nothing out of the ordinary. Whatever's on his mind always turned to wanting whatever stash I've got around, but"—she looked at me suddenly, fright filling her eyes and making them seem to want to leap from her face—"you know I'm clean, right?"

I nodded. And I did know by the very fact that she was speaking to us—letting us into her home with some ease—that she was sober for the time being.

She exhaled and her eyes settled into something vague and guarded. "So"—she waved her cigarette—"I told him for the thousandth time I was clean and that I didn't have anything around. Nothin'." She stopped rocking and began bouncing her legs up and down as if there was some force like a geyser inside her that she was physically trying to keep from erupting.

"What exactly, Ms. Boone, was Victor wanting?"

"Anything. Alcohol from the fridge"—she gestured to the kitchen, then paused and looked at the floor. "But, you know, glass," she mumbled. "Crystal. He was tweakin'. Went through my drawers, throwin' shit around all over the place, my clothes. Said he figured I'd, at least, have some pills or something, you know, some Dilaudid or something. Even broke my jewelry box." She set her Bible back on the floor again, went into her bedroom, and came out with a wooden box with a narrow drawer with a small silver handle at the bottom. "My mom gave me and my sister both one of these when we turned ten. Anyway, the asshole broke it." She lifted up the lid that was splintered on the edges and detached from the box, the hinges hanging off and twisted.

"Did he hit you?"

"No, but he pushed me. Dumped the kitchen trash all over the living room. He even threw my Bible against the wall." She looked at it lying on the lavender-colored carpet. "So when I heard what happened to him, I remembered how he threw it"—she nudged it gently with her toes, her foot clad in a striped brown sock—"that's when I knew that he had crossed his line."

"Whose line?"

"God's line," she said emphatically.

Monty glanced at me, then back to his notes. "What did Paul say when he came over to a mess made by Victor?" I asked.

Leslie turned to me, her head cocking to the side, her eyes narrowing. "I know what you're suggesting"—she pointed her cigarette at me—"but you're wrong."

I held up my palm again. "I'm not suggesting anything, miss. Officer Harris here and I"—I gestured between Monty and me—"we just want to figure out who did this to Victor."

"Well." She paced again. "Paul didn't come over until later and I had the place picked up."

"Did you tell him what happened?"

"Some of it. But not how he broke my jewelry box."

"Ms. Boone, forgive me, but I do need to ask you where you were and where Paul was on Thursday and Friday of this last week."

"We were together. Here." She held out her hands to her sides. "With Lewis. Watched a movie together." She pointed at the TV.

"On Friday, you mean?"

She nodded.

"From what time on?"

"I don't know, from like five or so."

"Paul too?"

"He came around six, after work."

"Where were you before that?"

"I was here with Lewis."

"So, you were here from what time on Friday?"

"Lewis rode his bike to my sister's house after school and she brought him by after a bit. We went and got a frozen pizza for dinner and a movie. That *Transformers* one. Then we came home for the rest of the night." She made the same kissing sound again.

"And Paul? Where was he before he came over?"

She shrugged. "I told you—work. But it's not like I know his every move."

"Where does he work?"

"Plum Creek."

"Okay. And what was your Thursday like?"

"Thursday?" She knitted her brow, then shrugged. "I worked most of the day. At the grocery store. I went right after Lewis left for school. I needed to clean the back supply room."

"The store in Hungry Horse?"

"Yeah, then I came home for lunch around twelve thirty and went to clean at Dr. Nieder's, the only dentist here in town, around two because that's their half day and they leave by one thirty."

"And how long were you there?"

"Until about three thirty or so. And when I got home, Lewis was already home from school."

"And then?"

"Nothing, we were in for the night."

"And was there anyone at the dentist's office who can vouch for your appearance there?"

Leslie put her hands on her hips and looked at me like I was an idiot. "Mister, you think they'd let me alone in a dentist's office with my history?"

"Good point." I smiled at her. "At any rate, I'll need the name and number of whoever was there with you."

• • •

"So what do you think?" Monty eliminated the whistle this time. I pulled out my quarter—noticing that it was still the Vermont—and began rolling as soon as we got back in the SUV. I had finished with Leslie by asking her if she knew Stimpy. She got completely close-mouthed and clammed up. Not uncommon for a former druggie, especially a female fearing for herself and her child. When you bring up a dealer, the trained response even if you've dried out is to quit talking as if the questioner suddenly puts a kink in the hose and the information flowing like water seconds before abruptly ceases. I figured we'd have to circle back to that one. Eventually, she'd talk. Each and every one of them always does. The unwritten rule among the users is to never snitch on anybody, and they don't. At first. But eventually, they all do.

By the time I'd brought up the animal torture, her sudden silence made her energy come out even more in the form of physical movement. She became too fidgety to address any other topic: sitting up and down; bouncing one leg; making that sucking, kissing sound; playing, twisting, and tangling her dark hair; rocking back and forth with a wild, distracted look in her eyes. I decided I'd get the lowdown from the vet before circling back to her on that one too. "I think she's telling the truth that she was home, in spite of the fact that addicts are good at lying."

"And why do you believe her?"

"Just a sense." I started the engine and put my quarter back in my pocket. I decided not to set Monty on edge for the drive back to headquarters. "You didn't believe her?"

"No, it's not that. It's just, I don't know, getting the Bible out like that and all. Just weird."

I shrugged. "It's her lifeline. Better life after death than death after meth."

Monty half-smiled. "But Bones Church? I thought that was mostly for teens."

"Teens. Young Adults. My guess is that it's pretty harmless. They target the *lost generation*, right?"

"I thought they targeted the skateboarders and snowboarders, not the addicts. The addicts don't have any money."

"Boarders have money?" I asked.

"If they're trust-fund babies, they do."

"True, but the more, the merrier. And boarders or not, the young are the future."

"I guess. So you don't think there's anything there to look at?"

"Gotta always be thorough," I said. "But it's not high on our list. Other things are, though, so this would actually be a good time for us to divide and conquer. I think you're ready to handle some of these people on your own. In fact, I've been meaning to tell you how great you were with Lou."

"Thanks," Monty said.

I believe he smiled, but I kept my eyes on the road.

· · ·

At headquarters, I made a list of all the things I needed done: checking the DMV for vehicles registered under Victor's name, checking with the bookkeeper at the dental office to verify Leslie's presence from two until close to four p.m. Checking with Hungry Horse Grocery for her hours there. I needed him to verify Paul Tyler's employment status at the timber company, to run a background check on him as well, and to look into the local hardware stores that sold duct tape on the off chance that the perpetrator had to go buy it and didn't already have it on hand. I wasn't quite sure what to make of the tidbit on the capsaicin traces Gretchen had found on the tape. Searching for all the capsaicin sold in the area was a futile endeavor.

I was off to see the veterinarian whom the dog was taken to while he did these things. But before I left, I looked at Monty, "You good?"

"Yeah, I'm good." He pressed a finger against the bridge of his glasses and set them up higher on his nose.

I stood for a moment, hesitant. Monty raised an eyebrow. "Yes?"

I shrugged and left. I'm not sure why I paused. Perhaps I'd gotten used to having him along. The truth was I was beginning to like his company. For me, a little human companionship in Glacier was like having a drink or taking some pain-relieving medicine to take the edge off. Or maybe I just lingered because I had an urge to ask him about Ford. Because for some reason, Ford's presence, even when there was no direct link, seemed to layer into all that I was trying to accomplish on the case. I didn't even need to hear from the guy or have a conversation with him, but I felt his existence, like a deceiving, barely visible layer of ice coating the ground I was trying to cross.

11

T HE NORTHWEST MONTANA Animal Hospital was between Whitefish and Columbia Falls on Highway 40. The assistant at the desk—a young woman with a pretty round face in a pale-blue uniform with a pattern of pink paw prints—told me that Dr. Pritchard was just finishing up with a patient, so I thanked her and drifted over to a corkboard plastered with thank-you cards and pictures of dogs and cats. One picture reminded me of Tumble, the black Lab my family got when we moved from Florida.

A door opened to my left. "Can I help you?" Dr. Pritchard asked.

He had a deep voice, which I expected, because he was at least my height, six-two or -three, and had fine features, almost effeminate: dark, but surprisingly kind eyes, high cheekbones, russet skin. But he wore his hair disheveled, so he didn't appear prim, and his face was weathered and lined in that Montana way—maybe from squinting in the wind, the cold, and the high-altitude sun.

"Dr. Pritchard," I said. "I'm Ted Systead. I work as a homicide detective for the Department of the Interior. I'm just here to ask you a few questions if you have a moment."

He looked to the gal behind the desk, and she looked back at him with wide doe eyes. His own appeared tired, heavy-lidded, but under the lids, I could see surprise and an ounce of curiosity since he had an unusual visitor, a break from the routine. "Okay, sure." He shook his head slightly in the way people do when they have a sudden shiver, but I think the move was to simply shift himself into a different and unexpected gear. "Who's waiting for me, Rose?"

"Just Mrs. Phelps, but I can send Elizabeth back with her to explain the phenobarbital dosage."

"Okay, that's fine."

He brought me into a small office where he had a laptop angled toward him. A picture of a woman and two children and another of him somewhere in the backcountry beside what appeared to be a wolf or maybe wolverine trap stood on the other end of the desk. He sat back languidly in his chair and motioned for me to sit. "What can I help you with?"

I told him about Victor and waited for his reaction, but there was no response. No *good, he deserved it,* as if he knew him or no overdramatic *What? Are you kidding?* Or *oh no, that's awful* As if he couldn't believe such a thing would happen in his neck of the woods. He just sat silently and waited, perhaps exhaled a little louder than usual, and I saw his body slump a bit as if he was used to carrying a good amount of the world's pain.

"I'm here because you treated a dog that was beaten badly last spring, and there's a small chance that there may be a connection to the victim."

"I see." He nodded, complete comprehension crossing his face; he knew which dog I meant. "A connection?"

"Yeah, it's a long shot, but in my job, I've got to follow up on everything."

"Makes sense. Well, here's what I know." He leaned forward, placing his elbows on his knees, and looked at me intently. "It was a shitty, shitty thing. One of the worst I've seen in my career." He looked down for a moment. "I've been a vet for twenty-eight years now and I've seen a fair share of animal cruelty cases: horses underfed and left in overly small enclosures, dogs left outside in the cold until their hearts have nearly stopped, cats left trapped in trailers, puppies and kittens tied up in plastic bags and thrown in Dumpsters. One guy thought it fun to burn his kitten's ears off on a stove burner . . . . But this poor Lab."

He shook his head and ran a hand through the wavy, gray-flecked hair above his ears. "Whoever did this beat the poor dog so badly with a bat that his intestines exploded inside of him, the contents poisoning him. His skull was fractured, his shoulder and hip fractured. His spine broken."

"Who brought him in?"

"Someone drove by and saw him tied to a fence. Collapsed and bloody on the ground. They stopped and checked his tags and saw my clinic's name, so they brought him here. It was a Sunday and they called me on their way over. I met them here, not knowing how bad the situation was. I figured a few bruises—that he'd need some stitches." He blew out a long breath, making his cheeks puff out with air. "They were a nice couple. Helped carry him in on a blanket they had in the back of their car and they stayed until I examined him. I knew I had to put him out of his misery as quickly as I could."

"And that's what you did?"

He rubbed his eyes as if he could smear the blackened bruise of the experience from his mind. He nodded. "I called the owner first. Gave him morphine intravenously to ease the pain until he could come. When he got here, I told him about his dog's condition, then I got his go-ahead and euthanized him."

"How did he take it?"

"Poorly. As you'd expect. He couldn't believe it. He, he"—Dr. Pritchard sighed heavily—"he wanted to pound my walls down once the reality that someone could have done this to his dog sunk in. But he contained himself and got through it. He comforted the poor thing as best he could as I administered the dose."

"Who was the owner?"

"Guy named Rob Anderson. Lives in Columbia Falls. Loved his dog." He knit his brow. "Logan. That was his name, if I recall correctly—after Logan Pass in Glacier."

Logan Pass was the passage for the infamous Going-to-the-Sun

Road that cut through the steep terrain and crossed the divide in the heart of Glacier. So much in the area was named after something in or about Glacier. You couldn't drive far without seeing signs with names like Grizzly Property Rental, Glacier Dental, Glacier Eye Clinic, Northwest Glacier Mechanics, Glacier Bank, Going-to-the-Sun Café . . ."Did Mr. Anderson have any idea who could have done such a thing?"

"Not that I recall. He was totally shocked. Very devastated." Dr. Pritchard nodded again. "We reported it to the police and they came here to question us, but they never found who did it. Not sure how much time they spent on it, although it did make the paper, and many of my clientele brought up how sickened they were by the whole thing. I believe the entire Flathead Valley was somewhat enraged that someone could, and would, do that to an animal."

For reasons I can't explain, I imagined the grizzly I had not yet seen trapped in his heavily fortified cage, still alive, his three- or four-inch claws curling around the thick steel wires. I shoved my hand in my pocket and felt for a quarter among several coins, what felt like a mixture of pennies, dimes, and quarters now. I gripped one of the quarters between my thumb and forefinger. "So," I said, "Mr. Anderson had no leads to give the police?"

"Not that I remember." Dr. Pritchard suddenly looked up like he understood why I was before him. "You think the guy who beat the Lab murdered the guy in Glacier?"

"Not exactly." I brought my quarter out, not sure if it was still the Vermont, and I didn't bother to check because I caught Dr. Pritchard glance at my hand, so I wrapped my fingers around it and pressed it into the point of my chin. I can't exactly say why I felt uneasy. I had no bad feelings or intuitions about the man before me. Perhaps it was simply the smell of animal mixed with the medicinal smell that always permeates a vet's clinic that somehow triggered something inside me: the distant sound of beeps and voices of orderlies somewhere in my memory bank. "As I said when I came in, it's a long shot, but what we're trying to discover is whether or not the guy who was murdered was one of the guys who actually beat the Lab."

"Oh, I see." He pursed his lips, his eyes murky with serious thoughts. Then he scratched the side of his cheek and I could hear the sound of his razor stubble like sandpaper. "Yeah, it was a bad thing to happen to a sweet animal. I hope you discover who did this, and if he's not your guy in the park, that he's punished accordingly."

"I hope so too, Dr. Pritchard." I stood and extended my hand. "Thank you for your time."

As I left, I glanced one last time and saw him turn to his computer. But he wasn't looking at it. He was staring at the floor, his head drooped as if I'd zapped his energy—as if he wasn't expecting to pause on this particular day to mourn the loss of one of his former patients.

• • •

The first grizzly bear I did see subsequent to my father's death came four years later, right after I graduated from high school. I was still dating Kendra, and her father, Jack, wanted to hike to Almeda Lake up the Middle Fork drainage, which is adjacent to the park, but not in it. Parts of the area where the trail cuts through have been logged, leaving broad, rectangular bald spots on the hillsides that provide thick, brushy areas with huge huckleberry bushes perfect for bears.

I did not know about the clear-cuts and figured the trail was similar to ones in Glacier, broadly buffed out and nicely maintained with open vistas as soon as you gain elevation. The Almeda Lake trail, however, meandered through lower elevation for some time, alternating between dense clear-cut areas where the bushes were over fifteen feet high and Hansel and Gretel wooded forest with green ferns and sturdy ponderosas.

Each time we strode through a clear-cut patch, my chest tightened and my breathing quickened because I knew that this was the most predictable spot to startle a bear. I carried my capsaicin spray as usual and hurried through the logged patches, the brush scratching my arms and legs. I was frantically expecting a large, furry beast to charge out from the overgrown bushes at any moment and felt calmed each time we made it through one with no surprises. Kendra kept asking me why I was walking so fast. I just ignored her until she got mad and decided not to speak either.

We had just come out of what I figured was the last clear-cut because we were about to hit a turn leading us up and away from the huge scars on the mountainside. I felt relieved, and in my respite, I was just about to reach out to grab her hand and say something sweet (*hey, babe, you put your sunscreen on today?*) when Jack stopped abruptly in front of me and slammed to a halt. I saw him fumble at the side of his fanny pack where the holster for his spray hung.

"Two cubs," he whispered with a forceful airy quality. "Up ahead. One just crossed right in front of me 'bout ten yards."

My chest and stomach instantly seized. I could feel my pulse hammer my chest and shoot through my neck in forceful shoves. I felt like I was suddenly being trapped in a shaft with syrupy darkness narrowing around me. I fought the urge to turn and bolt, to just keep running until some light at the end of the tunnel showed.

I felt Kendra dig her fingers into my arm. "Where?" she whispered back to her dad.

Jack pointed down the trail into the shade of the darkened forest. About twenty yards from us, two small moving blobs of fur crossed and disappeared into the brush beside the trail.

Then I heard the grunt—a low guttural sound somewhere between a bark, a woof, and some loud, deep incomprehensible forced exhalation. All noises ceased. I heard no hawks. No ravens or jays. No squirrels. I saw her rise up on her haunches, her height rising against the trees as if she might turn to stone and become one of them—a great sturdy statue in the forest among the firs. She sniffed the air, her head bobbing and slightly angling to the side, one, two, three, four times.

Her paws dangled before her as if she were getting ready to play some grand piano. She woofed again, and somehow I managed to raise my arm, heavy like lead, the spray in my shaking hand.

"Remove the cap," Kendra whispered.

I fumbled with the top and got the safety off with my left hand. Jack already had his held out before him. I couldn't speak if I tried. I'm certain I didn't.

"Let's go back," Kendra whispered, her high-pitched voice sending painful reverberations up my spine.

Jack shushed her with an urgency I'd never heard from him before. He placed his forefinger to his mouth. The grizzly stood before us, her broad silvery snout lifted, trying to read the air like braille. Then she dropped back to all fours. Her front feet hit the ground with a boom, and although in retrospect I'm sure it was just my imagination, I could have sworn that the return of her mass to the ground made the forest floor vibrate. She panted three very specific times: *huff, huff, huff.* Then she rocked back and forth, to show aggression, to signal *Don't mess with my cubs*, and turned and left.

I still couldn't breathe, and I stood frozen, thick, and trembling. Her skunklike odor strangled the air. We listened, the forest still quiet, save the sound of her large body moving through brush, branches breaking, leaves rustling. We could hear her making her way up the ridge, traversing to one side, then stopping and we'd hear her: *huff, huff, huff.* A heavy, breathy sound that seemed to swing with her body. Then she'd traverse to the other side and do the same. She continued to zigzag from side to side, moving her cubs along, panting three specific times with each pause.

"She's talking to 'em," Jack whispered. "Directing them higher up the ridge."

I was still holding my spray up, my hand shaking uncontrollably.

"You can drop that now." Jack pushed my arm down with two fingers and stared at me for a moment.

"That was so scary," Kendra said, then giggled and brought her hand to her mouth as if she could catch her nervous chuckles in her palm. "But cool. Haven't seen one that close up *ever*."

Her voice was too high and loud. I stared at her for a moment, deluges of blood surging in the sides of my neck and between my ears, still semitrapped in a dark shaft, but I could make out some light and that light took on the fuzzy form of her round, flushed face and buttery-blond hair.

I could hear Jack announcing that we'd wait ten minutes to give her and her cubs time to clear the ridge and then continue our hike. I tried to say something, attempted to form the beginning of my sentence starting with *I*, but couldn't form the word, my throat swollen with nausea and acrid fear. Somewhere in the back of my head I could hear the sound of crunching bone.

I quit trying to speak. Instead, I turned and began walking down the trail toward the car with Kendra yelling in a squeaky voice, "Where are you going? Wait. Jesus, Ted, what are you doing?"

I kept walking until her voice became a distant vagueness. I made it around the bend before I threw up what was left of my breakfast beside the overgrown trail.

A hint of nausea accompanied that image in my mind for a beat before it kindly vanished when I returned to headquarters. Ford and Monty were discussing something in the office. When I walked in, they both abruptly quit talking, and I couldn't tell if I was imagining it or not, but Monty's face seemed to flush and his eyes shifted toward the floor as if I'd caught him tattle-telling on me for god-knows-what.

"Hello, Systead." Ford stood. "Good to see you again."

Something bitter formed in the back of my throat, and I glanced at Monty, who was sorting through some papers.

"What can we help you with?" I purposely used the plural pronoun, although I can't exactly explain why, other than to somehow claim Monty on my imaginary side.

"Not a thing. Monty here's already been more than helpful." Ford smiled at him, and again, Monty looked shy, as if he'd somehow betrayed me.

"That right?"

"Yep, I'm all up-to-date. So about this bear." Ford blew out a loud breath of air. "We've decided that even if he doesn't produce this bullet you're searching for, that we will eventually be putting him back into the wilderness. He needs to begin heading for the high country."

"And this was your decision?" I asked.

"The committee's and mine. And don't worry, I've run it past Sean Dewey."

I didn't want to speak because I knew anger was boiling inside of me at the mere mention of Ford going above me to my boss and the idea that I might be without crucial evidence because of a decision prompted by Ford. Dewey knew that getting a slug was of utmost importance. I was certainly aware of the need to get this bruin back to his fall schedule, but there seemed to be something directed at me from Ford that smacked of a blatant disregard for what I was trying to accomplish. I was having a hard time not taking it personally. Ultimately, I knew final bear decisions rested with the super, but I was prepared to fight him because at this point I needed that slug even if I had to put someone behind that bear's ass with a plastic cup for the next week. "You mean the bear review group?"

"Yeah, Bowman, Smith, and that cadre."

Uh huh, I thought, who the hell uses the word *cadre*? Suddenly, I wanted him to leave. "All right then." I picked up a random file off the long table; I had no intention of having that bear let loose without getting my hands on the slug used to kill Victor Lance. "I'll talk to Bowman and Dewey."

"There's no need. We've already discussed it. We'll make sure he's got a GPS collar on him," Ford said.

"Good." I humored him and opened the file, still not taking in a single word from it. "Back to work then," I said.

"Actually, if you don't mind. How 'bout taking a little walk with me."

I raised my brow. "Sir, with all due respect, I'm a little too busy at the moment for a walk."

"Just a small one."

I glanced at Monty, who was still looking down at the papers before him. I tossed the file back on the desk and followed Ford out, thoroughly irritated that this guy had some in with Sean. I had to play nice with him because Sean wanted me to and because I couldn't afford to irritate any higher-ups in my department by upsetting park superintendents. We went out the back doors of the headquarters, across the parking lot to a path that led through a group of thin birches. Pale yellow leaves scattered the ground over a blanket of fallen tamarack needles. The crisp air hit my cheeks and a wet, earthy smell filled my nose.

"So," Ford began, "Monty's told me that Lou Shelton is Victor's uncle."

"That's right."

"And that when you questioned him, you got him a little riled up?"

"I'd say he got himself riled up."

"Well, Ted. Mind if I call you Ted?"

I shook my head. But I did mind.

"Here's the thing, Ted. You know that around Lake McDonald there are numerous estates not currently owned by the park?"

"Yeah, so?"

"Well, these estates, of course, present a problem because owners don't always play by park rules, right?"

"Look." I held up my hand. "With all due respect, I'm quite busy at the moment—"

"You must also know," he said more pointedly, "that it's in Glacier's and the tourists' best interest to have open shoreline unencumbered by any local residences. People come here for the beauty of the unbroken land, not to see cabins on the shoreline."

"So? Isn't it simply a willing-seller–willing-buyer policy with Glacier getting first right of refusal?"

"That's exactly right." Ford paused on the trail, not far from a barracks-looking structure that I believe was the Lakes District office. "And with Mr. Shelton here, he's close to becoming a willing seller."

"How so?"

"Well, Lou's father, Roger, specified that Lou would live in the cabin upon his passing. He died in 1999, a few years after his wife passed away. But beyond Lou, he didn't specify if or how the grandchildren would inherit the cabin when Lou's gone. Roger and Eloise Shelton had some eight grandchildren, all of whom are now over twenty-one and none of them giving a damn about the place the way Lou does. Anyway, I didn't know it until now, but apparently, Victor was one of the grandchildren."

I nodded.

"So." Ford's eyes narrowed under the shadow of his hat. "Let's just say it's in the park's best interest to keep Lou Shelton on our good side because he's this close"—he held up his fingers like he was about to pinch some salt—"to making a deal with the park."

"You mean a willing sale?"

"Precisely. With a life-estate agreement. So, of course, I'd never interfere with your work, but if you can try to not upset him in the meantime, that would be in all of our best interests."

"I'll try not to anger him, but when it comes to finding out who did this, a life-estate agreement's not going to keep me from doing what I need to do."

"Of course," Ford said. "But remember, the department isn't going to be too happy with you if you prevent them from getting their hands on shoreline property."

"I appreciate your concern," I said with mild sarcasm, fighting the urge to tell him to get the hell out of my business.

"You're welcome. And now, just as you said"—he smiled—"back to work then."

• • •

He left me standing there. I stood on the path, not moving because I was gathering my wits before heading back in, but then I heard it. It wasn't a very loud sound, but deep, and gruff. I knew instantly what it was. I turned and saw the twenty-by-twenty cage. He rocked from side to side and was looking in my direction. His silver-tipped hair thick and full—a heavy coat of armor against the oncoming winter. He grunted again, and the sharp taste of fear stabbed the back of my throat. I fought a childish urge to run.

Just like at a zoo, I told myself. Not the wild. In a heavy-duty cage sturdy enough to hold a grizzly in the headquarters district of West Glacier so he can crap a piece of evidence out. That's all. My breathing quickened in spite of myself. Not the wild, I repeated. The image of Oldman Lake with its stunted and wind-deformed high-line trees surrounding its deep-green water flashed in my mind. "Not the wild," I whispered it out loud.

But still, it was Glacier, and all the things that made her Glacier: white jagged peaks draped with golden morning fog; aspen trees with bone-white bark; crystal-clear frigid streams moving silently over large pastel-colored rocks; foamy, roaring waterfalls; red-rocked gorges with intricate curved patterns; cold, cold air—somehow crisper and more raw and desolate; and exquisite beauty surrounded me and seemed to mock me, whisper to me that I was somehow inadequate, incapable of solving a case while in her embrace.

I shook off the feeling and walked closer to the cage. I could feel my pulse in my ears. The bear stood on his hind legs and lifted his nose to the air. The sharp stench of wild animal seemed to cover me and nausea began to build in my gut. I stopped. A silky black raven flew by and cawed. I felt dizzy, like things weren't real and I was in a movie montage. I reached for a quarter in my pocket but realized I hadn't grabbed my coat. My hands shook.

Really—the bear was beautiful, with its full silvery coat, thick oval-shaped ears, and long, concave jawline. Suddenly, there were too many layers: Ford's presence fueling my anger, Glacier's breeze hitting my face, the case presenting many avenues, Monty and Smith feeling like unexpected friends, the ephemeral nature of the light, and under it all, a primitiveness locked deep inside of me scratching to break free . . . And here before me, less than thirty yards away, a magnificent, deadly grizzly bear grunting, sniffing my human odor, trying to make sense of me, trying to make sense of its cage. Its relentless presence filled the air.

It occurred to me—broke through the fog in my head—that I could simply walk away, not just from the cage, but from the case entirely, and go back to Denver. Tell Sean to send someone else to solve a case about an animal-torturing meth head. And although I'm certain I didn't define this with clarity at the time, something inside of me screamed that if I did, I would never be able to work another case in my life. And if that happened, I would be as caged as that bear by my own fear. In retrospect, I can describe this as if everything fit neatly into a pattern as perfect as the circular swirls of red rock around the Sun Rift Gorge on the east side of Logan Pass. But at the time, it was blurry and just a sharp sensation, like being deprived of air. And when that happens, you fight for it.

I wish I could say that the moment was a pivotal turning point for me. That I strode right up to the bear, inspected him calmly as he roared. That I smiled into his long snout and hot breath as if I were John Wayne. But I didn't. As anticlimactic as it sounds, I wasn't ready and probably never would be, not without completely faking it. I knew I couldn't quit the case, but I wasn't ready to face a grizzly bear that had only days before eaten a human being. I stood and fidgeted, then turned back. And when I did, I saw Ford standing in the parking lot, his hand with his car keys frozen before the lock as he stared at me, squinting as Lou Shelton had, like some quintessentially wise mountain man. When I think about it now, I'm sure his look was one of amusement—his brow furrowed as he watched me flustered on the trail and wondered why I wasn't going anywhere when I had so much work to do.

But to me, at the time, all I could see was that he was peering at me as a man who'd conquered great patches of wilderness in his own life, like a man who could see right through me as if I were a fraud, as if bravery was only stitched to the fabric of my DOI cotton-poly-blend shirt . . . and as if I had a neon sign above my head flashing the word *coward* over and over again.

12

I CALLED SEAN, WHO seemed a million miles away in a world so separate from Glacier Park that it suddenly made me think of my apartment in Denver and that I still needed to ring Rexanne, the landlady, to check on my plants sometime near the end of the week. I was lucky that she liked me because she was very helpful for a guy with my travel schedule. She watered my ficus, my jade, my coleus, and my weeping fig anytime I was gone for more than a few days, and sometimes in the dead of winter, she would make sure my heat was up from sixty to sixty-nine if I told her when I was returning. Unfortunately, I felt that some long shadow had marked me the day I set foot on the McGee Meadow path and that I would be in Glacier for longer than half a week.

"Systead," Sean said. "It's about time I heard from you. Guess you haven't been missin' those good ol' heart-to-hearts with Uncle Sean now?"

I chuckled. "I always miss those."

"Well, you'll be missing them forever if you don't get your act together."

"What's that supposed to mean?" My half smile faded.

"Bad joke. I just mean that part of your job is reporting to me, or did you forget that?"

"No, I didn't." I was loitering around the entrance to headquarters and had to back away from the door when it opened. Karen Fortenson and a male ranger I hadn't seen before came out the door laughing about something. I tipped my head and Karen held up her hand in a small wave and the other ranger tipped his head in return. "Look, it's just been busy here. No witness, no weapon, no ballistics, but time-consuming because we've got several leads." I shuffled over to my loaner SUV and leaned my hip against the hood.

"That so? Well, while you're in lead creek without a paddle, I've got the superintendent breathing down my neck about every move you make."

"I've gathered. And he called you about letting the grizzly go, which would guarantee a lack of ballistics?"

"Of course he has. And he's probably going to call me next to see if you wiped your ass this morning."

I laughed. "About the bear?"

"What about it?"

"You backed him that it should be let go even though it's probably carrying the slug?"

Sean laughed. "I wouldn't exactly call it *backing* him. I don't need to remind you that I back *my* men as long as they don't do anything stupid, and you haven't. Yet."

"Thanks for the vote of confidence."

"You're very welcome," he said facetiously. "Look." He changed his tone to be more serious: "I told Ford what you already know—that the final call on a federal bear belongs to the super, but that it would be highly unusual for the super to not be helpful in an investigation."

I didn't say anything.

"I'm no bear expert," he continued. "But there's a ton of pressure coming from the park to release it so that it has a healthy hibernation. Plus it's not like this Victor Lance was a senator or something."

"Probably had better ethics than a senator," I mumbled.

"I caught that. And you're probably right," Sean said. "Look, Ted, I'm no idiot, I know getting that slug can play a crucial role in nailing your perp."

"Absolutely," I stressed. "If I get it, we can define the weapon and we can check the lands and grooves, even if it's something totally generic like a Smith & Wesson and trust me, in this neck of the woods, everyone and their brother has one and not that many are in the ATF database. So at least if we have a slug we can still get a match if we come across the gun."

"And if you were really lucky, the gun was purchased recently from a firearms dealer, so that its serial number is in the ATF database. You might even find it was purchased by someone who's in *leadville* right now."

"I thought it was a creek?" I smiled.

"Creek. Ville . . . who gives a shit?"

"You're right. *If* they purchased from a registered dealer." Montana has no gun registration laws, but firearms dealers were required to run checks, and that meant the purchased gun's serial number would go into the ATF database along with the purchaser.

"Hmmm." I heard Sean flipping pages and figured he had some type of file before him. I waited for him to continue. "If we put this bear down to search his stomach contents, there's a chance you won't find anything, and even if you do find it, it's unlikely that the firearm hasn't been disposed of, right?"

"Can't say that. You know how many people hang on to their guns—keep 'em in their house even after a murder for Christ's sake. Although, you're right about disposing it. It's fairly common around here for people to toss 'em into the rivers. It's a quick way to get rid of the evidence, and we've got some of the county guys with underwater detectors lined up to search the corridors as soon as they're done with the job they're on." For some reason, my knees felt a little shaky, and I was glad I was leaning against the SUV. I wasn't just kissing ass. The chances were slim that we'd find the gun in the rivers or some characteristic in the bullet that would magically point me in the right direction. However, it has happened. The third case I solved involved a late-nineteenth-century buffalo rifle that only a select few in the county had registered. Once I identified all the owners, it was easy to see that one of the teenagers on my suspect list had had his grandfather's model in his possession at the time of the murder. It wasn't hard to get him to confess. But the bottom line was that no detective worth their salt would let a bear free with a potential slug in its digestive system. "Seems like the park would rather save this bear than find who did this."

"Right you are about that. If he weren't such a promising specimen, it might be different. Also, people come to Glacier, in part, because they know the grizzlies are there. The murder, well, probably a fluke tied to some meth deal. I'm sure they think this nasty business will all pass before spring."

The logical part of me agreed, but the detective in me cringed. It didn't matter who the victim was, my drive to solve the case surged through me like electricity. "So we aim to please the park?"

"Come on, Ted, how long've you been with us?" He tsked several times. "You got any other stupid questions?"

I didn't answer.

"The way I see it, we stall the bear committee and Ford for as long as possible to see if he eventually craps the bullet out."

"That's been the plan all along," I said. "It's not unreasonable to think he won't pass it. It's just a question of when he's ready for hibernation, and Ford's worried that we're messing with his instincts, that his body's delaying his natural instincts because he's caged, which also delays his digestive system."

"Yeah, yeah, I hear ya. Just play the game, will ya. And I'll do the same. Would it be the worst if we end up letting him go with a collar? That way, if we get into a bind, we track him down and get him then. With a collar on, we can't go too wrong. Then, everyone's happy."

"He'll be in the high country, and you know as well as I do that he'll most likely head for a north-facing slope with lots of snow, which will make it too difficult to get to him even if we locate the signal, which we'd be unlikely to do if he caves with the first blizzard. And if he craps it out in the woods, we'll never find it."

"Well, let's not get ahead of ourselves. Let's see what happens in the next few days. Why can't they give him some ex-lax or something?"

"Against park rules. It'd mess with the hyperphagic state he's in, and they can't have him completely losing his energy supply and changing the metabolic process in his gut before hibernation or he won't make it through the winter."

"Christ." Sean chuckled. "So tell me—how strong are your leads?"

I spent some time going through the five in detail: Stimpy, Leslie, Leslie's boyfriend, Lou Shelton, and Rob Anderson with the animal cruelty situation. When I finished, I heard him sigh.

"Well, at least you got some stuff to work with. Of course, you know which one of those my bets are on."

"Yeah. It's the obvious."

"It's unlikely someone in the meth ring will have a registered weapon."

"Yeah, but I try not to make too many assumptions. It gets me in trouble every time."

"Just keep the pressure up, Systead, and your head out of your ass and you'll get to the heart of this in just a few more days. By that time, the bear will have shit the slug out and you'll have cinched the case."

"Sounds like a plan," I said, maybe a little too tentatively and hoarsely. I wasn't comforted, but I forced a little humor in spite of myself: "And by the way, I did take care of it this morning."

"Of what?"

"My ass," I replied. "I wiped it. You can let Ford know that."

He laughed wholeheartedly, and after he hung up, I spent some time leaning against the SUV, staring at the trees through which I knew the bear's cage stood off another hundred yards. I couldn't see it from the parking lot since the forest blocked the view. Ford said they'd considered transporting him to the Logging Lake area, which had been closed for camping two months earlier and day hikes restricted just the day before in anticipation of this eventual move. Not many people visit Logging Lake during the summer, and even less during the fall, if any at all. It's deeper up the Inside North Fork Road, but still close enough to McGee Meadow that the bear should feel like it's still in its own territory. For years, park Bear Management would try to relocate troublesome bears, only to find they'd hightail it right back to where they came from. I figured it was like getting drunk in a bar in a different town, being drugged, and waking up the next morning and saying to yourself, *Where the hell am I?* Then heading home as soon as possible.

They would not need to sedate him. They would simply lead him into the culvert trap, drive him up the long, rutted road, then let the cranky thing out with a remote-controlled cage door so they could be safe in the cover of their vehicles.

I pictured him swaying from left to right on his forepaws. Looking around, glancing back at Bowman and Smith. Snorting, grunting, then trotting into the woods. Maybe drinking out of the cold lake after gaining distance, then moving on and up to the tree line where the terrain turns rugged—letting the wilderness provide a barrier from all human constructs. And sauntering away with the case's most crucial piece of evidence.

. . .

We didn't find Stimpy as effortlessly as I thought we would. For one, his run-down trailer at the address we had from the task force seemed abandoned—no recent footprints, dust at the base of the door, debris from a windstorm on the front steps. . . . It was down a dirt road just past the Lake Five turnoff, and we found the shithole easily. We figured he was probably taking up with a girlfriend.

I went back into headquarters and grabbed Monty even though I was conflicted over the idea that he seemed so cozy with Ford, an irrational thought, I knew, since he worked for the guy. I needed someone with me on this one in case Stimpy was all jacked up and ended up freaking out. I quizzed Monty on the way over to make sure he remembered some of the backup protocol from his early training days before he got all soft and converted to Ford's duties. Just the obvious and only just in case: going in single file, watching my back, covering opposite vision points, searching for fields of fire. Monty didn't seem insulted with my review and once again, I considered the fact that he was a good student.

I had a list of known users through the Regional Drug Task Force database and quite easily came up with Stimpy's whereabouts by threatening the first user, an undernourished, chain-smoking guy named Kevin Miller, whom we tracked down at a local hangout in Coram called the Elk Tracks Saloon. It was only a matter of convincing him that it was going to be his ass very soon and that I would make sure the sheriff's department made a full-time job of him if he didn't give me some information on our friend Stimpy.

He sang within minutes, giving us Stimpy's girlfriend, a Melissa Tafford, and that she ran a bar in Hungry Horse called the Outlaw's Nest. We headed there, and when we walked in, I rearranged my gun that I wear on a shoulder strap just because you never know how a paranoid drug user and dealer, usually with easy access to illicit weapons, is going to react to federal law enforcement. But when we entered, there were only about five people in the place—two older men with receding hairlines at the bar and two young women and a young man (possibly all underage) at a table. They were clearly drunk, speaking and laughing loudly in the quiet place. I knew that things hadn't changed in Montana—very few people called taxis as they do in the city when drinking heavily. They simply hopped in their vehicles and hit the roads in spite of the reverence-inducing American Legion practice of placing white crosses at car fatality sites.

Nobody in the bar even remotely fit Stimpy's description: a stout guy with a shaved head and a dark goatee. We walked up to the bar. The whole place gave off a tangy smell of stale cigarette smoke and alcohol mixed with the strong scent of bleach even though Montana had outlawed smoking in all food and drinking establishments. The two older men were having tumblers of whiskey, and the one closest to me turned and glared at me with narrowed, disapproving eyes. He threw his drink back, grimaced, and made a smacking sound, then looked back at his empty glass. I wondered if they were retirees from the aluminum plant when it was still going strong or if they'd been let go with the most recent closure. Or possibly old loggers out of work, their hands strong, rough, and scarred as they cupped their whiskey.

"Let me guess," asked a medium-size woman with dark, wavy hair and several deep acne scars pocking the pale skin on her cheekbones. She was washing beer mugs in a large sink with murky water. "You two aren't here for the whiskey."

"Come on." I smiled. "We don't stick out that much." I looked down at my jeans and my navy coat. I wasn't wearing my badges. Monty had on gray pants and a black windbreaker.

"Yeah." She picked up a cloth and began scouring the bar. "You do."

"Well, let's get right to it, then. Your boyfriend, Stimpy—can you tell us where he is?"

She gave me a blank stare and walked over to the older gentlemen. "Another?" she asked him. He glanced our way, then nodded and slid his glass to her.

"He's not in trouble; we just need to talk to him," I said.

"'Bout Victor Lance." She filled his glass partway with ice, grabbed a bottle of Crown Royal, and filled it halfway.

"That's right. And may I ask how you know that?"

She clutched her rag again, turned her back to us, and began cleaning the opposite counter. "Guy turns up dead. People talk."

"Makes sense." I smiled even though she wasn't looking at me. "So where might Andrew Stimpson be this afternoon?"

"I don't know where he went. He was in here earlier, then he left."

"You're his girlfriend and he didn't tell you where he was going? That wasn't very nice of him."

"I don't give a shit what you think." She pivoted back to us and put her hand on her hip, the dingy rag still in her hand. "Neither one of us did anything wrong."

Both of the older men stared at me, and the one who'd refilled his drink cleared his throat. "Melissa." He wagged his finger at her to come over. She went and he scooted forward, leaning over the bar, and whispered to her.

"It's okay, Bud," she said. "It's fine."

I politely nodded at him. "If that's the case," I said to Melissa, "that you've done nothing wrong, then why so nervous about us having a chat with him?"

Her face got pouty, and she shrugged.

"Look, Ms. Tafford. My partner and I aren't here to stir up any trouble; we just want to find out what Victor Lance was up to before this past weekend."

"How would I know that?"

"Like you said, people talk. Just thought you might've heard. Did you know him?"

She nodded.

"When was the last time you saw him?"

"I don't know." She bit her lower lip. "Last week sometime. Came in for a few."

"Was he with anyone?"

"No. He was alone."

"You sure 'bout that?"

"Yeah. I'm sure. He sat here"—she lifted her chin to the bar—"and we made small talk."

"Which day of the week was it?"

"Wednesday, I think."

"How did he seem?"

"Fine."

"Nervous or jumpy?" I asked.

"No more than usual."

"Where's Stimpy?"

"I told you. He left, but I have no idea where."

I turned my back to her, away from the old men, and leaned against the bar on one elbow and took in the rest of the place. A meager, dusty light filtered in from a greasy street window. A red-and-black psychedelic seventies-type carpet spread under old linoleum-top tables with metal legs and metal chairs. Several different blue-and-red neon beer signs hung on the walls, and the tiled floor in the short hallway to the bathrooms was buckling. Even though the place was bleak, it was nicer than some of the other taverns up the Line. "Nice place you're runnin' here. Bet it's not easy to keep it going."

She looked at me only for an instant.

"I'm guessing you don't want the local law enforcement making a project of this place?"

She still said nothing. Monty took a seat at the bar, and I stayed half-turned away from her. "Bet that might make the owners a little nervous, you know, 'bout the management of it. Kind of makes life real tough when you're a bar owner to have the cops breathing down your neck, checking to see if you serve to minors, overserve to people with too many DUIs, you know, that kind of thing." I turned back to face her. "Not to mention any drug deals that might take place—and I'm not saying that happens here." I held up my palm innocently. "But you can never be too careful these days. Especially when the boyfriend of the person you're paying to manage the place is listed with the local drug task force."

Her bottom lip stuck out even farther, like she was an angry, sulking teenager. I took a seat along with Monty and gave her a dose of her own blank stare.

"Look, I told you." She threw the rag into the sink after about five seconds of silence. "He took off."

"Why?"

"Because some guy came in here asking questions. Said he was investigating a murder in the park and that he'd heard from Victor's sister that Stimpy might have known Victor. Stimpy was pissed, so he left."

I glanced at Monty. "A police officer?"

"No, no one like that. He said he was a reporter, that he was just checking into things because he knew there was more to the story than the sheriff's office was letting people in on."

"Let me get this straight. So this reporter—he spoke to Stimpy?"

She nodded. "Stimpy said he knew nothin' 'bout Victor Lance. And I believe him; he didn't."

"So why did he leave?"

"He wanted to talk to Victor's sister. Find out why that reporter came to him."

"And how does he know Victor's sister?"

"I don't know. I guess through Victor. He was proud of her. You know, mentioning her a lot. He'd talk about her having her act together and working at that café in C' Falls."

. . .

"Where are we going? The soup place?" Monty asked.

"That's right. See if Stimpy's still there and see who this reporter is? Damn." I slapped the top of the steering wheel. "You can thank your boss for that."

"My boss?"

"Yeah, what the hell's a reporter sticking his nose into Stimpy's business?"

"How would I know?"

"I'll tell you why. This is the way it works: if you don't give the media enough information, they attempt to dig it up themselves and they go sniffing around where they don't belong."

"What's that got to do with Ford?"

"He arranged with the sheriff's office for them to defer all questions from the press to his PR department. You read the article. It didn't even mention a kidnapping or homicide. He should have at least given them that." I felt my grip on the steering wheel a little too tight. "If that reporter gets hurt by sniffing around meth dealers, you think your boss even cares?"

I could sense Monty's eyes on me for a long moment until finally, he looked out the window.

. . .

It wasn't the reporter who got hurt. It was Megan, but only mildly. We found her at her apartment hugging her arm with an ice pack. "My fucking brother." She sat down on her couch after she let us in. Then she paused and took a deep breath. I could tell she was holding back tears. She waited a second until she was free of the impulse, then added: "Still, even with him gone, I have to deal with his screwed-up life."

"How long ago did he leave?"

"'Bout thirty minutes."

"Did he say where he was going?"

"No. Can you believe it? That asshole grabbed my arm and twisted it behind my back." She took another deep breath, held it for a few seconds, then let it out, making a shaky airy sound, almost like a whimper. "Then he whispered in my ear." She shivered. "I could smell his nasty breath and he said that I'd pay for it if I ever mentioned his name to anyone ever again."

"Wasn't there anyone in the café with you?"

"No, it was past the lunch rush and I was reading a magazine when he came in. After he left, my boss came in with some supplies, and when I told her what happened, she let me go so I could come up and ice my shoulder."

"And who was the person that you mentioned Stimpy's name to?"

"To that reporter. From the *Daily Flathead*."

"Do you remember his name?"

"Will something. Will Jones." I saw Monty write it down.

"Why Stimpy's name?"

"Same reason I gave it to you. They asked who my brother might have been involved with on the drug scene. I guess I wasn't thinking. I feel so stupid." She shook her head. "I should know better, but he was young and seemed harmless, and after I gave it to him . . . after I realized that that might not be such a great idea, I asked him if he planned on putting it in the paper or using my name in the paper and he said he wouldn't. I never dreamed he'd use it with Stimpy or that he'd even go talk to the guy."

I sighed. "He won't mention Stimpy in the paper. A reporter, even a bad one, knows better than to spew out hearsay." I knew Megan was a tough girl, but I had also pegged her for being smarter than to give such details to the press. She was hard, but apparently, she was no criminal. "You were just trying to help. Did you tell him anything else?"

"Not really."

"Did he ask about the bear?"

She nodded and took a sip of water. She looked at us with those same hard hazel eyes, but this time they were darkened with fear instead of anger. I reminded her that she had my card and told her to call me immediately if Stimpy or the reporter showed up again.

. . .

Quickly, we checked the bar again in Hungry Horse, but Stimpy hadn't gone back. Melissa scowled when we waltzed back in. The place was picking up with the late afternoon, but at least the two older men had left, and I hoped the one who didn't throw his whiskey back so quickly was driving. Melissa still refused to give us any names of Stimpy's buddies. She probably knew he'd take it out on her if she gave that type of information and I'm pretty certain he would. I figured we'd get more from the Regional Drug Task Force and call Walsh at the county sheriff's office and see if he had more information on whom the possible dealer hung out with. This way, we could maybe save Melissa from a possible backlash from Stimpy. We also checked his trailer and Melissa's house, and there was still no sign of him at either place.

We headed back to headquarters, picked up a couple of to-go sandwiches from Carol at the café in West Glacier on the way, and ate while we waited for Walsh to do his digging around. Finally, when he called back, we got the names of four possible users who might know of Stimpy or hang out with him. We found them easily since three of them were roommates living in a prefab structure with a corrugated tin roof near the South Fork Flathead River, close to Hungry Horse. All three were high. All it took was threatening to take them in for some drug testing for them to tell us that Stimpy would be hanging with a mutual buddy of theirs named Trevor Fields. Coincidentally, Fields turned out to be the fourth guy on our printout, so we left without needing to get his address.

. . .

"Ma-fucking-lissa," Stimpy said, shaking his head after we introduced ourselves, as if he knew she was the one who directed us to his buddy's place. "Ma-fucking-lissa." I could tell by his enlarged pupils and his quick and random fidgety body movements that he was jacked on some form of amphetamine.

"Actually no," I said. "She wouldn't give us any names at all. Said you knew nothing about Victor Lance's death."

"Then you should listen to her, 'cause I don't. Ain't that right?" He turned to his buddy, Trevor, who wore a black skullcap and was watching some reality TV show, his jaw slack and his mouth hanging open. He stared at us blankly, didn't answer, then turned back to the screen, the right side of his mouth suddenly jumping toward his right eye. I resisted the urge to ask him if he'd caught any flies yet.

"When was the last time you saw him?"

"How should I know?" Stimpy sat in an ugly green armchair in the dim house, one leg resting across on old coffee table with beer cans scattered across it, the other bouncing fiercely up and down.

"Maybe if you think about it, you might remember." Monty stood next to me, his arms stiff by his sides. I casually folded my arms in front of me and tilted my head and gave him my best I'm-serious-and-I've-got-time gaze.

"I knew him, that's all," Stimpy offered.

"And the last time you saw him?"

"In Melissa's bar. Last week sometime."

"You have any words with him?"

He shrugged and laughed—that crazy meth laugh, and I felt a twinge shoot up my spine. "I guess I did." He took the other leg down from the table and began bouncing it too so that both legs bobbed frantically like he was some vibrating puppet. "I shot the shit with everyone in the place. Don't ask me the fuck what we talked about." He laughed again.

"Fair enough." I knew he wouldn't remember—was too doped up for any clear recall, so there was no point in asking. "What I need to know then is what you were doing this last Friday."

"I was at a barbecue all day at a friend's house in Columbia Falls, near the river."

"All day and evening?"

Stimpy nodded, his eyes large and bulging, a strange, almost goofy grin on his face, the corners of his mouth tucking downward. I looked away, at the filthy walls, at an empty bottle of Jack Daniel's in the dirt-caked windowsill and at scraps of wallpaper that had been pulled off in the hallway past the living room and left on the floor. "What time did you go there?"

He sucked in his cheeks from both sides for a moment and wrinkled his brow, then let the flesh pop out with a suction sound. "Don't know. Don't remember."

"How long were you there?"

He grabbed a beer can, tipped it, and when he found it empty, threw it with some force across the coffee table so that it hit the others and made a loud clanking sound. I was surprised because I don't think Monty moved a muscle, but I wasn't sure that I didn't ever-so-slightly flinch. "Don't know. Don't remember." He turned his gaze to the TV.

"Look." I stepped toward him. I towered above him and interrupted his view of the TV. He looked up at me, agitation in his eyes. "You gonna go to that place where you're too cool to help us out?" I asked. "Because, I mean, we could leave here together, you, him"—I pointed to Monty with a chin lift—"and me till we get some kind of alibi on you. Until we go huntin' down people at the party and try to figure out when you got there and when you left. You interested in that?"

He sneered at me.

"Huh, what do you say? You got other plans for the next few days? And while we're at it, I might as well talk to the county boys 'bout taking on yet another project on meth dealing up the Line. Apparently, that last one didn't quite get the job done now, did it?"

Stimpy hopped up, anger filling his eyes. He was a good five inches shorter than me, but he had girth and adrenaline already on board. He glared at me with one side of his lip turned up in disgust, his eyes bulging, and the veins in his neck popping. I was taking a chance by getting him riled up, but I wanted some answers. "You don't know shit about me."

"That's right, I don't. So fill me in."

"I was at that party all day."

"What time did you go?"

"I don't know, we went before noon and stayed until late."

"What's late?"

"Past two a.m."

"You got names of some of the people at the party?"

Stimpy nodded, his lip still curled in disgust. Then, as if he suddenly recalled something, he got that goofy wide grin back. He reminded me of a ventriloquist's doll. Then he started laughing crazily, a high-pitched maniacal laugh that prickled the hairs on the back of my neck. Trevor joined in, his facial twitch erupting into a full-on laugh. "Man, don't you guys do your homework?" Stimpy asked.

I felt something inside me wither.

"Coppy, coppy, coppy." Stimpy rocked from foot to foot with stick-straight legs like an excited child who needs to pee.

I stared at him, my eyes narrowed.

"The C' Falls cops came to our party Friday night because, ohhh"— he made a mocking circle out of his mouth and put a hand to it—"I guess we were being a little too loud. You can check with the guy that came. He knows me; they all do." He began laughing again, this time more a snicker than that maniacal cackle. "Surprised you guys didn't already know that."

• • •

That night I drank. I went to the closest liquor store I could find in Hungry Horse and bought some Jim Beam whiskey. I also brought home several of the files to mull over to try to get a feel for what my gut was telling me.

After leaving Stimpy, we checked with the Columbia Falls police station and verified that Andy Stimpson was at the party they visited. With no search warrants on hand, they didn't search for drugs, just for underage drinkers, which, lucky for the hostess, weren't there. This didn't account for whether he had left earlier in the day or for what time he showed up at the party, but it did verify that he was there around seven p.m., a time Wilson said was possible for the bullet to have entered Lance.

My rationalization about the whiskey was that it would cut through whatever static was clouding my brain and leave only my intuition to point me in the right direction like a compass finding true north. In-stead, I found myself going deeper into my neurosis, rolling the Vermont quarter incessantly over and over, and feeling sorry for myself and guilty for not having phoned my mother or sister since I'd gotten to Glacier.

That's when there was a knock. I shoved the coin back in my pocket and opened the door to find Monty with a yellow bag of potato chips. "Didn't have time to bake that pie." He held out the bag.

I moved to the side and gestured for him to come in. "I'll live."

"Oh, but I make a good one."

"I'm sure you do and probably balance your checkbook just as well. The question is, can you operate a chain saw?"

"Sure can." He smiled.

"And can you drink whiskey and fill up on those greasy chips"—I motioned to the bag with my chin—"and still be worth a damn in the morning?"

"We'll find out," Monty said.

I laughed in spite of my earlier disappointment in him. If this geeky guy was actually going to attempt to drink liquor with me instead of Shirley Temples, I'd have to give him some credit. I thought of the two old men in Melissa's bar, tossing back a couple tumblers of whiskey in the middle of the afternoon. I grabbed Monty a glass from the old oak cabinets, threw a few ice cubes in, and splashed the amber liquid over them, its dark color rich in the hue cast through the old 1950s-looking, rippled-glass light casings of the cabin. "So what brings you here?"

"Thought we could go over the case."

I nodded. "Workaholic, are ya?"

"I suppose. And you're not?" He looked at the papers spread across the rectangular table in front of the old couch.

"Actually, I'm not. I just don't have anything better to do in this place."

"This place? You say it with such disdain?"

"Nah." I shrugged. "Didn't mean to." But I did.

"I thought you were from here? Don't you have family in the area?"

"I am and I do." I took a sip of whiskey and winced out of habit even though I was probably already beyond the grimacing phase. "Now don't start making me feel guilty about that."

"You haven't seen 'em?"

"Actually, haven't even called 'em."

Monty peered at me through his glasses, his eyes seeming wider than usual, almost magnified, and I couldn't tell whether it was the booze or the eyeglasses he was wearing.

"What? You been noticing a lot of extra leisure time in the past two days?"

"True." Monty looked at the coffee table again. "Are there always this many leads?"

"There's always a lot of busywork, tracking things down, verifying details, but this one has a bunch of divergent avenues to go down." I sat in the chair I'd been sitting in for the first two nights and gestured for Monty to sit as well.

He did, set his glass on the coffee table, and ripped open the bag of chips.

"Let's see," I said, holding up my index finger, "we've got the meth connection." I added a finger and continued to do so with each lead. "We've got the animal torture thing, we've got a weird situation with a family member's truck seen closest to the crime, and I don't need to tell you, the family or the significant other's always the first place we look because nine times out of ten, there's trouble there. Which leads us to the girlfriend." I had four fingers in the air and was gesturing with them. "Who—Christ Almighty—happens to be Smith's daughter. And let's not forget that she's got a new boyfriend"—I opened my thumb— "who just might have a temper himself and just might have wanted to teach this guy a lesson or two." I put my hand down.

"Obviously," I said, "Smith's daughter doesn't know how to pick 'em. And now"—I looked Monty in the eye—"your boss tells me that Victor's uncle is trying to get a life-estate agreement out of him because the grandchildren are all feuding over how to deal with the Lake McDonald cabin, which is probably worth, what, a few million now?"

"Hard to say what the land is worth at this point. It's not like the Park Service is dripping with money these days, but usually they do buy anything they can get in the Lake McDonald area. And for Lou Shelton's lot, anything in that price range is a lot of money. Somehow they always scrape the funds together, whether they use TPL." He raised his brow to see if I knew what he meant.

"Yeah, Trust for Public Lands."

"That's right. Often we use them for bridge funding or we sometimes use LWCF, you know, the Land and Water Conservation Fund."

"You work a lot with this stuff?"

"I do."

"That what you do for Ford?"

"Partly."

I studied Monty sitting on the old forest-green couch that sunk with anyone's weight, even his small frame. I had somehow come to trust him in a very short span of time, but I wasn't exactly sure why. Probably most significant to me was that he seemed to lack the prevalent overinflated ego and the cockiness that often accompanied law enforcement. Plus he stayed quiet in all the right places. But after today, with Ford, it was clear whom his loyalty resided with, so I wasn't sure I'd been wise. Of course, it's not like it was a bad thing that he was loyal to his boss. It just bugged me that his boss was Ford. "You like working for that guy?"

"That guy? There's that disdain again. You really don't like him?"

"Don't know him enough to know."

"Well, it's an absolute joy." Monty made an overexaggerated smile, all teeth. "By the way, he's not my boss. Smith is."

"He's the super and you've been assigned to him. Same difference."

Monty shrugged. "You think that life-estate deal might have something to do with this?"

I looked at the paperwork on my desk and picked up Shelton's file. He had no criminal record, and his financial records were decent except for a Chapter 11 financial reorganization that he filed for in the early nineties. "Probably not. It's a far-reaching and highly unlikely scenario, especially with all the trouble our victim was capable of getting into all on his own. But let's just say, for example, that since he was such a live wire, that a cousin wanted him out of the possible inheritance pool? Again, it's far-reaching, but maybe Victor was threatening Lou or one of the other cousins with something. Maybe Victor knew that Lou was talking to Ford about giving the place up and knew that he'd never see a dime of it. And being the druggie that he was, he might have been counting on living in the place once Lou was gone. All those homesteads are long since paid off."

Monty shrugged. "Sounds like a bad movie."

"It does." I chuckled. "Must be the whiskey. Speaking of which, your ice is melting." I lifted my chin to point at his glass. I felt like an older college student trying to corrupt his younger roommate. To my surprise, Monty grabbed his glass and finished the entire amount in one swig. He cringed, then he grabbed a handful of chips and threw the bag across the table toward me.

"I like to stay away from the far-fetched." I grabbed a few. "Another?"

"Why not?"

I brushed the salt off my palm on my jeans and went to the kitchen to grab the bottle and felt how noodlelike my legs were. Honestly, this was the best I'd felt in the last sixty-some hours. I refilled Monty's drink and went back with the bottle. "How come you didn't tell me about Lou Shelton before we went to see him?" I asked.

"Tell you what?"

"That you knew Ford was attempting to get a life estate out of him?"

"Didn't know about it. Never even heard the Shelton name before."

I eyed Monty, tried to read if he was being straight with me. "And you don't think that's strange?"

"What? You mean in terms of Ford or Shelton or me?"

"All three."

"I didn't work on the west-side projects. I've been working mostly on the mining claim inholdings east of the Continental Divide, which were part of the Ceded Strip."

"The Ceded Strip?"

"Yeah, you know. George Grinnell bought the strip in about 1895 from the Blackfeet and sold it to the government for conservation purposes, although, of course, at the time, before Taft even signed the bill to make the park in 1910, the government was mainly interested in mining, laying roads for that, and trapping into places like Quartz Lake or even Cracker."

"So, what work do you have with that now?"

"You'd be surprised. By Cracker Lake in the St. Mary region, there are mining claims in court because the Park Service still doesn't own that strip of land even though it's in the designated border of the park. It's still part of the Ceded Strip. The Blackfeet are still fighting for it because the government didn't uphold its end of the bargain, you know, we'll give you X amount for this land and we'll also do Y and Z. Then the government doesn't do Y and Z."

"Sounds like a familiar story."

"Yeah, but the court cases are a waste of time. They'll never get that land back from the government. Then there are other claims, like from the Cattle Queen's lineage. You've heard of her."

"I suppose." I had a vague notion that I'd heard of her in some Montana history book in college.

"She ran a cattle ranch near the town of Choteau in the late 1800s and had a mining claim on a creek that ran through the park, Cattle Queen Creek."

I hadn't heard Monty talk this much since he'd joined me and I wondered if the historical element of the park is what drew him to working with the superintendent. "And what about this side?" I asked.

"Even the west side has a few old mining claims, but mostly, it's the homesteads and some ranches up past Polebridge where they used to have cattle that have the inholdings."

"And what's the main deal with the inholdings around West Glacier?"

"Just that the people who own private lands that are locked inside the park usually have lineage that goes way back. That's the reason they have the land. For years, the Park Service has been trying to buy most of the inholders out with not a whole lot of success. People underestimate the value of family heritage. And for these people, their land and what they decide to do with it often is very different from what the Park Service wants to do with it."

"Like the unbroken strip by Lake McDonald?"

"That's right."

"Before the wildfire of 1920, Lake McDonald was starting to look almost as crowded as any old lake in Montana at the time and people were constructing more and more cabins on their own property. But the fire wiped some eighteen of them out and then the Park Service went in and bought up as much of the land as they could. People thought they were getting a good deal after losing their cabins in the fire. But the homesteads that hung on now know how priceless what they have is. To the inholders, the land has economic and family value—the priceless value of home. To the park, it's about the wilderness and drawing the public in to enjoy it—the whole point of the park."

"So you don't know much about the Sheltons?"

"Not until just today after Ford told me about him"— he gave a sly, sketchy smile and held up a finger—"so I looked at his file." He pulled out a folded sheet of paper. "I copied Ford's notes."

I leaned in, surprised that he'd done this. "And Ford knows you've done this?"

"I didn't say anything to him. But why should he care? If the guy's a suspect, then he's a suspect. Right?"

"Absolutely." I reached for the paper and scanned it. There were just a few notes scribbled down by Ford, noting the background with Roger and Eloise Shelton, that the cabin would be Lou's for his life span and that nothing had been designated as far as the grandchildren were concerned. On the second page was a note on an incident in June of 2010 stating that Lou Shelton refused to allow the Park Service to test his septic system. "Why do you suppose he didn't want his septic tested?"

"I don't know. Most of the inholders hate some of the regulations the park imposes, so they take a stand. All the test involves is putting some bright-blue dye in the system and if the dye shows in the lake, then the park demands they clean up the system. Most people around here hate the interference. They despise having government tell them what they need to do with their own property."

"I bet." I took another sip of my drink. "And Shelton definitely strikes me as an antiauthority kind of guy. Thought he was going to rip my DOI badge right off of me and flush it into that system you're talking about."

"Yeah, and it's the DOI that sets the septic regulation, so when the Park Service goes in, it's the department that gets mentioned."

"So judging by his financial records—his Chapter 11 filing in the nineties, he might just not be so good at managing his money and he might not have had anything to spare if his system was leaking into the lake."

"Could be the case." Monty grabbed a few more chips, wiped the grease on his pants, and took another sip of whiskey. "Which tells us what in terms of the case?"

"Not much really. Just speculation. But really, what we need to do is to refocus on the crime." I leaned back in my chair and rubbed my forehead. "What I can't figure out is whether we're looking for one person or two. The fact that he was out there for over eighteen hours is confusing. Gretchen hasn't found evidence to suggest that someone was hanging around with him for that entire time, no clothes fibers on fallen logs or nearby large rocks big enough for sitting and waiting. No obvious prints. So assuming that whoever bound him left—was it the same guy that returned to do him in? Or was it someone else doing the dirty work for him?"

Monty shook his head. "That's way beyond my expertise."

"Well, I'm not a profiler, but I've learned a lot in all my background analysis work, and here's what I think."

Monty quit chomping on a chip and looked at me like a kid ready to hear a good story.

"I think whoever did this wasn't quite sure about whether they actually wanted Victor dead or not."

"And why do you think that?"

"More of a hunch than evidence." Monty's eyes were on me, waiting intently for me to say more. "The fact that the shot was fired so close and from a strange angle"—I held my hand up like I was holding a pistol and pointed it downward toward my rib cage—"it . . . it makes me wonder if the killer went back to talk to him again. Maybe he needed information and he left Victor out there to torture it out of him. And when he went back to get it, something went wrong and he shot him instead. Maybe Victor said something that angered him, or maybe Victor wouldn't give him the information he needed, or maybe Victor tried to grab the gun because the guy got too close—in his face. After all, his arms weren't bound, just his waist and chest. His wrists were bound, but his hands were capable of grabbing for something."

"Sounds so mafia-like."

"It wouldn't be the first mafia incident in a national park. There's still a presence up in Eureka, although very much watered down. But Victor Lance was a lowlife. Forgive me for saying, but these meth dealers aren't the brightest of the criminals and the mob wouldn't waste their time with 'em."

"I'll forgive ya." Monty half-smiled again, and I began to laugh. I was definitely feeling tipsy and thankful for it—the relaxation of my chest and gut—even though I knew I'd pay for it the next day.

• • •

Before the night was over, I made a fire because the cabin was getting cold. Monty and I continued to go over some of the files, and, of course, rehashed what happened with Stimpy.

"You think that guy's it?"

"He's no angel. That's for sure."

"What about his alibi?"

"That's why you need to go get some rest because that's what you'll be working on tomorrow. Along with a million other small details."

Monty nodded and lifted up his notebook to show me. "I know. I'm keeping a list."

"Good," I said. "I don't know. I don't have a strong feeling. He's weird. Typical. But he didn't act guilty."

"Then why did he go see Megan?"

"Like I said, he's typical. He's an out-of-control goon who needs to throw his weight around and because he doesn't want anyone sniffing around his business."

"But he didn't seem too concerned about the local police, and he didn't seem to care that much that we were there. He wasn't nervous or on his best behavior with us."

"He was nervous, even with the drugs. The drugs just disguise it. But still, there's a part of him that feels special, important, because he's the big guy in the neighborhood now. And because of his ego, he's too stupid to be humble around the law, especially when he's got a friend around to impress."

Monty chuckled. "You're pretty good at reading people."

I shrugged. "How hard is it to read a meth dealer?"

13

Headquarters seemed busy the next morning when I arrived. While getting some water from the cooler for some Tylenol, I noticed Bowman, Smith, and Ford arguing over something in one of the conference rooms. Then I heard someone up front announce his name was Will Jones and that he was a reporter from the *Daily Flathead* and wanted to speak to Savannah Williams, Ford's lead PR manager.

I quickly swallowed the capsules and hurried up front and introduced myself.

"So you're the detective working the case?" Jones asked. He seemed young, maybe twenty-five, had a Denver Broncos cap on and shoulder-length hair curling out from underneath. He looked completely harmless—boyish—and I could see why Megan felt like she could say anything.

"That's correct."

"And you're with the sheriff's office?" He was looking my clothes over. I was wearing my navy DOI jacket, but other than that, no clothes that would look like a uniform. I had on jeans and a striped shirt under my jacket.

"No. The Department of the Interior."

"How does that work?"

I explained to him how it was with Series Eighteen-Eleven, and he began to jot the information down.

"I thought the FBI would be called in since it's federal?"

"Sometimes they are, but usually we get called because local FBI is working on other issues. Look." I held up my palm. "I'm sure you can appreciate how dangerous it is for you to ask questions in places where things are a little touchy."

"I'm not sure what you mean."

"For one, meth users might be a bit on edge about people snooping around their business, no?"

He didn't say anything.

"You could potentially jeopardize this entire investigation, not to mention endangering Victor Lance's sister by dropping her name around the wrong people."

He continued to give me a stupefied look. "Well." He shifted stances, then cleared his throat, and I could tell he hadn't considered such a thing. "I'm, I'm just trying to do my job. It was obvious once rumors started flying that the sheriff's department wasn't giving us the full story."

"May I ask which rumors?"

"In the department. You know, I go there every day to check the log. Don't you think someone's eventually going to say something to me?"

I nodded. "No, listen, I agree. You should've been given more, but you need to understand that there are sensitive situations here. All I'm asking is that if you need any information in the future that you're not getting from the park's PR department, make sure you come to me before investigating on your own." I handed him my card. "I promise to make your job easier."

Jones smiled widely as if he'd just won at poker. "Deal."

. . .

I found Monty in our office down the hall. He was drinking coffee and going over his list of things to accomplish. He had fetched me a cup as well and pointed to it on the desk. "Heard you down the hall," he said. "Figured you could use some."

I paused, the small act of kindness on Monty's part making my brow furrow for a brief moment. "Thank you." I picked up the mug. "I appreciate it."

"No biggie," Monty said. "Needed to stretch anyway. Been at it for a bit."

"You got it covered?" I was referring to the long to-do list.

"Go over the victim's phone record, check the dental office and the grocery store, check the timber company and the hardware stores in Kalispell and Whitefish. The hardware stores in Columbia Falls had no recent sales of duct tape to anyone suspicious in the last week. And by the way, there's no record of Victor owning either a Toyota or a motorcycle."

"Figures," I said, then paused and looked at him, at his youthful energy permeating the room. "You feeling all right?"

Monty smiled. "Feeling good, sir. You?"

He didn't appear to be remotely affected by the whiskey like I was. Suddenly I felt old and pushed away the voice reminding me of how tired and shaky I was beginning to feel. "Fine," I said. "I'm off to track down Rob Anderson, the owner of that dog. Call me if anything interesting at all turns up."

"Will do, sir." Monty took another sip of coffee, and I wondered how the hell one keeps their teeth white if they're a coffee drinker. I walked away picturing him using those silly-looking plastic trays filled with some type of bleach, then admonished myself for being such a prick for thinking such a thing after Monty had been nice enough to fetch me a cup of coffee.

．．．

When I walked into the rental car agency by the county airport in which Rob Anderson worked and saw a tall man with thinning blond hair punching away at keys on his computer at the front desk, I was surprised to realize that I knew him. Of course, Robbie, Robbie Anderson, who went to Whitefish High School. Even though Flathead High was Double-A and Whitefish only Single-A, our basketball teams sometimes played each other for local rival fun. Robbie was a forward. I played a guard. I never considered myself any good, but since I was tall, everyone told me I should try out, and my ma insisted, saying that the exercise would be good for me. At that point, I would do anything she asked if it made her feel better. Plus I figured basketball was reams better than the therapy I had tried.

When Anderson looked, I'm not sure if he recalled who I was, just that he recognized me. I introduced myself, mentioning basketball, and saw it come together for him. "That must happen quite a bit around here for you, seeing someone from the old days." I thought of how age had a way of pronouncing people's flaws once the youthful baby fat was gone. His nose seemed bigger and his lack of chin more obvious.

"Every once in a while." He gave a one-shouldered shrug. "And what are you up to these days?"

"Working," I said. "Mostly out of Denver—where I live."

"What do you do?"

I filled him in, and he said he vaguely remembered that I used to work on the local force. I told him I was on it in my twenties and asked him how long he'd been working for the rental agency. He said for about five years and shrugged, saying it wasn't the greatest job, but it beat construction or logging and came with health benefits, something very difficult to get in the Flathead unless you worked for one of the chain stores or restaurants or had a full-time position at the community college or one of the hospitals. Then things fell silent.

"So you're not here to rent a car?"

I shook my head. "I'm really sorry to hear about what happened to your dog last spring."

Rob furrowed his brow. "How did you know about that?"

"I'm here investigating a crime in Glacier Park. You hear about it?" I studied his face.

"Sure, read about it in the paper. Weird thing." He furrowed his brow again. "And that has something to do with my dog?"

"Not necessarily. Just following all leads."

"Leads? And you've got something that connects this to my dog?"

"We're not sure, but there's a chance that the victim may have been involved."

"You've got to be kidding?" Rob stared at me, his mouth hanging half open.

I didn't answer.

"Fuckin' A," he said. "Really?"

"Possibly." I held out my hand. "Again, not a hundred percent sure, but a few fingers have pointed in his direction."

"Fuck me." He stood abruptly. He began pacing behind the counter. "Jesus, so the guy who was found dead was one of those bastards that hurt Logan?" His voice was high-pitched.

I gave a half nod.

He stared at me, then slammed the flat part of his fist on the counter. "Yes," he hooted like his favorite team just scored. "Serves the asshole right. You have any idea what they actually did to my dog?"

"I do," I said.

"Well, then you know"—he nodded—"you know how bad it was." Intensity and hatred flooded his eyes.

"I got your name from your vet." I wanted to suggest that he sit back down, but I knew he was wired now. "I just need to ask you a few questions to just make sure we have it on record that we checked out all avenues."

He stopped pacing and looked at me. "You mean you think I had something to do with that Glacier Park thing?"

"Like I said, just have to cross all the *t*'s and dot the *i*'s or else we pay later when we get to court. You follow me?"

He studied me, then sat back down and folded his arms before him. "I never even knew who did it." He softened his voice and furrowed his brow. "He was just left there." He looked down again. "By the fence like that."

"You said, 'one of those bastards,' so you think that there was more than one?"

"Not for sure. I'd heard a few rumors around that there were two guys involved. But I never heard names."

"Do you remember where you heard the rumors?"

"I think it was from a friend of mine that works in town at that sandwich shop on the highway. She'd heard from her boyfriend or something that he'd heard from who-knows-where that more than one guy was involved. You can imagine how much I talked about this when it happened, to anyone I knew."

"Have you ever heard of Victor Lance?"

Rob brought one hand to his mouth and waited a moment before responding. "I have."

I lifted my brow.

"But never met him, just heard the name around. Not sure where and definitely not in conjunction with what happened to my dog. I'd remember that."

"You can't remember where you heard his name?" I prodded.

Rob looked at the ceiling, thinking, then shook his head. "Really, I don't know how I've heard that name. Maybe in a bar in C' Falls or something. I live up that way, you know. I tried to recall when I saw his name in the paper but couldn't then either. You remember how it is around here—names being thrown around all the time and you think you ought to know someone since it's such a small world, but you don't."

"Do you recall what you were doing on Friday evening around seven p.m. of last week?"

"You've got to be kidding me?" He shook his head.

"Again." I shrugged. "Just dottin' the *i*'s and—"

"Crossin' the fuckin' *t*'s," he finished. "I was home. Making dinner. Watching TV."

"Anyone with you?"

"No, but I was online for a while, if that helps."

I grabbed a card from my pocket and held it out to him. "If it comes to you how you know Victor's name, do me a favor and let me know. Anything at all can help during an investigation."

. . .

When I was sixteen, two and a half years after the loss of my father, we still lived in the same neighborhood out of the Kalispell city limits among thick pines and tall tamaracks near the Columbia Mountain Range. It spread out for miles and was more like a wilderness area than an actual neighborhood. The whole place always seemed as if the woods barely tolerated the houses that tried to squeeze in and exist without nature's permission. Homes were built against hillsides and on top of large, rocky hills as if some houses had won king of the mountain, while others were relegated to hide in the trees below.

Our house happened to be one of the ones on top of a knoll. My parents picked it because they loved the deck that had the illusion of poking right up to a mountain peak even though we were at least ten miles from its base. Because we were on top of the hill, we shared a driveway with a house below us, our drive starting out with theirs, then continuing on and wrapping up and around the back of their house. I only mention it because of Tumble, our black Lab. She would get confused about the house below and sometimes amble into their property as if it were her own front yard. We had a large chain-link kennel for her, but she would sometimes dig out of it during the day when we were at school. She was harmless; she'd just sniff around, then meander back home. But one day, she didn't come home.

My sisters and I searched for her for a day and a half before we found out what happened. We went to our neighbor's to ask if he'd seen her, and he told us that he hadn't, but guilt seemed to spread across his face.

The first evening, when we saw Tumble had escaped her kennel after Mom had fetched us at the library and brought us home, Kathryn and I walked around calling for her as dusk fell on the tall pines, creating a dim void into which Tumble seemed to have disappeared. We kept calling as twilight surrounded us, the air turning cool and the sky a pale, pearly color behind the mountains. The smell of pine permeated the air. We searched until it got completely dark and knew that Ma would be beside herself if we didn't get home.

Ma told us not to worry, that Tumble would come back by morning or that we'd get a call from someone saying they had her, but I could see the uncertainty in her eyes, the same eyes that were unwavering previous to my dad's death, now forever changed the way a small pond is never the same once an algae bloom takes it over.

But the next morning, a Saturday, came and went with no calls and this time, Natalie and I went looking because Kathryn had a ballet recital practice. We walked the hilly, curvy streets in the warm spring sunshine, thinking every movement we caught in the corner of our eyes might be her, but would turn out to be only the shadow of a black raven taking flight, someone else's dog or cat crossing a yard, or a child playing between houses. We visited house after house, until on our way back, luckless and defeated, we decided to stop again at our neighbors.

We walked between his truck and his green-camouflage ATV in the driveway, the late-afternoon shadows from the trees making long, dark velvety shapes across his newly mowed spring lawn. Since our family's loss, I could feel the strange undercurrent of things not being right, of this world's pain standing so readily behind a mask of everyday normalcy, of fresh-cut grass in the middle of wild woods, spring sunshine on my shoulders, and my sister's tennis shoes scraping gravel as we walked. I felt as if I wasn't fully present and things weren't completely real. And even though it was a bright day, I knew that if you pulled the sunny veil off my sisters' and my existence, only a raw, bruised dream world of fear, loss, and sadness would remain.

I knocked on the door, the wood hard under my knuckles and the sound of my pounding flat. When he answered, he looked annoyed. "Excuse me, sir." I swallowed hard. "We were just wondering if you've seen our black Lab around yet."

"I already told you I didn't," he said gruffly, his hair short but greasy.

I swallowed hard. "It's just that we've been looking around today and we thought—"

"If you would've kept the damn thing on your property in the first place, it wouldn't be a problem now, would it?"

Natalie and I stood quiet. I could hear anger in his voice, and even though I didn't recognize it then for what it was—a lack of compassion, something he'd killed in himself somewhere along the way in his own life—I knew there was something more: a type of disgust and antipathy. "I know, sir, but she's a good dog. She wouldn't bother anyone."

He laughed. "If she's so good, why does she pick on mine?"

"I don't think it's serious, sir, when those two go at it. They're just workin' it out the way dogs do."

"Let me tell you something." He leaned in and pointed a finger in my face. "Your dog was a bully. And she crapped all over my property." He gestured to the expanse of the yard.

I shook my head but didn't say anything. I could smell something bitter and sour from his breath. The hot sun had moved between two trees and bore down on my back. I could feel sweat pooling by my belt. The word *was* rang in my ears. I continued to shake my head as if I had no control over it.

"You disagreeing?"

I wanted to scream at him that his little dog starts the tiffs every time by nipping at the back of Tumble's legs. That my mom was religious about picking up Tumble's droppings if they were in his yard, but I didn't say anything. I could only shake my head even though I could see I was making him angry.

"Is that right. Look, you little . . ." he sneered, then spat over me into the bushes to the side of the walk. "Young man, you don't know the first thing about animals." He reassumed his position, leaning toward me and pointing his finger in my face. "I wasn't gonna tell ya, but maybe you should know. Maybe I should teach y'all a lesson 'bout keeping animals." He looked at me sharply with eyes close together like a gator. "I had enough. That's right. I had enough and I shot your goddamn dog, so there, now ya know. That's right. I had enough."

I was vaguely aware of Natalie bringing her hand to her mouth and a small sound escaping the back of her throat. She began to wail and ran out the drive to where the two dovetailed. She screamed the whole way up the hill, her sneakers kicking up dust from the gravel. My body felt heavy like cement. I wanted to follow her, say something to her, but I felt like I was underwater, so I stood still and held my breath or else I was certain to drown.

He stared at me, the half grin on his mouth had slowly turned to a fearful look. When my sister screamed and ran, I'm sure he wasn't expecting that. "Now go on and run home yourself. Go tell your mammie. She can't do nothing. It was my property and she should've kept the damn thing off it."

"Where is she?" I managed.

"Your mammie? How the hell should I know?"

I shook my head fiercely.

"The dog?" He looked surprised, then pointed to the corner of his property toward the main road. "I buried her over there. Now git, go on home, and the next time you get a pet, keep the damn thing on your own property."

I went home, my chest tight and burning with anger. We called the county sheriff's office to report it, but there was nothing they could do. A female sheriff interviewed us, then him, then came back to tell us that he had claimed it was self-defense. I had never seen my ma so angry. She raised her voice and went on about how messed up Montana was, about people caring more about their property than people's pets.

She kept it raised even after the lady sheriff held up one palm and told her to calm down. Ma said that Tumble had never growled at a person in her life. This was true, Tumble was sweet, always wagging her tail for any stranger, but I secretly had the feeling that she had growled at this man. And I hoped that she had at least done that because I knew that he would have shot her either way. I'd like to think that Tumble knew what I knew: he was a bad apple.

. . .

Mindy Winters was exactly as I expected, a flighty, strung-out basket case with overly enlarged pupils. She couldn't keep her dates straight when discussing Victor, but in general, her story matched what Megan had said about their relationship: on and off again and highly dysfunctional. Her hair was greasy and appeared to be dyed with some overly strong peroxide mix out of a box. Her features, besides homely, were lackluster, probably from doing drugs during adolescence and from a lack of decent nutrition. At one point, I forced myself to push the thought away that Victor must have known she wasn't worth keeping around for more than the sole purpose of getting his rocks off, and considering Victor's lack of morals, this wasn't a compliment. By the time I completed my questioning, she had grown whiny and teary-eyed and was laying out the rationale that Victor might have treated her better if he only understood how much she loved him. I patted her slumped-over and bony shoulder and told her to get herself a tissue and a cup of water and promptly left to go find Daniel Nelson.

Daniel, on the other hand, turned out to be quite composed and together. He worked for a local appliance center and managed the delivery and hookup department, making sure appliances got installed correctly with no gas leaks or water damage to anyone's kitchens. He was quite proud of his managerial position, and I thought of my conversation with Rob and how hard it is to get a decent, long-lasting job with benefits in the valley.

I found him at his work, a nicely built (as far as strip stores go) medium-size building with brick accents and blue awnings. Kitchen appliances and washers and dryers stood on one end of the store and agreeably lit stereo equipment and big-screen TVs on the other. One of the salespeople on the floor called Daniel out from a back room and he sauntered up, his movements smooth, and shook my hand. When I introduced myself and told him why I wanted to chat, he motioned for me to follow him through a back door to a small, cluttered desk. It wasn't an office, just a desk in the corner of the warehouse storage area with a phone and a computer so he could probably arrange pickups, deliveries, and repairs and manage his employees' work schedules.

When he pulled up a spare chair for me beside his desk and took his own seat, he told me he'd seen Victor's name in the paper and that he couldn't believe it. He ran a hand through his sandy-blond hair and even though his movements were fluid, I could see a hint of shock in his eyes. "Can I get you some coffee or something?"

"I'm fine. You okay?"

Daniel shrugged. "It's, it's just . . . I wasn't expecting it. No one called me."

"Megan didn't phone you?"

He shook his head. "I called her after I read it in the paper. I asked her why she didn't let me know. She didn't know why. I guess she's pretty stunned by it all."

"Understandable."

Daniel nodded back rhythmically, hugging his chest and staring at his feet. "Did you see him? I mean, what happened out there?"

"Yes, I was at the scene on Saturday morning. Unfortunately, a grizzly got him. The medical examiner said it was fast and he was in shock."

"Tied to a tree?"

"Afraid so."

Daniel bit a cuticle on the side of his pointer, his eyes slightly glazed.

"I hear you two have been friends for a long time?"

"Yeah, we went to school together."

"You were close?"

"When we were younger. But not so much since adulthood. We just checked in with each other now and then. Vic, well, you've probably heard, kind of went his own way."

"How so?"

"Drugs. Some bad stuff. Screwed him up pretty good. He got into drinking really young, after his dad left. I did too, but I kept it at alcohol and some—" He paused and looked at my face as if to consider whether to continue, then decided it was all right. "Some pot, you know, stupid teenage stuff. I never got into the hard stuff like he did. We drifted apart, but I don't know." He shrugged. "He always came to me for help and I always had a hard time turning him away. You know, childhood friends—it's hard to not see those differently. Plus he'd had a hard life with no dad and all, and I swear, he'd help me out if I ever needed it."

"When was the last time you saw him?"

"Let me think. Not since July."

I wrote it down. "How did Victor's life seem then?"

"The usual mess—no job, impatient with everything and everyone around him."

"Was he involved with anyone suspicious?"

"He brought up Stimpy but no one else."

I nodded. "You know Rob Anderson?"

"No, sir, I don't. Should I?"

"Not necessarily," I said, watching his reaction. "He's an owner of a dog that was beaten up a while back."

Daniel shut his eyes. "I heard about that."

"Who did you hear it from and what did you hear?"

"I heard it from Rick Pyles. A buddy of ours from school. Ran into him at some bar and we got to talking about Vic. He said he'd heard he was involved in that but didn't know for sure."

"Was it just Victor that he mentioned?"

"No, he mentioned another guy. Tom Hess."

"You know him?"

"No. Not personally. I've seen him around here and there, but I don't really hang in those circles. Victor would make an easy target for that guy, though."

"How so?"

"When we were young, a lot of the kids bullied Vic since he was on the small side and somewhat insecure. Vic really just wanted to fit in, and he'd do anything to please guys like Hess."

"Would Victor do something like that to a dog?"

"I would have said no. Not the Victor I knew." Daniel shook his head slowly. "But the drugs made him crazier than he was. The Victor I knew wasn't that bad. I mean, he could be a really cool guy." Daniel looked tearful suddenly. "He did have a heart. There were lots of times when he was a really good friend to me."

"I'm sure there were."

"And Megan doesn't admit it, but he adored her and would have done anything to protect her if she ever needed it. She just never did, self-sufficient as she is. But Megan, she didn't take the brunt of their dad's poor parenting like Victor did. He used to say that his mom, Megan, and I were his family and he'd do anything for us. I mean," he said, "I'm not making excuses for him, but people get it wrong sometimes for why people like Victor are sometimes cruel."

"How so?" I lifted my brow.

"It's not that Vic didn't like people or animals. He just didn't like himself, and when people don't like themselves, they usually have to find someone other than themselves to hate, or else fess up to their own self-loathing." He shrugged, then looked vacantly at me.

I could see that he wanted to be left alone to process, perhaps to remember a more trouble-free and happy Victor Lance from childhood. The picture of Victor and Megan swimming and laughing popped into my mind. "Do me a favor," I said, handing him my card. "Give me a buzz if anything else comes to mind that might be helpful."

. . .

I didn't find Hess at a local tannery in Columbia Falls where Daniel said he worked. His boss, Reggie White, was there: a short, plump guy with about ten strands of hair above each ear. He was working in the dismal and smelly lime pit, in which he treated the hide after it soaked. He said that Tom had taken a week off and, as far as anyone knew, had gone hunting.

"East or west side?" I asked, because I knew that if he was east of the mountains hunting deer or antelope, then he was probably going to be away all week. If he was hunting on the west side of the divide, then he might be going home in the evenings.

"East side." He shrugged. "I think anyway. Said he'd be gone for a week, maybe two." He told me that Hess had his ways, and he never asked him much of anything. Then he started to give me an earful of local stories about poaching and never getting caught. About people waking up and seeing ravens circling above, only to go out on their property to find the smelly innards covered with buzzing flies. I couldn't tell for sure if he was referring to Tom or not, but figured he was. I did get it out of him that Tom owned an ATV and that he and his buddies liked to head east of the mountains, out past Lewistown, as far as Winnett even, to run down antelope.

And *run down*, I was certain, was exactly what a guy like Tom Hess probably did. It was common practice with some to chase antelope, animals designed for high-speed running. With an ATV, you can run them through the wide-open sage fields until the antelope are fatigued, then blast away.

I thanked Reggie and was more than ready to leave the dank and acrid-smelling atmosphere of the tannery. When I walked to my car, I breathed the fresh air deep into the lower lobes of my lungs. Even though I'd never met him, I had this image in my mind of Tom and his buddies drinking cheap beer and whiskey, eating junk food, and haulin' ass on ATVs, hootin' and a'hollerin' with their pride blooming—kings of their own universes. Then I imagined it as a warm afternoon with the sun baking the sage fields. I pictured Tom not paying attention, going too fast, and skidding out, falling off his ATV into a nice, large, and active rattlesnake pit.

• • •

When I returned to headquarters, it was late, and I was surprised to see Ford. He came down the hallway holding a rolled-up newspaper, his pointy frame swaggering as he walked.

"Just now getting to the daily news?" I offered.

His face looked slightly agitated, his eyes seeming beadier than usual. "I've heard that you've told that reporter to come to you if he needed information."

"I told him that he should come to me before getting himself in the middle of my investigation."

"I thought we already discussed this in Missoula."

"We did." I held up my hand. "And trust me, I'd like nothing better than to not have to deal with him. But when something interferes with my investigation, I'm going to take a stand."

"Orders are orders, Detective. And our office is handling the press, not you." He flicked the paper with his free hand, "You had the nerve to mention kidnapping and murder on top of a mauling?"

I looked at him, my brow furrowed. Then I laughed, and Stimpy's crazy laugh echoed in my mind. "I didn't mention a word about any of those things. The guy had already gotten all he needed from snooping around locally. It's investigative work 101: give the press just enough to keep them out of the way. Bottom line—your office didn't give that guy enough. To make matters worse, Harris and I found him pestering the victim's sister, and a local meth dealer turned around and pestered her for mentioning his name. Do you have any idea how dangerous that is?"

Ford glared at me—trying to sum me up. His lips pressed together and his eyes squinted. He even lifted his chin a bit, and if I wasn't over six feet, he'd be looking down the line of his face at me. "Of course I do, but I have a job to do here."

"And so do I, so if you'll excuse me—" I gave a curt nod and left him standing there, just as he had left me on the trail.

. . .

I went back to our makeshift office and sat. I thought of Ford's tightly wound face, and suddenly I felt very tired. I looked around. It was early evening and I could hear a slight breeze. Monty had left. Joe had invited me to dinner with him and his wife, but I politely declined, saying I had too much to do. He had smiled and said maybe later in the week and I had told him that by then, hopefully it was a celebration for a closed case.

I sat in the quiet of our office and listened to the battery-operated clock on the wall tick out an almost achy beat that made me feel a bittersweet pang deep down, as if the ticking persistently tapped into the exact moment in my childhood, when I realized that not only would everyone, including me, die, but that you go it alone from your own tangled path. I remembered reading "The Solitude of Self" in college, the line always staying with me: "We come into the world alone, unlike all who have gone before us; we leave it alone under circumstances peculiar to ourselves."

A vehicle started its engine outside and I wondered who was leaving. I leaned back in my chair and looked out the window. I could see the branches of the maple tree reaching across the window, its golden leaves making a vivid collage in the paling light outside. Once the car drove away, everything stilled, and I was reminded of the bottomless quiet in the park.

I thought about Rob Anderson. How the anger and hatred filled his eyes when he thought about what had been done to his dog and whether the crime against Victor was committed out of revenge. I'd been around homicide enough to know the degree of loathing that occurred toward a person or institution responsible for the harm of a loved one. Family members of victims, in weak, helpless moments, would sometimes confess to me that they were capable of spending entire nights awake conjuring up detailed and violent fates for the person who took their loved one. That they'd like nothing better than to see them dead: run down, tortured, incinerated, crushed down to nothing . . . But, of course, imagining and doing are two separate things.

. . .

I continued having trouble sleeping and would often find myself lying awake in the chilled cabin, the tip of my nose cold and the covers pulled high. I could hear every sound Glacier had to offer: the wind caught in the fireplace fluke, an owl screeching, the scuffling sound of deer hooves crossing through fallen leaves, an intermittent high whistle of a cow-elk call or a lower, deeper, bull-elk bugle, a train passing by in West Glacier and an occasional honk of a vehicle from Highway 2 in the distance.

But what was more penetrating and irritating to me was how Glacier held back sound. I would hear nothing at all for hours: no car tires swishing on a road nearby, no honks, no animals, no wind, no raindrops, no voices, no nothing, as if I had been transported into the dark void of outer space. I would toss and turn, often finding myself halfway falling asleep, then dreaming of some person who'd come to the cabin (perhaps Monty, who needed to tell me something important, or Gretchen because she had new evidence or Sean, who wanted me to hurry up and solve the case). They'd let themselves in without my permission, stand in my room near my bed, and try to tell me something important that I couldn't make out, something essential and purposeful, yet unspecific. I would desperately try to move my arm or lift my head, but felt like I was in a sleep paralysis, aware that I was half-dreaming and also aware that I was attempting to rally myself out of the dream state, but incapable of it. When I'd finally wake, I'd feel impotent and panicked that I'd turn out to be utterly useless for the rest of the day.

On the fourth night of the investigation, I finally fell asleep around two a.m. and dreamed I was face-to-face with some large beast, not exactly a bear, but something similar, that snorted and grunted. I pulled my gun out and tried to shoot, but it jammed, and in an endless tangle of fear and frustration, I'd keep trying to fire my weapon unsuccessfully, yelling at Shelly, who was behind me to get clear, to get out of the way. I kept trying to push her aside to get her behind a wall for safety, but each time I reached out for her, she'd vanish. When I finally got a shot off, I only angered it, and no matter how many times I fired, the beast kept coming for me. I frantically ran through the woods, hitting sharp, spindly branches and slipping on thick, long roots of prickly Caragana bushes that snaked out in every direction over the forest floor. While I struggled, falling and slipping on the wet branches, Shelly screamed and called for me from the distance.

I woke up startled and out of breath to a shrill cry and sat up instantly in bed, my T-shirt soaked with sweat. It took me a moment to realize not only where I was but who I was, and another few moments to recognize that the strident and eerie cry in the distance was only coyotes yipping and calling into the frigid night void.

14

——

THE NEXT MORNING, I was on my way to the office when Karen Fortenson came down the hallway, her shoulders tall in her gray-and-green ranger outfit and her eyes the color of dark chocolate.

"Agent Systead," she greeted me. "How's the investigation going?"

"It's going well." Not a lie, but not entirely true either. By now, we should have narrowed in on someone more closely instead of thrashing around in so many different directions.

She looked at me with an energetic hope bouncing in her eyes. "Glad to hear that. So you have an idea who did it?"

"The butler." I smiled. "I'm almost positive."

She laughed. "I take it that means you don't want to tell me."

"I'm sorry," I said. "I don't mean to trivialize matters. We've got some very good leads, but nothing definitive yet."

"I see. Well, the paper ran another follow-up article and you were mentioned quite a bit."

I looked at her.

"About how you work for the department, how you're a special agent, and all that good stuff."

I sighed. "A real double-o-seven, huh?" I chuckled. "Do you have it?"

"It's on my desk. I'll get it for you."

I watched Karen walk away, her demeanor much calmer than the first time I met her after she'd discovered the body. Yet, with the tranquility, she was still energetic with a slight bounce in her walk. She seemed in equilibrium—content with herself, her job, and her life. I chalked it up

197

to how much nature she took in most days. You could see it in her smile, not overbearing but not timid—entirely genuine in the way that always made me feel like I lack something crucial in my own life. I thought to myself that I'd still enjoy having that cup of tea with her and perhaps some of the magic would accidentally sprinkle onto me like dust.

· · ·

After she returned with the paper, I sat down in Monty's and my office and read the follow-up article by Will Jones. My name was mentioned with some information about the Series Eighteen-Eleven position, which not that many people are aware of. He probably got the gist of the information off the Internet.

Honestly, there was only one good reason for why I cared that I was named, and that was that my ma and sister, Natalie, would realize I was in town and would be wondering why I hadn't called earlier. For that, I had no good excuse other than just being busy. I made a mental note to call them as soon as I had some privacy.

I glanced at Monty, who was on the phone with another hardware store inquiring about duct tape and bear-spray purchases. He was jotting down notes and saying, "Ah huh, ah huh." I got up and headed outside with my cell phone, thinking it would be as good a time as any to call my ma, but before I even got to the door, my phone started buzzing and I looked at it to find my sister's number on the screen.

"Theodore Systead," she said loudly.

"Hey, Nat, what's up?"

"You're what's up." She sounded excited. "I wondered if you might come when I read about there being a man found dead in the park. Then I figured it wasn't you since I didn't hear from ya. How long have you been here?"

"Since Saturday morning, but it's been crazy."

"Yeah, yeah, yeah."

"Really, it has." I felt like a child defending myself.

"I suppose," she conceded. "It definitely looks it from the article."

"Does Ma know I'm here yet?"

"I don't know. One of us will probably get a call from her any second. Be nice if you called her first."

"I was actually just going to do that."

"Like I said, yeah, yeah, yeah." She laughed.

"I was." I smiled. "I was walking out with my phone in my hand when you rang. Scout's honor."

"Tell you what, you call her now; then I'll call you back later and let you know what time to come for dinner tonight."

"Nat—"

"I don't accept no."

"Natalie," I tried again. "I've got a lot of work—"

"Oh, come on. You've had your forty-eight."

"Forty-eight?"

I shook my head. With this day and age, it was hard to say whether she got that from a CSI-type show or from reality TV.

"Maybe later this—"

"I told you; I don't accept no."

I wanted to protest further, but then the thought of being another night in the cabin trying to make sense of this crazy case hit me like a wet blanket. "Give me a time," I said. "And I'll be there as close to that as I can."

I sat down on the sidewalk outside. The sun just peaked high enough to escape tree branches and warmed the parking lot. It had to be getting close to fifty and it was still morning. The day was glorious. I'd been too busy to really take it in, but it occurred to me that the foliage must have turned late in comparison to other falls since the entirety of each deciduous tree—each and every leaf—still burned rich with color. I saw a bright yellow birch leaf drift by and settle near the end of the parking lot. I called my ma.

She didn't answer, so I left a message and immediately felt better for having done so. I wondered why such little things, like making a phone call to a family member, felt so difficult to execute at times. I pictured her with her golfing buddies having coffee. It was too late in the season to golf, but she was close enough with the three of them that for years they got together once a week at a café in Kalispell for coffee after the golf season ended. I stuck my cell in my pocket and headed into the office.

. . .

Monty was off the phone.

"What have you got?" I asked.

"Not much to go on as far as duct tape or capsaicin purchases so far. And everything Leslie told us checks out—the store, the dental office."

"What about the timber company where her boyfriend works?"

"That checks out too. He was on his shift until five that evening. All week, in fact, including Thursday, and the manager confirmed that he didn't leave. Had lunch with the coworkers every day. His only day off was Tuesday. So if he was with her by six, that wouldn't leave him much time for taking a little jaunt to the Inside Road."

I took a seat, placed my elbows on my knees, and rubbed my face. I could still see the brightness of the sun under my eyelids in the form of red squiggly lines when I closed them.

"What time did she leave the store on Thursday? Around noon?"

"At twelve thirty. One of the checkout clerks verified it."

"And she got to Dr. Nieder's office at two?"

"That's correct. The office manager there verified that as well."

"So she had a break from twelve thirty until two."

"Yep."

"That enough time to get out there and back?"

"It is, but it sounds so unlikely. I mean, I asked the gal at the dental office how she seemed when she came in. If there was anything strange at all and she said no, nothing at all."

I propped the side of my forehead on my fist, my elbow still on my bony knee. "Yeah, and she's so small. She'd need help."

"Yeah, and Tyler was at work on Thursday as well. And according to Leslie, she and Paul were home with Lewis on Thursday evening."

I grabbed a dry-erase marker and went to the whiteboard and wrote *Thursday* and *Friday* down with a line between them. Then I wrote Leslie's, Paul's, Lou's, Stimpy's, Rob Anderson's, and Megan's names down and began filling in where they were on most of Thursday and at the key times on Friday: between twelve and eight p.m.

"If I might offer some help," I heard Monty say behind me. I turned. He unrolled a large poster-size paper and spread it on the table. "I took the liberty of already charting the information that I've been acquiring." He raised his brow as he waited for my response.

"Oh." I walked over and looked down at it. It was color-coded to each suspect, blue for Leslie, red for Stimpy, green for Lou, and so on. I cocked an eyebrow at him. "You get up early to do this?"

"Been doing it as I go." He grinned.

"You want your scout points now or later?" I said dryly. The smile on his face faded. "Actually," I added, "this is useful. Very useful. And it saves me a bunch of time."

His smile reappeared. "Thought it might."

"I owe you a beer for this one." I grabbed the rollout and some tape from a drawer under the counter. "You mind?"

"Help yourself, by all means." Monty was still smiling, his teeth still irritatingly bright, and I thought of cop shows where the IA guys are always thin and clean-shaven with wire-rimmed glasses. I taped it to the wall and sat down to look at it. I definitely recognized its usefulness, but something petty inside me reared its ugly head, and the chart instantly got on my nerves for reasons I couldn't quite pinpoint. I began bouncing my right leg up and down, but then the manic quality reminded me of Leslie or Stimpy, so I stilled it. I suppose it was the fastidious and tidy nature of the damn thing. Even though I could've told you from day one that Monty was the type to make a visual aid like this, with the first forty-eight over, I was beginning to feel like I was missing something, that I wasn't being careful enough, and the chart seemed to accuse me of the very thing I woke up feeling. I had a strange subconscious notion that I'd walk up to Monty any hour now and he'd look at me laughing and say, *Why didn't you tell us about Oldman Lake? Here, let me put that piece of information on my tidy chart as well.*

"Damn." I slammed my hand down on the table hard.

"Whoa." Monty snapped his head to look at me. "What was that for?"

"No witness, no weapon, no ballistics except in a grumpy, constipated grizzly bear. Shit, we haven't even been able to pinpoint who the last person to see the guy alive was."

Monty stared at me.

I grabbed my quarter. "Okay, okay." I held up my free palm as if I were calming Monty down instead of myself. "At least they're searching some of the water today. Maybe we'll luck out."

"Maybe," Monty said.

"Let's spend some more time on these phone records." I handed Monty a few of the printouts and kept half the pile for myself. His cell service had been cut by the end of September, so we were winging it in terms of finding something we could sink our teeth into. At this point, we were looking for patterns. It was clear that Victor and Leslie were seeing each other from the previous fall until August. Leslie's number showed consistently during that time frame with a mixture of long- and short-duration calls. A number, which we determined belonged to Stimpy, showed up arbitrarily pretty much every month, which didn't surprise me. And there were consistent calls to another number, which turned out to be Mindy Winters, and other random calls to several other girls, including a Tara Rhodes, whom Megan had mentioned.

I was looking at the report closely and one number in particular caught my interest. "This one here," I said to Monty, "this two-one-two-five-nine-seven-four, shows up in kind of a weird pattern."

"How's that?" Monty asked.

"Well, I'm seeing it only in January until March once a week on the same day of each week, a Monday, and then again from August until the phone was disconnected, once a week, again same day."

Monty ran his finger down his copy. "This two-one-two number?"

"Yeah." I picked up my phone. "Let's see whom it belongs to." I left a message for Monica while Monty studied the pattern. "In the meantime," I said, "we still don't know where Lou was on Thursday evening. I guess I'll be paying him another visit today."

"You want me to go?"

"Nah, you finish the stuff you're working on. We still need to know if Tom Hess was really on the east side hunting when this happened, and I need you to verify that Rob Anderson was really online when he says he was."

"Roger," he said. "But don't you need the good cop?"

"What? You nervous 'bout the way I'll behave with the guy?"

"No, it's just that you look, well, like you might need a small break."

"Break? Shit, it's not even noon."

Monty stared at me through his glasses. He definitely knew when to keep quiet, and I reminded myself why I had begun liking his company.

"Well," I reconsidered. "I'll take one later. After I go talk to Lou." I thought how a jog or something might make me feel better—to sweat out the whiskey. "Don't worry." I stood and walked to the door. "I'll behave."

. . .

On my way to go talk to Lou, Monica called.

"I have your number," she said.

"And?"

"It belongs to Louis P. Shelton."

"No kidding?" I said.

"That help?"

"Considerably," I said, immediately feeling lighter. "In fact, I'm going to see him right now."

. . .

This time I met Lou's wife, Becky. She answered the door looking like she had the day off, her hair in a messy braid, and she wore a pair of baggy, faded jeans, but she was surprisingly pretty. I only took note of this because I was having a hard time imagining any woman interested in Lou, but perhaps I wasn't being fair.

"Hello, Mrs. Shelton. I'm—"

"Deats. I didn't take Shelton when we married."

I noticed that she still had a cute figure for her fiftysomething age, a small nose, big doe eyes, and I could see that if she let her hair out of its braid, it would be full and wavy. "Thank you. Ms. Deats." I bowed my head as I tried to place in my mind whom she reminded me of, maybe some TV actress. "I'm Detective Systead, and I spoke to Lou the other day about his nephew's death."

"Yes, yes," she said. "I know. He filled me in."

"Is Lou here?"

"No, he's in Kalispell getting some stuff at Costco."

"I see. Would it be all right if I asked you a few questions in the meantime?"

"Me?" Her eyes widened in surprise.

"Sure," I said nonchalantly. "Just a few simple things to help us get a better understanding of Victor?"

She pulled the door back to let me in and led me to the dining room table that was directly off the living room. I took a seat, and she offered me some coffee. I asked if it was already made, and when she said it was, I said I would.

She went into the kitchen, which smelled of something having been cooked, maybe onions and potatoes. A washing machine whirred in the background from another room. I looked around at the knickknacks on the shelves: glass figurines of deer, elk, and mountain goats, earth-toned pottery, and some pictures of a young boy with wavy blond hair who I assumed was her son. "Nice photos of your son—I'm assuming your son—anyway," I called out toward the kitchen.

"Yeah, that's Tanner." She came back with the cup of coffee for me, offered me cream and sugar, and told me it was her day off. I said I was sorry to bother her.

"It's okay, just catching up on chores," She smiled nervously. "Sorry about the mess. You caught me in the middle of laundry." She gestured to a basket full of a tangled bunch of whites that she'd set down on the floor. In whichever way Lou had filled her in about Monty's and my visit, this woman didn't seem to have an attitude about me. "So what would you like to know about Victor?"

"Did you know him very well?"

"Not really. I didn't see him much."

"When was the last time you did see him?"

"August. At Lou's birthday party. The whole family was over here."

"Lou told us about that. How long have you been with Lou?"

"'Bout nine years now."

"And you've known Victor all this time?"

"Yeah, but like I said. Not a lot of contact. He irritated most of the family members—asking for money and such all the time."

"Are you aware of any contact between Lou and Victor since the August party?"

She furrowed her brow and looked around the room. Avoiding eye contact, I considered. She pushed a strand of her auburn hair behind one ear. "No, I'm not aware of any contact." She shrugged, a small twitch of a motion. "Why does that matter?"

"We're just trying to find out what was going on in Victor's life before this mess. So no contact, not even by phone?"

"I wouldn't know that, sir, but I don't think so."

"He hasn't stopped by asking for money?"

"No, nothing that I'm aware of." She pursed her lips and I wondered if she was holding something back, maybe protecting Lou.

"So if he was always bugging his relatives for money, why do you suppose he's stayed away all this time?"

"Because he was a coward—afraid to show his face—and Lou told him to not bother us for money. He's made that clear to him over the years."

"Was there a time when Lou *was* giving him money, then?"

Again, the small twitch of a shrug. "I really can't remember, but yeah, probably. Everyone in the family has given him money at one time or another. Mostly Penny, though. Besides . . ." She looked intently at me. "Why don't you ask Lou, Penny, or Megan these questions?"

"I will, Ms. Deats. That's what I came to do. When do you think he'll return?"

She glanced at the clock on one of her kitchen walls. "In a couple of hours or so. He was going to run some other errands while in town."

"I don't mind coming back later, but just one more thing, were you and Lou having an argument last Friday late afternoon to early evening?"

She looked at her lap and clasped her hands, "Yes, Detective. We were."

"And he left?"

"That's right.

"Do you remember at what time?"

"Sometime after four." She shrugged. "I didn't really pay attention to the time. Lou was angry. Needed some time to himself."

"Mind telling me what you were fighting about?"

"Yes, yes, I do." She looked at her lap again. "It's on the personal side."

"Personal?"

"That's right. Personal." She narrowed her eyes. "You never have a personal argument with your significant other?" she asked, sarcasm in her tone. "Or don't you have one of those?"

I ignored her remark. "Look, Ms. Deats, Lou doesn't have an alibi right now, so anything you can tell us would be helpful."

"Are you telling me that Lou is a suspect in all this?"

"I'm not saying that either. I'm just checking all avenues of everyone involved—all family members, all friends . . ."

She began laughing. "Well, I'm no detective and I'm not telling you how to do your job, but if I were you, I'd focus on those meth heads Victor hung out with."

"We're doing that as well," I said. Her laughter died, and she fidgeted in her chair. I scratched the razor stubble building on the side of my cheek and said, "Thank you for the coffee, then." She walked me to the door and on the way, I stopped at their gun cabinet, a unit made from some type of oak, darkly stained, with glass doors. A padlock hung from the looped handle in front. Two rifles and two shotguns lay in order, propped between each wooden rung. At the bottom of the cabinet lay a pistol in its brown leather case, but I could see by the handle that it was a Smith & Wesson. "Lou hunts?" Becky nodded. "And nice." I pointed down to the floor of the case where the pistol lay. "That a Model 19?"

"I think it is," she said. "A .357 Magnum."

"Very nice," I said. "Can't be in this business without admiring guns," I lied.

When I got down the porch steps, Becky said, "Are you talking to the other family members as much as you are to Lou?"

I turned and looked into her hazel eyes, "Yes, Ms. Deats," I lied again. "We are. It's part of the process."

"I suppose that means you don't have any real suspects?"

I stared at her. Was about to speak when she saved me by saying, "No, I know." She held up her hand. "You can't say."

. . .

On my way out of the driveway I called Joe and ordered him to have
one of his men from Park Police pull Lou over as soon as he crossed the
park entrance station and bring him to headquarters so I could speak
to him. I wanted to get his story alone and then check back with Becky
before they saw each other and were able to compare notes.

I drove to headquarters and looked back at the phone records.
"Once a week," I said to Monty. "Once a week Victor called Lou for
three months in the spring and again in the fall. Selling or buying
meth? Placing bets?" I looked at Monty.

"Basketball in the winter. Football in the fall?" Monty pushed his
glasses up.

I leaned back in my chair and scratched my face. I definitely
needed a shave.

"Would someone on meth care about betting on sports?" Monty
asked.

"Addictive behavior is addictive behavior. What else can you think
of? January to March. August to when the phone is cut off?"

"Could Lou have entered the meth ring somehow—been buying
from or for Victor?"

"Possibly, but I'm not getting that vibe. Although it's entirely possible that Victor had become a runner."

"How about Victor calling Lou for money, nothing more?"

"That's possible. From the sounds of it, he hit all the family members up most of the time."

. . .

Officer Ken Greeley was chomping on a piece of gum again, just as
he was the day I questioned him the first time. He still chewed it a
little too vigorously, as if he couldn't control his excitement to have
the chance to apprehend a guy and bring him in for questioning. I had

thanked Ken at the reception area of headquarters and said, "I've got it from here."

He stood for a moment, not wanting to go anywhere until I thanked him a second time, at which point he finally got the hint to leave.

I held out my hand to an angry-looking Lou, who refused to shake it, so I dropped mine and led him back to a little room across from the one we were using. It had a smaller table than ours and was cold and bare-looking with white walls. I left him there to get a couple of coffees and chat a bit with Joe, giving Lou time to sit and seethe.

"Hello again," I said cheerfully when I went back in. I offered him coffee.

"No. No, I don't want coffee. I want to know what the fuck some asshole park officer makes me come to park headquarters for when I haven't done a goddamned thing?"

I held up my palm. "No need to get worked up here."

Lou crossed his arms before his chest and set his jaw into a rigid position.

Monty came in and made a production of setting up the small handheld video recorder I had requested onto a tripod and pointed it at the table where Lou sat. "Thanks," I said to Monty and sat back down. "Want to join us?"

"Sure," Monty said in a chirpy voice.

"Agent Systead and Officer Harris, interviewing Louis P. Shelton," I said to the recorder. Lou glared at the camera, not moving a muscle. "Just a precaution." I smiled at Lou.

"Why am I here?" he asked.

"You sure you don't want some coffee? I know you must drink it. Becky makes a good cup."

He shot me a piercing look.

"I went to your house, but you were shopping, so I had a cup with her. Had a nice chat."

His look turned sarcastic. "Good for you."

"Actually, it *was* good, in terms of our investigation." I glanced at Monty. I was, of course, bluffing since Becky hadn't given me anything useful, but it didn't hurt to keep him wondering. "Now, Lou, once and for all, we just need to make sure certain details are straight because we have reason to believe they're not"—I cleared my throat—"all that straight, that is."

"I have no clue what you're talking about," Lou said.

"Where were you on Friday evening?"

"I told you." He shook his head in irritation. "Becky and I were in an argument. I left and went up to the entrance to the Inside Road."

"At what time?"

"At around quarter to five."

I wrote this down, more for show than of necessity. I knew his answer squared up to the one he'd given before and to what Becky had said. I continued questioning him, making him cover the rest of his activities while he was near the Inside Road. All his answers were consistent with the ones he gave previously, and the repetition seemed to make him wary and more annoyed, but not nervous as I'd hoped. "Listen," I said, getting up and leaning my back against the small counter against the wall. "What's the story on the willing sale you might have going on with the park?"

Lou laughed and let his head hang as he looked at the ground. "Are you for real?"

I sat back down and shrugged. "I don't know; I'm curious." I looked to Monty. "Aren't you?"

Monty still had the nice little connection he'd established with him the first time and leaned forward with a pleasant, interested look as he set his chin casually on his fist. "Actually, Lou, I do quite a bit with the inholdings on the east side of the park. I'm not all that familiar with what's going on here." He sounded utterly sincere, as if he were only having a beer with Lou. "What *is* the deal with your place?" He knit his brow in a confused way.

Lou sighed. "Then I don't need to tell you. It's the usual story in the park and I have no idea what this would have to do with Victor."

"Not much really." Monty shrugged. "Other than we know the grandchildren aren't really into taking care of the place the way you have and that they're all suddenly taking an interest in it now that it's dawned on them that it might be worth something." Monty leaned back. "It's just an interesting topic to me more than anything."

"I told you. There's not much to tell," Lou said. "Same old park story—the likes of you guys want the lake front and are willing to pay for it. It's my choice what I do with it and until then, it's nobody's business but mine."

"Lou," I said sternly, "what about Thursday night? Where were you?" I asked, taking him off guard.

"Thursday?" He squinted at me as if he was calculating the time frame in his head. I could see that he was shocked that Victor might have been out there since Thursday evening—that he thought this was only a Friday ordeal. "With Becky," he said. "And Tanner, at home."

"When was the last time you had contact with Victor?"

"I told you, in August." His jaw stiffened, almost imperceptibly.

"Really, August?" I shuffled through several of the files I had placed in front of me when I came in. I made a show of opening one with crime scene photos, giving him glances at the bloody mess, but not a close look at any of the pictures. Then I closed it and tucked it under another file. I opened the top one and pulled out the cellular records. "No contact at all since August?"

I could see his shoulders stiffen ever so slightly.

"That's not what these records show."

"I told you I hadn't *seen* Victor since August."

"No, I've actually got it on the recording." I hit rewind and played the part where Lou answered my question regarding *contact* with Victor. "Do you know what that means, Lou, when we catch someone lying to us in a federal murder investigation?"

Lou jutted his chin out. "I didn't lie. I thought you meant the last time I saw him."

"That so? Well, we're not thinking you're that dumb. So"—I stood up and peered down at him—"lying by omission, withholding, whatever you want to call it . . . I won't go into all the details, but often that kind of deceit leads to a search or two, sometimes to an arrest, unless we understand why the suspect is not being up-front with us. In fact, I should probably tell you at this point that you have the right to stay silent unless you'd prefer not to, and anything you do say will—"

"Christ Almighty." Lou pushed back from the table and stood. "You want to arrest me for killing my nephew?"

"I don't *want* to arrest you for anything, but your vehicle seen in the vicinity of the crime combined with no alibi and now, Lou"—I paused until he looked me straight in the eyes—"you not being up-front with us about the amount of contact you've had with your nephew is obstruction of an investigation and I hate to tell you, but that's a federal charge." I sighed, holding my palms up and glanced at Monty to take over. I had briefed him earlier on this part.

"Wait, wait," Monty offered calmly. "Let's just back up a bit. Let's not split hairs here. Please, sit down." He gestured to the chair. Lou looked to the chair, then to each of us. He sat down slowly. "When was the last time you spoke with Victor?"

Lou pursed his lips for a moment, then exhaled forcefully. "On and off on the phone early in the fall. I don't remember any exact dates."

I picked up the phone records and read them. "How 'bout September twenty-fourth?"

Lou nodded. "I guess that sounds right."

"So why was Victor calling you?"

"He wanted to borrow money. Like usual."

"How much money?"

"Whatever I had to spare."

"And what did you tell him?"

"What I always tell him: to stop calling."

"I have records here that show you spoke frequently from January to March and from August until Victor's phone got shut off in late September. How do you explain that?"

"The same way. He called for money often. He was persistent, and I kept telling him to leave us the fuck alone."

"You speak to relatives that way?" I asked facetiously.

"To *him* I did," Lou said. "Come on, even you have gathered by now that he was a pest."

"Yeah, pesky enough to take out and tie to a tree in the woods to teach a lesson to?"

"No." Lou smiled a half smile—the same kind that I do when I'm most calm and I took it as a very bad sign. This was not our man. He was too calm and confident. "You've got it wrong. All wrong. He wasn't pesky enough for that. No one's pesky enough for that."

. . .

I kept Lou there for another hour and a half so that I could go have another chat with Becky. I had Monty give him a twenty- to thirty-minute break with some coffee, then go back in and go over all the details two or even three more times, recording and writing them all down to see if his story stayed the same with each retelling. I knew this was not going to make Lou happy, and Ford's words to not piss him off rang somewhere in my ears, but really, I couldn't have cared less.

Becky had cleaned up since I'd seen her earlier. She looked showered with her hair neatly pulled back in a shiny gold hair clip, a hint of makeup on, and a nicer pair of jeans and a sweater. But behind the cleaned-up version of herself, her eyes showed strain. She said she needed to leave in about twenty minutes to pick her son up from school. I told her it wouldn't take long.

She nodded, folded her arms, and leaned against the porch railing without inviting me in.

"So you got the call from Officer Harris that we've got your husband at headquarters?"

"Yeah, why there? You said you were coming back here to visit Lou."

"Let's just say that there were some unfortunate discoveries on our part that are leading us to believe that your husband has been less than truthful regarding his level of contact with the victim."

"Less than truthful?" Her voice suddenly smaller than when I arrived.

"That's right. Seems your husband has been having fairly regular contact with Victor last winter and again in the fall. Did you know about that?"

Becky's face hardened, and she peered out toward the lake, the water like glass.

"Mrs. Deats?"

"So what? Big deal—he talked to his own damned nephew. Where's the crime in that?"

"Unfortunately, it's not that simple. Your husband has no alibi at the time of the murder, his was the only vehicle in the area as spotted by a witness at Fish Creek Campground, has lied about having contact with the victim, which is obstruction of an investigation. And if I find out that you're not being truthful, it's the same charge . . ." I looked at her with wide eyes.

She didn't speak, and I could see in her busy eyes that her mind was racing, weighing options, considering possibilities.

"So, Mrs. Deats, if you have anything to add that would make us feel better about letting your husband return to you by the time you and your son come back, now would be the time to offer it."

"I told you, I didn't even know they were speaking."

"Why were you fighting?"

"The same reason ninety percent of the couples in the world fight—over money."

"What about money?"

"'Bout there not being enough."

"Not enough?"

"Is there ever enough for anyone around these parts?"

I shrugged. "Look, let's stop toying around here. I'm going to give it to you straight: your husband could very well end up arrested for the murder of Victor Lance before this afternoon is used up. Now, before you say anything, let me tell you that I work in homicide. Gambling, drug trafficking—those are no longer my deal. In other words, I don't care about 'em. What I do care about is who killed Victor Lance, and I don't really think for one second that your husband killed his own nephew."

I didn't really know if I believed what I was telling her. A part of me had already nailed Lou Shelton from the day I met him, but another part of me sensed that we were barking up the wrong tree. "So let me put this straight, Mrs. Deats," I said. "I need to understand why your husband and Victor were having consistent and regular phone conversations from January to March and from August until Victor's phone got shut off in late September."

Becky sighed, and I could tell she was close to breaking. She glanced nervously at her watch. "I really need to get my son," she said softly, almost a whisper.

"I understand, but it hasn't been twenty minutes yet."

She nodded and sat down in one of the Adirondack chairs. "Betting," she whispered and sighed again with more force.

"Goddamn betting. Basketball in the winter. Football in the fall. Some bookie in Buffalo. Lou's gotten into trouble with it before." She tossed her hand to the air. "He quit for a long time, but fairly large sums have been missing from our savings, so I figured he was at it again. That's why we were fighting that night."

"And did you know about the phone calls with Victor?"

"I did." Becky looked up at me, her eyes drooping at the corners as if they were surrendering. "I figured he was dealing with his bookie, but I had no clue why Victor would be involved, but I knew he was because I saw his number come up several times in September."

"And you asked Victor about it?"

She nodded. "It just ended up in a horrible fight with him denying everything. Just like the old days."

"Did he say that Victor was betting too?"

"He didn't say that exactly, but yeah, I could tell that Victor was calling Lou to have him place bets to Lou's bookie."

"Have you talked about it since the fight?"

"No, I've not had the nerve to bring it up with all this going on."

"Thank you, Mrs. Deats." I stood and looked at my watch. "We'll get to the bottom of this. In the meantime, you better go get your son."

She didn't stand, didn't nod. Just sat still with her eyes fixed intensely on the gray planked wood of the porch. She looked deeply afraid, as if the natural markings in wood held secrets that would forever damn her and her marriage.

· · ·

On the way back to headquarters, I had Monica fax Lou's cell phone records to headquarters so that I could verify the calls to whoever his New York bookie was. Turns out that he was a guy named Donny Welsch, so when I went back in and saw Lou's jaw set like stone, I started by leading into that tidbit of information.

"So turns out that we have reason to believe that you're still not being completely forthright with us."

Lou had his arms crossed and glared at me. Monty had followed me in, and I made a show of the fax papers in my hands, shuffling them loudly. Then I set them in a neat pile in front of me after I pulled out a chair and sat. Monty did the same. Lou said nothing.

"We have some new information that makes us think that Victor wasn't simply calling to ask for money. Can you tell us more about that?"

"I'm not saying anything without a lawyer," Lou said flatly.

"That can be arranged. We can get you to the phone and you can call him or her. Or maybe you need the Yellow Pages to look one up?" I lifted an eyebrow. "Yes? No?"

He nodded.

"We can do that. Monty," I said. "Would you be so kind as to fetch a phone book for Mr. Shelton?"

"Sure, no problem." Monty walked out.

I sat and waited patiently until he came back, not saying anything either. I could hear Lou's breathing whenever he took a deep breath, and I detected a slight shakiness whenever he did so. Monty came back in and handed the phone book to him, but he didn't pick it up or open it. He just sat with his arms still folded and stared at it.

"Look, this doesn't have to be so difficult. I'll tell you what I told your wife, I'm trying to solve a murder here. I don't care about drugs, gambling . . ."

Lou looked at the floor.

"For example, I could care less about what Donny Welsch is running out of Buffalo, New York."

He looked up, and I shuffled the fax papers again.

"So why don't you tell us why Victor was *really* contacting you?"

Lou exhaled loudly, then nodded slowly. "Victor knew I bet on basketball and football. I had quit for a while, but then got back into it over the past two years. I'm not proud of it, but it's just one of the few things I haven't completely kicked in my life. Victor latched onto it around the fall before last and said he wanted in on the action, but I told him absolutely not. But he kept pestering me about it, so I finally gave in."

"So you placed bets for yourself as well as for him?"

"Yes," Lou said.

"How much did Victor bet?"

"Not much. Sometimes fifty, sometimes a hundred or two. Sometimes he'd come out ahead, sometimes not."

"And so your foolish nephew, who you knew needed money all the time, was betting through you. Who paid his debt when he came up short?"

Lou shrugged. "That was his problem. I told Welsch that I wasn't covering for the guy. That if he wanted the weasel's bets, that he had to deal with him himself."

"But you placed the bets for him. Why didn't Victor just call him himself?"

"Donny's particular about how many clients he has calling him. He didn't want me to give his number out, and I knew better than to fuck with Donny's request. He said he'd take Victor's bets and see how payments went for a while, but if it didn't go so well, that it would be my responsibility to get Victor out of the game."

"And so how did it go?"

"At first okay, Victor was on a winning streak for the first part of the season, but then he started to lose and owe Donny money."

"How much money?"

"About eighteen hundred or so."

"And did he pay up?"

Lou shook his head.

"So Donny never got paid?"

"No, he got paid."

"You paid him?"

Lou nodded.

"So you covered for the guy even though you said you wouldn't."

"Look, he was my nephew, good or bad, and I felt responsible since I placed the bets for him. I paid and figured I wouldn't place any more for him."

"And did you?"

"Only one or two more in the fall, before his cell got cut."

"And why did you do that?"

"I don't know." Lou shook his head. "'Cause I'm stupid, I guess. I'm a gambler. We do stupid shit." He looked at the floor, shaking his head back and forth.

"Did Victor come out ahead on those last bets?"

"Yeah, but I told him he owed me the money and anything that came from Donny would be payback for the eighteen that he owed me."

"Did he come to see you after his phone was disconnected?"

"No, I told him that if he came by my place, I'd never place a bet for him again."

"And he listened to you?"

"Yeah, honestly, I didn't think he would." Lou looked sincere, his eyes wide. "But you have to know Victor. He was like a kid with ADHD, crazy and wired on the drugs. Always going from one thing to the next. He had forgotten about me for the time being, but I knew he'd be back."

I looked at him, my eyes narrowed, and I think he must have sensed what I was thinking—that he'd taken care of it so that Victor wouldn't be back—because Lou looked at me wide-eyed, then Monty, and back to me. "No, no, it's not what you're thinking." He held up his hand. "I swear to you, I have no idea what happened to Victor in those woods. I wasn't forthright with you only because of the gambling. Becky doesn't know and, well, we've been fighting a lot and, I just . . . I just . . ." Lou hung his head, deflated. "I just didn't want to get in trouble for the gambling. I've quit before; I will quit again. In fact, I sent Donny what I owed him and haven't placed a single bet since your visit earlier in the week. I swear to you."

I looked at Monty, his face showing no emotion, then back to Lou, his expression sincere and pleading. I nodded once, then stood up and walked out. Monty followed me into the hallway.

"What's your gut telling you?" I whispered.

"That he's telling the truth."

I bit my lip. "Mine too. Plus we don't have anything specific to tie him to the crime. You can go back in and let him go home. In the meantime, we'll see what else we can come up with." I grabbed my quarter. "Damn, if I could get just get that damn slug, we might be able to tie it to his weapon."

"He had a gun?"

"I saw it in its case when I talked to his wife. He owns a .357 Magnum Smith & Wesson Model 19. Which, as you know, is a revolver where the casing stays in the gun. So the slug would be hugely helpful, and if it looks like it could be a match, then we could get a search warrant."

"But his wife will tell him that you saw the gun, won't she?" Monty asked, pushing up his glasses. "Then he'll just get rid of it."

"Maybe, maybe not. She's scared since she ratted him out for the gambling. I have a feeling she's afraid to say that she's betrayed him by giving me any information at all. Plus it was only chitchat when I saw the gun, and she has no idea that Victor was shot. Only that he was bound and eaten. But still . . ." I rubbed the back of my neck with my other hand. "It's the chance we take. We can't get a search warrant without something more specific than betting on sports games. We need something to tie him to the scene of the crime."

. . .

I fit in a jog—actually more than once—during the investigation, which, according to Monty, Park Police and rangers had begun calling Investigation Bait—a title started by Ken Greeley. After dealing with Lou, I decided Monty was right, I needed the stress relief, and Natalie was nice enough to not expect me before seven thirty or eight.

I ran from my cabin, past headquarters, by the pay gates, past the bright red Bear Country sign—All Wildlife Is Dangerous—Do Not Feed—and up to Apgar Village, only about two and a half miles. I had a sharp knifelike pain in the side of my knee when I got to the tiny village and slowed to a walk to Lake McDonald's shoreline. A small cherry-red building with bright white trim that used to be a school for park employees' children at the beginning of the century stood now as a souvenir shop. A lodge, a motel, and some motel cabins with a white freezer for ice between two of them lined the road before reaching the lake. All were boarded up.

When I reached the Boat Rentals sign, I passed several tall cotton-woods and some birch trees, the leaves shimmering in the late after-noon light. I looked at the shoreline as I stretched my legs and noticed that the floating docks were pulled for the winter. The glassy lake pro-vided a mirror image for the already snow-covered peaks. The Belton Hills gradually rose to my direct right, and Gunsight, Edwards, Little Matterhorn, and Mount Brown reached for the sky at my one o'clock. Mount Cannon, the Garden Wall, stretched out before me at twelve o'clock, and Mount Vaught, Stanton, and Rogers Peak popped upward at ten and eleven. To my left tapered the small and burned-out Howe Ridge, with its skinny lodgepole pines making the entire flat ridge look like it had a bad crew cut. To the north of Howe was the Inside Road area, which held Fish Creek, McGee Meadow, Logging Lake. . . . I thought of the bear, that if they'd gone ahead with initial plans to let him go, where he'd have made it to. I imagined him crashing into the woods without looking back. Then I thought of Lou, destroying his marriage with a silly addiction. And myself, letting my marriage fall apart because I couldn't open up. Humans, we were all so damn predictable.

Shelly knew only bits and pieces about Oldman Lake—mostly scraps of information from Ma and Natalie and one-word answers and shoulder shrugs from me in response to her probing questions. *Did you suffer post-traumatic stress? For how long? Do you have nightmares still? Maybe you've never fully grieved the loss?*

One time I came home from work and she showed me some self-help books that she'd bought for me, books titled *Victims No More* and *Secrets to Grieving.*

"Trust me," I told her. "My mom has already given me plenty of these types of books."

"Did you read them?" she pleaded, tucking her blond strands behind her ear.

"Yes," I lied. It was a hot summer afternoon in August, and our house in Kalispell felt small and stifling. The fan spun at high speed, pushing warm air around. I went into our bedroom next to the living room to take my uniform off, and she followed me in.

"But these have exercises that you can do."

"So?" I unbuttoned my work shirt.

"So it might help?"

"Help what?" I threw it on the bed.

"Help you become, I don't know, more open."

"What's some silly book going to do? Change who I am?" I looked at her—her round eyes pleading. Her flimsy tank top clung to her stomach, and I could make out her belly beginning to swell with the beginning of pregnancy. "If you can't accept who I am, then we have a problem."

"It's not like you're broken, Ted. You might have some cracks, but you're not broken, and all marriages take work. I want more for us, for myself, for . . ." She looked down at her stomach. She never finished her sentence, as if she'd had a premonition even then that it wouldn't work out. I turned away and dug around in the dresser for some shorts. She waited for me to look back at her, to say something, and when I continued to take way too long to find a pair, I heard her sigh deeply and leave the room.

I found a boulder to sit on and stared out at the placid water. It felt good to run, but I was tired, some kind of exhaustion that had nothing to do with the physical and everything to do with the mental and the emotional. Not that the case was testing my intellectual capacity to its fullest, yet. It was more a deep-bone exhaustion that came to me unexpectedly, as if I was someone who couldn't swim and had lived the rest of my life since Oldman Lake trying to stay away from the deep end of the water—away from riptides—and suddenly found myself in the wrong current, frantically treading water and pushing back with feet and arms to stay clear of the drop-off. Living in Florida had taught me early that when you get caught in a riptide, the best thing to do is swim sideways with it, not fight it, until you can find a place to swim to shore.

Still, the day before me on the Continental Divide, many miles from any ocean, was glorious. Nearly painful because the colors were pure, the air fine, the lake cobalt, the leaves so poised in their golden glory . . . Even two bald eagles flew above, fishing, circling together as they rode gentle air currents as if they were performing a choreographed dance. I watched them for some time until my neck began to stiffen. None of it felt real because it was too polished, like some overcolorized movie.

"Damn," I whispered. I had to work this case quickly, get it over with, and get the hell out. I wanted to get up, but I didn't. I sat still in the sun, let its slanted rays hit my face. They provided only a low-grade heat at this point. The memories are put away and locked up, as if in a steel vault. Only at certain times do I crack that vault and let a few spill out. I suppose so much pressure builds up behind the door that it has to open a bit or there will be an explosion of sorts.

That fall day came too quickly after an abbreviated Montana summer. The summer of 1987 gave only forty-two frost-free mornings and never went above eighty-five degrees. It was peppered with heavy, gutter-filling rains, obnoxious, demanding windstorms, and cloudy, cool days, even in August. A funnel cloud formed on Flathead Lake's waters. My sisters and I drove my ma crazy complaining of boredom. *Go outside*, she'd say. *It's too cold*, we'd yell back. *It's too wet*. So when the still-tawny Indian summer came, the people of the Flathead Valley were spring feverish, cabin-bound, and dying to get out and catch the sun's rays, even as oblique as they were in late September. Hungry for sun, fun, and life: that's the way the dawning of that long-needed, brilliant, and deadly weekend was all those years ago.

My dad wanted to take me camping, and I thought, yes, finally something fun to do. Get away from my sisters and all the arguing over stupid stuff like whose turn it was to take out the trash, set and clear the table, sweep the garage, or walk Tumble. Dad was busy in the lab all the time, so to go with him alone and get away from my sisters was like a true idyllic *Leave It to Beaver* situation. I got ready, remembering my knife and pushing it into the front pocket of my shorts.

I didn't have one of those red Swiss Army knives with the small blades, the narrow pair of scissors, tweezers, or a corkscrew, that some of my buddies from Scouts had. For my eleventh birthday, my dad gave me a pearl-handled jackknife with only one six-inch blade that was significantly longer and larger than your average pocket blade. He said I needed to be careful with it because the blade was very sharp, but that I would need a proper knife if I intended to gut fish.

When my line got tangled while we were casting for trout on some jade-green lake toward Libby, he told me to use my knife to cut the line. When I told him I forgot to bring it, he made a face like he was disappointed in me and told me that one should always be prepared when out in the woods. Afterward, whenever we went camping or fishing, I always took it with me.

I did have that knife at Oldman Lake. And I can't say I'm very superstitious, but sometimes those little things just get the best of me. I continued to carry it even after Oldman Lake until I saw that grizzly with Kendra and her dad on the Almeda trail. With the renewed pangs of fear and loss settling in my stomach like acid for weeks after the incident, I decided that maybe the knife brought me bad luck, so I put it away in the top drawer by my bed.

But that particular day before we left for East Glacier, I did have my knife. We also packed turkey and cheddar sandwiches, beef jerky, filled canteens of water, trail mix with peanuts, M&M's, raisins, cashews, and dried coconut flakes. I remember oatmeal packets we took for breakfast. I rerolled my sleeping bag several times to get it tight enough to fit into the impossibly short and narrow bag. I shoved my warm clothes, including heavy cotton long johns, into the pack. Not much of the fancy polypropylene stuff was out then.

When we got to Glacier's Two Medicine campground, snow that never melted over the summer and new layers that had arrived in late August and early September coated Sinopah and Rising Wolf Mountains. The golden aspen leaves scintillated in the sun and twitched nervously with the breeze. Even then, I remember feeling strong undercurrents of anguish. They came on suddenly and in a rush as if those sensations had been put in a syringe and given to me intravenously.

I've always wondered if my dad felt them too. If there was a moment when his radar picked up on the oncoming danger, if he paused briefly when he looked out with his raven-sharp, deeply intellectual eyes toward the passage between Dawson and Ptimakan Pass, at the massive structures in the distance—the backbone of Montana—as the Blackfeet referred to it.

When he scratched the razor stubble on the side of his face (I remember he hadn't shaved that day), had he wondered if we should just stay in the campground and not go into Oldman Lake? Or had he chalked it up to the fact that that's just the way the eastern front felt to everyone most of the time—wild, untamed . . . ominous?

And if he hadn't and I had, should I have said something and would it have mattered? Should I have told him that the gently lapping water of Two Medicine Lake had given me goose bumps for no good reason, that when the aspen leaves shook in the light breeze, I felt nervous, not calm? All of this, in retrospect, is essentially to say I had some tabs on the future, some radar picking up on events about to occur, which I didn't.

· · ·

The police didn't find anything under the first two small bridges on the way out from McGee Meadow, a relatively shallow creek that was easy to search with metal detectors and no divers. Now Walsh's men were working under the McDonald Creek Bridge on the way out from the Inside North Fork Road, a medium-size, much deeper body of water flowing out of the Lake McDonald and feeding the Middle Fork drainage.

After my jog, I had just enough time to shower and visit the dive site with Monty before heading to Nat's. The sun set softly through the trees as we parked before the McDonald Creek Bridge, and the temperature dropped quickly. We stepped out and walked toward the riverbank where the divers had set up their operation. The underwater search unit consisted of four divers, one of whom is a dive supervisor. Essentially, all of them are regular county officers who fulfill their diving roles as an additional duty for a small amount of extra pay. Now two divers still slinked along the river bottom in the freezing water in their dry suits and with their underwater metal detection devices. The supervisor and one other diver stood on the side with several gear bags and two bright yellow tanks lying on the bank.

I glanced at the deep and darkening jade-colored water sliding past. In the spring, during the runoff phase, I knew McDonald Creek turned bright turquoise, and at the point where it met the Middle Fork, you could see a clear demarcation between the bright, milky turquoise water from Lake McDonald and the brown muddy water of the Middle Fork. Now the water was clear and mysterious, and the smell of damp soil rose to my nose. I introduced myself and Monty to the supervisor, a man named Otto Burns.

"Any luck?"

"Nope. The usual—cans, a beer bottle or two. A kid's toy truck." Otto pointed to an old rusted, metal army truck, covered with a growth of green algae. "And a pocketknife; don't suppose that could have been your weapon?"

"Nah." I shook my head. "How much longer?"

"We're pretty much done here." He looked to the setting sun. It was getting dark quickly, and the sky was turning a deep lavender. "If we come up with anything, I'll let Walsh know immediately."

"Thanks, I appreciate you guys doing this. I know it's extra work for your men and that you've been busy lately over in Flathead Lake."

"It's our job. No problem."

Monty thanked him too, and we walked up to the bridge and halfway over it. We peered down into the clear water and could see the bubbles from the divers farther out as they quartered back and forth. "My father used to say," Monty spoke in a low voice, "never trust a guy whose name can be spelled backward and forward."

"That so? Well, he looks pretty trustworthy to me." I smiled.

Monty chuckled.

"What does your dad do?" I asked.

"He runs a construction company in Kalispell."

"And you didn't get sucked into that business?"

"Nah, I did my time with it when I was younger, before I got into this." Monty rested his arms on the bridge railing and peered into the water. I had been curious as to Monty's roots. But I made it a habit not to pry into the history of any of the partners temporarily assigned to me. I often thought of detectives I remembered on the Kalispell force, officers who partnered for life and knew each other's moves and comments like married couples, who'd fight over some significant detail in a case, then slide right back into a routine the next morning as if nothing happened. A part of me envied that, but my job didn't afford that kind of partnership. And even if it did, I didn't know if I'd understand what do with that kind of companionship. In general, I'd learned to not get into anything too deep or personal. However, with the bubbling sound of the river and cool breeze in my hair, a dozen other questions for Monty popped into my head out of nowhere, about where he lived in the valley, which high school he went to, whether he shared any of my same teachers, which college he attended, and how he came to choose Park Police. Yet instead of probing, he asked me, "What about your family? You call yet?"

"Headed to my sister's in Whitefish for dinner now."

"Good boy." Monty nodded.

"It was definitely past time." I leaned on the railing as well and looked up the river to the mouth of McDonald Lake. The yellow larch framed the opening of the lake from both sides.

"Beautiful," Monty said. "Never ceases to amaze me how incredible this place is."

"Yeah," I offered. "My family used to come here for picnics after we first moved to Montana."

"When did you move here?"

"In the early eighties." I pointed into the now dark gray water. "Bet there's some trout down there," I said, then added, "You were probably an infant then."

"Actually . . ." Monty smiled. "Thanks for the compliment, but not quite. I was born in '77." Monty lifted his chin to the bank where the two divers surfaced, slick and black. "Looks like they're done, and"— he glanced at his watch—"you better get to dinner."

I was about to ignore his comment, ask him about how he got into law enforcement, but something inside me made me stop. The damp smell of the cool breeze piggybacking over the cold river water and its wet banks swept up and onto the bridge and filled my nose, wild and full of the park's ancient layers as if it was casting spells. I shook off the urge to keep talking and realized that he was right. I did have to get to Natalie's, and I was beginning to get very hungry.

15

SECOND-GUESSING EVERYTHING DOESN'T always make you the kind of guy people want to hang out with, and sometimes you end up not even liking your own company. I don't consider myself irrational, but when you're always in the critical zone, a good dose of superstition, whether you want it or not, comes along for the ride. Also with questioning comes a ton of self-analysis, the kind that, after enough years of doing it, shows in your eyes like thin venetian blinds pulled down over the pupils, dulling the brightness.

My sister Natalie didn't have eyes muted from self-analysis. Hers were childlike and joyful in spite of our childhood tragedy, and I considered it some kind of genetic trait that she got such a happy demeanor. When she opened the door at her house in Whitefish, she immediately enfolded me in a vigorous hug, reminding me of how she also possessed that enthusiastic no-holding-back quality that didn't seem to come from the family I remembered being a part of. Kathryn, Ma, and what I recall of my dad, and I all had that amicable, semidistant politeness that showed itself in awkward moments like around greetings and compliments. There was always a pause before a hug hello, good-bye, or before an *I love you*. Not with Natalie.

"Come, come." She ushered me in, taking the flowers and bottle of wine I'd brought with a big cheerleader smile, her cheeks bunching up into doughy balls. "You must be exhausted, getting into town like this and going right to work."

"I'm used to it. That's what I do: fly in and get right to work. I'm sorry I didn't call earlier."

She waved her hand in front of her as if shooing off a fly. "Here, give me your coat. Mom's up with the boys." I could hear the sound of kids upstairs, the patter of feet running down a hall and some louder thumping. "What can I get you?"

I smiled. "I'll have a beer if you've got one."

"Of course I have one." She walked down the hall and I followed her. As she passed the base of the stairwell, she yelled up, "Ian, Ryan, your uncle's here"—then turned back to me—"Budweiser okay?"

"Great with me."

"They're bottles, not cans."

"Doesn't matter to me."

"Luke's not here?" I asked.

"He's working."

"As I should be."

"Well, you have to eat."

"So does Luke."

"Trust me." She laughed. "He eats plenty. You, on the other hand"— she opened the refrigerator door and paused before it, scanning me up and down—"could use a good home-cooked meal."

"You're wasting energy." I lifted my chin to the open fridge.

She turned back and reached for a bottle. "Plus he'll be here in about an hour." Luke owned and managed a glass company in White-fish that he'd bought about five years before.

"Boys," Natalie yelled again. "Your uncle's here. Mom."

They both came crashing down the stairs, and, as always, I genuinely showed my amazement at how much they'd grown as I gave them each a hug. The older, Ian, was nine in September, if I remembered correctly, and the younger, Ryan, turned six in February. Ian had gotten taller and a bit lanky, his shoulders bonier than I remembered, like

mine when I was his age, and Ryan still looked completely proportion-
ate as far as kids go, like a nimble little gymnast.

"Uncle Ted, Uncle Ted," Ryan said loudly, "you want to come play
Mario Cart with us?"

"Are you kidding?" I smiled. "Do I ever. But let me say hello to your
Nanny Mary first."

. . .

Ma likes to talk about my work. A lot. Almost too much for my liking.
She wants specifics, but I prefer to speak about it in the most general of
terms. So after our hugs and kisses and *you're looking great*s, the boys
went back upstairs to play Mario Cart on the Wii, and Ma began to finely
chop a garlic clove and slice some tomatoes. Natalie motioned for me to
take a seat at the counter. Once Ma found her chopping rhythm, she
dove right in. "So your first murder case in Glacier after all these years?"

"First and only," I said. Natalie grated cheese into a pot filled with
what looked like a creamy mixture of green beans and mushrooms. "Go
figure. Not a lot of homicides in Glacier in the last decade. A lot of ac-
cidents: drowning, climbing incidents, disappearances." I left out maulings, but it would be on all of our minds without me saying. "And some
potential suicides, but not much in the way of foul play until now."

"So?" Ma said sharply. "What's the case about? Some kid from up
the Line was kidnapped?"

"Something like that."

"Then mauled?"

"I hate to admit that I don't really understand what happened yet."

"That can't be good. It's been a few days already."

"What? You been watching the same crime shows as Nat?"

She pointed her knife at me for a second and made a funny face
in a mock scold, then tossed the stem of the tomato in the sink. "How
many of these you want cut?"

"Two's enough." Natalie looked over her shoulder.

Thinking Ma might drop the subject and focus on her slicing, I asked about her golf buddies.

"They're fine." She waved her hand before her face. "Up to all the usual boring stuff. You've got anything to go on?"

"I've got some good leads."

"Which are?"

I shrugged. "The usual—friends, family. Need help cutting some of those veggies?"

"Of course not." She looked at me like I was crazy for asking, her brow crinkled and her chin pulled in. She paused for a moment. I could feel some tension subtly insert itself into the room like a change in the lighting or the air pressure. "You've seen that Ford yet?"

I considered saying *not yet*—just to keep it simple. "Yeah, I've seen him."

"And?"

"And what?"

"Still the same creep?"

"Don't really know him," I said. "I'd never met him before." I took a sip of beer. Ma set aside the tomatoes, pushed a clump of thick graying hair behind her ear with the back of her hand, and began chopping cucumbers, more vigorously than she had the tomatoes, the blade hitting the cutting board too hard, no coincidence after mentioning Ford's name.

"I don't know him either, but I can read people and it doesn't take a genius to see that that guy's no good."

"Someone likes him, or at least thinks he does a good job up there," Natalie offered. "Otherwise he wouldn't be around for so many years . . . decades."

"Well, I . . . I just never liked that man," she said.

"No kidding?" Natalie said dryly, then smiled.

"What? It's not a joke," Ma said. "How he portrayed things with your father and all."

"That was a long time ago." Natalie looked at me, her eyes wide. I couldn't tell if she was looking for backup from me or just curious about my reaction.

"He know who you are?" Ma asked carefully, gently. Suddenly, perhaps because of the unexpected softness in her voice, I felt something fragile welling up.

"I don't think so. Like Nat said, it was a long time ago."

She looked up, her eyes serious. I fidgeted in my stool. "How could he not if he knows your name?" The edge back in her voice. Time, apparently, had not taken care of it.

I shrugged. "Doesn't recall the name, I guess. Can't say I'm hurt."

Natalie smiled, large as always.

Ma threw the butt of the cucumber in the garbage disposal and turned it on, the loud grind speaking for her.

She was complicated. She didn't escape the weltschmerz Kathryn and I had, but she always had a way of buoying herself above it and keeping a sense of humor, or at least a large dose of sarcasm. When Dad died, she lost her playfulness for a number of years, but she pretty much regained her old self after a decade or two, if you can ever fully do that. Losing a loved one changes people. Period.

"I don't care how long it's been. If you're a park superintendent, you shouldn't forget the names of . . ." She looked down and I sat quietly while Natalie opened her pot again and poked at the beans. She had just finished stirring a moment earlier, so I knew she was only doing this to escape whatever discomfort was occurring. "You shouldn't forget significant events that happen in your own damn park," she finished.

I took a sip of my beer and felt the familiar clench gather below my breastbone. I turned and tried to peer through my sister's sliding glass doors. It was going on eight, so it was dark out, and I could see our reflection: Natalie before the stove, her dark hair in shoulder-length waves, Ma now at the sink washing the cutting board. She had gained a little more weight around her center since the last time I saw her. And myself, sitting languidly but inside, wound up. I looked thin, tired, and the reflection made my face seem more elongated than usual. I turned back to Natalie. "Can I set the table?"

"No, no, I've got it. You better go up and play a game or two of Mario before dinner or the boys will be upset."

"My pleasure." I grinned and headed upstairs.

. . .

We had a baked chicken dish with Parmesan cheese and rice along with the green beans. Luke had arrived after we started eating and quickly washed up to join us. I'd always liked Luke, an easygoing and avid fly fisherman. We caught up on the best fishing holes around the valley and up toward Eureka, near the Canadian border. We discussed proposed measures to control the lake trout that were squeezing out bull trout and new legislation on reopening cyanide mining techniques in Montana that could potentially harm streams and rivers. The boys got bored listening to us, and after they cleared the table, went back upstairs to get their PJs on before they could have the apple pie Ma had brought.

Against Natalie's and Luke's protests, I insisted on Luke staying seated and helped Natalie rinse the dishes and put them in the dishwasher. Ma stayed at the table and chatted with Luke. "Ma baked this with the fruit from that apple tree in her backyard." Natalie worked at the plastic wrapping from underneath the pie plate.

"Excellent," I said.

"Oh, and guess who I ran into the other day?"

"Couldn't say."

"Shelly. At a grocery store in Kalispell."

I lifted an eyebrow. "That so? How is she?"

"She's good. She recently got divorced."

"That's too bad." Nobody had brought Shelly's name up to me in years, and I had had no reason to mention it myself. Just the sound of it made me feel oddly shy. "She has a couple kids now, doesn't she?"

"Two girls. I think 'bout seven and nine."

I shook my head. I wasn't sure how it made me feel, other than sad for her, for her kids. Some pang of nostalgia shot through me, and I wondered if her second husband communicated with her. When Shelly had gotten pregnant, it was unexpected, and I found myself reeling with fear that I'd make a terrible parent and that the world was too unstable a place to bring a child into. But as several weeks passed, I'd wrapped my head around the idea—even became excited. Shelly was giddy, but wanted to wait a few weeks before telling her parents or my mother. When we finally did, as if on cue, the miscarriage hit us, a tornado railing into our marriage at full speed and crumbling the already weakened pillars and walls we'd managed to construct.

Two months after the miscarriage, I discovered calls on our cell phone bill (one Shelly usually paid and I rarely looked at) indicating that she was talking into the late hours of the night with some over-muscled bozo from the local gym. When we fought over whether the baby had even been mine, she'd yelled, "I didn't even begin talking to him until you clammed up and ignored me." Through choked cries, she said she only confided in him because she needed someone, any-one, who could talk to her, whose sentences didn't trail away in midair like mine, whose eyes didn't glaze over and not see her, whose silences made being with someone a lonelier prospect than being by herself. And guilty I was. I thought if I could just walk away from it, not look directly at the pain and tears in her eyes—just go to work, set my mind on other things, that it would all pass. Time. It helped me get over my father; time would heal her wounds as well. I couldn't do it for her.

"Just thought I'd let you know," Natalie said. "You should give her a call while you're here." From a drawer beside me, Natalie grabbed a silver pie knife, the kitchen light glinting off its shiny surface.

"Oh, you think so?" She looked at me with her signature smile, and I laughed. "I take it that means you really do think so."

Natalie nodded.

"You're something' else." I pinched her arm lightly. "Come on, cut that pie before everyone starts yelling."

. . .

Natalie was getting some whipped cream out of the fridge and bringing it to the table when the boys came down, Ian in flannel and Ryan in some blue cotton PJs with a picture of two crisscrossed baseball bats and a ball on the chest. I felt another twinge of something achy sift through me when I looked at them—a type of longing or homesickness for something forever lost. Both were younger than the age I was on the fateful day I went camping with my dad. At the risk of sounding trite, I couldn't help but recognize the innocence shining in both sets of eyes. When Ryan climbed onto Luke's lap, his body looking taut like a Gumby doll, but cuddly at the same time as Luke's big arms held him in a warm bundle, I tried to remember my father's lap but couldn't.

Ian sat across from me and asked me what was white and black and red all over. When I said a newspaper, he told me to try again. "A toad in a blender," I said.

"Yuck," he screeched. "No, *an embarrassed zebra*." His smile was huge like Natalie's.

I laughed.

He and Ryan continued to tell me silly jokes, and I laughed on cue until they finished their pie and Natalie shoved them off to bed. I gave each of them a good-night hug and as I smelled their soft, silky hair, an overpowering urge, sharp as a blade, to be sweet, trusting, hungry for life and giggling uncontrollably at silly jokes just once again, cut through me. The yearning caught in my throat and I had to cough to dislodge it. I pushed my hand in my pocket and felt for a quarter but came up short, so I wrapped my fingers around my thumb and squeezed tightly until Ma said, "They're sweet boys, heh?"

"I take it you haven't wagered any money yet on one of those Wii games."

Natalie insisted I stay the night on their couch, but I told her absolutely not, that I needed to get back to the cabin so I could get on the job early. A part of me wanted to stay, curl up in their family room with the rest of them soundly sleeping upstairs, their rhythmic breathing providing some invisible shield from the outside world. How I admired Natalie for the simple, but hard-won irreplaceable things she'd created and fostered by having a little trust and an ounce of faith in the world. The willingness to take leaps in spite of knowing how fragile it all is, how easily everything can break—how it can fall and shatter like broken glass in an instant.

Yes, a part of me wanted to stay in the warm cocoon of their family life and not go back to Glacier, but I had the feeling that if I stayed one night, I'd want to stay two, then three, and not sleep in Glacier again as the case progressed. And for reasons not completely understood by me, that would be unacceptable.

16

Victor ended up with a small family gathering at a depressing funeral home in Evergreen not too far from his mother's place. I stopped in on the off chance that some strange person or weird characters whom I hadn't considered would pop up out of the blue.

The ceiling was low, the lighting dim, and the carpet a rusty burgundy color trying to look royal but failing miserably. I had been in the same funeral home about fifteen years earlier for a friend who'd lost his life in a heavy-equipment accident while paving a highway east of Kalispell. Victor's father wasn't there, and according to our records, now lived somewhere in New Mexico. Megan had informed us that they'd tried to contact him all week but had been unsuccessful. They left messages on the only cell phone number of his they had, but no longer had his voice recording on it, so were unsure if it was even his any longer. I made a note to make sure Monica checked his current number so he could be notified.

I stood at the back, trying to fade into the wall and stay unobtrusive. There was no coffin, only flowers next to a tripod stand with a photo board filled with pictures of Victor, mostly when he was a boy and still had some fat and color on his cheeks. I recognized one of the pictures—the one of Megan and Victor swimming—and figured Penny must have taken it from its frame from her side table.

Penny looked glassy-eyed and numb, going through the motions and being pleasant to everyone who came. She wore a dark-green dress and Megan, in black trousers and a sweater, stood next to her with her

239

arm woven under her mother's. With her jaw set hard, Megan appeared stoic, as if she had her guard up and was there to offer protection for her mother, not to grieve her dead brother. When she noticed me, she gave me a stiff, curt nod, her dark eyes darting around, ravenlike. Eventually, she and Penny sat with the other family members: Lou and Becky, another uncle on Penny's side whom I hadn't met named Mark and his wife, Angela, and a few of their kids who all looked older than twenty and had a few toddlers and various-aged children of their own.

Candles glowed steady and created oblong shadows beside the altar. I felt a little shaky again, which I chalked up to another sleepless night and the fact that I drank too much coffee before coming. Lou glanced at me when he took a seat behind Megan, then looked away. Daniel, a few rows back, noticed me as well and gave me a small wave.

The service was short with a few hymns and one or two sentimental eighties songs, including "Wind Beneath My Wings," which seemed grotesquely out of place, given that Victor didn't seem to provide wind for anyone's wings other than his own attempt to fly high in some altered state.

When everyone rose from their seats and filed outside, I followed. The sky had turned bruised, the temperature dropped, and the wind picked up and stirred some fallen leaves. I found Penny first and offered my condolences. She thanked me for coming, then stood on her toes and whispered to me, "Have you caught who did this yet?"

"Not yet," I said, stooping down to her level. "We're working hard on it."

Sadness broke through the dull glassiness of her gaze. She pursed her lips, nodded, and opened her mouth to speak, but one of her friends came up and grabbed her around the shoulder before a word escaped. I smiled politely and turned to see Megan.

"Surprised to see you here, Detective Systead."

"Have you been able to contact your father yet?" I asked.

"Yeah, we finally got ahold of him this morning through a former landlady of his who had a current number."

"Had he known?"

She shook her head.

"How are you holding up?"

"I'm fine. Any closer to finding who did this?"

"It's progressing," I offered. "Anyone here that you weren't expecting or that seems out of place?"

"Besides you?"

I smiled. "Besides me."

"No, whoever you're lookin' for wouldn't be *here*." It was almost a question; her brow furrowed.

I nodded as I scanned the crowd. "No, most likely not."

• • •

It was late afternoon, and the wind had picked up even more. When I returned to headquarters, I sat outside in the car for a moment with my eyes closed and listened to gusts of wind cut through the mountains, stir the leaves, and rattle the outer branches of the trees by the building.

I thought of how it must have been for Victor Lance out alone in the woods for an entire night, strapped to a tree, scared shitless: wildly looking around, the wind in the creaking trees, shaded objects that you can't tell are real or your imagination, not knowing if a wild animal might wander upon you. Just the act of breathing must have been a challenge—trying to calm it down, but trying not to focus on it. It's the first time I'd let myself go there and immediately felt the familiar clench below my breastbone. I opened my eyes and shook the images away.

I went inside, where I talked to Monty more about Lou and Victor gambling—that it just didn't sit right with me. "Why in the hell would

Lou place bets for a guy who he knew would be an albatross around his neck, who he'd tried so hard to get rid of in the first place?"

"Maybe he didn't try as hard as he claims."

"No, he did. His wife confirmed that, in general, that was the way it was, and I can tell she's not lying."

Monty looked at me thoughtfully, his head cocked to the side.

"I'm going to go talk to him again," I said.

"Now?"

"Nah, it can wait till morning. Havin' another home-cooked meal now."

"That so? Lucky you—your sister or your mother?"

"Neither, Joe and his wife."

"Nice." Monty smiled.

. . .

Joe and his wife, Elena, lived in a two-story farmhouse on ten acres by the Flathead River outside Columbia Falls. They still had several horses, but according to Joe, he decided he was getting too old to have so many responsibilities, so they sold the four head of cattle they'd owned.

Elena was a petite woman, and I could easily see that Leslie got her mother's frame, large eyes, and pale porcelain skin, while Heather got her father's larger, Scandinavian build with fairer, ruddier skin and blond hair. Elena looked quite a bit younger than Joe, and I wondered what the age difference was. I knew Joe had to be in his midsixties, while Elena looked to be in her early fifties.

"Nice place you have here," I told Elena as I handed her the bottle of wine I'd picked up in Columbia Falls on the way over.

She thanked me, took my jacket, and brought me into the living room, which was painted in a tasteful, deep silvery-blue with white trim. White bookshelves framed the fireplace, and I could see family pictures lining the mantel, many with the two girls when they were younger, a dark-haired beauty next to a light-haired one. Pictures of them riding horses, sitting on wooden field fences, bundled up and standing beside a Christmas tree they had picked out in the woods, and school pictures with perfectly combed hair and gap-toothed smiles. In the pictures, in spite of the light and dark, tall and little contrasts, it was obvious they had similar features in the shape of their jaws, their cheeks, and their smiles. Joe came in and greeted me, and we hadn't chatted for more than five minutes when the doorbell rang. "Oh, that's Monty." Joe smiled. "Ran into him on the way out and thought he could use a good meal as well."

Monty came in clean-cut, smelling of cologne, and smiling. He gave Elena a big hug and handed her the bottle of wine he'd brought. I could see that this wasn't the first time he'd been over for dinner. Monty turned to me. "Guess I'm having a home-cooked meal as well."

"I guess you are," I said. "Glad you could make it."

"Ran into Joe after you left. I suppose he felt sorry for me."

"Speak for yourself." I smiled. I couldn't tell if I was pleased or pissed off that he was coming to dinner too. I had decided earlier that I was looking forward to spending an evening with Joe and meeting his wife after all this time.

"Not that anyone should feel sorry for either one of us," Monty added.

I held up my hand to signal for him to say no more. The two of us followed Joe into the kitchen to chat with Elena and to see if we could help her with anything while she finished last-minute preparations. Elena shooed us away and said that we absolutely could not help her. She told Monty and me to sit, and put Joe to work opening both bottles of wine. Monty and I took seats at a small counter dividing the kitchen from the dining area.

"I'm making corn chowder for us tonight for starters," she said, her eyes large and brown. She had that sophisticated, Audrey Hepburn look with her dark hair pulled back in a bun at the nape of her neck. She moved gracefully around the kitchen, but I could sense that there was an energy to her small frame that bristled and revved, waited to escape as soon as she felt more at ease with her guests.

Joe gave us each a glass of wine and we sat at the counter and chatted. Joe was talking about his acreage and how it was to raise cattle when out the kitchen window, an older, white Toyota truck rusting near the front bumper drove up, and Elena said, "Oh, hon, did you invite Heather?"

"Nope." Joe stood to go greet her. In the fading light, I watched as Heather got out of the car. Then I saw the passenger side open and a young boy hopped out. A minute later, they all came into the small kitchen, and Joe introduced Monty and me to Heather again and to Lewis for the first time.

"I'm so sorry," Heather said to her mother and she bent, because she was much taller, to kiss her. "I didn't know you had company tonight. We just stopped by to say hi before heading to get some ice cream for a certain person with a big sweet tooth." She smiled at Lewis.

"Don't be silly." Elena threw a dish towel over her small shoulder. "Please, stay and join us. It's too cold out for ice cream. Plus it looks like rain."

"Can't. We're on a mission." She poked Lewis. "A chocolate-chip-mint mission."

"Well, at least have a drink with us before you leave," Joe offered, and Heather agreed, so we moved to the dining area and sat, while Elena continued to fiddle around with dinner preparations in the kitchen. I began to figure out how to gracefully ask Lewis about his relationship with Victor without upsetting any of the other family members.

"So, Lewis," I said, "what grade are you in now?"

"Fifth."

"That makes you"—I squinted—"eleven?"

He nodded.

"You must like martial arts?" I asked. "Judging by that mean roundhouse you gave your grandpa outside."

Lewis smiled; his bottom tooth in the center was angled crookedly against the one next to it. "I take Tae Kwan Do."

"That's awesome," Monty said. "Where do you do that?"

"In town, that gym up by the post office."

"That's so cool," Monty said, genuinely excited, and I could see a brightness, a twinkle, in his eyes when he looked at Heather. Suddenly, I wondered if the separation might be a sure thing after all. I decided to hold off on asking Lewis about Victor and made a mental note that I would circle back to visiting him at his mother's in the afternoon after he finished school.

. . .

When it was time for Heather and Lewis to leave and they said their good-byes, I made a quick decision to follow them out. I wanted a moment to ask Heather about visiting Lewis at her sister's.

When Heather heard my hurried, scuffed walk to catch them on the driveway, she turned, her eyes electric and filled with a startle.

"Sorry," I said. "Didn't mean to spook you."

"Oh no, it's fine. You didn't really."

Suddenly I felt shy and sheepish. "I, I was just going to ask you about your sister."

Heather glanced at Lewis. "Go ahead and hop in, honey. I'll be right there."

Lewis did as she said and I added, "I mean, nothing much." I lowered my voice so Lewis couldn't hear me. "Just thought it would be good to talk to Lewis actually." I twitched my head toward the car. "Possibly sometime tomorrow. I wanted to get your input before I surprised them."

Heather frowned and shrugged. "I'm not sure what I'm supposed to say. I mean, you need to do what you need to do."

"What I meant—do you think Lewis is mature enough to chat about Victor a bit without upsetting him? Nothing major, just a few questions."

"I guess. I suppose it would be fine. You're not going to get too detailed about—" She looked down. "About things?"

"No, just some general impressions. That's all. It's just general procedure."

"My sister might be a little tough to convince."

I nodded. "Well, we'll give it a shot. I'm sure she won't mind that much."

Heather shrugged again and looked down at the keys in her hand.

"Better get that boy some ice cream." I smiled, holding my hand out toward the car door to signal that I didn't have much else to say. I felt silly for following her out. I had the gentlemanly urge to open her car door for her but realized that would be totally ridiculous.

"Yeah, you're right. I better." She smiled back at Lewis, then looked at the ground as she shuffled by me. I was probably just imagining it, but I felt a frisson of excitement as she passed.

"Drive safely, then."

"Thanks, I will."

Just as she opened her car door, Monty stepped out onto the landing and waved. A big grin spread across his face. Heather waved back, and I saw Lewis waving through the passenger window as well. As she slid into the driver's seat, her blond hair a pale flashing flag in the dim light, a pang of something I hadn't felt in a long time shot through me. It occurred to me that maybe the world was full of women whom things could actually work with; that maybe my experience with Shelly was not a blueprint for how each and every one of my potential relationships would turn out.

I watched Heather and Lewis back out and drive away, then turned to go back to the door, where Monty stood with one eyebrow raised in question.

"Just checkin' to see if she thought Lewis was stable enough to chat with tomorrow."

Monty smirked. "And?"

I nodded. "No problem."

"That's good." Monty was still smiling, peering down the drive where Heather had departed.

. . .

Elena refused to let us help her clean up in the kitchen, so after we had the chowder and grilled steaks that Joe claimed were the half head of cattle he'd gotten from the neighboring farm, and at least cleared the table, we moved into the living room to sit by the fire Joe had made. Joe offered me some brandy, and the three of us sat staring into the fire. "I've spoken to Walsh about getting the divers back out to search the South Fork Bridge."

"And?"

"Not happy about it. Says they've already done the two most probable bridges in the park and see no reason to spend the resources on the third bridge all the way in Hungry Horse."

I sighed. "But even though it's on the highway, it's actually the most concealed by trees and the deepest. It would be my first choice if I were going to toss it."

"Yeah, I have to admit, mine too," Monty added.

Joe nodded that he understood.

"I'll call him tomorrow," I said. "See if I can talk him into one more dive."

"Suit yourself. In the meantime, I've also spoken to Ford about the bear, as you asked me to," Joe said as soon as he handed me the glass of brandy. Monty turned it down, saying he needed to head home soon because he was short on sleep.

I thanked Joe. "And?"

"I've bought you guys some more time." Joe sat in an armchair beside the couch I was seated in. "I told him we'd set up some heat lamps to change the temperature in his cage for a few days to try to fool his system."

"You think that'll work?" Monty asked.

"We'll find out," Joe said.

"And if it doesn't," I said. "You know I may need to take more drastic action? You know that, right?"

Joe turned as if he were peering past the reflection into the darkness outside. He sat thinking.

"I just can't let this bear go without the slug," I reiterated.

"I know that." His eyes were intense, but calm, his mouth slightly open. Suddenly I couldn't help but think that there was something in them that reminded me of my father's, but I couldn't tell if I was recalling his expressions correctly or simply conjuring false memories.

"What did Ford say?"

"He's fine. He's not particularly happy. He wants this bear released as soon as possible. And so does the committee. He says he's simply following the committee's recommendation."

"But you understand law enforcement. You know I can't have this bear set free without that slug."

"I know."

"Even if it means I go higher up, which I don't want to do. I don't want an all-out fight with Ford over this."

Joe nodded. "I know," he repeated. "Hopefully, it won't be necessary. The heat lamps should trick his system into a little more regularity."

"And what's the committee saying about that?"

"They're not thrilled with that either, because it screws with his system right before hibernation. They believe he could have already evacuated and is in need of forming his intestinal plug for hibernation as we speak. But if it's a matter of cutting him open or doing the lamps, they'll take the lamps."

"Has Ford always been such a stickler about this stuff?"

Joe shrugged. "He made the call to put that old sow down last summer that was getting too friendly with the tourists and teaching her cubs the same behavior. He got a ton of flack about it. I don't think he wants any more bad press over putting another one down, especially one that's done nothing wrong."

"And that's all to it?"

"Yeah, why? What else would there be? You think there's something else?"

I wanted to tell Joe that I thought Ford had something against me, that he simply didn't like me, but I knew I'd sound petty and childish—perhaps paranoid. "No," I said. "Nothing else. Just curious. You know how it gets when there are too many cooks in the kitchen."

"Yes, yes I do." Joe smiled and took a sip of the rich amber liquid. "Why do you think I'm out here and Elena's in there?"

17

It had been exactly six days since Victor Lance was found tied to a tree in the middle of the woods near McGee Meadow. And even though it had felt like weeks to me, I knew those six days were too long to be mucking around with the case. I should have solved the damn thing within the first two days.

I had turned down an extra glass of brandy at Joe and Elena's, got home at a decent hour, and woke early to drizzle the following morning. I had called Walsh first thing and gotten a big, fat no on getting another dive going in the South Fork River. Then I made sure I was on Lou's doorstep by seven a.m. "I need to speak to you again."

Lou sighed. "Let's take a walk." He grabbed his coat off the hook and glanced back over his shoulder into the house. "Becky just got up. She'll be getting in the shower in a minute."

"Fine with me." I lifted my head to the drizzle I'd woken to. "I've got a hat."

Lou put on a baseball cap as well as a jacket. We walked out into the light rain, down the driveway, and took a left toward Lake McDonald. I could feel raindrops splat on my nose. I zipped my coat up further because the temperature had dropped at least fifteen degrees from the day before. Lou shoved his hands into his pockets.

"What do you need to know now?" Lou asked, resigned.

"I need to know why you placed bets for Victor. I'm not buying it that you'd just do that for him, knowing full well what a wild card he was and that you'd end up having to cover for him."

Lou stopped and squinted at the sky, letting the drizzle cover his face. "Looks like it could turn to snow by this evening. Definitely getting cold enough." He began walking again. "It's a long story."

"I'm up for it," I said.

He sighed. "I probably should be in a confessional for this."

"Well"—I gestured to the mountains—"it's as good as any church around here. I'm not as good as a priest, but I'll have to do."

"Age-old story, I guess." Lou rubbed his temple. "About two years ago, I had a fling with another woman. Becky still doesn't know. It was brief, and, like all affairs, a mistake, but it happened. I'm not proud of it, but it is what it is."

I shrugged. "And?"

"Victor found out about it, and when he came to me wanting to bet and I said no, he confronted me with it. Said he'd tell Becky if I didn't let him in on the action. He'd heard from Megan that I'd won about eight grand the season before."

"So you took him seriously?"

"Absolutely. He was so obnoxious and a total wild card. There's no question that he'd tell her if I didn't do what he wanted me to. And the same with the eighteen hundred—he insisted I pay his debt or he'd tell. And"—he shook his head—"I couldn't have that. I love Becky, and I know this would have been the last straw. We'd been through a lot with me gambling, and I planned on stopping, but to find out about this affair, I know she'd leave me. I was drinking a lot too when it occurred. I was a mess, but I got that under control, and I quit the gambling as well. I don't know why I started again, other than we needed some money. We were always fighting over finances, and I figured if I could just have another good run, it would be the last time I would do it, and it could really help us out if I got ahead."

"How did Victor know about your fling?"

"I think he found out from Leslie, his girlfriend."

"Leslie? How did she know?"

Lou paused and stared at the lake. The clouds had crept in low and the rain fell quietly on the still water. Two mallards floated, dunking their heads and flapping their wings near the dark shoreline. I heard geese calls from high above somewhere to the north. "I don't know for sure."

"Then why do you suspect her?"

"Because the woman I briefly got involved with was her mother."

And there I had it. Lou had just spilled his guts to me and in the process provided himself with a major motive for getting his pesky nephew out of the picture. Still, now more than ever, I didn't think Lou had committed the crime. Perhaps I was being a sucker, drawn in by the very fact that he was confiding in me, telling me his darkest secrets, so I was being overly generous. Shelly used to say that I was a sucker for other people's problems. Still, I did not believe the person who tied Victor Lance to a tree for an entire night was Lou Shelton.

I tried to picture Lou with Elena. Elena. Graceful and poised, cheating on Joe with Lou. It made my stomach turn. I overwhelmingly wanted to protect Joe from any of this nonsense, and suddenly I could feel my generosity fade and my anger begin to rise at the thought of him sleeping with Joe's wife.

We walked on to McDonald Creek, which drew from the lake and fed the Middle Fork River. We paused by the creek. "So you think Leslie found out about you guys from her mother?" The sharpness in my voice betrayed me.

"I'm not positive." Lou hung his head. "I know that Leslie's not welcome at the house. Mainly because of Joe, and it's a sore point in their marriage. Leslie's been a handful for them her entire life, but it hurts Elena to write her off like that. I think that once in a while Elena visits Leslie without mentioning it to Joe."

Elena, I thought again. What would drive her to someone like Lou Shelton? How many years younger than Joe was she? Was Joe working too much? Getting too old? Not paying enough attention to her? Lou looked together, the mountain man type with a bit of mystery, a bad boy, replete with gambling and drinking. I could see how he might be a draw to a bored housewife with some midlife issues. Suddenly, an image of Elena looking down at her plate during dinner the previous evening when Lou's name came up in relation to Victor made perfect sense. "You know Lou?" I had asked Elena. She had glanced at Joe, then sliced her steak with her knife. "Just from around the park. It's a very small world around here, Agent Systead." I had laughed because I'd heard the cliché so many times by now, that the song "It's a Small World (After All)" was starting to play a running track in my head.

"You think Elena would have actually told Leslie something as personal as that, though?" I asked Lou.

"I really can't imagine it, but maybe. It's the only thing I could think of. Unless someone saw us together and told Victor. But like I said, the whole thing lasted no more than two weeks before we figured out what selfish, unrealistic assholes we were being and called everything off, including our friendship. During those two weeks, we were extremely careful. We probably only got together a few times."

"And this was two years ago?"

"Yeah, just about." Lou kicked some mud with his boot.

I heard the flock of Canada geese getting closer, who were honking louder, now to the west, but couldn't see them. The drizzle was getting lighter, and a milky-white mist that had lain over the lake had lifted and collected at the base of the mountains. I felt like we were in some dream world.

"As far as Victor, though," Lou said. "The betting's not all he was blackmailing me for."

"Oh?" I turned to him.

"He also knew that Ford has been offering me a willing sale."

"You told him about it?"

"No, are you kidding? I wouldn't tell him anything if I could help it. I think he found out from his mom because, besides Becky, my sister was the only one I spoke to about the sale. I mean, I thought she ought to know, being my sister and all."

"Not your brother, Mark?"

"I didn't say anything to him. He'd find out soon enough, but I didn't want to involve him. He can be overbearing."

"Would the place be split between the three of you?"

"My dad left it to me, not to be unfair, just because he knew I loved it, worked it—always took care of it for him. He left other things for Penny and Mark, but it's kind of a sore spot with Mark."

"So you decide who it goes to?"

"That's right."

"And you have a will with the decision already made?"

"I should, but I don't. Just procrastination, I guess. Becky and I have been talking about it for some time."

"And?"

"And we've been talking about the sale because we know that very few in the family appreciate this place the way we do. It might just be better off with the park. But we haven't decided that yet."

"And?" I repeated.

"Victor knew that the place is worth a lot and that if I go through with the sale, that when I go, the place goes to the park, not to Penny, Mark, or the grandchildren. And if I don't do the sale, it would go to Penny if I go before her, then the grandchildren even though the will wasn't specific beyond me. Victor knew that was a losing proposition for him because not only did that mean years of waiting, but if the place was eventually handed down to the grandchildren, including my own, they'd just fight over it, and if they sold it, the profit would be split many different ways. Victor wanted me to accept the willing sale—to take the money up front and split it with him. And, of course, if I didn't, he said he'd tell Becky about Elena and Joe about me."

I whistled. Like Monty, I couldn't help it.

"Yeah, crazy little shit he was. He was pretty much blackmailing me on a few levels."

"Do you realize what kind of a motive this gives you for wanting Victor out of the way?"

Lou nodded. "I do, and it's why I've been so nervous about talking to you. But I swear on my life"—Lou turned to face me, placed a fist against his chest, his knuckles white and wet from the drizzle—"I had nothing to do with Victor's death."

. . .

I wasn't sure what to make of my conversation with Lou. In a way, it had been like talking to a criminal or someone very adept at manipulation. Still, in spite of all the games Lou had played, I had a sense that he was telling me the truth, at least about being innocent of Victor Lance's murder.

On my way to see Elena, I called Monty and filled him in. He'd been surprised and bummed about Lou's fling with Elena and was having a hard time imagining it. "They've always seemed so great together, so content," he had said. I thought of Joe and his fatherly eyes. The thought of his own wife hurting him rankled me deep down.

After telling Monty to meet me later in the afternoon to visit Lewis, I mentioned that I wanted a better sense of Victor's relatives, specifically, his uncle Mark and his cousins, including Lou's kids, who might be in line for the Shelton cabin when Lou was gone. I told him he was perfect for the job since he knew so much about the inholdings. I told Monty to let them do the talking; that he'd be surprised what people offer up when you listen quietly and don't bombard them with questions.

I found Elena at the catering business in Evergreen called Tasty Peaks Catering. Her business wasn't far from Penny Lance's neighborhood, and when I entered the store that was part of a larger strip mall on LaSalle Road, the smell of baking cake, chocolate, and something lemony hit me. I stood at the counter, where one of those silver bells stood for me to ring, but I didn't hit it because I hate those annoying things. I waited a moment longer for someone to come out, and just as I hovered my hand over the bell, Elena stepped out from a door near the back carrying a large box, which, judging by its elongated shape and serrated edging on the flap, was a warehouse supply of cling wrap. She smiled when she saw me, placed the box down, and came over.

"Hello, Ted." She lifted her chin. "What brings you here? Did you forget something at the house last night?" She was as poised and elegant as the night before, even in a thick-cloth navy apron plastered with baking flour tied around her slight waist.

"No, no," I said. "I wanted to thank you for the great dinner though." I rubbed my belly. "I haven't eaten that well in a while."

"It was our pleasure. But"—she cocked her head to the side—"something tells me you didn't come all the way to tell me that."

"I confess. I did want to chat with you about Leslie, you know, since she was involved with Victor Lance. Dang." I lifted my nose to the air. "It smells good in here. What are you making?"

"A wedding cake for tonight." She glanced at her watch. "That's the trouble with my business. I have to work on weekends. I can chat for a few minutes, but then I need to get cranking on the canapés. Come on back to my office."

I followed her to a small room cluttered with stacks of papers and envelopes. A laptop lay on a small black desk, which she sat before. She motioned for me to sit in the chair next to the desk. "What can I help you with?"

"I'm guessing you're aware that Leslie and Victor had a relationship. If not, forgive me for intruding."

"No, I know. Joe filled me in."

"Is that the first time you knew about it?"

Elena looked down at her lap and tucked a loose strand of hair that had escaped her ponytail behind her ear. "No." She looked back at me, heavy-lidded through long lashes. I could see a sexy quality in her that I had not noticed at dinner the night before. "No, I knew about the relationship, but I never told Joe. You have to understand, there's been a lot of, shall we say" —she bit her lower lip— "dysfunction in our household when it comes to our second daughter. She's pretty much put us through hell over the years."

I didn't say anything.

"In order not to enable her," she continued, "we try to keep the contact to a minimum, and let's just say that my husband's better at doing that than I am."

"She's your daughter," I said. "That's understandable."

"She is that all right." She looked down again, this time to her side, to the imitation-wood laminate flooring. I sensed a great sadness.

"And is there anything you can tell me about your daughter's relationship with Victor Lance that might be useful? Anything at all that struck you as strange?"

"There were a lot of things strange about Victor Lance from what I understand. Or maybe not strange, just despicable and predictable. Leslie wouldn't admit it, but I think she gave him money. Money," Elena said sharply, "that should have been used on Lewis for new shoes, clothes, food, anything but on him." She said *him* with disdain. "Heather and I are always buying things for Lewis to keep him in clothes that fit. See"—she stood up and leaned against the door jamb—"that's what I mean—enabling."

"Well." I had to shift in my seat to face her. "He is your grandson."

"That's right. And I'm not going to watch the poor boy walk around in clothes two years too young for him because his mother was giving money to a boyfriend who just squandered it away on drugs."

"How did you know that was the case?"

"Leslie's been on and off drugs since she was thirteen. She's been trying to stay clean for the past year or so."

"Was she using with Victor?"

"I'm not positive, but I think she was clean when she met him.

She'd been through some treatment, but"—she sighed loudly and walked around me and sat back down at her desk—"it's hard to say. It's probably impossible to stay clean if you're an addict and you're hanging out with an addict. Both Heather and I tried to talk her into dumping him after we found out about him."

"And how did you find out about him using?"

"Heather knew somehow, through the grapevine and by just observing their relationship. It was obvious—his erratic behavior, things that Lewis would mention to Heather, like parties at Leslie's home and the people there, bruises on Leslie's face . . . plus word gets around in a small community like this."

I thought about the possibility of her and Lou having long, confiding conversations about Leslie, about Victor. "Do you know why anyone would want to hurt Victor? Did Leslie ever say anything to you about something that might be bothering her or him?"

"No, we didn't discuss him. Most of what I knew about Victor was from Heather. Leslie confided in her sister more than me. Even though I still have contact with Leslie now and again, it's slim because things are so strained between her father and her. Like I said, I just end up enabling her despite my best efforts. It just causes a fight between Joe and me. Heather, on the other hand, well, you know sisters."

I nodded. "Is Heather married?"

"No, not anymore. She used to be—in her twenties. She was with him for about nine years and got divorced in her midthirties." Elena shrugged, and I felt slightly embarrassed for asking something that didn't really pertain to my line of questioning. "She dates here and there," she added with a slight smile.

"Did you know Victor's uncle?"

Elena looked slightly confused, and I saw a twitch—a quick fluttering of her lashes, at the mention of his name. "Yes." She pursed her lips. "From around. I catered a function that he was organizing a few years ago—for Ducks Unlimited or something like that."

"Did you know that Lou was his uncle?"

"Yeah, I think I knew that somehow. It's a small community."

I'll bet, I thought. *Really small.* "Did you ever speak to him about Leslie and Victor?"

She paused, then shook her head. "No, not that I can recall. Why would I?" She stood up again and began pacing around the small room, and I could see the energy or nervousness I'd noticed in her in her kitchen begin to flare. Leslie obviously inherited some of her mother's high energy, then, unfortunately, got in the habit of ramping it up even further with meth. "I don't think Victor and Leslie were even involved when I did that event." She fiddled with the tie on her apron that was wrapped around her back, brought to the front, and tied at her slender waist. "Agent Systead," she said, and I noted that she had reverted back to my title instead of using my first name as she'd done when I came in, "are you thinking Louis Shelton had something to do with this horrible crime?"

"I'm thinking I need to check all avenues."

"But you wouldn't be checking on him unless something was pointing in his direction."

"We've got a lot of directions that we're going in right now. I'm just trying to narrow things down. Like I said, if you have anything at all that could be helpful, please let me know." I slid my card across her desk. "And if you have any leftovers from that cake"—I held my nose up to the air and smiled slightly—"you can also let me know that."

She smiled back, but it was a weak one. Her large, suddenly busy eyes revealed that thoughts raced across her mind. "I can't imagine that Mr. Shelton would have anything to do with that horrible business," she added.

"Yeah, I know. It's hard to imagine *anyone* having anything to do with it even knowing the victim was not very well liked. Did Leslie ever mention an Andrew Stimpson to you?"

"No, why? Was he a friend of hers?"

"He was a friend of Victor's." I stood.

"A dealer?"

I didn't answer.

"No." Elena peeked out her office door toward the front of the shop. I assumed she was signaling that she needed to get cranking on her work. "She never mentioned names of anyone to me. She'd be too afraid I'd tell her father, and with him in law enforcement in the park, she knew better than to talk to me, especially about dealers."

18

WHILE I WAITED for Monty to return from talking to some of the Shelton family members, I sat in our office and had a cup of coffee and spread the Saturday local news out. I was immediately surprised to see an article on the front page with the headline "Waiting for Caged Grizzly to Provide Evidence."

I felt something instantly wither inside of me. "Shit." It came out as a whisper. I read on, hoping there was no mention of the damn bullet. I'd not made it past the first two paragraphs when Eugene Ford stormed in my office with the paper in hand. Apparently we were on the same page, in more ways than one.

"Did you give them this information?" he asked.

"I was just going to ask you the same thing."

"How the hell do they know we're holding this bear? I've allowed no such information to go out." He looked at me with disdain. He really thought that I had filled the media in.

"Do you think I'm that stupid? You think I want to ruin my chances of getting the guy because he reads this and gets rid of the weapon?"

Ford shook his head. "This is all I need. People breathing down my neck for why we have this grizzly in our possession instead of out where it belongs."

"If you don't mind my saying"—I cleared my throat—"I think you're reading too much into the public's sympathies for this animal. Bears are put down all the time around here, and it's always in the news."

"This is different." Ford set his jaw and glared at me. "The public knows this bear did nothing wrong. The last time we put a bear down without doing anything wrong other than teaching her cubs risky behavior, the public was outraged."

"The Lake Ellen Wilson bear?"

Ford nodded, then looked me in the eye. "Look, Systead, I know my park. I've been here for a long time."

"And I know investigations. Might as well have a headline that says 'Get Rid of Your Gun Now If You Haven't Already.'"

Ford continued to glare at me, his eyes in narrow slits like he was in some Clint Eastwood movie. I almost felt like laughing and might have honored the urge if I wasn't so upset over the mention of evidence. I looked down at the paper. "I haven't read more than a few paragraphs. Does it mention a slug?"

"No, but it's quite obvious for anyone with half a brain. Although you never know with the public. It's possible they believe we're waiting for him to crap out a wallet or a keychain or something. Who knows." He threw the paper on the table where Monty and I had all sorts of files, charts, field reports, and diagrams of the site spread out.

I scanned the rest of the article with Ford still standing before me—read that the grizzly was in a compound under surveillance for unknown reasons, most probably to observe its behavior, to get DNA samples, and to check for any other possible clues in the bear's scat.

Suddenly I laughed. Something about it sounded utterly ridiculous. I couldn't help it.

"You think this is funny?"

"Not the situation," I said. "Just the way, I don't know, the way it sounds."

"Well, I don't really care if he's falling short of some journalism award or not. I just want this to stay under our hats. You were the one saying we didn't give enough information in the first place." He scowled. "Well, you got your wish. Plenty of information is out there now."

"You know that's not what I meant." I stared straight into his eyes.

"It's a fine line. I just didn't want the reporter poking around where he didn't belong, which it looks like he's still doing. It's possible he just walked around the place and saw the bear on his own."

Ford shook his head as if he had decided that was unlikely. He stood silent for a moment, then picked the paper back up, rolled it into a cylinder, and pointed it at me. "I'll find out who's talked and get back to you."

"I'd appreciate that," I said in as even a voice as I could because at this point, my urge to laugh was gone and my blood boiling.

• • •

Monty showed up at two thirty as I had asked him to. I had to admit that I felt relieved that he was his usual punctual self because it gave me something I could count on—some certainty. Monty filled me in on who he'd seen so far: Mark and Angela and their kids. "They have four, all grown now, so it took me a while to track them all down."

"Anything interesting pop up?"

"Not really, Mark is kind of arrogant, maybe a little pissed off that daddy left the cabin to Lou and not him, but according to his wife, Angela, he got the house Roger and Eloise lived in C' Falls, which he's sold already and made some money off of. Mark wasn't all that chatty, but Angela was, so most of what I got was from her."

"What about the kids?"

"I only spoke to the oldest daughter, Sara, a cousin of Victor's. You probably saw her at the funeral. She lives in Whitefish now and works at a hair salon. She and her husband have three young children."

"She say anything of interest?"

"Nothing in particular. But she did mention that she was never su-perclose to Victor or Megan. That they were kind of weird. She said"—Monty raked his fingers through his hair and crinkled his face—"that she always wondered if the two of them had been abused when they were younger."

"Physically, sexually?" I asked.

"She didn't say, but I got the feeling she meant sexually. Said that Penny dated a few interesting men that kind of gave her the creeps when she was a teenager. Victor and Megan were younger than she was."

"So not by the father?"

Monty shrugged. "She only mentioned the boyfriends."

"Well, it wouldn't surprise me. It would explain Victor's drug use and abusive tendencies." I looked at my watch. "Good work," I said and meant it. Monty must have done something right for a family member to give that much personal information to a cop. "Think you can be as smooth with Lewis?"

"I'll try," Monty said.

• • •

When we got to the mobile home, no one was there. We poked around, then sat in the car in the driveway, out of the chill and the light drizzle. I kept wondering about the collapse in Monty's home life, so I asked him how it was going with his wife. He said all was cool for the time being. That it was amazing how much pressure was relieved the minute you got two people not getting along out from under the same roof. I thought of Shelly and how we couldn't speak for months after the split, but eventually became cordial.

"Suddenly, some manners come back—you know, some decency. It's amazing how that all seems to go out the window and be taken for granted when you're together in the thick of it."

I listened, rolling my quarter, watching its shiny surface cascade over each knuckle, then I broached the subject. "The separation, your idea or hers?"

"Hers. Definitely hers."

"Why?"

Monty made a long sigh. "Oh man, it's complicated, right?"

"Always is, but there's always that last straw, that one thing that makes someone take action."

"You sound like you've been there?"

"I was married before. When I lived here."

"Oh." Monty leaned farther back in his seat. The vinyl squeaked as he shifted. "When you were on the force?"

I nodded.

"What happened?"

"She had a miscarriage, and I guess we . . ." I stopped my quarter, moved it to my palm and squeezed. I surprised myself that I gave that information up so freely because I've told no one about the miscarriage besides Ma and my sisters. "We," I added. "Or maybe not we, maybe I should say *I*, I wasn't much help in how we dealt with it."

"Sorry to hear that."

I shrugged. "It's history now."

"You never remarried?"

"Nah, man, are you kidding? With this job and all the traveling I do, it's definitely for the best that I stay single."

Monty furrowed his brow as if he was considering that for himself, weighing what a big decision that actually was. I had made it sound so simple—as if being alone was weightless and easy and exactly as it should be for a detective. No questions asked, spoken like a teenager with the world before him. "That's a pretty big sacrifice," he said.

"Well, it's not as hard as you think. It's not like I'm meeting lifelong potential mates that I'm having to turn away constantly."

Monty blew out a stream of air again. "Marriages are hard. They're really hard. No one tells you that when you're young. Even when you watch your own parents go through their shit, you think it will be different for you, riding off into the sunset and all, but then you end up making a mess of everything in spite of your best intentions."

I sat quietly in case he wanted to continue, wondering what kind of mess Monty—Mr. Tidy—could possibly make.

"I mean, it's not like she didn't know my deal when we got married."

"Your deal?"

"That I didn't want to start a family."

"Because of your work?" I couldn't imagine his duties at Ford's desk somehow precluding him from raising a family, but then he said, "No, that's not it."

"So that was the *thing*—the last straw?"

Monty nodded. "I guess that's a big part of it, but it's never really just one thing." Monty flicked his finger over the edge of the window control.

"Why don't you want to have kids?" I wanted to add that I thought he was definitely the father type. Careful, controlled, and thoughtful. Maybe too serious, but kids would probably loosen him up a bit, make him giggle and laugh, but I didn't. I thought of Ryan in his dad's lap, tickling him under his armpits, and Ian's huge smile and bursting laughter.

Monty shrugged, a sliver of a shadow suddenly inserting itself into the air between us, mostly settling on him, for a change. Since I'd stepped foot on this case, I felt that shadow cling to me like resin. "That's a whole other story," he said.

I looked down the empty drive. "Looks like we've got time."

He continued to flick at the control. "Let's just say I don't trust my family line."

"What, your dad into alcohol or something?"

Monty laughed. "Oh, *hell*, yeah he's into alcohol. I *wish* that was the only issue."

Again, I waited, looking down the road. The shadow settled back between us, and I thought maybe Monty would offer more, but decided it best not to pry. Out of my peripheral vision, I could see Monty shaking his head slowly. "Nah, this issue tends to skip a generation and go right to your offspring."

"Oh," I said, "that sounds fairly serious." I glanced at him, then looked back down the road, nonchalantly rolling my quarter again.

"It's serious enough to not fool around with." Monty followed my gaze down the drive. He didn't offer any more, and I didn't ask. We sat silently for another moment or two, the quiet needling me and making me fidget. I shoved down the stubborn little voice telling me I was an idiot for mentioning my private life with Shelly to anyone other than my family. I started to pull out my phone to check to make sure it wasn't on silent mode and that I hadn't missed any important calls, when a silver car suddenly turned onto the drive. Monty sat taller, and I put my quarter in my pocket. We both opened our doors and stepped out.

Lewis and Leslie got out of the car and Leslie ordered him to go in and change out of his dobok. She opened her trunk and grabbed a bag of groceries. She looked better than the last time we saw her, as if she'd put on a pound or two and her hair seemed—I wouldn't say shinier— but at least less dull and less stringy.

"Need some help?" Monty offered.

She didn't answer immediately, just studied us with suspicion. "Why are you here?"

"We were hoping to speak to Lewis."

"Lewis? What for?"

We explained that it was nothing serious and that we just wanted to speak to him since he was involved with Victor, even minimally. "It's perfectly fine for you to be present," I said. "Although if you were okay with it, I have Officer Harris here with me since it's procedure to not speak to a minor alone, and the two of us could talk to him if you have other things you need to be doing."

She eyed us both, suspicion fully returning to her face. "What are you going to ask him?"

"The usual. How long he knew Victor, if he liked him, and if he didn't, why not?"

"I can answer all that. He knew him the amount of time I had him in our lives, and no, I don't think he particularly liked him."

"And I'm sure he'll say the same, but again, if this ever gets to court, we need to have it on record that we spoke to all of the people who were involved in Victor's life."

"That's a bunch of shit." She set the bag of groceries back in the trunk and looked at the front door Lewis had just entered. Then she grabbed at her purse around her shoulder, and I was thinking she wanted to get a cigarette or her Bible or both. "What does my son have to do with any of this?"

"So you're not giving us permission to speak to him?"

Leslie brought her free hand to her mouth and chewed her fingernails.

"I'm kind of thinking that you don't want it going on record that you wouldn't let us talk to him, that you maybe were afraid—"

"I'm not afraid." She let go of her purse, letting it swing back under her arm, and picked up the grocery bag again.

"Here, let us help you with those," I offered again.

She nodded and we each grabbed two paper bags and carried them into her kitchen and set them on the counter. Even the mobile smelled less stale than it had the week before. Immediately, she grabbed a cigarette out of a pack that she'd retrieved from her purse and lit it and deeply inhaled, her cheeks going hollow.

"Lewis just came from a Tae Kwan Do meet in Columbia Falls at the high school," she said proudly. "I was just there." She seemed to calm considerably with the cigarette, even wore a small smile as she described her whereabouts, perhaps pleased that she was acting like a normal mom attending her child's event. "My sister was there too."

"Your sister—she teaches Lewis, right?" I didn't think it wise to bring up the fact that we had a chummy dinner with Leslie's ma and pa the night before, given the strain between them all.

"That's right." Leslie set her cigarette down in an ashtray. "She's certified to do that. You know, black belt and all. And Lewis loves it. It's, it's probably a good thing for him." She picked her cigarette back up.

"Leslie," I said softly so Lewis couldn't hear from his room, and my voice must have resonated a seriousness because she looked at me, fear in her eyes, "did Victor ever hurt Lewis?"

Her eyes stayed wide and she glanced at Monty, then back to me. "No, no, sir. He just hurt me. He never touched Lewis. Thank God."

· · ·

Finally, Leslie agreed to let us chat with Lewis and we offered to wait outside. He came out in a pair of high-water jeans, old, ripped sneakers, and a blue jacket in need of a washing. I thought I detected a slight limp. "Hey, you hurt yourself at your meet?"

"A little," he said. "My aunt says I've just pulled a hamstring."

"You did that while sparring?"

"Yeah, I felt something while I was kicking, but it didn't seem bad at the time. It got worse later. My aunt gave me some cream for it."

"At your age," Monty said, "that should heal right up."

"Have a seat, Lewis." I motioned to the porch step and he sat down on the dirty green turf covering the step, not looking like his leg was too stiff. Monty and I sat on one of the porch steps as well. "How did you do in your meet?"

"Okay, I lost one round and won two."

"Awesome," I said. "That's great. Hey, do you know who we are and why we're here?"

"Yeah, you were at my grandparents. You're working with my grandpa—the guys investigating Victor's death." He picked up a twig off one of the steps.

"That's right. In case you forgot our names. This is Officer Harris." I gestured to Monty. "And myself: Agent Systead."

He gave a small nod.

"And since your mom dated Victor for a while and since you knew him too, it's standard procedure for us to talk to most people who knew him, sometimes even when they knew him only for a little bit."

Lewis rubbed the twig between his thumb and forefinger.

"Did you like Victor?"

"He was all right."

"Did you do a lot with him?"

"Yeah, I guess." He shrugged. "He was over here a lot when my mom was with him."

"Was he nice to you?"

"Yeah, I guess. Sometimes we played cards and stuff. Sometimes watched TV."

I glanced at Monty. I'd forgotten how difficult it could be to question a kid. It could either be really simple because they could ramble on and give you all sorts of interesting bits of information without even asking for it, or they could do the opposite, answer with short clips with many quiet spaces between. I looked back at Lewis, at his wavy, blond hair that I figured he'd either gotten from his dad or from his grandfather. He definitely had Leslie's and his grandmother's large, dark eyes. I momentarily felt a wave of gratitude flow through me that I had had a father for fourteen years. "And you liked him and your mom together?"

With the twig, he started sketching imaginary shapes on the faded green turf covering the step.

"Lewis?"

"Huh?"

"I asked you a question."

"Sometimes he could be pretty angry," he mumbled, his head down.

"You mean, lose his temper?"

He nodded.

"And what was that like?"

He shrugged and looked up at me. "Kind of scary, but it would always blow over and they'd make up. He usually lost it when he was drinking a lot."

"Did you see him hurt your mother?"

"I guess." He lowered his gaze to his stick again.

"How so?"

"Slaps and stuff. Sometimes he'd twist her arm."

"And did you tell anyone about it?"

"Victor said I'd get into trouble if I did. He said he didn't mean to hit her. I was kind of glad when they broke up, though. I like Paul better."

"I probably would too."

"Did you know Victor?" His eyes were curious.

"No, no, but I've heard a lot about him. I know he could be kind of volatile."

"Volatile?"

"Yeah, angry. Fly off the handle, like you said."

He nodded and went back to drawing shapes.

"Did he ever hurt you in any way?"

He stared at his shapes, kept drawing. "Can you tell what this is?"

I squinted at the step. "Do it again."

He drew the shape again.

"A flower?"

"Nope. You?" He pointed at Monty with the twig.

"Let me see it again," Monty said, and Lewis drew it two more times.

"A guitar?"

Lewis smiled a gap-toothed grin and nodded excitedly. "How about this?" He drew a different one.

"How about you finish answering Agent Systead's questions and then I'll guess again?"

Lewis glanced at me, and I asked again: "Did Victor ever hurt you?"

He looked down and shook his head.

"Did you ever hear of anyone talking about hurting Victor?"

"Nope," he said and drew another shape. "What's this?" he said to Monty.

"An airplane?"

Lewis smiled and nodded again.

. . .

When Heather returned after feeding the horses, I was waiting for her. The door to her house was unlocked, but I stood outside politely, watching her out in the field. She was carrying a large bale of hay and setting it down for a mule in an enclosed area near the barn. When she finished, a dog trotted crookedly beside her as she walked up a gravel road from a faded barn. It was evening, and the sun's rays shot under the chrome-colored cloud cover, illuminating Heather's hair and turning the hay field stretching away from the wooden fence along the road golden.

When she spotted me standing there, she cocked her head to the side, her blond mane falling to one shoulder. I could tell she was squinting, trying to make out who I was. I held up my hand. "Hello," I called out. "It's Systead."

She nodded but didn't change her pace as the dog, which I could make out was a type of border collie, black and white with a little brown on his pointy snout, ran toward me with a pronounced limp, but its tail wagging.

"I saw your car here." I held my hand out for the collie to smell, then pet the crown of his head, knobby under my palm. "So I knew you must be around." She was tall, maybe five-eleven, and I could see she was muscular from hauling hay, working the land, teaching martial arts.

"Welcome to my place." She pushed her hair off her shoulder and smiled a small, nervous smile as she came closer.

Suddenly the same shyness I felt at Joe's washed over me, so much so that I felt the need to look away for a moment. I glanced down at the collie. "What happened to him?"

"Got in the mule's area. Learned his lesson not to taunt her."

"I guess so. Poor guy." I knelt down and stroked behind his ear.

"Fractured his spine. He couldn't walk for a few days, but he's doing better and better. Swimming helps a lot. The doctor says to keep him moving." She pushed some hair behind an ear. "How can I help you?"

I refocused on why I'd come. "I thought I'd swing by to ask you a few questions about your sister, you know, just to try to cover all angles regarding Victor Lance." I stood back up, and the collie scratched my leg with his front paw for more attention. Heather snapped her fingers. "He's okay." I scratched behind his ear again. "I spoke to your mother earlier today, and she mentioned that you and Leslie are fairly close."

Heather shrugged. "As close as you can be to a lying addict. But yeah, I suppose. She's my sister after all. Would you like to come inside?"

"That'd be nice." I took off my cap and peered across the stubby hay field to a line of tall pine and cottonwood trees in the distance that I knew stood by the bank of the Flathead River. "You own up to the river?"

"Yeah."

"Must be hard work." *For someone on her own*, I thought but didn't say and thought of her mother smiling and saying that she dated once in a while.

"I manage all right. The horses graze the field. The winter's tough, keeping them fed and exercised. Sometimes I hire a little help if things get crazy. I need help with harvesting the hay, and keeping the weeds back in the spring and summer gets to be a full-time job." She walked up the porch steps and opened a sliding glass door that led directly into a small mudroom off of the kitchen. Open shelving stood on one side and was cluttered with tack, tools, different-size rucksacks, water bottles, flashlights . . . "Sorry about the mess." She removed her heavy boots, her jacket, and told me that it was fine for me to keep my shoes on.

The house, an old farmhouse, was modest with old, dated linoleum countertops, oak cabinetry, and a tiled kitchen floor that looked as if it had been redone more recently. She motioned for me to sit at the kitchen table and asked if I'd like something: tea, a beer, coffee. I told her I had a late lunch and didn't need a thing. She grabbed herself a beer, took a seat across from me, and pushed more blond strands of hair behind her ear again.

"You've lived here long?" I asked.

"'Bout five years. I lived closer to Columbia Falls before that. After my divorce, I was happy to get some acreage and the horses."

"Similar to your folks' spread?"

"I guess so, yeah. It's what I grew up with. I like the space."

I was deciding whether to ask about her marriage or about Leslie, but a part of me simply wanted her to talk about her life, to let her take the lead and fill me in about living alone near the Flathead River with a dog and horses and a couple head of cattle. But she didn't say anything, just stared at me with her green, unreadable eyes and dark eyebrows. I thought I noticed tiny flecks of gold reflecting in the light. "This business with Victor Lance," I said, "did you ever spend time with Leslie and him?"

"I was around them a few times. Sometimes they'd bring Lewis over to hang out with me while they'd go to do something." She began picking at the corner of its label.

"Lewis. He's a sweet boy."

Heather nodded. "He's a good kid. Deserves better than the mom he got, but she's doing her best to stay clean, and I think things are going pretty well. He's doing better in school now that things are a little more stable. How did it go with him?"

"Oh fine. Perfectly fine." I gave a half smile. "Was he not doing so well before?"

"He struggled for a bit, as you'd expect with a mom who goes through stages of not being very"—she shrugged—"present or tuned in to her child's needs. Leslie's does her best, but she's sick. Call it narcissism, addiction, or bipolar disorder—I don't know what the hell the label is. She's been called it all. All I know is that when you get hooked on drugs when you're a teen, in my opinion, it seems to screw up your chemical makeup forever. Warps your mind, makes you immature, unable to cope well, always putting your own needs first like a teenager."

"You spend a lot of time with Lewis?"

"A bit. I try to help out as much as I can. I don't want to enable her, but I like to be in his life. I try to provide as much stability as possible."

"Enable. That's what your mom said too."

Heather chuckled. "Hang out with addicts for a bit and it doesn't take long to speak the psychobabble."

"Leslie went through treatment?"

"For a month. At a local inpatient facility in Kalispell."

"Before, during, or after her involvement with Victor?"

"About seven or eight months before Victor. She'd been doing really well." Heather looked down, her eyes heavy, and when she looked back up she appeared more tired than I first noticed when she walked up from the barn with her cheeks flushed from the cold. Now I could see faint dark shadows under her eyes, and I wondered how difficult it must actually be to hold down a farm on your own with little help. "She did okay with Victor for a while and even influenced him some, got him to settle a bit, but eventually, it just got out of control."

"Out of control?"

"Well, come on, two meth heads having a relationship?" She lifted her brow to me. "A little here, a little there until both were using pretty regularly about three months into their relationship."

"What made her break it off with him?"

"He was abusive, and it got worse when he was using."

"She told you that?"

Heather nodded. "She didn't need to." She took a sip of her beer, and I wished I had accepted the offer to have a drink. "She'd show up with a hurt arm or a bruised eye, always making excuses, saying she bumped into something. You know, classic behavior for that kind of shit."

I was slightly surprised she swore; she seemed too poised for that, but she also seemed tough and not afraid to say what she wanted. "And she had the wherewithal to get out?"

Heather stood up and walked to the kitchen. "You sure you don't want anything?"

"Actually, I'll join you for one of those." I pointed at the bottle in her hand.

She fetched one out of the fridge. "Would you like a glass?"

"Bottle's fine."

She grabbed the opener off the counter, opened the bottle, handed it to me, and sat back down. "She broke it off with him more than once. I'm actually speaking of the first time, back in, oh, I don't know, I guess it was January. It took lots of questions and prodding before she opened up, but one night, it got really out of hand and she brought Lewis to me because she was getting afraid. After Lewis went to sleep, I pinned her down, wouldn't let her leave without telling me what was going on." She took a swig of beer, then licked both of her lips. "So she agreed to tell me only if I didn't say anything to Mom or Dad. I agreed and she spilled her guts about his temper. I did my best to help her. In large part for Lewis's sake."

"How did you help her?"

"It's a long story." She ran a hand through her hair, raking it away from her forehead and letting it fall back down in a golden wave.

"I've got time and"—I smiled my signature half smile and held up my beer—"I've got a beverage now."

"First step was simply supporting her, getting her to wean off the meth, and getting her to open up. Once she cleared her head"—she looked toward a hallway, which I assumed had a spare bedroom—"she stayed here for a bit. Anyway, once she saw the light, I simply supported her in the breakup, which she did much better and stronger than I imagined she would. I was guessing that the year of counseling was paying off a bit because once she decided that she would get out of the relationship, she held pretty strong, at least for a month or so."

"Only a month?"

"Maybe a month and a half or even two. It's kind of a blur, but yeah, probably more than a month. He was pretty pesky and hard to get rid of, and he kept coming around, so after several weeks of that,

I convinced her that we needed to go through the correct channels, through the police to get a restraining order placed against him. But that got messy because my sister is on record with social services for being a user and let's just say, she didn't have a lot of credibility with the system, and . . ." Heather tore the label even further off and started scratching at the remaining thin film of glued paper.

"And?"

She shook her head with a disgusted look. "She got back in the relationship before we even fully looked into the matter." She stood and went into the kitchen again and tossed her bottle in the trash. I thought she might grab another from the fridge, but she didn't. She simply leaned against the counter by the sink and folded her arms in front of her as if she was done with our conversation.

I stayed seated but turned sideways in my chair to face her. "And that was in February?"

"Near the end of February, I guess."

"And she stayed with him until summer?"

She nodded, her face blank but serious.

"And he continued to abuse her?"

"I think he was on his best behavior for a while, but then it started again, and I'm assuming that is why she ended it the second time, although, as I told you at headquarters, who really knows why. I'm sure it didn't hurt matters that she got interested in Paul, and who knows who was in his life at the time."

"And you like Paul?"

"Yeah. He's much, much better than Victor. Leslie's doing really well with him."

"Is he a user?"

"No, thank goodness. Not that I know of anyway."

"And Lewis?"

"What about him?"

"Did Victor hurt him?"

Heather glanced at the ceiling, then back at me, her arms still crossed before her. "I'm not positive, but I don't think so. He doesn't say much when I ask him."

I got up and went into the kitchen and leaned against the counter on the other end. "Do you know of anyone who would do this to Victor?"

"I'm sorry, I can't help you, Mr. Systead."

"Please, it's Ted. You know, I'm a friend of your dad's."

"I know." She looked down again as if she was shy, at the floor. "You're from the area."

I nodded.

"He speaks highly of you. But, as far as Victor is concerned, he was a real asshole. A lot of people might have wanted to hurt him, but I don't know who actually would."

"Paul?"

"No, I can't imagine. Why? Is he a suspect?"

"No, not really."

Heather looked out her kitchen window toward her barn. "I have a sick mare with a swollen ankle that's not eating," she said, and I felt a sinking sensation at being dismissed. I fought back the idea that my motives were not completely professional, that I really wanted to stay longer to get to know her better. "I was actually coming back to the house to grab her antibiotics," she said. "If you don't have any more questions, I'd like to get back out to her before it starts to get too dark to see if I can get her to eat with her medicine."

"Oh, no, that's good. Sorry to keep you." I drank the last of my beer and motioned that I would throw it in the trash under the sink, but she stayed where she was and held out her hand to grab it. "Thanks," I said. "If you don't mind, I'll need your number in case I think of anything else."

"Of course." She began opening a drawer for a notepad and wrote her number down for me. And when she handed it to me and gave me the same small, nervous smile as she did earlier, I felt shy all over again.

19

TWO DAYS BEFORE my twenty-fourth birthday, I read a front-page story about a grizzly attack on two men in a backcountry Yellowstone Park campsite. I know exactly where I was when I read the news—in a coffee shop in Missoula near the university surrounded by the buzz of the early fall semester energy. In fact, I always remember precisely where I am and what I am doing whenever I hear about a grizzly attack, the way people recall their whereabouts when they heard about Kennedy's assassination or 9/11.

The article said that the attack happened in the night near a lake about a mile and a quarter in from one of the main roads. The two men were each in their own tent on opposite ends of the site. With the first victim, the grizzly had torn open the tent while he slept, took him out of it, and dragged him about fifty feet away from his campsite, where his remains were found. Apparently, there were some screams, but judging by the tent, there didn't appear to be much of a struggle.

The second victim heard some of the commotion and screams off in the distance and wasn't sure what to do. By the time the grizzly came for him, he was still in his tent, and when the bear went for him, he screamed and thrashed. And the louder he cried out, the harder the bear bit down. He could hear his bones breaking. Then, as I can only imagine when one undergoes a traumatic event—his adrenaline pumping, his mind slowing down and putting things in some strange, perhaps logical perspective, he decided not to fight it. He mentioned

281

that it took all his strength to go completely limp, but when he did, the bear loosened his bite and left him there, injured. Luckily, there were two other people camping at the site: two male college-age students who helped him. One stayed with him and one ran back to their car to get help.

· · ·

Mom didn't ask about the park or about Ford anymore after that evening at Natalie's, which surprised me, given her nature to dive right into things without beating around the bush. I'd caught up with her on the phone a few times since dinner, and she'd simply ask, "How's the case going?" I'd usually give a one-word answer, like fine or good, and she'd get off the subject and go into details about her job or the grandkids. On our most recent chat when I returned back from Heather's place, she asked about the cabin and if I was comfortable there. I said it was fine.

"Do you ever go out?"

I assumed she meant for dinner. "Pretty much for all meals. Once in a while I cook, which in fact, I'm just about to do." I had picked up a steak and some fresh mushrooms at the grocery store in Columbia Falls on my way back from Heather's.

"I mean," she said, "on a date?"

I got off the subject as quickly as I could. I was pretty certain that Nat and she discussed my lack of a love life on a regular basis, but she wouldn't let it go, so I told her that I dated someone two months ago, but that it didn't work out.

"Why not?

"She was still hooked on her ex." I took the frying pan I'd used once before to make some eggs out of the drying rack by the sink and opened the old fridge and grabbed the butter I'd bought earlier in the week.

Ma went silent.

I found a colander, threw the mushrooms in, and turned the faucet on to wash them. I knew there was nothing she could say since it wasn't my doing that it had ended. I waited for her to say something, but she didn't. "Ma." I turned the water off. "You don't need to worry about me."

"I'm your mother; that's my job."

"I know. But I'm fine with or without someone in my life."

"I know you are," she said. "It's just that . . ." She trailed off.

I waited for her to say more, but didn't push for it. When she didn't, I promised her I'd come by soon.

. . .

While I was eating my steak and sautéed mushrooms, the worry in my mother's voice started to needle me. I chewed my steak too long until it felt thick and hard to swallow. I had no appetite and pushed my plate aside. I began pacing the cabin, unable to sit and relax. I poured myself a whiskey but didn't drink it. I tried to sit and read but couldn't focus on the words.

I pictured Aubrey, the last woman I'd dated, with her dark bobbed hair and round eyes. I had brought her to my apartment after dinner, put on some tunes, and poured some Cabernet. We talked for some time, laughed a bit, although probably not enough in retrospect, and when I kissed her it was nice. No sparks really, but nice. When I tried to go further with her—ran my hands under her shirt along her spine and eventually circled the butt of my hands so they were touching the sides of her breasts—she started to weep. I kissed a tear away and asked what was wrong. She poured it out then, that she'd been badly hurt by her last and still missed him.

That was pretty much the end of it. She called me three or four times after that wanting to go out again, saying she was better and that she regretted ruining things between us, but by then I'd thrown sturdy walls up. Decided I didn't need it in my life, and because of my traveling, she didn't need it either. I thought of Monty. *Marriages are hard. They're really hard. . . . Even when you watch your own parents go through their shit, you think it will be different for you. . . .*

From what I remembered, my parents made it look easy, but maybe I just was remembering our family history incorrectly. The thought of my memories being imperfect, that time morphs all events in our minds, stabbed at me more than usual.

I thought of Heather. A good-looking woman who seemed to be my age, living alone, not remarrying. Embarrassment over the fact that I wanted to have another beer with her, ask her about what went wrong for her, prickled me. I thought of Monty and how he seemed to pop right out of his sorrow over his separation and to light up around her. All men are such fools around attractive women, I thought.

I lay in bed for over an hour, restless and unable to drift off. I got up and paced some more, my mind or heart aching with some nameless want or need. The wind was picking up again outside, making the cabin creak. I opened the door and stepped out into the dark to take a deep breath. The cloud cover had broken and the stars shone above like billions of false promises. I went back in and threw on a pair of jeans and a sweatshirt and went back out to look at the night sky. Instead, I found myself walking up the driveway from my cabin's light and onto the dark road, where the night consumed me, enveloped me.

I could feel my breathing quicken and my sternum clench stronger. Maybe it was just the conversation with my mother getting to me, but suddenly I felt a wave of anxiety crash over me: me telling Monty about Shelly's miscarriage, Lou's confession about Elena, the caged grizzly with his beady eyes out there less than a mile from where I stood, Ford and our dislike of one another, Aubrey weeping under my kiss, Shelly divorced after two children. . . . All of these unrelated things pressed in on me from every direction, looking for cracks to leak into and gain momentum. I wanted to scream into the cold air, to scare every living thing out there in the brush and trees behind the cabin away.

I strode back into the cabin, determined, even though I had no specific goal. I grabbed my flashlight and went back out and started walking, a deliberate stroll, heading for headquarters while the forest vibrated around me.

About halfway there I began to hear a moaning, a low-pitched and eerie part-groan, part-whine sound that rippled through the woods. As I rounded the last cabin on the block, I could see a reddish glow in the darkness: the heat lights from the bear's cage. Someone had left them on. Surely, I considered, they were supposed to be off at night. The bear's whining seemed to grow louder, and I couldn't tell if it was because I was getting closer or if he was actually moaning more intensely.

I kept walking, slower and with more trepidation than I had been, but onward. My limbs felt as if they were on autopilot, carrying me through the dark toward a grizzly cage I could scarcely approach in the light of day with all sorts of park employees around. I barely noticed the leaves rustling or pebbles crunching under my feet on the gravel road that bypassed headquarters and led to the path to the cage.

When I reached the trail, the red glow and the moaning became more surreal—and for a moment I thought I was in one of my strange dreams. I walked down it—the one Ford and I had walked, past where I had stood frozen earlier in the week, and up to the cage. The wild smell of grizzly filled my senses, seemed to enter my pores, my eyes, my nose. My heart pounded in my chest. The bear had been pacing the length of the enclosure, and now that I stood before him, he paused only for a second to hold his snout to the air, then returned to his pacing and moaning as if he didn't care anymore who turned up beside his cage. One step—turn, one step back—turn, one step—turn, one step back—turn. Wailing the entire time.

I stood and looked at him. I could see his hot breath in the cold air. I wanted to run, but everything felt like it was slowing and speeding up at the same time. My scalp felt like I was in the middle of an electric storm, but my mind went sluggish, like molasses was leaking into it, my vision going tunnel-like and dark on me with the red glow on the outer edges. My legs went limp, my knees buckled, and I fell to the hard ground to a kneeling position. Grotesque images tumbled through my mind and unheeded voices whispered in my ears. I thought I heard something loud in the distance, a train or a truck, and then the grizzly made an even higher-pitched wail, blocking all other noises out.

Except my father's voice. His screaming. *Oh my God, a bear, he's got me.* I hear the rustling of his sleeping bag and screaming. *Get out of your sleeping bag, Ted. Get out of the tent.* I try to move, but I can't. I'm a block of cement.

If he comes for you, don't move, Ted, play dead. I hear more screaming and I'm still frozen, my heart exploding in my chest. *Don't move, Ted, play dead. Go limp if it goes for you.*

Something is being dragged. I hear the breaking of branches, underbrush, bushes, and brambles suddenly as loud as a Mack truck barreling through the forest, and I think it can't be him, but somehow I know it is. And still my father's orders between screams, now from fifteen or twenty yards off to the side of the campground: *Ted—if—* He gets only part of what he's trying to say out between ragged cries. *If—*there's more screaming and I just lie there. *If . . . if he comes for you—go limp.*

I try to answer. I try to say, *I will, Dad, don't worry, I will,* but I'm frozen. I can't speak. I'm tangled in something wet. I try to get out of my wet bag, kicking and frantically fighting it, my arms and legs flailing and finally I break out, stagger into the unspeakable night toward the sounds: the crunching, the ravens screeching like blades being sharpened, the unbearable shrieking. Then it all goes quiet. *Dad?* I manage. *Dad?* But there is no answer. *Please, Dad, please, go limp. You play dead. Please, Dad, stop talking. You play dead.*

My lips are moving, I'm sure, but I'm not certain that sounds are escaping. I look frantically around, but it's so dark and all I see are millions of stars in an inky sky and shadowy phantom, twisted and gnarled objects that I somehow figure are trees even though everything is all wrong and all order is lost. There are too many levels for order: frigid air, water gently lapping by the lake, bright stars, stunted trees, the soft flutter of a bat's wings, no human voices . . . and the horrible snap of bones.

The hollow moaning yanked me back, along with someone's hands pulling at me by the arm, shaking me, the smell of bear still in my nostrils. "Ted? Are you all right? Are you all right?"

I tried to stand, but my legs kept giving.

"Jesus, Ted, are you all right? Are you drunk? What the hell's going on here? Just stay seated."

I fell back hard on the cold, wet ground and put my head between my knees and breathed, gulping in the dank air sodden with the musty smell of earth.

"Just stay seated, will ya? I'm going to call an ambulance."

I managed a loud "*no.*"

"Well, stay there. I'm going to turn these lights off. I'll be right back."

In I don't know how long—a minute, five, ten—Joe returned and crouched by my side. "Do I need to call a doctor?"

"No," I said, my vision sharpening, my breathing trying to slow. "No, I'm fine, really."

"Fine is not how I'd describe this."

"I just want to get back to the cabin for some rest."

"All right, then, let me help you." Joe grabbed my arm as I stood, and after a few steps away from the cage, I felt sturdier. I turned and looked back. The red glow was extinguished, and the bear's moaning had subsided. The forest surrounding us felt still. I turned back and kept walking.

"My car's in the lot."

"The walk," I managed. "It'll be better for me."

Joe stopped and looked at me, his face etched with deep concern. "I think I should drive you."

"No, really. I want to walk."

"You sure?"

I started down the path.

"The lights," he said. "Kurtis called me since I'm closest and he's in Kalispell. He told one of his men to turn them off, but the guy forgot and remembered about an hour ago, so Kurtis called me and asked me if I could come out and turn 'em off. Not good for the guy to have lights on him all stinkin' night."

"I guess not," I said.

"Did you hear him moaning from your cabin?"

"Not from the cabin, but I was out for a walk. Couldn't sleep. I heard him when I got closer and came over to see what the deal was. I could see the lights were still . . ." I quit talking because I felt it begin to rise, the same damn drill, the nausea building, breaking through the clench in my sternum. I broke away from Joe and made my way to the side of the road.

• • •

After Joe got me some water and I sat on the couch, he sat in a chair kitty-corner to me. I could feel that my butt was damp from being on the ground. He wore an old pair of jeans and a thick red-and-gray-checked flannel shirt. Razor stubble covered his pointy jaw and his thinned white hair stuck straight up in a fuzzy mess. I thought of the tufted hair on a baby duck. He had poured himself a glass of whiskey.

"I see you found the good stuff." I looked at my glass of water. "I could use one of those."

He cocked his head to the side and eyed me for a moment. "I'd hop right up to grab you one, but I'm trying to figure out if you've already had too much, and I'm thinking you haven't since I don't smell alcohol on you."

"I'm not drunk, Joe."

"No." He stood. "I'm not thinking you are. I didn't smell it on ya out by the cage either. Which begs the question then of what the hell is wrong with you? Should you even be here right now and not getting some tests run in the ER?"

"I'm fine, really. I just . . ." I shook my head. "I just had some kind of an anxiety attack."

He peered down at me, studying me, his eyes narrowed in concern and confusion. "You get those often?"

When I didn't answer right away, he went to the kitchen and grabbed another glass and the bottle.

"No," I said when he came back in. "I don't. That was, well, strange. I guess I just haven't been sleeping well."

"Insomnia and anxiety?" He handed me the glass and sat back down.

"More like insomnia causing some anxiety." I took a big gulp, relished the sting of it cutting through the acrid taste of my own vomit.

"Hmmm." Joe's eyes were like my father's again.

I turned away, stared at the floor. My hand shook and I saw him looking at it, so I put the glass down and set both palms on my thighs above my mud-stained and wet knees, Abe Lincoln–like.

"What's really going on here, Ted?"

I thought about telling him. I really did. It would have been a relief, but here's what I ran through my mind: if I told him, he'd probably feel obligated to fill Ford in, who in turn, would fill Sean in, and then my ass would be in hot water for not mentioning it earlier to Sean. Not that

I'd done anything wrong by not mentioning it. In fact, I felt extremely embarrassed that there was anything to talk about in the first place. After all, what happened when I was fourteen had no bearing on a murder case I've been called in on. Unless, of course, the thing that happened affects my mental ability to get the job done. Before this evening, I would have said, absolutely not. After what had just happened, I was no longer so sure. All I could think was that I needed that bullet and I needed that bear released. "It would be good if we could get that slug," I mumbled.

"Yes, yes, it would," Joe said in a monotone voice and stared at me. "But if you don't mind me asking, what does that have to do with you shaking like a leaf on your knees out in the middle of the night in front of the bear's cage?"

"Nothing, I guess. It's just, well, you heard him moaning. We need to either put him down and get that slug, or we don't get it and he goes on his merry way to hibernate. It snowed heavily this morning in the higher elevations."

Joe rubbed his chin, his face serious.

"But," I said, "there's no way I can let him go without getting the evidence."

Joe sipped his whiskey and licked his lips, exactly as his daughter had done earlier. The prior events of the day seemed a million miles away, and suddenly I felt exhausted, so drained that I didn't feel like I could say another word. "You should get some sleep," I mumbled to Joe.

One corner of his mouth lifted upward in a wry smile. "I think," he said, "*you* need to get some sleep. We'll talk about this tomorrow." He stood, grabbed his glass, and went to the kitchen with it. When he came back in, he asked, "You need help getting to bed?"

It was my turn to smile wryly at the thought of Joe tucking me in like a child. "I can manage."

He turned to go, and when he got to the door, he stopped and glanced back. "If you want to talk, you've got my word that I won't say anything to Ford. I know how you feel about him. I don't know why you feel that way, but I'm pretty sure I can respect it, whatever it is."

"Thanks," I said, then lifted my hand to give a wave good-bye, which ended up looking weak and pathetic and I'm certain betrayed how spent I felt.

Joe bowed his head and shut the door behind him.

20

I‍T WAS HIGH TIME I revisited the murder site. I'd only been there twice so far. Usually I make a habit of checking it numerous times on an investigation because it keeps my mind fresh and active and prevents me from conjuring up ideas that aren't possible since I've forgotten the layout of the site. I knew I was overdue in paying it a visit, so I grabbed Monty, and we headed up the Inside Road to McGee Meadow.

The morning had a milky fog hanging over the mountains, making them disappear and changing the landscape into some eerie limbo state, some parallel universe where nothing is crystal clear and the edges fuzzy. We drove the bumpy road, even more grating on my nerves than the first time we did it—when I had the feeling of a new investigation before me, the case filled to the brim with anticipation.

Monty kept glancing at me with his wide-eyed, are-you-sure-you're-okay look while I drove because I'm certain I looked like pure death after my panic debacle the night before. When I didn't say much, he began filling me in on what he'd come up with so far on all the Shelton grandkids.

"They're an interesting bunch, as you can guess."

I didn't respond.

"There's Mark and Angie's four kids, whom I've already told you about, Lou and his first wife's kids—Trish and Benjamin, Lou and Becky's son, and, of course, Penny's, now only Megan. And then, there are the kids' kids, the great-grandkids, that is."

"How many total?" I asked.

"Grandchildren or great-grandchildren?"

"Grandchildren?"

Monty began to say their names, counting on his fingers as he went, "Let's see, there's Kendall, Mica, Paige, and Jordan. Then there's—"

"Did you make me one of those charts?" I stopped him because the names blurred in my head.

"Uh, no, not yet." Monty curled his four fingers back into his palm but still held his hand loosely in the air. "I can though."

"Have you found anything else useful?"

"Not yet, but the ones I've spoken to definitely have their own ideas about what ought to be done with the place once Lou is out of it, and most of 'em seem to act like they're fairly entitled to it. Something interesting might pop up. But you're right." He nodded his head firmly. "A chart with the family tree would be useful."

I was thinking of what to say, maybe telling him not to bother unless he came up with something more useful or to say the complete opposite: to go ahead and make a chart because it could come in handy. But just as I was about to speak, a moose trotted across the road, and I hit the brakes.

"He's a big one," Monty said.

"Yeah, he is." I felt a grin spread on my face. It felt odd because I wasn't expecting a smile, a moment of joy brought on by such a simple thing. Suddenly, I recalled a time camping at Therriault Lake with my dad the first summer we were in Montana. We saw a moose and her calf trot along the shore, bright moonlight scintillating on the lake behind them. Dad didn't say a word, just tilted his head in their direction to make sure I saw, a small smile on his lips and his eyes uncluttered with intellectual thoughts.

"There's just something about them," I said to Monty, thinking of their large, cumbersome bodies and broad, flat antlers, how they move gracefully in spite of themselves. I rolled down my window and peered through the trees in the direction he ran to see if I could make him out in the distance. "You see him?"

"Nah, he's gone," Monty said. "Already over the ridge."

I nodded and slowly applied pressure on the gas pedal and drove the remaining five minutes of the drive feeling better than I had all morning, but it didn't take long to wipe the smile off my face and a deep-bone exhaustion to return. The walk out toward McGee Meadow was muddy, cold, and wet, and even though I knew there was no grizzly around, I still felt that with each breath I took, I could taste the same strong stench accompanying the unusually warm afternoon when we found Victor just eight days earlier.

Water droplets lay on the yellow-and-red leaves of the ground cover, and the trees continued to make a ghostly creak with every slight and chilling breeze that crept through them. My boots got stuck in deep mud every other step and created a suction effect when I pulled my foot up.

I grabbed my quarter, held it snugly in my palm as we walked, and began rolling it when we got to the site. I stood before the tree where Victor was bound, the bark still stained from his blood, and thought of that day, when Gretchen and her CSS techs and photographers went at it all day and into the evening, scraping every leaf, pinching any stray hair off bark, taking molds of any possible prints.

The trees scraped against each other again, and I looked over my shoulder as if someone had spoken. Monty peered at me with his brow furrowed as if to ask, *What the heck do we do out here?*

"We're just looking, sensing. That's all," I said as if he had asked out loud. "Seeing the place might make you consider something new, something you couldn't think of the first time since you didn't know much about anything. Now we know a thing or two about the victim's life, his family, his girlfriends—"

"His cruelty," Monty added.

"That too." I turned and walked away from the large tree toward the woods to the west where Gretchen had found the boot. "So just look around," I said over my shoulder. "Observe."

Monty walked toward the trail we'd come in on and turned and looked back to the tree to gain perspective. I searched the ground with my eyes, hungry for some clue that Gretchen and her team overlooked, although I knew that wouldn't happen. Besides, the heavy rains had altered the ground. Funny enough, the grizzly prints were still in the same place, appearing even larger than before because the rain had made them expand in the mud.

I thought of the night before—of standing in the red lights before the grizzly's compound—as if there'd been a pair of spectral hands to my back, pushing me, guiding me to the cage. My breathing quickened and my heart began to speed up, but just a little. I was still extremely exhausted, and my fatigue seemed to override any automatic panic response that seemed to be occurring too frequently these days. My nerves felt splintered, and I was enough on edge that when the trees rubbed together and groaned again, I jumped, accidentally flinging my quarter into the bushes to my side. "Damn it," I swore.

"What?" Monty came over.

"I dropped my quarter."

"Oh Jesus. Call 9-1-1."

"I glared at him, then bent to the bushes to look around for it.

"It's just a quarter," Monty said. "I've got another if you want."

I wanted to scream, *I don't want another. I want this one—the Vermont one*, but I was aware of how ridiculous and childish I would sound.

"Besides," Monty added, "it's probably a habit you ought to stop anyway. Especially when you're driving. It's not good, you know."

"What? You my mother now?" I turned back to the bushes, separating dripping branches to find it, looking for a shiny edge but not seeing one.

Monty began to laugh.

I turned to him. I felt momentarily stunned at first, then felt the urge to join him, but not sure I could find the energy. Then a forceful welling up of pressure pushed against my jaw muscles and images flooded my mind, seemed to gather and create an inertia as if at the top of a hill: my moment with Ford in which I wanted to laugh after reading the paper, my humiliating performance before the bear cage, Joe wondering if he should help me to my bed, myself suddenly grinning about seeing a moose, losing my Vermont quarter . . . and I began to laugh with him. Then we gained momentum and laughed even harder like we were in junior high and unable to stop ourselves. I held my stomach and bent over and without expecting it, my eyes began to water. My laugh started to turn to a cry, and I wasn't sure what the hell I was doing.

I turned away from Monty. I could tell that his outburst had begun to subside. It felt like I was the only one in the world, bent over, laughing and crying, but that I was listening to someone else, my own voice tinny and distant. For a moment, I wondered if I was going crazy, becoming schizophrenic. I sat down on the ground, put my head on my forearm, and tried to rein it all in.

Monty said nothing. I could tell he was confused, trying to figure out if I was still laughing or crying and perhaps taken aback at seeing a grown man losing it suddenly and weeping. I wiped my eyes, shook my head, and stood. I didn't dare look at him, just started walking back up the muddy trail to the SUV.

• • •

Monty followed me out of the woods, and when we got to the car, he held out his hand for the keys. "I can drive."

"No," I said firmly. "I'm fine."

He stood with his hand stretched out, and I ignored him and hopped in. I could hear my rattled breathing, and I didn't want Monty hearing it too. I tried to slow it down, which felt like a difficult task that required more strength than I actually had. He paused for a bit, then went around to the passenger side and climbed in. We sat in the restless silence for a moment; then I shifted in my seat and put the key in the ignition.

"Excuse me, sir," Monty said all polite as if it was his first day on the job again, "but what's going on? Is something up?"

I let my hand drop off the keys onto my leg, leaned my head and shoulders back into the seat, and sighed. "You didn't sign up for this, but I'll tell ya because otherwise, I just look plain nuts."

Monty said nothing. He rotated slightly sideways so that he could look at me as he leaned his shoulder against the inside of the car door.

"I don't really know how to start other than to just get it out." I tried to take a deep breath, but it was nothing more than shallow and shaky. "When I was fourteen . . ." I looked out the window at the cross-country ski marker on the tree and paused. I'd like to say that telling someone came easy for me—the simple act of announcing what happened that night. But after all the years of distancing and numbing myself, I was out of practice in the disclosing department. I hadn't told anybody about the incident since the sketchy version I gave Shelly and my Missoula therapist.

"Yeah?" Monty waited.

I stared at my feet and at the gas and brake pedals. The air in the car felt stale and warm. "I lost my father to a grizzly in this park."

Monty's eyes widened. "You're serious?"

"Yeah, the eighties. Oldman Lake. We were camping. Just the two of us."

Monty stared at me.

"Go ahead," I said.

"Go ahead?" He lifted his brow.

"Go ahead and whistle."

"What?"

"Whistle. You always whistle over stuff. Doesn't that warrant one?"

Monty didn't whistle. "Jesus," he said instead. "That's, that's—I don't know—horrific."

I stared straight ahead. My whole body felt itchy and my heart pounded in my ribs. My face felt hot and flushed. I could easily have dropped the whole thing now that I'd put it out there.

"What happened?"

I lowered my head, tried to hide my flushed face. I realized I'd have to continue, and I didn't particularly want to.

Monty cleared his throat and shifted in his seat. I fidgeted. The vinyl felt like tack paper, as if it was keeping me captive. I needed to either open the door and get out or begin talking, the air turning so thick I could slice it. Something needed to give before I'd lose it laughing or crying again. "We'd gone in the day," I said, my throat dry. I swallowed hard, found very little saliva. "Fished the lake—just catch and release. Then made a fire when it was close to getting dark. We'd made some dinner, some of those premixed camping packets where all you do is add boiling water for stew. It's not like we were careless; we weren't cooking steaks or brats or anything out in the middle of bear country."

"Had the area been having problems?"

"No, not like the Many Glacier area. There'd been no trouble sightings in the Two Med area that fall."

"It was fall?"

I nodded. "Not late fall. It was September."

"That's spooky," Monty said.

I didn't respond, just scratched the back of my hot neck.

"You were a kid?" He had that sympathy look on his face that I'd come to hate when I was a teen—that droopy look that always made me feel like I was on the brink of falling off the edge of some great precipice into a pit of complete human rawness and emotion.

"Yeah. Fourteen. We sat by the fire for a while after dinner." I shut my eyes. "Just chatted before going to bed." I could remember the smell of the smoke, having to squeeze my eyes tightly shut when the breeze blew it straight in my face, then the wind changing directions and blowing it away from both of us. I pictured my dad putting his forearm before his eyes until it blew the other way.

"We slept in a three-man tent that my dad had packed in. I remember thinking how heavy it looked." I swallowed hard again, considering what to say next. I drew a blank. I ran my hands through my hair while Monty sat patiently. "After, after the attack," I said. "After it dragged my dad into the bushes, I don't know how far, off to the side of the campsite, I was completely frozen with fear, didn't know what to do."

"Jesus," Monty said again. "Were there other campers out there?" Monty wrapped an arm around his gut as if the thought of it was making him ill.

I shook my head. "Just us."

"Your dad, he didn't make it?"

I shook my head again. "Just me."

"How the hell did you get out of there?"

"It's a blur, really. But I have memories of frantically searching for a flashlight, finding the lighter in dad's pack, and remaking the fire, getting it going again. I sat in front of the fire with one thought and one thought only, that I needed to keep it going, to not let it die. That if the fire died, I would die."

Now I thought I could hear Monty's breathing, loud and adenoidal like a child focused on building something. His lips were pursed, and he was still wrapping an arm around his waist.

"At the first light, everything was quiet. I tried to find my dad, at least, I think I did. The mind's funny that way. You know how unreliable witness accounts are? Anyway, I'd like to believe I searched, but I guess I was in shock."

"You'd have to be," Monty said.

"I ran the trail with only a flashlight. I remember stumbling, over and over, on autopilot, I guess, until I fell. I must have run and walked close to six miles, because they said they found me only a mile in from the Two Medicine Lake. I'd stumbled and fallen, crunched my skull on a rock so hard that I was knocked unconscious. Some hikers found me, got me emergency help. I was in the hospital, actually in a coma for a short time. Subdural hematoma. Never even came to in order to fill anybody in on the attack, but I guess they thought it through, sent out a party to hike up the trail, and found our site."

I looked at Monty, his eyes like quarters and his face sheet white. I cleared my throat.

Monty began to slowly nod. "You spent hours by the fire by yourself after the bear took your dad?"

I bit my lower lip, looked into Monty's intense eyes and gave a nod, then turned back and fixed my gaze on the floor of the car. The itching had ceased. I just felt hollowed out and exhausted.

"This case," he said. "These circumstances with the bear . . . tough duty to—"

"It's not that big of a deal." I cut him off, holding up my hand. "I'm fine. Really, what happened all those years ago has no bearing on this case, and I'm fine. I've just not gotten much sleep lately and I guess I just needed that"—I lifted my chin to the woods, to the direction of the murder site—"that laugh or whatever the hell you want to call it."

"I guess you did."

I shrugged; then wrapped my hand around the car keys hanging in the ignition to start the car.

Finally, Monty whistled.

. . .

The next hour with him—driving back to West Glacier in the silence, grabbing another cup of coffee to go and a couple of pastries in the café, getting back to headquarters so that Monty could begin his family tree on the Shelton's children—felt like half a day. It was the aftermath of confiding in someone—the total discomfort. What I thought might be a relief at filling him in was quickly beginning to look like an ever-growing colossal mistake on my part. With each glance from Monty, like a concerned parent with a closed-lip smile full of pity, I felt weakened, melted like the Wicked Witch to a puddle of water. First, exposing my personal life with Shelly to him, and now this. I felt pathetic. If it wouldn't have rattled my nerves to hear my own laughter again, I'd have almost cracked up at the irony: Monty like my student in the beginning of the case and now a concerned partner handling me with kid gloves and a mouthpiece to Ford to boot.

I recalled the service for my father, which had been delayed for a month until I recovered fully and was discharged from the hospital. I remember the picture board with images of him hiking, biking, holding up a large bass he'd caught in one of the warm Florida lakes. There were refreshments afterward—trays of cold cuts and cheeses, platters of cakes and doughnuts that made me queasy just to look at. There'd been a quiet and pleasant air of both sorrow and warmth, but what I remember most were the people's uncomfortable glances at me and the comments about how lucky I was to have made it, then the awkward pause from the person who'd said it as they realized how cold that must sound to a fourteen-year-old boy who'd just lost his father. I felt weak and exposed when other parents and my father's friends forced fake smiles full of sympathy. I had to leave the funeral home, walk outside just to escape the pity because it made me feel too fragile to even breathe, as if I was suffocating.

I threw the files I was going over down on the table because I couldn't think straight. I left Monty in the stuffy office working meticulously on his diagram to go to the bathroom and maybe step outside for a breath of fresh air. I'd only made it a little ways down the hallway when I ran into Ford.

Great. What now? I hadn't said anything out loud, but he spoke as if he had read my mind.

"This business with that reporter . . . what's his name?"

"Jones."

"No one under my or Smith's watch is admitting giving the guy information, although both Nicholas Moran and Karen Fortenson said he'd tried to get details out of them. That he'd swung by to find you, but since you weren't around, started questioning whoever he found."

"Makes sense," I said.

"Yeah, well, I've spoken to him."

"I'm sure you have," I said.

Ford caught the smugness in my voice, and I could tell was about to say something, as his mouth opened briefly, then shut, his lips twisted in disgust. It was an understatement to say that this man and I made no music together and never would.

"The bear," Ford said. "I've made a decision. He goes back to the wild tomorrow."

"We can't do that," I said.

"Oh, yes we can, and will. It's been long enough, and we are not putting him down. Besides, with the public now knowing we're looking for evidence, we can be pretty sure that whoever had the gun to begin with has gotten rid of it by now."

"You can't make that assumption."

"You said it yourself; no perpetrator is going to hang on to it at this point after that article."

"The article wasn't that clear. You said *that* yourself—keys, wallet?"

Ford looked up at the ceiling, then back at me. "Tomorrow, Systead, he's being released." He continued down the hall.

I forgot about the bathroom, just turned and walked to the exit and went outside into the cold and damp air that hung heavy. Heavy like my head, as if was full of wet sand. Yet somehow it also felt clear, as if my anger was burning through my fatigue like sunlight through fog. I shook it like a dog trying to throw water off his snout, to snap myself out of the funk. Big fucking deal. I'd told Monty about my past. It wasn't the end of the world. Aside from the bear dilemma, the investigation was proceeding, and a small part of my brain or something in my intuition, like the very beginning of a pearl formation inside the soft body of the oyster, was starting to shape. You never know why or what makes it come on in the absence of any strong clues, but it still can come, and I recognized the sensation, one all homicide investigators know. I didn't have the answers, but I sensed they were close.

I would have to get support from Sean on preventing the bear's release because I still needed the damn slug. I whipped out my phone, dialed his number, and left him a message that I needed to speak to him as soon as possible.

. . .

On my way back in to use the restroom, I got a call from a female officer at the Columbia Falls Police Department who said they knew we'd put out the word requesting to be apprised of anything suspicious involving Andrew Stimpson and that they had him and Daniel Nelson in their custody. Apparently, the two had been brought in by Officer Pontiff for fighting in front of one of the bars on the main drag in Columbia Falls.

Monty and I found Officer Pontiff in a small office on the other side of a recently added two-way mirror looking into the only interview room the station has. Apparently, Pontiff was very proud of the new addition because he stood, leaning against one wall with a smile, sipping a cup of coffee. He said, "I love these two-ways, don't you?"

"They're nifty all right," I replied. "What happened?"

"According to the other guy, Nelson, he—" Pontiff lifted his chin to point at Stimpy, who was glaring directly back at Pontiff as if he could see him. Stimpy had a cocky look on his face and his arms folded before his chest. One knee bounced ferociously, and his eyes had that crazed I'm-larger-than-life-'cause-I-don't-care-about-shit look that comes from popping a few pills, snorting a line, or shooting up a vein. "Stimpson instigated the whole thing. Started teasing him about the fact that his longtime buddy Victor was no longer with us. Nelson said he tried to leave the bar without any trouble, but that Stimpy followed him out, started pushing on him, and asking him why his mama didn't teach him enough manners to not walk away from someone when they was talking to ya. He was pretty ramped up when we got him. Pretty sure he's on something."

"Anything on him? Drugs? Weapon?"

"No."

"Where's Nelson?"

"He's in one of the cells. Figured you'd want a shot at this moron first, so I brought him to the interview room."

"I'll let him simmer and speak to Nelson if you don't mind. He sober?"

"Yeah, seems perfectly fine. That's why I relayed his story to you."

"And Stimpy's story?"

Pontiff broke into a huge grin. "That Nelson was making eyes at his girlfriend."

"Melissa?"

"Yeah, that's her. I guess she was taking a break from the Outlaw's Nest and was hanging with Stimpy at the Bandit."

"Is she here too?"

"No, but I'm sure she'll be by soon to post bail for her oh-so-stellar boyfriend."

. . .

After I talked to Daniel and found nothing all that interesting other than to confirm that what Officer Pontiff had parlayed was accurate, I went in to Stimpy. By the time I got to him, he'd started scratching. He was no longer the poised and cocky master of his universe as he was earlier—sitting fairly composed (other than the shaking leg) and glaring through the two-way mirror. Now he paced and scratched behind his neck, the side of his chin, where he'd broken a scab and smeared the blood. He was wearing a leather vest with a faux-fur collar with no shirt underneath, so I could see his bare arms with all his tattoos: a buffalo head, a rainbow, and an eagle on one arm, and on the other, a crucifix with the words *Jesus Listens* underneath.

Monty and I walked in and took a seat each. I began: "So," I said, "if Jesus listens, I guess there're no secrets."

Stimpy stopped pacing and looked at me, then shook his head as I'd done earlier after talking to Ford, as if he could shake things into a different order, clear the Etch A Sketch, and start with a new design.

"I ain't got secrets from no one."

"That's good, then. So let's start with where you're getting the nice little concoction that's so healthy for your skin."

"Fuck off."

I clucked my tongue. "Remember, Jesus is listening."

"I don't give a fuck. Maybe he needs a little educating on what it's like in a Columbia Falls jail."

"Where's Melissa?"

"She'll be here."

"Look, you can keep your secrets about where you get your drugs because we don't care. That's being handled by the police anyway, and from what I've heard, they're not far from nailing you and the sorry lab you're getting your supply from. Guess it doesn't help that your connection in Mexico is too stupid to not be using the same drugstore for his Sudafed supply over and over again. That he's willing to roll on you guys. In fact, right now, they've got a sheriff's car parked right up in those trees across from your skuzzy little lab, and they're taking pictures. Maybe you guys should check the IQ of the people you hire."

"Fuck off."

"They've even got videos of you walking in and out of the lab. Hey, you're a real celebrity!"

Stimpy's face contorted in disgust.

"But, again, I don't give a rat's ass about any of that. What I want to know is why you were messing with Daniel Nelson, one of Victor Lance's old friends?"

He looked away, scratched his arm, and bounced both knees.

"Because going to jail for dealing meth is a whole lot different than going to jail for murder?"

He stood up and started circling the room, around Monty and me. I slammed my hand down on the table and made both Stimpy and Monty flinch. "Sit down," I said loudly. "Quit pacing and—SIT—DOWN."

Stimpy did what I said, like an obedient child.

"There, that's better. Don't you think?" I said to Monty, and he nodded.

"Now, let's start with why you felt the need to pick on Daniel Nelson?"

"He was hittin' on my girl."

"Cut the bullshit," I said. "Your dick that small that you're worried about a glance or two at your girl?"

One side of Stimpy's lip went up, and he clenched his teeth.

"So let's back up. How did you know that Daniel knew Victor?"

"I'd heard they were buddies in school."

"From whom?"

"From a dude named Tom Hess, who knew Daniel."

I nodded.

"And you knew Tom and Victor were good friends?"

Stimpy nodded.

"You hear about the dog beating that Victor and Tom partook in?"

"I heard about it."

"What exactly did you hear?"

"Just that. That those two were drugged out and beat the shit out of a dog somewhere, but what the fuck does that have to do with me?"

"You get them high for that beating?"

He didn't answer.

"You know the owner of the dog they beat?"

"I heard he runs a rental car agency by the airport."

"Who'd you hear that from?"

"Don't remember. Could have been anyone. Besides, it's just gossip."

"You know that guy?"

"Nah, man. I ain't got nothin' to do with that dude."

"What about Hess?"

"Haven't seen him. Heard he's huntin' or somethin'."

"What about before he went hunting?" I asked. "You know what he was up to?"

"Got no clue."

"You don't know if he and Victor had a falling-out of some sort?"

"Nah, I wouldn't know that."

"You know Leslie Boone?"

He nodded.

"You runnin' to her lately."

"Nah, man. I'm not runnin' shit."

"Look." I sat back and folded my arms across my chest. "I told you that I don't care about the makin' or the runnin', I just want to know about Victor. If I were going to get you for that, I'd have a tape recorder on you as we speak."

"Probably got one behind that glass."

"See that camera"—I pointed to the corner of the room—"you see some kind of light to indicate that that thing's on?"

Stimpy didn't respond.

"There's no light on, 'cause I told 'em I didn't want to tape ya. I just want information on Victor Lance, that's all. And the more you cooperate, the quicker you get out of here so you can go make as many mistakes as you want in that little entrepreneurial world of yours."

"You going to give me some kind of immunity?"

"Depends on what you got for me?"

"Leslie's trying real hard to get out of the shit. Last I saw her, she said no, thanks, that she didn't go through the dry heaves, the shakes, and hallucinations for nothing. Said she'd even had a seizure and it scared her shitless."

"Was Victor a runner?"

"Hell no." Stimpy laughed. "If he was a runner and not just a user, he might have had a pot to piss in. Victor was broke. I don't think he could even buy a tank of gas near the end there."

"So he got into trouble with you for not paying up?"

"God, no. He usually came up with something. He wasn't perfect, but Jesus, no one killed the guy over that, if that's what you're thinking."

"So why were you pickin' a fight with Daniel Nelson?"

Stimpy shrugged, one corner of his mouth twitching into a slight smile.

I eyed him, rubbing my chin. I could see it in that one corner of his mouth in his minuscule grin, and although it was small, it held the answer to my question. Somewhere in the back of my mind, I heard his crazy laugh to accompany it. He was messing with Daniel Nelson just because he could, because he was the type to mess with anyone in the quest to make himself feel bigger and better than he is. "I'm going to leave Monty here with you so he can go over all the details again."

"What fuckin' details?"

"About where you were on the Thursday and Friday before Victor Lance turned up dead?"

"What about immunity from any drug busts?"

I chuckled. "I couldn't do that if I tried, you know that. Besides, you gave me shit. Not one useful bit of information to help me find Victor's murderer."

• • •

Monty ran Stimpy through it for another hour and a half, rechecking his whereabouts and driving him absolutely berserk, this time with the little green light on the camera flashing its presence over and over.

I watched part of it from behind the two-way and left, making Officer Pontiff view the rest for Monty's safety. I went to see Daniel off and to tell him that I thought it'd be a good idea if he got out of the area, maybe found himself a place to rent in Kalispell, and got away from some of the knuckleheads in town. He smiled at me, thanked me, but said that Columbia Falls was where he grew up, where his mother and father grew up, and he intended to stay.

I thought about the folks in the area, even Joe and Elena and now Heather, and the Sheltons, who could look back at the procession of farm families, aluminum-plant workers, and logging families with a haze of nostalgia—who could commit themselves to the endless routine knowing that prosperity would be small and that the pinkish-orange sunsets peeking under the cloud cover and illuminating the golden wheat were payment for all their hard work.

"I hear ya," I said. "Your loyalty is commendable."

"Thank you, sir." He gently touched the shiner on his left eye with his pinky finger.

"Sorry you had to run into him. If it's any consolation, the police might be getting closer to his little ring."

"That'd be good."

"You watched Victor go to shit on that stuff?"

"I did. Don't get me wrong. Victor always had personal problems, but the drugs made it so much worse, and he got on them before he had a chance to grow up."

"You ever meet Leslie?"

"Just once or twice. At a bar or two."

"Your impressions?"

"That she was a nice enough girl but screwed up like him. I heard, though, that she was trying to stay clean." He shrugged. "Good for her, especially since she's got a son."

"I know when we talked before, you said that you could imagine a lot of folks hating Victor, but that you didn't know of anyone in particular that would want him dead enough to do it. Do you still feel that way?"

"Yeah." He nodded. "Even that prick in there." He motioned to the department to our backs. "I don't think he did it."

"And why's that?"

"Just the way he was teasin' me, saying that it was too bad I didn't hang out with Victor more often, that maybe I could've kept him alive. So I said to him: 'Why? You would've been afraid of me when you went to take him out?' He looked surprised at first. Then laughed, as if he hadn't considered that. Then he said, 'Nah, man, 'cause maybe he would've stayed a Goody Two-shoes like you.' "

"I don't know. Maybe I'm naïve, but I didn't get the feeling that he'd done it, not 'cause of what he said—I know he wouldn't think twice about lying—but the look of surprise in his eyes when he realized that I'd thought he'd done it."

"All right." I held out my hand for a shake, thinking that wasn't much to go off. "Good luck to you. I'll call you if we need anything else."

21

MELISSA FINALLY BAILED Stimpy out, and we drove back to West Glacier, where Monty said he needed a break to go back to his place. I agreed that he did. An hour and a half going over a druggie's whereabouts for two days would tire anyone. Fighting the profound exhaustion pulling at me from every angle, I called Walsh to see if Tom Hess had returned yet from his hunting trip and found that he hadn't. I was beginning to wonder if he was on the run and not coming back at all.

I drove back to the office, went in, and stared at Monty's color-coded poster with the time line and alibis, which was growing more and more crowded with the addition of the Shelton grandkids. Then I began to make my own diagram, a type of flow chart with all the possible leads we'd come across so far. I'd been working it—circling items of interest and connecting lines between them, pressing too hard into the paper—for half an hour and my stomach began to ache from the numerous cups of coffee I'd drunk all day to keep me awake. I thought I'd better get a bite to eat and was just about to grab my coat when Ford came in.

"You have a minute?" He looked even more severe than usual, with a grimness in his eyes that seemed to mean business.

I motioned for him to have a seat.

He grabbed a chair, sat down, and all went mouse-quiet. "I'm not sure where to start other than to just say it—that I know who you are."

I sat still.

"I mean"—he steepled his fingers and continued before I responded—

"I finally figured out why the Systead name rang a bell with me: 1987. Your father and you. Oldman Lake."

I glared at him now, something sour rising in my throat. I didn't need this now, not ever, from this man. My mother wanted the satisfaction of his recognition of her son. But now, before me, I didn't want shit from him other than to leave me alone. His paltry remembrance of the recount of Oldman Lake, of what happened out there in the dead of that night all those years ago, was a sour pill for me to swallow at this stage of the game.

"I've not spoken to Joe and Sean yet, but needless to say, that should I feel the need to do so, that they'd have to agree that there's been some, shall we say"—he cleared his throat—"credibility lost here."

"How so?" I managed after taking a hard swallow.

"*How so?*" He pulled his head back incredulously, tucking his chin. "I don't believe you're that stupid, Agent Systead. The obvious is that it compromises your ability to make sound judgments about a case that includes a grizzly bear that, because of your insistence, we've got cruelly caged while you continue to botch this case."

"Botch?" I could feel my anger rise with a vengeance, a geyser about to blow. I had a flash of me throwing him against the wall by the scruff of his collar, him dangling like a puppet under my grip. I stayed still and waited for him to answer.

"From what I'm gathering, you're not exactly making much leeway. You're no closer to the killer now than you were a week ago."

"You have no idea how an investigation works." Something dark and insatiable with sharp teeth seemed to grip at my chest. I almost felt the need to glance down at my sternum.

Ford pursed his lips and cocked his head to the side, then he did the worst thing he could do: he let his eyes fill with pity. "Now, don't get me wrong, I understand what you must—"

"You don't understand shit." I stood from the table so fast the chair flung back and fell over. I leaned over, my face before his. "This investigation is going just fine, and if you prevent me from completing what I've begun, I'll . . ." I held back. My heartbeat—a mallet striking my ribs—arrested me. I actually didn't know exactly what I wanted to say. What? That I'd beat the shit out of him—an old man? That I'd make his life hell? But it didn't matter because a modicum of common sense lay somewhere inside of me, and I didn't finish. I straightened myself up and backed away, my face hot with rage.

Ford stared at me with a combination of disdain and anger, all the fake pity gone.

"You've been here for a long time," I said. "But you know, you don't know as much as you think you do."

"Oh, I know quite a bit. You'd be surprised."

"Yeah, well, so do I and I know that your credibility is not at its highest either. That you'd like nothing more than for me to hurry up and whitewash this case—call it closed or unsolvable." The thought of Ford forever staining my father's death with a lie for the public and the park to make itself feel better, superior—as if there's a tidy reason for every tragedy in this world—savagely bit into me with even more force.

"Whitewash?" He pulled his chin in again, his eyes narrowed.

"Just like you did in '87. I'm well aware of how you lied to the press about my father."

"Lied." He laughed. "What crazy ideas are you conjuring now? Listen, Systead, if I were you, I'd be very careful because you're starting to sound, well, a little cuckoo." He made imaginary circles with his pointer by his temple. "How in the hell would you know what you did or didn't take to bed with you?" Ford continued. "You could have had candy bars in your pockets for all you know."

My breath caught. I stood silent before him. I stared back into his narrow eyes, waiting for him to give more information, not wanting more, but wanting it as if my life depended on it. "You have no clue what we found out there," Ford added with contempt in his voice. "How could you? You were fourteen and totally clueless."

His words penetrated me to some deep place, and every ounce of vitality siphoned out of me. "*Could have had?*" I said. "What the hell does that mean?"

"Like I said—you were only fourteen."

"Yes, I was," I managed. "That's definitely one piece of truth." I stood for a second—stared down at him, my face hot, my knees going weak, my jaw clenched. "If you'll excuse me," I finally managed. "I've got work to do." I strode out and left him to my diagram and my notes with one small, petty thought in my mind: that when I stood and knocked the chair over, he flinched.

. . .

I drove to Kalispell in the dark. I'd lost my temper with the super, and now I was furious with myself. I stood on Ma's doorstep sometime well after dinner. She had already gotten ready for bed and was in a pale-blue bathrobe and slippers. She grabbed me by the wrist and pulled me in.

"Holy Mother of Mary," she said once I was inside the front door. "You look ghastly. Haven't you been eating?"

"I've been eating. Just not sleeping."

"Well, good Lord, there's help for that. Have you forgotten that your mother's a pharmacist?"

I shook my head.

"What can I make you? Soup? I have some leftover chicken in the fridge. I could warm it up?"

"I'm fine. I'm not really—"

"Don't be ridiculous. You need to eat."

I didn't feel like anything, but I knew there was no getting away from her making me something. "Either sounds great."

"Sit down, sit down. Make yourself comfortable."

I took a seat in front of the gas fireplace, which she'd converted from a wood-burning insert about five years before to make life easier.

Otherwise, the place was the same. After the incident, we stayed in the house Ma and Dad built together after moving to Montana until Kathryn left for college. Then Ma insisted that we needed a smaller place and that there were too many memories haunting the old house, not to mention how unbearable it became to drive every day by the neighbor who shot Tumble. So we moved smack into the center of Kalispell on the east side of its main drag, where sidewalks and maple and chestnut trees lined the streets. For me, it was a relief to leave the woods and the foothills.

Ma hadn't changed the place much over the years. The white mantel with the tall silver candlesticks in the center, the antique rocking chair my parents brought up from Florida, the nautical coffee table with the hinged flaps on each side were all remnants from my childhood. The same striped wallpaper was in the dining room, although she had had the kitchen and the living room repainted several times over the years. And I noticed that the area rug on the oak floor and the throw pillows on the couch looked new since my last visit.

"Why didn't you call me and tell me you were coming?" Ma called from the kitchen.

"I'm sorry, I know I should have. I just had a lot on my mind. Just kept driving and thinking."

"If I'd known, I'd have waited and had dinner with you—made you something good."

"No worries. I just thought I could use a visit."

She didn't answer, and I could hear the pots rattling, the fridge opening and closing. She made some tea when I showed and brought out two cups that she set on the dining room table. Eventually, she brought me chicken and rice that she'd heated up and broccoli that she'd steamed fresh. When I told her that she shouldn't have, she shushed me and told me to eat, so we sat together at the dining room table. I ate while she drank her tea, her hands folded neatly around the base of the cup. "So what's going on with this investigation?"

"Oh." I sighed. "Answers just aren't coming as quickly as they should."

"But you're getting there?"

"I think so. You read the paper about the grizzly?"

She nodded.

"What was your take on that?"

She put her hand to her chest. "*My* take?"

"Yeah? What was your first reaction?"

"That you were doing what's necessary to figure out this case. I mean, the bear ate part of the victim, right?"

I nodded.

"I figured you're taking all necessary precautions by keeping him for a bit, studying him—getting DNA or whatever you do."

I chewed the broccoli, actually happy to eat something healthy.

Ma studied me. "Is that Eugene Ford giving you a hard time?" Her voice was pointed.

"Why do you keep thinking that? He doesn't even remember who I am," I lied.

"I don't mean that; he doesn't need to know who you are to give you a hard time. Like I said, he's just not a good guy in my book."

"Well, lots of people really like him."

"What's the problem, then? Why do you look like you haven't slept in a week?"

I smiled. "Because I haven't slept in a week."

"Let me rephrase that. *Why* haven't you slept?"

I finished chewing a piece of chicken, took a sip of tea. "I don't know. It's been weird being up there after all this time."

Ma looked at her hands, then tucked a loose strand of hair behind her ear. "I can imagine."

"Do you still have those old clippings?"

"Of the incident?"

I nodded.

"I do." She studied me. "You can see them if you'd like."

. . .

After I ate, Ma poured more tea and we moved to the gas fire. She had gone into her bedroom for a bit and reappeared with a faded-blue pocket folder, then sat down beside me on the couch and set the folder on the table before us. It was soft and bent at the edges from years of being stuffed in a drawer. She opened it, and I could see a number of thin, yellowed clippings. I felt strange sitting with her as if we were simply going to go over some old high school basketball write-ups or something equally nostalgic. Only the fact that we were stone quiet gave us away.

Of course, I'd seen the clippings before, when I was still in high school. I'd gone into her room and looked through her top drawer for no good reason, only that I knew she kept family pictures, school photos, our report cards, and other sentimental items in it. I was drawn to the drawer as if it held life's answers and would go through it several times a year, but I never really could bring myself to read the clippings. I'd just quickly thumb through the folder and move on to other items—pictures of our family with Dad still in them.

The gas fire hummed in the background, and she carefully began to open the first article on the top of the pile. She smoothed it out before us with her palm, and I could see it held its sharp creases from years of being folded. I had to hold back from grabbing the ones underneath and spreading them all out as well. It was more my style—to see it all at once—to take it in and see how it all fit together in my mind. Ma was different, more meticulous from years of grinding, cutting, and counting pills. She pushed it toward me—an article from a local Billings paper. The ink on the headlines looked as if it had darkened over the years, while the background had turned a brownish-yellow sepia tone, the color of unbleached grain. The ink on the front-page pictures had faded, and the headline stood at the top: "Fatal Grizzly Attack in Glacier Park." There were no pictures accompanying it.

The date was September 24, 1987, so it was one of the first reports. I scanned the article, and neither of us spoke. It mentioned that a man had been taken in the night and dragged some one hundred and fifty feet from his tent and fatally mauled by a grizzly bear. It said that the man was with his fourteen-year-old son, who was in critical condition in the Kalispell hospital recovering from sustained injuries while trying to get back to the Two Medicine campground. It mentioned the emergency helicopter that retrieved him and flew him to the hospital as well as the couple that found him in the a.m. on their way to hike Dawson Pass.

Mom pulled out several more, still slowly, one at a time: the local papers in Kalispell, Missoula, Great Falls, and Bozeman. All of them were from the same date with similar accounts. Then she pulled out one from Missoula, dated September 25, the day after the others. This one's headline made my pulse speed up. Ma shifted in her seat. The headline read: "Possible Careless Camping Habits Leads to Glacier Park Grizzly Attack."

I fidgeted in my seat and ran a hand through my hair. I couldn't wait any longer for her to pull them out one at a time. "If you don't mind?" I grabbed the thin pile left underneath and began unfolding them, spreading them out before us.

Ma said nothing.

I had them laid out: the age-stained, putrid-looking thin sheets of newspapers. I could smell a dry, musty scent from them. I took in the headlines: "Careless Camping May Have Caused Glacier Bear Attack." "Mauled Father's Careless Camping Habits Lead to Tragedy." "Fatal Mauling Brought on by Careless Camping Habits." All were from local Montana cities, though two were from Sheridan, Wyoming, and Denver, Colorado. "Where did you get all of these?"

"You know, the old news shop." She pointed to the northwest wall of the house to its direction. "It's still there, you know?"

I grunted some response. The last one I opened was the *New York*

Times, with a similar headline: "Possible Careless Camping Brings Grizzly Fatality in Montana."

"Go ahead." She waved her hand in the air. "Read them." She stood and grabbed our cups. "More tea?"

"Sure," I said, without glancing up. I chose the Kalispell one first: "Fatal Mauling Brought on by Careless Camping Habits." I ran my hand over it, my palm moist against the aged surface, now grainy and fuzzy from the slow disintegration of the fibers. Briefly, it ran through my mind that the paper would be completely decomposed someday, but that it would still exist long after the Systead family was gone.

Saturday's fatal mauling of a camper by a grizzly bear in Glacier National Park, the first killing since 1976, has raised concerns of many camping enthusiasts due to the suspicion of park officials that the victim may have been less than careful in keeping a clean campsite.

The victim, whom park officials have identified as Dr. Jonathan Systead, a pathologist who worked for Kalispell Regional Medical Center, and his fourteen-year-old son, Theodore Systead, from Kalispell, Mt., had hiked about six miles in from the Two Medicine area to fish and camp at the Oldman Lake backcountry campsite.

Judging by the ripped state of the tent, in the night the grizzly dragged Jonathan Systead one hundred fifty feet from the tent, where there was sign of a struggle.

According to Glacier Park superintendent Eugene Ford, park officials have reason to believe that techniques for avoiding encounters were not closely followed. He refused to give further details in an effort to respect the victim and the victim's family members.

Theodore Systead is in critical condition in Kalispell Regional Hospital for a serious head injury sustained while staggering out of the woods alone in the early hours of Sept. 23. Glacier Park officials emphasize that bear attacks remain extremely rare and that no visitors have been injured by bears in the park in the last decade and that Sunday's killing was the first bear-caused human fatality in Glacier since 1976.

    Rangers are in the process of trying to capture the grizzly responsible for the fatality to take appropriate measures against it.

I read the others, all with similar accounts. Ma brought me the tea and sat down again, this time in the rocking chair. "So, you see?" she said and began rocking, the wood chafing against the oak floor. "He painted it like it was your father's fault."

"I know. We've known that for years." I rubbed my forehead. "What I'm wondering is why you're so sure that he's not correct?"

"Of course he's not correct. You told us that you were careful. *You* told us that, and you had no reason to lie."

"Maybe I was wrong. Maybe I just wanted to believe it was clean. Maybe we did something stupid, like going to sleep with the clothes we cooked in."

"No." She shook her head stubbornly. "No. I remember. You told us that you didn't. You told us the site was clean."

"But memory is tricky. I know that now. I see it all the time in my line of work. Witnesses make stuff up constantly—their brains bend and fill in the details, and they truly believe them. Like, for years I believed I searched for him, but now I'm not so sure I ever did. How could I have? It was dark and I had to make a fire." I looked into her eyes. They were moist; the brown had lightened as she'd gotten older. They looked more tea-colored than coffee-colored in the fire light. They were intense, not brimming with pity, but concentrated and crowded with something, perhaps love, perhaps horror. She was imagining it all over again—her boy in the night making a fire, sitting in his own urine, praying his father would walk back out of the trees. "Maybe they did find evidence that we were sloppy?"

"No, it wasn't like that. You told us in the hospital what happened. You were right out of a coma; you had no time to make stuff up. You had no time for memory to play tricks on you. And it's not like I hadn't camped with your father countless times. I know how careful he was, and I know that he'd be even more cautious in the fall in Glacier. Plus why doesn't one single article mention what was found to indicate that there was any carelessness?"

I didn't answer.

"Not one of those gives any details and that's a bunch of bologna about wanting to respect the family members. When have you ever seen that in all the prior and subsequent grizzly attacks written over the years?"

"I haven't," I admitted. I sat back in the couch, laid my head back, and sighed. "You really think he made it up? It sounds so crazy."

"I think he made it up to ease people's minds about the park. To make them think that bears only go wild if there's a good reason, and if there's no reason, you're safe. And for the most part, people are, but not that time. For whatever reason, not that time."

"But does it really matter that he lied? Why do you care so much? Why haven't you let it go? Why haven't you thrown these away?" After my rage with Ford, I felt sheepish for asking, but had to anyway. I sat up, rested my elbows on my knees, and gestured to the table.

Ma sat and stared at the fire, her jaw set. She didn't shrug; she didn't move. "I'm not sure why," she finally spoke so quietly that I barely heard.

"Then maybe you should," I said softly.

"I called the man, you know, and confronted him. I wanted to know what they'd found to suggest that your father had been careless."

"And?"

"And nothing. He blew me off; said he didn't have permission from the DOI to discuss detailed findings with me."

I looked at the table. The dark headlines blurred and smeared together. My eyes hurt. I began to pick up the clippings, fold them neatly back up, and place them in the folder.

Ma leaned forward to help me, and I could hear her breathing. It was more labored now, and her face was very serious. I wanted to ask her if she was feeling all right, but suddenly I felt too exhausted to say anything more.

She stood and tucked the folder back under her arm. "You're sleeping here tonight. There's a spare toothbrush in the bathroom. I'll make sure there are fresh sheets on the bed in the upstairs' room."

. . .

I woke to the creaking of the walls as the wind continued to gust, but could see a pale-blue sky through the small side window of the upstairs bedroom. Ma had given me some pills, some Sonata or something, before I went to bed. I told her I didn't need them, that I was exhausted, but she said it would keep me from waking in an hour or two and that I needed that. And other than a groggy head, I'm guessing she was correct—I did need it. I felt human for the first time in days. But judging by the angle of the sun through the window, I figured I'd slept much later than I'd wanted to. I sat up, rubbed my face, my chin prickly with stubble.

I found my phone in my pants pocket and saw that I'd missed several calls from Sean and one from Monty. I took a big breath and blew it out loudly. *Here we go*, I thought. Sean was either returning my call about the bear or he was going to ream me out because Ford had called him. I put the phone away. I'd call him on the way back to the park.

After I showered and shaved, my hand only slightly shaky, I went downstairs and had a cup of coffee with Ma. I told her I was late and needed to get going and would have to skip breakfast, but she refused to let me leave without two scrambled eggs in my belly, telling me that I looked even thinner than when she saw me at Nat's. I scarfed those down and thanked her, but before I left I asked if she still had some of the things I used to keep in my bedroom in my top drawer of my dresser.

"Of course I do," she said. "Everything's boxed up in the basement."

"Do you remember the knife Dad gave me? The one with the pearl handle?"

A half smile came to her lips. "That's not in storage. It's in with the articles I showed you. You want me to get it?"

"Yes, please," I said. "I do."

I waited for her to return with it, and after she placed it in my hand, I stood quietly for a moment, feeling its weight through the smooth pearl and observing the rust on the edges. I didn't open it in front of her, just kissed her good-bye. "I'll visit again before I leave," I said at the door.

"I'll expect it." She was dressed in a pair of burgundy cords and a striped sweater. Her hair was neat and her cheeks slightly rosy. I thought she looked good for her age, even pretty. Suddenly, a pity washed over me that she'd never remarried or found another partner.

"What?" she said curiously when she saw me pausing.

"Oh, nothing." I turned and got in the car and started it while she stayed at the door. The blue sky had already turned a bruised gray in the short time it took for my breakfast and flurries of frigid wind tossed the dead leaves in the front yard. I started to back out, then stopped and rolled the window down. "Thanks again, Ma," I said.

"Why are you thanking me for nothing?" she called through the gusts. "I'm just doing what any mom would do."

"It wasn't nothing," I said. "I needed that." I waved again and backed onto the avenue and headed north.

• • •

I called Monty first on my way to Glacier. "What's up?" I asked him.

"Walsh's boys finally searched the South Fork and guess what?"

"They found it?"

"Yup."

"You're kidding?"

"Nope. I'm not. A Ruger Blackhawk."

"But it's Sunday. How come I didn't know they agreed to search?"

"Guess he had some guys willing to work an extra shift this weekend, and he knew you'd been wanting it done. Guess he rethought it. Deep down, Walsh is a softy."

"Good to know." I chuckled in spite of my irritation at Monty.

"He left a message here at headquarters last night."

I was relieved by this surprise, but I still was feeling uneasy about telling Monty about my father. It had occurred to me that he had to be the one who filled Ford in. The timing seemed a little too coincidental, and I was kicking myself for confiding in a guy who I knew all along was Ford's right-hand man. Even Monty had enough sense to not go on about whatever it was in his family that made him not want to bring children into the world. The thought of exposing the events of 1987 to anyone else ever again made a ball of acid expand in my stomach, so when I called Sean after telling Monty how to handle the evidence until I arrived, I was doubly relieved when Sean didn't chew me out.

He said he was returning my call to talk about the bear. I let out a pent-up breath and felt my pulse slow back down. He said that after some consideration and a few chats with other officials in the department, he had decided that it was, indeed, important to get the slug regardless of what had come out in the paper and regardless of what the park's bear committee had decided.

"Well, that's good to hear because the county guys have found a gun in one of the rivers outside of the park."

"You're kidding?"

"Nope. Just got the call right now."

Sean was pleased, and since his mood was calm, I knew that I should tell him about Ford and my history in Glacier because it was inevitable Ford would. Sean had said that he'd call him to make sure he didn't release the bear, and I pretty much knew that when that happened, it would irritate Ford enough that he'd spill the beans. But I stubbornly, and perhaps foolishly, held back. I was clinging to the idea that my past was nobody's business but mine. Other than lose my cool a time or two, I had done nothing wrong or unprofessional. The worst I'd done was making a fool of myself by the bear's cage in front of Joe Smith.

So when I entered the office and saw Monty, I had already conjured in my head full conversations between Ford and him about my past. I pictured Monty, his eyes full of pity for the poor fourteen-year-old boy, but with the same upward curled lip as Stimpy, slightly smiling as he enjoyed furtively dishing out the juicy details to Ford like a good little minion.

"Hey," Monty said when I entered.

"Let's see it." I held out my hand, and Monty handed me the gun wrapped in thick plastic. I inspected it through the wrapping. Its barrel was narrow and about six inches long, the handle a rich brown. The serial number and other markings lay etched on the barrel and the frame under the cylinder. "Have you checked to see if it's in the ATF database?"

"Not yet," Monty said.

"We need to do that first." I rotated it and checked out the barrel. "Fingerprints are probably unlikely after being in the water this long. Looks like it's stainless, though, and not blued, and with the cold water, the barrel shouldn't have rusted."

"How quickly can that happen?" Monty asked.

I shrugged. "The inside of the barrel isn't usually treated, so it can rust pretty quickly in warm water but less with stainless. After we check for registration, we need to get this to Missoula quickly and see what they come up with." I sighed. "Obviously now, more than ever, we need the slug." I set the gun on the table and eyed Monty suspiciously. "It's Sunday," I mumbled. "Why are you in here?"

"Don't have anything better to do. Tried to get Lara to spend some time with me, but she's not interested." He gave a small shrug. "Besides,

I wanted to organize some of my notes." He tilted his head toward my diagram. "I see you've been working on your own."

I grunted.

"I was going over all interviews with the Shelton grandchildren when the call came in from Walsh."

I swallowed my irritation at the fact that Walsh didn't call my cell phone to let me know firsthand, and I wondered why Monty always seemed to be in the right place at the right time. I dialed Walsh and asked him how quickly Gretchen's officer would transfer the gun to the ballistics lab in Missoula.

"How quickly?" Monty asked after I hung up.

"By early evening. Gretchen's guy should be here any minute."

"You need for me to record the info on the gun?"

"No, I got it." I took out my notepad and wrote down the serial number and the other etchings.

"Figure anything out?" Monty asked, pointing to my diagram.

"No," I said. "Been busy dealing with a few other issues."

"Such as?"

"Such as making sure we get the slug from our bear before your boss lets him go."

Monty leaned back in his chair and placed his hands behind his head. "I heard he wants to do that, like today."

"Yeah, well, obviously now that we have the gun, he can't. We need the slug."

"But it's over a week already." Monty furrowed his brow. "What if he'd already threw it up or crapped it out in the woods before we got him?"

"The bear's not crapped anything in over a week. That's why I doubt he did it before we picked him up."

"So you really believe it's still in his digestive tract?"

"I do. It could very well stay in there all winter, but I'm hoping the heat lights will work."

"And if they don't?"

"We'll have to cut him open."

Monty pushed his glasses up. "From what I've heard, I don't think the committee's going to let you do that."

"I'm sure you've heard all sorts of things," I said resentfully. "But bottom line is that it depends on the chain of command in the DOI at this point."

Monty lifted an eyebrow. "Everyone knows the parks make their own calls on their own bears, not the department."

"But this is different. This involves a federal murder investigation, and like I said, now we have the weapon."

"And you think that will trump the park's decision?"

"Look," I said. "As much as I know how much you like the guy to be happy, I'm afraid I *do* think it trumps his decision."

"Happy?" Monty furrowed his brow.

"I know you like to please the guy." I could hear the accusation in my voice. I tried to cover: "After all," I added, "he's as good as your boss."

"Smith's my boss." He stood up to face me. "I'm just doing whatever job I'm assigned to because that's who I am. It's not like I'm trying to kiss anyone's ass." He spread his hands out to his sides as if to add, *Come on now*.

"Oh, please." I knew I should back off, but I couldn't just yet. "I know the only reason you've been assigned to this case is to keep tabs on things and report back to him."

"Really? I thought the reason I was on this case was to help you out. I am a Park Police officer."

"Hmm. Well, I'm not sure why they'd take a desk guy who's practically Ford's secretary to do real police work."

"Maybe I'm good at both?" Monty's mouth was half open.

"Well, if you're good at both, maybe you ought to start acting like a real officer and start making it easy for us to solve this case rather than harder." I knew I was being completely irrational and unfair. Monty did, indeed, act like a good officer and was extremely helpful, but I couldn't set my anger aside.

"How the hell am I making it harder?"

"By trying to undermine me." I picked up my diagram, rolled it up, and placed it under my arm.

"Undermine you?" He furrowed his brow.

I gathered the files filled with photos of Victor and the crime scene and shoved them in my case. "It's neither here nor there at this point. Let's just keep plugging along and get this thing solved." I let out a loud sigh and went to the door. "I'll be back in a little while."

"Wait. I want to know why you think I've undermined you."

I turned to him from the doorway and saw that his brow was still deeply furrowed, his arms crossed before his chest. "Let's just say that I really didn't need you filling Ford in on what I'd told you about yesterday." I turned and walked out the door without waiting for a reply.

22

As soon as I got in my car, I called Monica and gave her the serial number and tracked the initial registration to a Robert Stein from Kalispell who often bought guns at one gun show, then bartered them for other things he needed at pawnshops or other gun shows. I visited Mr. Stein at a nice home in Whitefish near the ski resort. He claimed to have traded the Ruger for a piece from a local artist and showed me the painting above his rock fireplace, a rich landscape of an eastern Montana coulee cut into a buttery wheat field lit by a fiery sunset and adorned with handsome pheasants.

I then tracked the artist down to a residence in Bigfork at the south end of the Flathead Valley on the north end of Flathead Lake. His name was Davis Riggs, and I found his number in the phone book back in my cabin and asked his wife if he was there. She asked who was calling, and I told her the truth. He came right to the phone, no stalling, and I figured he had nothing to hide.

"How can I help you, sir?" his voice was pleasant and warm.

"Ah, Mr. Riggs, I wonder if you can help me. I'm wondering if you still own that Ruger Blackhawk .357 you traded one of your paintings for at the Fairgrounds Trade Show two years ago. I believe." I looked down at my notepad. "It was in August?"

"The Ruger?"

"That's right."

"You know, I rarely keep those for more than a week. I take them to a pawnshop and get cash immediately."

"Why's that?"

Riggs laughed softly at the other end. "It's the best way to make money during an economic downswing. It's hard to sell a painting outright during tough times, but everyone wants a gun around these parts when things get pinched."

"I see. Do you remember which pawnshop you used and when you took it there?"

"Sure, First National Pawn, on Highway 93. Like I said, I never typically wait more than a few days. So if the gun show was in August, it was probably still August."

The owner of First National hemmed and hawed and made no promises that they had a record of who bought what from that long ago. "You know, most people buy with cash," he said, but did kindly agree to go through all his August records from two years ago and get back to us with any purchase of a 1970 stainless .357 Ruger Blackhawk. I gave him the details, politely asking him to write them down. "A 1970 stainless," I repeated, "with a six-inch barrel and an adjustable rear sight and composite grips with 'Sturm, Ruger and Co., Inc.' and 'Southport, Conn. U.S.A.' stamped on the left side of the barrel. And," I added, "it has 'Ruger .357 CAL' and 'Blackhawk' on the left side of the frame beneath the cylinder, and the trademark phoenix logo to the right of the words."

In between pacing around the cabin, I tried to study everything I had and not think about Tom Hess, Ford, or even Monty now. Since I'd been at Ma's the night before and hadn't had the heat on or a fire going, the place felt cold and fusty. I turned the electric heat up and sat on the couch to look at all the photos of the crime scene with the tree and the corpse bound to it, shot from every conceivable angle—close-ups of the bloody duct tape, his chewed-up cheek and jaw, his skull, his ripped arms and legs, and his abdominal area, where large gaps of flesh were taken. When thoughts of my father started to creep in, I shut the file angrily and hoped like hell that the ballistics lab wouldn't take long to call with some useful information on the Ruger.

I unrolled my diagram and continued to work on it, unsuccessfully attempting to brainstorm anything that came to mind. I knew there was a connection somewhere right in front of me. I felt as if I was peering through a kaleidoscope, and I only needed to make one or two more turns and a different pattern, the right one, would emerge before my eyes.

I spoke to Gretchen to see if anything else had come up, and she said that there was nothing new to report. I spoke to Dr. Wilson again to recheck my notes on everything he had told me: the gunshot, the angle, the amount of time the victim spent bound to the tree, the possible time of death.

I went back over Tom Hess's file. As bad as Stimpy seemed, a guy who could beat a dog to near death was probably worse in terms of violence. I made myself a turkey and cheese sandwich, read more notes, then began pacing, and when that started, I knew I needed to get out. I grabbed my coat and headed to the Inside Road.

When I parked and got out, I could see my breath. Mosquito-size flakes of snow started to slowly drift down from the sky, and I held out my palm to let one land on it and watched it melt. There was something comforting about the snow, how just a touch of the flaky white stuff drifting and swirling in the dark, empty forest could alter the fall mood and make it seem less eerie.

I walked on the overgrown trail and expected a raven to caw, but all was silent except for the creak of the trees and the rustling of a ground squirrel somewhere off in the brush. The ground had become firmer as the mud began to freeze, and I could feel the cold, bumpy earth poke the soles of my shoes.

By the time I made it to the site, a thin veil of snow layered the forest floor. White flakes gathered on golden and red bushes, on dead leaves, pine needles, and old leftover yellowed grass from the summer.

It began to dust the baby firs springing up, as well as the crisscrossed jumble of fallen branches.

I walked slowly to the tree, to the bloodstained grayish-brown bark and stared at it. The trunk had a thick triangular, naturally caused groove that exposed a lighter-colored ash-gray part of the tree underneath. I suppose it grew that way, around some disease or ailment.

It was a tall tree. There were no branches until the top, and it seemed to stretch a long way up to touch the sky. It looked solitary—a one-man show. I walked away from it, to the side where a fallen log lay, and brushed off the film of snow and sat, not caring if my pants would get wet. I opened my thermos and poured a steaming cup and stared at the tree in the clearing. Suddenly, an owl sailed by, its wingspan long, brown, and silently flapping. I thought of how that same owl might have flown by Victor during his night of hell, maybe shrieking to prompt its prey to startled movement. I tried to imagine who brought Victor and bound him. How he endured a night of torture—a child's worst nightmare: alone in the woods, freezing, unable to run and coming off a high, the rough bark against his skin, and the tape too thick and tight to wiggle out of. Bait for anything that wanted him. My heart rate began to rise, and flashes of Oldman Lake shot through my mind. I pushed the thoughts away.

My butt began to freeze. I stood and tossed the last cold bit of my coffee onto the ground, shook the thermos cup out, and screwed the lid on. I brushed the gathering flakes, rapidly growing bigger and now the size of moths, off my pants. I knew that I had come to the spot to tackle at least one thing: to see if anything new came to mind about what happened to Victor Lance. I stood silently, waiting for an epiphany, hoping each small twitch in the forest held an accessible clue.

I walked around the tree studying the blood spatter on the bark. Then I continued around it wider and wider until I increased the circle beyond where Gretchen and her crew had worked. I climbed over fallen logs and parted branches, carefully studying them for any signs of blood or breaks. I looked for dislodged logs or flattened foliage not already noted. I tried to put myself in both the perpetrator's and Victor's position.

How did they get Victor back here? Did they force him? Did he fall? Were his hands bound? I saw nothing out of the ordinary. The woods formed a tangled pattern. Branches were intertwined, and people and animals had traipsed through the area, including the rangers checking for bear scat, but I found nothing that obviously broke the interwoven network. I thought about the motivation.

Anger, I considered. Revenge. A combination of both? I thought of Anderson and kept coming back to Tom Hess and the dog. Anyone nasty enough to do that to an innocent animal must be—and this is an understatement—difficult to have a friendship with. I wondered how he and Victor got along and if something went wrong enough for Hess to take his partner-in-cruelty to the woods and leave him there. It almost seemed too restrained, too controlled, for a poaching, instant-gratification personality. We'd already notified Highway Patrol on the east side of the mountains to keep an eye out for Hess, but I decided to again stress the need to locate him and to also put the word out to all Fish Wildlife and Parks game wardens working the hunter-access areas. The vastness of eastern Montana provided a multitude of places to hide.

As I circled back in, I found myself by the bush where I'd dropped my quarter. Its leaves were fire-red and now covered in white. I thought of Monty and me laughing. I bent over and peered through the branches to the dark ground not yet touched by the snow. No quarter. I walked around to the other side, stepping through thick clusters of underbrush, yellow, red, and brown. The legs of my pants were soaked. I separated the branches again and searched.

In the mud, I saw an edge of silver. I smiled, grabbed it, and rubbed its wet and muddy surface to a clean sparkle. Its tactile exactness amid all the unanswered questions churning in my mind gave me a vague sense of hope. I walked out of the woods with my thermos and no answers. But for that moment, I had my Vermont quarter and only a moment or two of an increased heart rate.

· · ·

I drove back to the office. I figured they'd be completely empty now that it was turning dark, but Monty was still in, and when I entered, he lifted his chin and gave me a curt dip of his head. "Ted," he acknowledged me.

"Didn't think you'd still be here."

"I'm just leaving." He shuffled his work together. Then he carefully slid his files into his satchel and left without another word or eye contact.

Again, I stared at his color-coded poster as if it held the answers. Getting no smile and the cold shoulder from Monty hit me square on. I knew I deserved it. I sat without taking my coat off. A numbness began to take hold of me, and I continued to sit still, chilled in my wet pants, for I don't know how long until my phone rang and made me snap out of it.

"Ted, what the hell is going on up there?"

It was Sean. I didn't answer—tried to collect my thoughts.

"I get a call from Ford about your goddamn history in Glacier. Are you kidding me? A grizzly attack in 1987?"

"So?" I said.

"Why didn't I know about this?"

"I don't know." I stood up and began to pace the room, but my legs felt weak, so I sat back down. "Why should you?"

"Why should I?" His voice was getting louder. "If you've got a water phobia, I shouldn't know about it?"

"I don't mean to be disrespectful, sir." I tried to take a deep breath, but it caught high up near my throat. "But it's just something a long time ago. There's no phobia and it has nothing to do with the present. Seriously, what does it have to do with anything now?"

"Let me think," he said sarcastically. "Maybe because you're in charge of a case in the same park that it happened in? Maybe because this case involves a grizzly bear?"

"So?" I said again, trying to sound cavalier, but not sure I was pulling it off.

"*So?* That's all you've got to say?"

"Look, sir, I honestly don't see the relevance. I've been working this job over ten years and I've been in many parks with grizzlies around: Yellowstone—"

"You've never been this close"—he cut me off—"to . . . to a situation like this before."

"It's not like anything is wrong, sir." I ran my fingers through my hair and squeezed my eyes shut for a moment. "If my father had died in a car accident that I'd been in with him when I was a teen, would I not be able to investigate a murder at a car dealership?" I knew what I had just said was completely ridiculous.

"That's different and you know it. Besides, you should have solved this by now."

"It's happening, just a little more slowly than some. But definitely not the slowest. We've taken longer, a lot longer," and I almost said *and some have never been solved*, but stopped myself when I imagined the rage he might go into about me thinking that was acceptable. In fact, I didn't think not solving a case was acceptable at all, and the few in the department that went that way, one involving a thirteen-year-old boy, bothered all four of us deeply.

"Look, Ted. Clearly, we originally missed something in your initial psych evaluations."

I knew what he really meant: *clearly, you did not give all the information you should have about your background*, but I appreciated his tact amid his anger.

"You need to wrap this thing up quickly, and as soon as you do, you're coming back for another evaluation and a committee review.

And if you don't solve this case soon, like within the next week, you're coming back anyway, and I'm sending LaMatto in."

. . .

For the next two days, Monty and I hardly spoke, as if we were in some lovers' spat. I have to take responsibility for it because I am somewhat stubborn and was still angry that he told Ford about my history. I felt broody and quiet, and worse, knowing a psych evaluation was looming in the near future made me withdraw even further into my shell.

At the risk of sounding like I'm some kind of Holmes and Monty my Watson, I can say that I actually sort of missed him and felt a little lost without his eagerness buoying me up. Not making any further head-way on the case wasn't helping either. The place felt tense, stifled, and awkward, and all I could think about was Jeff LaMotto coming in, hav-ing Monty bust his ass to bring him up to speed while *opportunity and preparation intersected*, so that he could come in last minute as the hero when I got transferred to border patrol with my tail between my legs.

Monty and I did communicate but only to exchange whatever trickles of information we garnered regarding the case and the efforts to find the owner of the Ruger. The report from the ballistics lab in Mis-soula had come up with no fingerprints, and at this point, we needed the slug to verify a match between weapon and bullet so that we knew we even had a link between the weapon and the actual crime. Marga-ret, one of the lead ballistics specialists at the university, told me that it was a pre-1973 model and like all other older Ruger single-action revolvers, it didn't have a transfer bar between the hammer and the firing pin, so that the gun is less safe to carry loaded with six rounds when the hammer is down. "With this one," she said over the phone, "there were four cartridges left in the cylinder with only one round fired, so that means whoever fired it knew enough to not carry it with six rounds but didn't know that the empty chamber should be directly under the hammer."

"So that it won't accidentally go off if the hammer gets hit." I thought of the angle of the shot fired—how an accidental discharge would account for the strange trajectory of the bullet.

"That's right," she agreed.

I thanked her and told her to call if anything else of interest came up.

Monty informed me that there'd been no leads from any of the local stores on duct tape purchases that seemed like potential suspects. There'd been just a few purchases by credit card here and there from random people: a mother from Kalispell, a man from Oregon who'd just been passing through, a general-contracting business from Whitefish, and the rest untraceable because cash was used. He was still focusing on the grandchildren, trying to find some possible in, but was coming up short.

In addition to still searching for the owner of the gun, I was attempting to track down Hess on the east side, but no one had seen him, and he'd checked into no hotels. Other than that, I was climbing the walls. I could hardly be in my cabin without pacing, could hardly focus at headquarters, and I was drinking too much whiskey at night and waking up with massive headaches and shaky hands after having bizarre and dark dreams. On some level, I knew I was coming apart, and a strong voice in my head kept urging me to keep it together.

My cabin didn't even have a TV so that I could channel surf and settle on something mindless. Instead, I'd listen to the radio, mostly to National or Montana Public Radio, where I'd catch political pieces on world news, like Afghan talks between Karzai and Taliban leaders to end the war. Or something light, like shows featuring unique African music. I'd lost my appetite completely, and what I did eat was cruddy and devoid of anything nutritious.

On about day thirteen of the investigation, I was in the office with Monty going over information on Rob Anderson's computer records to see if there was anything that could corroborate his alibi when Monty read a headline from the local news: "Bear Kills Hunter," he said.

I looked up, the clench below my sternum instant.

"On the Montana–Canadian border," he offered.

"Grizzly?

"Yes."

"Bow hunting?"

"No. Rifle—black-bear hunting. A group of three guys."

"The bear?"

"One of the other hunters killed it."

I nodded, heard the tick of the clock and a murmuring of voices down the hall. Monty put the paper down.

"You know," he said, pushing his glasses up. "In spite of what you think, I didn't tell Ford."

I nodded, not sure what I wanted to say. I tried to focus on the notes in front of me, then began to say, "You making any headway on—" when Bowman came in, his face flushed from the cold and high energy jumping from him and permeating the stale, dismal room.

"The slug," he said. "We've got it."

Monty and I looked at each other, then back to Bowman. "You're kidding?"

"No." He smiled. "He finally went. And there it was, right among all the grass he'd been eating to form his intestinal plug and a good mix of bits of plastic and shreds of cloth from the victim's clothes."

I stood up. "Where is it?"

He held up a plastic bag and grinned.

• • •

We got the slug immediately to Walsh, who would send it to the ballistics lab in Missoula just as he had the gun. Even though I should have been ecstatic to finally get what I'd been waiting for all this time, I was still on edge. A humming vibration shot up the back of my skull and settled between my ears. Now we had the gun and the bullet, and once we confirmed the match, we would have solid evidence to convict a perpetrator. We just didn't have our killer yet, and without other leads giving us probable cause to search a suspect, we weren't going to get much further. The clock was ticking before I would have to head back to Denver to face my fate and let LaMotto take over my case. At least, I thought with relief, the damn grizzly could be released and everyone would be happy, especially Ford.

In fact, within the hour, I ran into Karen Fortenson, who told me that after the immediate release, a group of rangers were meeting at a bar in the Chalet in West Glacier to celebrate. She invited Monty and me, and I told her I'd try to make it, but I knew I wouldn't. I had no intention of going to celebrate the grizzly's release. It's not that I wasn't glad to send him on his merry way to the high country. Something just struck me as strange about my attendance at such a function—the kid whose dad was killed by a grizzly—and I was sure word had gotten around, judging by some of the hushed conversations and the furtive glances I was receiving whenever I came into headquarters or walked by any park personnel.

I had better things to do, like solve a murder.

Monty, on the other hand, liked the idea and packed up immediately, saying, "I could use a beer and some company."

I suppose I was envious, but determined not to show it. I told myself I could use coffee instead and that I needed to get out of Glacier.

"You should come," Monty offered.

"Nah, I've got work to do."

"Come on." Monty frowned. "We need a break, and this is the perfect excuse."

"Thanks," I said. "Maybe. I'll think about it." I packed up my notes as Monty walked out, saying he hoped he'd see me there.

. . .

By the time I hopped in the car, I reconsidered. Monty was right; it was something I should do. At the very least, in the most minimal of ways, it would be like getting back on the horse—facing a party for a grizzly around a group of people who knew my history.

I headed to the little bar in the Chalet in West Glacier, and I could almost feel the atmosphere as I walked through the lot and up the deck stairs toward it. The music blared, and more bodies than I expected stood behind the steamed windows. When I pushed the door open, a waft of warm, steamy air poured over me and again, I was surprised at how many people had shown in the middle of the afternoon. There were women, men, rangers, and park employees I'd never seen. The mood of the crowd was giddy with people singing along with loud music. Bowman casually leaned against the old richly stained wooden bar, laughing loudly with his head tipped back and a mug of beer in his hand. Karen sat next to him, and beside Karen was a big-breasted woman I'd not seen before, talking and giggling at Monty. Ken Greeley and a group of young rangers were conducting some drinking competition with shots of clear liquid and there, in the middle of them, sat Joe, one arm draped languidly over the back of his chair, his eyes bright and happy. A pang shot through me for no good reason. All I could think of was that I wanted that same contentedness that emanated from him in my own life.

I raised my hand to wave, but he didn't see me, so instead of trying further to grab his attention, I went to the other end of the bar, away from Bowman, Monty, and crew, and bought Joe the best Scotch they had in stock and watched the bartender carry the drink over and set it on the table in front of him, pointing over to me. Joe raised his chin, smiled, and waved me over, but I shook my head and held up my palm that I was fine.

I looked down the length of the bar and saw Monty waving me over as well.

"Glad you could make it." He grinned and introduced me to Wendy, a secretary at the Chalet who'd just gotten off her shift.

"Decided you were right." I gestured at the scene all around. "Is it me or is it a little strange that there's so much energy over this in the middle of the afternoon among a bunch of strait-laced rangers and Park Police officers? You'd think we solved the case, but apparently the bear was more important."

Monty cringed. "Maybe to some of these people, but you'd be sur-prised—any excuse for us Montanans is usually a good one." He took a swig from his mug. "Who the hell you calling straitlaced anyway?"

I held up my palm. "Sorry, no offense."

"Word of celebration spreads fast around here.", Bowman added, smiling.

"I suppose it does."

Monty handed me a mug of beer. "It's Bud. Cheers."

"Good with me. Cheers." I looked around, and as I took a sip of the cold brew, the door opened and Ford came in. I noticed Monty throw me a cautious glance. "How'd it go with the bear?" I asked.

"I guess smoothly. Ask him." Monty tilted his head to Bowman.

"What?" Bowman said.

"How'd it go with the bear?"

"Aw, man, it was great—Ford and I drove him out past McGee to the Logging Lake area. The moment we opened the door, he hit the woods running north." Bowman slid one palm across the other, one hand shooting out ahead to imitate the bear breaking speed. "Didn't even need to pepper his ass with pellets to get him going. And he's col-lared, so we'll have an idea where he ends up."

"I'm sure he was one happy bear."

"Yes, yes, he was."

"Good work." I nodded approvingly. "With the bullet and all."

"Thank you." He held up his drink to toast mine, then took a sip and turned back to Karen.

I looked back to Ford, who had now joined Joe. He glanced at me, then said something to Joe and laughed. I turned back around and faced the bar. Some high-pitched country music singer wailed in the background. I tried to relax and enjoy the music and the vibrating atmosphere I hadn't felt since I'd arrived.

"Too bad he didn't bring his daughter?" Monty said, looking toward the table with Joe and now Ford.

"Who?"

"Joe."

"Joe?"

"I mean Heather, of course. Not Leslie."

"Why?"

Monty shrugged. "I don't know."

"You interested in her?"

"Are you kidding me, with the shit I'm in the middle of, I can't afford to have an interest in anyone. But . . . " He took a sip of his beer.

"But you do anyway?"

Monty wiped his mouth with his knuckles. "She's, well, she's nice. Got some class, you know. But I was thinking about you." He lifted his chin to me.

"Me?" I cringed. "With the shit *I'm* in the middle of?" We both laughed, and I excused myself because I felt my phone vibrate. I stepped around the corner to the hallway, where it was a bit quieter. It was Walsh. He wanted to let me know that they'd just sent the slug with another shipment of evidence the county needed to get to Missoula to the lab with one of his officers. They'd have the slug by tonight and would be able to study it tomorrow.

"And," he said, "I've got something else for you."

"Oh?" I waited.

"Your man Hess has finally made it back from the east side. I've had one of my boys checking his place regularly, and suddenly there's some dead antelope hanging from his back porch."

I thanked him and went back and told Monty about the slug but not about Hess. I didn't want to pull Monty away from his fun, and something made me want to go see Hess alone.

"So by tomorrow we might have solid evidence," Monty said. "What then?"

"We'll still need the owner of it. And that's where we'll continue focusing."

Monty looked serious and nodded.

"Listen," I said. "Thanks for inviting me. I'm actually enjoying it here, but I'm just not going to be able to relax until I can find the owner of this gun. You stay; enjoy yourself for a bit."

"But there's nothing to do but wait to hear if it's a match. You should stay."

"Nah, I appreciate it, but I've got some things I need to do. But again, you stay." I looked at my watch. It was still business hours. "Maybe give the pawnshop guy a call when you leave and see if he's had a chance to check his records yet. I've already given him all the details."

"I can do that." Monty nodded and smiled his white grin. "It was big of you to stop in."

I set my empty mug down and pulled out a twenty and left it on the bar for him to do whatever he wanted with it.

"No, man, take that."

"No, get another round. It's on me." I playfully slapped Monty's back, turned to go, and found myself looking straight into Ford's eyes. He didn't say a word, just glared at me for a moment before making his way to the bar.

I gave a curt nod and began to move past him as the loud rumbling and whining of a freight train barreling by on the Burlington Northern Santa Fe consumed the place. It ran through West Glacier, across the street from the Chalet. I didn't catch it if he nodded back or not. I made my way to the exit as the bar grew louder and people raised their voices to compete with the deafening train. When I got to the door I waited for it to pass, paused to distinguish between the pounding of my heart and the loud *click-clack* of the wheels rolling over the joints in the rail. I saw Joe watching me while the train's diesel engine roared so loudly that it drowned the music. People quit trying to compete and halted their conversations as they waited for it to pass. Joe smiled at me and waved me over again. I pointed to my phone to indicate that I had business to attend to, and he pointed to the drink I bought him and mouthed "Thank you."

At that moment, with the arresting and vibrating howl in my ears and the kind look in Joe's eyes, my defenses melted. I felt shaky, and my heartbeat reverberated in my chest. Somewhere between Ford, Hess, my visit with Ma, and my trip to the woods, I was beginning to realize that Ford was never going to give me any satisfaction or release from my own demons. But even with the progress on the case—finding the gun and finally getting the slug—something needled me, and the train seemed to crash that unease and angst deeply into me at full speed.

Finally the freight passed and the sound subsided, leaving only the music as the patrons' voices tried to fully recover their cadence. I caught Monty, Bowman, and Karen smiling at me and laughing playfully at something. I ignored the clench in my sternum, put on a nice grin, and nodded back, then opened the door and stepped out into the cool air.

· · ·

Of course, we'd run Tom Hess through the system and came up with a few poaching complaints, but no real evidence that it was with him, so he was never charged and fined. But if there was one person whom I was going to lose it with, it was him. His cold, hazel eyes coated with arrogance, his shit-eating grin filled with bad teeth, his lopsided sneer, and his militant stance with his chest pushed out so far that his shoulder blades must have touched in back, all made me want to rip his throat out. But I knew that the only way interrogating him was going to work in my favor was to try to get along nicely with him. But he must have known one of Walsh's guys had been keeping tabs on him since he'd returned because when I got to his small house with faded-brown peeling paint and wood gone to dry rot, we were already off to a bad start in spite of my best intentions.

Tall dead weeds choked the lawn and the sides of the house under the windows. An ATV sat on one side under a slumped overhang with an aluminum roof. I'd stopped and talked to one of Walsh's guys around the corner before walking down the block and found that Hess had gotten home a few hours before and that he'd only left once to go to the store. He informed me that the place had two doors and that Hess had been using the back one. Also, he said that Hess had at least four or five dead antelope hanging from the top of a porch overhang covering the back concrete patio.

I strolled casually to the front door with a pleasant face in case he was watching and knocked several times. On the third attempt, he answered, his eyes narrowed in anger.

"What do you want?" He was the same height as me, if not a bit taller, his nose turned up.

I ignored the rude greeting and gave him my best smile and friendly tone. "Hi, I'm Ted Systead. If it's all right with you, I'd like to ask you a few questions about a friend of yours, Victor Lance."

"It's not all right with me," he said. "I'm busy."

I swallowed my irritation. A wet chill hung in the air around me and bit my cheeks. "I appreciate your candidness, but"—I pulled out and showed him my badge, which I wasn't wearing but had in a small leather case—"I'm afraid I misspoke. I *will* be asking you a few questions about Victor Lance."

Hess stared at me for a second, one side of his upper lip raised in disgust. Then he dropped his hand from the knob, left the door ajar, and walked down the hall without saying anything more. I slowly followed him into the dark hallway, placing my hand on my gun, which I can honestly say I hadn't felt the urge to do in nearly a year, not even with Stimpy.

At the end of the hallway, the house opened up into a small kitchen with an old, round Formica-topped table. Two dirty kitchen windows showed a junky backyard filled with old engine parts and trash, and the windows to his right all had the shades drawn. I suspected he had shut them to hide his antelope from my view. Hess leaned his backside against a dirty counter next to his old stove and crossed his arms before him. "What do you want to know?"

I stood at the kitchen entry and noticed a door at its other end, which I assumed led to the backyard. I began by asking him some simple questions: how long he'd known Victor and whether he even knew what had happened. He said he'd known him about two years and yes, he knew he was dead.

"Do you know when he was killed?" I asked.

"Over a week ago, right?" His smile was too large and fake, a few of his teeth missing, as if he was pretending to be a proud student in a classroom answering a question correctly.

"That's right. Between Thursday afternoon and Friday evening. That's why I need to ask you where you were during those two days?"

"That's easy." He continued to smile a wicked grin. "Huntin' antelope. Been on the east side for ten days now."

I nodded, lifting my chin toward the pulled blinds. I was pretty sure that if I stepped out the back door and asked him for the tags, he wouldn't have them. When I looked back, his top lip had resumed the curled-up-in-disgust position as he eyed me. His face appeared amorphous, constantly changing like it was made of clay or rubber.

"You stay at any motels over there?"

"Hell no." He looked indignantly at me like I was a total pussy for even suggesting it. "We slept in our trucks."

"I'll need the names of the guys you were with."

"Whatever." He began to laugh, and I could feel my blood begin to boil. I bit my lower lip and stared at him. "You find this funny?"

"Sort of," he said. "You rookies obviously haven't found much."

"You'd be surprised."

"Then why are you here?"

"To see if you have anything to add. Do you have anything that might help us out?"

"Hell no," he repeated and started laughing again. Not a crazy maniacal laugh like Stimpy, just a smug, condescending chuckle. "Even if I did, why would I help you?"

"Why wouldn't you?"

"'Cause I've never liked your kind, that's why." He rolled his fat lower lip around his tongue and pushed the skin below the lip out. I thought he looked grotesque, and I couldn't tell if he intended that for my benefit or if that was something he did often, no matter whose company he kept.

"You wouldn't want to help catch whoever did that to your buddy?" I know I sounded naïve, but I was still trying to keep it civil—to get answers.

"Shit." He laughed. "I could care less. Victor's too fuckin' stupid to not get killed, that's his problem." He shrugged. "All I care about is getting my motorcycle back."

"Motorcycle?"

"Yeah, the asshole had been using my '82 Honda this fall 'cause he was too poor and stupid to have his own car."

"You don't speak very highly of him. And here, I'm thinking you two were close?" And then I couldn't help but add: "Dog-beatin' buddies and all."

Hess's grin got even wider. "Oh, the good little detective's been doing his homework around town. Catchin' all the gossip and everything."

"Pretty certain it's not gossip."

"At this point, who gives a *fuck*?" He yelled the last word and I had to work not to flinch. The wispy hairs on the back of my neck prickled against a cold draft behind me. I widened my stance.

"A lot of people do."

"I bet." He laughed again, then licked his lower lip. "All them treehuggin' assholes. Boo-hoo for them." He puffed his purplish, pink lower lip out as fat and as far as he could into a ridiculous pout as if he were a mime.

"You and Victor have some falling-out over that dog ordeal?"

"Fuck no." He pulled his lip back in. "Victor was a pussy. Besides, that's old, old news."

In spite of the cool air in the hallway behind me, my anger was heating me up and I broke a sweat. "Great, so you're the one with all the experience, and you figured you'd teach your protégé?"

"Why not?"

"And I suppose Victor would've jumped off a bridge if you did that too?"

"No." He gave me his shit-eating grin, his eyes empty and cold. "Beatin' a dog's a whole lot more fun than jumpin' off a bridge."

At that moment, Hess began laughing again. Only this time, his chuckle sounded farther away because the blood was surging into my head. My breathing quickened as everything seemed to slow down. In one sudden and deft move, I grabbed my gun and dove across the kitchen. I slammed into him and rammed my forearm under his chin, bashing the back of his head into one of the kitchen cabinets so hard that it took him a moment to recover. As he began to regain his senses, he lifted his arm and made a fist. I rammed the butt of my Glock .40 under his chin and snapped his head back. Then I grabbed his wrist and twisted it around his back until the elbow was locked and he was bent at the waist, his cheek smashed into the ugly yellow linoleum counter. "I guess you're big on pain," I said into the back of his head, my voice breathy, but on edge as I spoke through my clenched jaw. "Maybe this isn't enough for you." I tugged on his arm so tightly that I was sure he had to feel that it could shatter at the shoulder. He was breathing hard, and I heard him grunt, trying to hold back a yell. An image of this guy beating the dog so badly that the animal's intestines exploded blazed in my mind.

"You fucking dickhead. You fucking asshole," he said.

With my free hand, I put the gun against the back of his skull. He shut up and all went quiet except the hum of the refrigerator. I pushed the tip of the barrel even harder into the back of his head until I could see an indentation in his grayish-white scalp through his dark and greasy hair. The instant effect of having a gun in my hand—the power—washed over me, surged through my veins like a drug. For a long moment, I wanted it badly. I wanted to pull the trigger—for that defenseless Lab, for Tumble, for all the defenseless victims I'd seen over the years, for all the injustices that seemed to take shape in the guy's ugly, amorphous face . . . but, in the back of my head, I thought I heard some small voice whispering something low and deep, or maybe it was just the blood swishing between my ears, but it was enough to make me take a breath.

I lowered my gun, tightened my grip on him in one more painful twist, and released him. "Better have tags on those." I pointed the barrel of my gun to the closed blinds. I backed down the hallway so I didn't turn away from him and left through the door that I never closed behind me in the first place.

．．．

When I got to my car, I was shaking. With trembling hands, I dialed Walsh's office and told him to call FWP and have them come and check on Hess's kills to see if they were legal. Then I called Monty and left him a message to see if he could find any information on a 1982 Honda motorcycle owned by Hess. I drove past headquarters and back to the cabin, forcing myself to take deep breaths. I sat staring at the cabin, unable to go in, so I pulled out and drove out to Highway 2 and turned east.

I kept driving, around dangerous curves with steep mountain banks plunging to the river below. At first I wasn't sure where I was going, and a steely loneliness and unease settled upon me—frightening and desolate. The feel of my gun against Hess's scalp rushed over me again and stunned me. Somehow I realized that my most strongly held delusion—that I could always keep my cool as Agent Systead—was cracking through and through. That the shots of anger flooding through my veins could be like an addictive drug, robbing all control and good sense. As I surged forward through the mountain pass, it came to me full-on what the distant, low voice at Hess's was murmuring. I could hear it clearly now. It was the voice of my Missoula therapist: *Your anger is the part of you that becomes the perpetrator, and that means the bear. As the bear, you'll suffer no consequences for your actions.* Just as he didn't, I thought.

Ford's words from the day before in the office came to me also. I unsuccessfully tried to push them aside. *Could have had candy bars . . .* I knew it was bullshit and that I needed to get it out of my head and think about the case. Then it hit me where I was headed, where I *needed* to go, and because I knew, I felt a wild rush pushing me forward. I could feel it pulsing through my veins as the gas propelled the car, the SUV hugging the windy mountain road leading to Two Medicine Lake, the entrance to the Oldman Lake area, better than I expected.

The total drive took about two hours, but it felt much faster. When I think back on it, I can barely remember the scenery; can scarcely recall passing Essex, the Izaak Walton Inn area or Goat Lick, the natural salt lick where mountain goats gather on the side of a steep ridge to get their fill of the briny mineral. Can just recall making it over Marias Pass and stopping in East Glacier to fill my thermos with coffee, grab a sandwich, some snacks, and a bottle of Jack Daniel's. I headed that way, through the pale white sunlight folding in on the ominous mountains surrounding me. It was only four thirty, but the soft light held the sigh of winter.

Dusk was beginning to fall when I arrived at Two Medicine Campground, and a rosy radiance infused Two Medicine Valley and turned the ripples in the lake pinkish gold. Several hearty fall camping parties took advantage of the more primitive camping conditions—no park bathrooms or running water available—and I saw two campfires already burning in different campsites not far from one another. I drove around the curving drive of the campground, checking out small vacant openings with fire grates and picnic tables nestled in among fir trees as if it was my job. I felt oddly comforted and less ridiculous that my park vehicle labeled me professional—as if I was only checking the campsites and making sure all was well when the deep prickling reality inside me was an entirely different matter.

I found a spot overlooking the lake, pulled in, and parked. The silence overtook me, and the presence of Sinopah and Rising Wolf Mountain bore down on me. I had no idea why I had come. I just knew—with the fierce energy needling my being—I needed to be at the spot my father and I camped before hiking to Oldman Lake the following day. I had no idea what I expected to accomplish, so I sat, silly in the paling light, taking in the view of some of the most sacred Native American territory sprawling before me. Rising Wolf towered above the lake and Sinopah's massive, dark point pierced the indigo sky. I didn't just see them there; I *felt* their presence before me like angry gods. I got out and softly shut the car door.

I walked to the pebbled beach and found a long, bleached piece of driftwood to sit on. A small breeze made me shiver and rippled the darkening water and somewhere in that breeze, chilling and filled with painful yearnings, I could sense the jagged-edged magic of Glacier Park. I could smell the campfire smoke in the distance and something dark and treacherous nibbled at the corner of my mind. I shook it off and looked around. A few trout rose in the lake, making soft rings that slowly blossomed farther and farther out. A group of geese honked in the distance and flew in a practiced, well-honed V-shape, with only two on one side flying a little too far behind. I stared at the water— took in every pinprick of its changing hue. I felt a brisk breeze switch direction and heard each small noise around me—a rustle of leaves, a delicate break in the water from a rising fish, soft voices in the distance—as if my nerves and sensory channels were enhanced. I picked up a handful of pebbles off the beach and felt their cool texture in my palm. I dropped them to the ground, watching them cascade down my lax fingers.

We had fly-fished here, walked carefully into the icy water with our waders on. We had cast Royal Wulff and caddis flies, and I had gotten the line caught and tangled in a branch of a fir tree behind me. Dad had used my knife to cut the line, then helped me untangle it from the branch so we didn't leave the monofilament in the forest. We had caught cutthroat for dinner and cooked them up at our site, savoring the fresh taste of firm-fleshed trout from icy mountain water.

When I stared at the shore, I could see us there, carefully tying on the Royal Wulff I'd made at home with the fly-tying kit I'd received the Christmas before. Dad had on his multipocketed fishing vest that held his angling paraphernalia and a green cap. We laughed at stupid comments as if we were invincible. As if we had eternity beyond that day. But now, in the chill, I felt the strong hands of time bearing down on my shoulders, felt its bony, fingers pressing into my flesh, each one a reminder of the eons occurring before: Precambrian, Cretaceous, Tertiary, Paleozoic, Quaternary...

I went back to the car, grabbed the silver space blanket out of the emergency kit, turned the engine on, and let it idle for some heat. I inclined the seat back and nestled in. Several bats had come out and zigzagged and dove erratically around for insects. I pulled out my cell phone and confirmed what I already knew: there was no cell service in this area. I almost left at that point. Being here was all so pointless and I shouldn't have left the case behind without letting anyone know where I was. I knew how irresponsible it was and if something happened and I wasn't around, I could be done, finished. Something about the reckless thought—the abandonment, throwing it all to the wind—tantalized me but scared me silly too. I'm not that big of an idiot; I knew that on many levels, my job was my anchor. I even reached for the key and turned the engine on, and if it wouldn't have been so dangerous to tackle Marias Pass again at night, I might have left. Instead, I sat and let the heater warm the car. I poured myself some hot coffee, spiked it with Jack, and drank it meditatively. Slowly I began to drift off, and just a modicum of sense prompted me to turn the ignition off before dozing off. I could hear soft voices from the other campsites, even a few crackles of their fires as I drifted in and out until reality mixed fluidly with dreams.

My mind slipped and slid between images of Two Medicine and Oldman Lake. The two mixed, then came into focus on Oldman with Flinsch Peak, Mount Morgan, and Ptimakan Pass casting my father and me into deep shadows and turning the jade-green of Oldman Lake a dark gray.

Cutthroat with flaming red colors under their gills grab our flies one after the other, effortlessly snagging them. We pull the fish gently to shore, where we cup their streamlined, slippery, and wiggling bodies in our palms, take out the hooks with care, set them in the cold water, and let them slowly glide away over the richly colored shale bed.

Aren't we going to keep a few?

No, we had our trout dinner last night at Two Med.

Yeah, but I'm game for it two nights in a row.

Dad peers around. Something crosses his face momentarily, like the slim shadow of a trout over river rock. *Not here. I don't want the smell of fish anywhere near us. We should wrap it up anyway. I've got some good packaged stew for us.*

I make a face.

It's not that bad. Put your gear away. He lifts his chin to point at his pack resting by a rock. *There's some lake-safe soap in my pack. Make sure you wash the smell of fish completely off.*

Thin necklaces of soap bubble briefly on the water's surface, then disappear. The water makes my hands numb and pink. I throw the bar to Dad when I'm done. After he washes, we sit by the fire. I watch him carefully handle a pot of water he boiled. He grabs the hot handle with an old cloth and slowly pours the steaming water into two tin camping bowls with premixed, freeze-dried stew. In the red glow of the fire, his face looks ruddy, his eyes focused, and his lips pursed, the same expression I'd seen on him when he peered down at slides under a microscope. He hands the bowl to me to stir and pours his own with the same concentration.

Look, he says and again, uses his chin as a pointer, lifting it to the mountains. *It's unbelievably beautiful, isn't it?*

I shrug. At fourteen, I'm not into the subtleties like he is. He and my ma seem to be always commenting on the how the light skids across the mountaintops, describing its various hues—rose, lavender, reddish-yellow, orange-pink, gold. My sisters and I made fun of them.

There's nowhere like this place, my dad says. I can see a slight plume of his breath in the chilled air. *It's sacred, you know, to the Native Americans. Makes you feel mighty small, huh?*

Yeah, I guess, I answer.

Dad peers back over his shoulder at the forest. *You know*—he turns back to me like he has a massive secret— *in the early nineteen hundreds a fungal disease from Europe called Blister Rust was accidentally introduced through nursery seeds and killed all of these trees?*

So that's why they're all deformed and creepy-looking?

Yep, they're dead whitebark pines. I guess about half of the original ones in Glacier are already dead and an estimated seventy-five percent of the remaining are infected and may die in a few decades. Tell me, Ted—he looks wistfully at me, his mind obviously no longer on the whitebark pines. *I know this is way off subject, but you ever consider going into biology or forestry when you go off to college?*

Jeez, Dad. I have no idea what I'm going to do, but no, probably not that.

Why not that? A bit of irritation slides into his tone, probably in response to the sudden annoyance in mine. He holds a good-size stick and pokes at the log on the fire.

Because I'm not good at science.

He shakes his head. *But you've loved being outdoors since you were tiny. Being outdoors and studying it are two different things.*

Well, your grades, he says. *You know . . .* He doesn't continue.

I don't want to go anywhere near the subject of my grades, but the thought of him not finishing a sentence prods me on. *What about 'em?*

Never mind. He looks around.

You brought it up.

I know, I'm sorry. Forget it. He pokes at the fire. *Let's just enjoy the fresh air.*

I sense his disappointment. The year and a half I'd spent since we'd moved from Florida, my grades hadn't risen. It wasn't because I didn't understand school; I just didn't feel comfortable yet and I missed my friends in Florida.

It's just that I know you can do better. I know you're reams brighter than what you're producing in school and something about that just strikes me as wrong.

I don't say anything. A blast of smoke hits my face. I slam my eyes shut and turn my head into my shoulder like a bird tucking into its wing.

And I don't mean lazy. I just mean wrong.

You do too mean lazy. I open one eye to see if the smoke has changed back to the north.

No, Ted. Really, just wrong. Not living up to your potential. That strikes me as foolish and selfish.

Selfish? How the heck is it selfish?

Because when you don't allow yourself to blossom, I don't know. It's like a flower that refuses to open. It's selfish.

What? I squinted. *Flower?*

Come on, Ted, you know what I'm gettin' at.

No, really, I don't. Flowers don't refuse to open. If they don't open, it's because something's wrong with them.

See, I told you that you're brighter than you let on to be.

I let out an exasperated sigh.

Okay, a musician then, not sharing music. Or a comedian, not making people laugh.

But those are specific things that people are good at. I'm not good at anything.

That's not true. You're a teenager. The trick is to find what you're good at. Plus you can be good at a lot of things. He gestures, palm up. *It doesn't have to be one thing. Sharing well-roundedness is just as important. You get my point?*

No, honestly, I don't. You just said it yourself. Look around. We're just specks out here in the scheme of things. What does it matter?

I get what you're saying, but it does. It matters what you do with yourself. What kind of a trajectory you send yourself on. This out here—he gestures to the lake and to the peaks. *It's right in our faces that it's billions of years old. And you're right, each of our imprints seems small against that, but really, each one of our imprints is fascinating. And just like those rings in the water that those fish make, we make them too, and what we do reverberates way beyond what you can ever imagine. I've mentioned before, studying the small is representative of the grand.*

Yeah, well, even in your job. Looking at all the dead tissue. Another life down the drain. At what point does each of those lives matter? The second I say it, I know I am pushing his buttons.

Look, Ted, I'm going to hope that that negative talk doesn't really run that deep.

The tone of his voice says he is very serious. I stay quiet.

Look, it's important to have empathy for others and to see each life as sacred. If you think that each body that I study doesn't matter, then think again, because there isn't one single cell I don't look at that, in my mind, isn't linked to a human being with interesting and important traits and histories.

I sit silently. I feel sick to my stomach, maybe from the smoke, maybe from knowing I hit a sore spot. I stare out over the black lake, the sky now dark, the fire fading to embers. Dad reaches over and grabs a log from the pile we'd gathered. *Let's just enjoy this,* he says brusquely, setting the log across the embers and stirring them up with his stick. *It's beautiful out here. I'm going to make some tea before it gets any darker. Want some?*

I shake my head. I feel sulky. Irritated. He tries to make small talk, but it doesn't help. I'm in silent mode and keep pouting until I tell him that I'm tired and want to go to bed. He points to the tent. *Help yourself. I'll tend the fire for a little while longer, then I'll be there myself.*

I stand up and fake a stretch. Dad stands too. *Here,* he says, holding out my knife. *Forgot to give that back after cutting your line last night.*

Thanks. I grab it and shove it into my jeans pocket.

Good night, Ted. I love you.

I mumble *Good night* back but don't say "I love you."

Gradually I became aware that the vehicle was getting cold and that I needed heat. My space blanket felt inflexible and crinkly on my lap, my spine stiff, and my butt cold on the vinyl seat, but I couldn't wake. A part of me wanted to roust myself away from my dreams and another part kept trying to push further into them to part and peek behind some heavy, dark curtain blocking my view.

Cool air bites the tip of my nose. My dad has come to bed. I hear his steady breathing. My sleeping bag is warm and snug, but the ground feels hard and lumpy and slightly slanted so that I fall toward the side of the tent wall and my pocketknife is still in my pocket, digging into my hip. I need to pee, but I'm snug in my sleeping bag and don't want to move. My shoes are just outside the zippered entrance to the tent. I find my flashlight beside me and, carefully and quietly, I unzip the tent, crawl out, and slip on my sneakers. I feel frightened. The night is black, and when I look up, millions of stars dot the black canvas of sky. The Milky Way sprays right across the center, dazzling, miraculous—unreal. Everything seems quiet, except the water, gently lapping on the pebbled shore. The baby hairs on the back of my neck prickle, and I decide not to go. I slide my shoes back off and crawl back in. I can hold it until morning.

Dad stirs, asks me if everything is okay, and I say it is. I hear him immediately drift back to sleep, his breathing returning to a steady and thick pace. I dig the knife out of my jeans pocket and toss it to the side. I snuggle back into my bag and scoot away from the side of the tent wall. Slowly, I slide back into the side of the tent, feel the cold fabric on my face, and fall back to sleep.

A knocking sound begins to catch in the corner of my mind, rising and drawing closer, like someone is trying to get in, but it can't be. The knocking resembles tapping on glass, but we're in a tent.

I hear Dad's yelling. *Oh my God, a bear, he's got me.* I hear the rustling of his sleeping bag and screaming. *Get out of your sleeping bag, Ted. Get out of the tent.* I can't move no matter how hard I try.

Give me your knife, Ted. Your knife. Oh Jesus, he's got me.

There's more screaming. And tapping. Loud tapping, and I think I hear voices that aren't my dad's. Something pulls me out of the dream, but I can still hear my dad. I don't want to lose my dad—his voice, his presence.

Your knife, Ted.

I can't move. I'm frozen and tangled. I'm trying to get out of the bag. Finally, I get my legs to move, but I just flail, my legs caught inside like I'm in a web. My bag is wet. My pants are wet. I frantically pat my hand around the fallen, tangled tent fabric trying to find my knife.

If he comes for you, don't move. Play dead. I hear more screaming, deep, raw, penetrating sounds, and I'm still frozen, my heart exploding in my chest. *Don't move, Ted, go limp if it goes for you,* he manages between screams.

Adrenaline and fear coursed through me, my heartbeat drumming against my ribs. My breathing was too fast, and my head turned rhythmically from side to side on the car seat. My neck hurt. *Knocking*, I told myself with whatever thread of reality was still attached to my mind. *It's just knocking. Tapping on the car window. That's all it is.* I tried to open my eyes. The darkness before me swirled and converged into tangled shapes. *Or scraping. Claws scraping. Scratching.*

I threw the space blanket to the side, frantically grabbed for the car door, but couldn't get my fingers on the latch. I pawed at the window controls with my left hand and reached for my gun with the other. Finally, in an eternity of seconds, I found the latch, swung the door open, and stepped out and saw the beast before me. I grabbed for him, throwing his heavy body against the side of the car.

"Are you fucking crazy?" I heard.

I had him under the neck, by the scruff of his collar. I aimed my gun right at his face. I could hear my breathing permeate the cold air around me.

"What the fuck, dude. Calm down. What the hell?"

The light from my car showed he had a beard and wore a dark-colored down jacket. I slowly lowered my gun and stepped away. I was panting.

"Holy fuck. You scared the shit out of me."

"What the hell are you doing?" I managed, shapes still shifting before my eyes. I was beginning to see this guy—simply a tourist—more clearly. Red flannel under the down. Brown wool cap on his head. Freaked-out, wide eyes.

"I was up by my fire late. Saw you had your running lights still on and figured you'd wake up to a dead battery if I didn't let you know. Don't know about you, but I wouldn't want to be out here with a dead battery."

I took another deep breath and nodded rapidly and rhythmically, like some ridiculous bobbing toy that you find in a gift shop. I tried to get my breath under control.

"Honest." He fanned his hands out to the sides, surrendering. "Honest, I didn't mean to freak you out."

Embarrassment flooded my face. I'd never been so relieved that it was dark out. My head suddenly felt overwhelmingly hot against the cool air. I swallowed hard. "I'm sorry. I, I . . . I was out of it, dreaming. You caught me off guard."

"Shit," he huffed. "I guess so." He looked down at my gun hanging in my hand by my side and fidgeted.

I slid it into the holster.

"All right if I go now?"

"Yeah, sure. Again, really sorry about giving you a scare. I appreciate you telling me about the lights. You just caught me completely off guard. But you're right." I swallowed again. This simple talk took more strength than I thought I had left. "I definitely wouldn't want to wake up to a dead battery."

"Okay, then. Right." He carefully edged off to the side and backed away, his hands still up, more to shield himself from me this time than to surrender. "Sorry I bothered you."

"It's fine. Really. Thanks," I said.

He didn't answer. Just kept backing away until he faded into the darkness, turned his flashlight on, and walked to his campsite, where I could see the glow of his fire. I climbed back in my car and turned my running lights off by turning the key all the way to the left. For the first time in my adult life, I wished I smoked and could have a cigarette to calm me down. I took a swig of my coffee, now lukewarm and still spiked with whiskey. When my breathing calmed down, I realized that when I turned the ignition off while I dozed, I hadn't gotten the key completely to the off position. The guy had done me a big favor.

I held my breath when I tried to start the car. When the engine roared, I laid my head back against the seat and thanked my lucky stars. I buckled up, pulled out, and drove all the way home, over the treacherous pass until I got to my cabin and collapsed at five a.m. Many thoughts prodded me, penetrated through the descending fatigue on my drive back to West Glacier. But mostly one image tugged at me more than any of the others: how tender and pink, how youthful my hands appeared under the cold water holding those trout.

. . .

When I returned, I slept until three p.m., ten whole hours of delicious, drenching, dreamless sleep. When I woke, I felt less frayed, less crazed. Invigorated, in fact. Maybe it was just good ol' rest, but strangely, after all my craziness, my panics, pulling my gun on Hess, then on an innocent civilian, my insane, stupid drive through the night, I felt both a gentle caress on my back that things would be all right and a powerful push forward to get back to the case.

I had a message from Monty and one from ballistics. I called Missoula immediately and found that the bullet was a complete match to the Ruger. I showered, shaved, and for the first time felt calm. There were several things about my past that were slowly dawning on me and beginning to make sense: for example, it never occurred to me that I turned my grades around after my dad died for him. And ultimately that I went into the force not just to nudge up to some half-ass notion of being a mountain man, but because I needed to try to prevent more of those dead bodies from turning up under the pathologists' bright lights.

I called Monty next. I told him I'd come down with a bug the night before and needed to sleep it off, but that I was feeling better and would be in by the evening. He informed me that he'd found nothing useful on the Honda yet and that there'd been no progress on finding the owner of the Ruger. He said he'd called the pawnshop guy again earlier and he wasn't very helpful. I told him he didn't need to wait for me to come in before he went home for the day. "Are you sure you're good?" he asked before we hung up.

"Yeah," I said. "Really, I am. And do me a favor. Bug the pawnshop guy one more time before you leave the office. I just think he needs us to light a fire under his ass. Threaten him that if he can't come up with something helpful, that we're coming in tomorrow with a subpoena for all his records."

I drove southwest, out of the park, through Martin City, Hungry Horse, and Columbia Falls. I pulled into a Starbucks, went in, and ordered an Americano with cream, and I took a seat at a small round table near the window by the parking lot. I had my carrier bag with me, so that I could review files, see if anything new hit me, but I paused before taking them out. I sat quietly sipping my coffee, read the paper that was left at the table next to mine, and saw another piece on the hunting incident that Monty had mentioned, then decided I was ready to retackle the case.

I pulled out the file with all the interviews and began rereading them and hoping a new perspective might hit me. After getting through several, I sensed someone approaching. I glanced up to see Dr. Pritchard. "*It's a Small World (After All).*" It was true. It's one of the reasons I'd left. You couldn't go anywhere—the grocery store, the movies, restaurants—without running into someone you knew. I just didn't expect it to be someone I'd interviewed for the case.

"I thought that was you," he said—no coffee cup—so I figured he either was waiting for his order or hadn't placed it yet.

I stood and we shook. "Nice to see you again."

"How's your case coming?"

"We're getting there." I offered him a seat and he took it.

"That's good. One of my sons is playing hockey in Kalispell. My wife sent me on a coffee run."

"Hockey. That's a tough sport on parents. All that standing around in the cold."

Pritchard smiled. "You have kids?"

I shook my head. I had a vague notion suddenly that Shelly could very well walk in any minute. As far as I knew, there was only one Starbucks in the Flathead Valley. I asked him how many kids he had, and he said three boys, and then the barista called out his drinks. When he returned, he stood above me, a drink in each hand, and just when I figured he was going to leave, he sighed and sat back down. "I'm sorry," he said, looking slightly embarrassed, and placed the coffees down. "I just have to ask: have you discovered who beat the black Lab you asked me about?"

"I've gotten no direct admission of the crime, but I'm certain I know who did it: the guy who was killed and another guy who lives outside Columbia Falls. You probably don't know him." I wanted to tell him to keep an eye out for the local police blotter on who's been charged with poaching antelope, but then reconsidered.

"Will he be charged?"

"Possibly," I said. "If not for that, then hopefully for other things."

He shook his head. "I know this is a silly question coming from someone scientifically inclined, but why would anyone . . . ?" His eyes were flooded with questions.

I grabbed my quarter. "I don't know," I said after a moment. "I suppose you can always fall back on genetic makeup or some type of injury or deficiency in the brain. I know scientists working with PET scans have written up studies on how the brain lights up differently for violent people."

He nodded and reached out for his cups. I knew he wanted something more, something profound, and I felt that unsteady shift inside of me, as if a crumbling floor I'd been standing on had fallen away—that familiar sense of how it can all pass into nothingness. I shook it off; I had work to do. "I just thought," he added, "that with your line of work, maybe you had some insight . . ." His voice faded and he shrugged.

"It's a mystery," I offered. "Unfortunately, it's an age-old question that no one can answer."

"I read in the paper that you've got a bear on your hands."

"*Did*," I said. "And if it wasn't so weird, it would be one hokey story, but luckily, we've studied him enough, and he's been released just yesterday."

"He ate evidence?"

"I'd like to discuss the situation, especially with a man of your expertise. Unfortunately, I can't."

"I understand."

"Someone at work mentioned that Joe Smith, the chief of Park Police, was on this case."

"Not necessarily working it, but since he's chief of Park Police, he's definitely around. You know him?" I was curious if he knew that Joe's daughter had been involved with the victim. Again, small world, but fortunately, nothing had come out in the paper about Leslie yet.

"I do. A lot more of my practice used to have a large-breed focus. As my own family's demands have gotten greater, it's gotten harder for me to make the house calls that large animals require, so I've scaled way back on those and stick to what I can do in the clinic. Plus—" He shrugged. "It's more economically feasible for me to stay in the clinic."

I took a sip of my espresso and waited for him to continue.

"I used to help Elena and Joe out with their horses. Joe's a great guy."

"Did you know the daughters?"

"Not well. I'd seen them around a time or two when they were younger, and I've dealt with Heather's animals some. In fact, getting back to the topic of animal cruelty, she had a problem not too long ago." He shook his head.

I lifted a brow. "Problem?"

23

W<small>HEN A DETECTIVE</small> starts to think they really understand a case, he or she can almost hear a clicking sound as small elements fall into place, like a finely tuned lock that ticks with every correct number, allowing the opening mechanism to slide into place.

I sat quietly after Dr. Pritchard had left, not hearing any of the sounds in the coffee shop as my thoughts raced, turning around and around as I tried to put it together. I could almost hear the clicks as my mind adjusted its calibrations. But you have to be careful, because sometimes hunches are not correct and hearsay is not fact. If you start getting desperate to solve a case, you can run wild with an incorrect hunch based on a few small clues that are not as significant as they should be.

For example, Lou had lied and didn't have an alibi, but I couldn't prove that he'd killed his nephew. Now, after talking to Dr. Pritchard, I was aware that someone else had lied to me, only this time, unlike Lou, I felt like the dam was about to break.

I gathered my things, left Starbucks, and headed back to Glacier. I had a lot to do. I needed a search warrant, but I wasn't sure I had probable cause. I racked my brain trying to remember what had been right there before me.

As negative as I say I am and how I typically imagine the worst, I wouldn't have predicted the outcome of the case to be so wounding. Ultimately, I guess it was the eyes—not just one pair, but several—the shock and sadness in all of them—drained and burned out like hollow shells—that have stayed with me.

On my way back toward the park, Monty called and confirmed my deductions. After he got ahold of the owner of First National Pawn again as I asked him to, he called back within the hour with a name of the buyer of the Ruger two years ago in August—a Kevin Fuller. "Ted," he said, his voice low and slightly strained, "I've got the most recent owner of the Ruger and it's no longer Kevin Fuller."

"I'm pretty sure I know who it is." I sighed, and after Monty confirmed my suspicions, I said, "I'm headed there right now."

•   •   •

Instead of driving all the way to the park to grab Monty, I took a chance that the house would be empty and rolled slowly in and looked for vehicles in the driveway. I parked and went to the window and peeked through, then I knocked. When no one came, I knocked again.

I looked around. The sun was setting and the fields burned with an amber glow—the perfect photo with tall, yellow-leafed cottonwoods in the distance and the bluish-green mountains in the background. A transient paradise holding so much radiant promise, so much ineffable beauty, but one that would pass in moments.

I thought I spotted movement at the barn—someone going through the large wooden doors, so I headed up the dirt road, zipping up my coat. When I got to it, I stepped in and saw Heather's blond hair falling around her shoulders onto a dark wool coat. She didn't turn to say hi, just kept stroking her horse and gently pushed his head toward the floor. "This releases their spine," she said, her back to me. "They love it."

"What releases their spine?"

"Pushing their heads down"—she looked over her shoulder at me—"and keeping it there for a bit. It's kind of like yoga for them. When they pull back up, they make a smacking sound with their mouths. Wait just a few more minutes," she said.

I shuffled closer, took in the musty smell of old wood and the sweet smell of hay and oats.

She gently nudged the horse's head back upright, and within a minute or two, he started smacking. She smiled. "See, they love it."

"I see that." I wanted to smile too, wanted to ask the horse's name, but I knew that type of personal conversation was not in order. I felt a great weakness fall upon me, and I wanted to sit down or lean against a wall. It took all my strength to force myself to say: "Heather, I need to ask you some questions."

Her eyes looked large, maybe filled with some fright, maybe a certain numbness or even petulance like a teen caught coming in late, but it was getting dim, and I couldn't really make it out. I did catch an intake of breath.

"About what?"

"For starters, about your mother."

"What about her?" She began to brush the horse, not mechanically, but with affectionate, smooth strokes.

"Did you know about Lou and her?"

Heather stopped brushing the horse's neck and turned toward me. She nodded.

"Did you know that Victor knew as well?"

She didn't answer, just stood by her horse. Her eyes narrowed as if she were trying to assess me.

"Did you?" I pushed it.

"Yes," she said. "He was trying to blackmail them."

"Both of them or just Lou?"

"First Lou, then my mother." She walked over and put the brush in a bin.

I had suspected that Victor may have gone to Elena too, but had no evidence. "Did Leslie know?"

"I don't know."

"What about your father?"

"No," she said, and this time, I could see fear in her eyes, even in the twilight. "And he can't know. It would kill him."

"Heather, there are things that are going to hurt him more," I said gently and walked closer to her.

She backed away, the whites of her eyes and her blond hair bright in the pale twilight. "What's that supposed to mean?"

"Look, the tape on the victim had traces of a heating rub or spray used for sore muscles, just like the kind you gave Lewis to use. And now we've got the gun and the bullet from the bear."

She stared at me, her arms by her side and her body stiff. I could see faint plumes of her breath in the cool, damp air of the barn.

"I saw both the tape and the spray in your mudroom on the shelf. I've got a warrant," I lied. "Even though I don't really need it now that we have the weapon and the matching slug."

Her breath caught and came out as a choked cry. She put her hand to her mouth. Her eyes filled with anguish and a wildness I'd not seen before. Suddenly, she darted for the wide-open barn doors. As if in slow motion, I saw her silhouette encased by the pale light streaming in through the doors as she dashed through. I ran after her, out into the evening light, which seemed bright compared to the inside of the barn but wasn't. The golden hue had disappeared and transformed into a pale, silvery pallor. She ran toward the river, across the close-cropped hay field—the wheat no longer on fire but beige and bland.

She was fast, and I ran hard, tripping on divots and gopher holes in the field, my legs and arms whipping and cycling around to try to regain control like some comical pantomime. I got my legs back under me, gained speed, and caught her by reaching out and grabbing a clump of her hair.

Her head jerked back, and we both tumbled to the ground. She tried to get onto her knees to get back up. I lunged forward again and pinned her underneath me. I don't know why she didn't use her skills in martial arts; she could have possibly taken me since my training probably paled in comparison to her routine. I figured she must have already surrendered in some way. I was breathing hard but managed to say, "Heather, Christ, where you gonna go?"

Her body went weak below me, and I knew there would be no more fleeing or fighting. She looked at me, a deep pain and fear in her eyes. I could smell the damp wool of her coat, the pungent soil below and her shampoo, some kind of coconut smell. She didn't run. She got into a crouched position, her knees before her. Her expression dazed and her eyes welling with tears, she just sat on the wet field. "I didn't . . . I didn't intend for it to happen this way. I didn't . . ." She dropped her head into her hands.

I kept my distance, fought the urge to go put a hand on her shoulder. But then she started crying harder, and I knew I couldn't let her carry on for too long. I went over and reached for her arm and helped her up. "I'm going to need to take you in," I said. "And I need you not to fight. It will just make it worse." I grabbed my handcuffs and clasped them on her wrists and led her across the field and up the dirt road to the house.

In those moments of walking back, the pale light meekly hanging on and straining my perspective, my fingers wrapped around her upper arm, the gravel on the dirt road scuffling under our feet, the smell of wood smoke in the cold air, my mind racing with the horrible consequences to follow—even under all those layers—it occurred to me that I felt a kind of deep contentment with her because she was like me: a decent person, but she had the bear in her.

As we came closer to the house, a car drove up, and Heather stopped in her tracks. "It's my father—please, he can't see me like this." She held up her wrists.

I thought about going for my keys in my pocket because I knew I wanted to not hurt Joe more than I wanted to make sure I handled the suspect properly.

"Please," she pleaded.

I really did think about fumbling around for the small key that opened the cuffs, but it was too late. Joe had slammed his car door and had come running. "Jesus, Ted. What's going on here?"

"Joe, I'm sorry." I shook my head. "But . . ."

"Ted, what's going on? Let my daughter go right now." His face was contorted with confusion. "Heather? What is this?"

"It's all right, Dad, I have some explaining to do."

"What do you mean? What the hell? Ted." He looked to me, to the cuffs. "Get those off."

"I can't. I'm sorry. She's a suspect."

"Bullshit she's a suspect. Get them off now."

"I can't," I repeated. "I'm sorry."

"This is crazy." Joe started to go for his gun.

"No, Joe," I said loud and firmly. "Don't do that."

He froze with his elbow cocked and his hand on his pistol still in its holster.

"Dad, it's all right. For right now, it's okay."

"No, it's not." His voice was louder and shakier than I'd ever heard it. "It's not okay. Why are those on you? You haven't done anything." He stared at her, pleading, his brow in deep creases.

She looked at her feet without answering.

His face, illuminated now by the porch light, went sheet white. "No." He shook his head. "Not you, not this one." His voice got smaller, and he dropped his hand away from his gun.

I swallowed hard. "I just have to take her to the station for some questioning. It would be best if you waited here. I'll call Monty and tell him to swing by for you. He can bring you. You shouldn't be driving right now."

Joe stared at me blankly, his eyes like I'd never seen them, engulfed by pain, haunted and choked by the cruel realization that this might be the beginning of the loss of yet another child.

• • •

I took Heather to the station in Kalispell, then sat her down in one of the interrogation rooms and had an officer at the station grab her a cup of tea. I excused myself and called Monty and filled him in briefly. He was silent, didn't whistle. I told him to go to Heather's place and check on Joe, then come to the station to meet me. I told him it was all right to bring Joe if he insisted, but that he must stay in the waiting area and not come back to interfere with the questioning. I also made sure Monty bagged the tape and the bottle of muscle spray at her house from her mudroom. In light of her partial confession, I was able to swear in telephonically as soon as I got to the county jail so that I could get the warrant immediately. We needed it to acquire the items from the suspect's home to corroborate the confession. Then I told him to come to the station when he had finished.

I went back in and asked Heather if she needed anything—coffee, water, more tea, and she just shook her head. "Please, I need to get this over with." She was hugging her knees to her chest, her feet on the edge of her chair, as if she could form a protective cocoon away from the harsh lights. She looked smaller than usual—pale-skinned in the fluorescents.

"That would be good," I said, not feeling particularly eager to get down to business. I stayed sitting casually back in my chair in an effort to keep things at ease. The sadness I felt for Joe and her overwhelmed me, but I needed for her to tell me everything and not clam up. We would need to corroborate her story with the evidence we had to make sure she wasn't confessing to save someone else's ass. The gun, the tape, and the muscle rub would go a long way in terms of corroboration. "I'm going to need you to start from the beginning, explaining your association with Victor. Obviously, I know he was involved with your sister."

She nodded. "He was, and as you know"—her voice was shaky and small—"he treated her poorly. The entire time he was with my sister, he used to make lewd comments to me and anytime she wasn't around, tried to make the moves on me. He, he"—she shook her head and closed her eyes—"was disgusting. I don't know what she saw in him and how she could have exposed Lewis to him. I guess"—she frowned—"he was some kind of a charmer to her."

"This was how long ago?"

She covered the same things she'd already told me in her kitchen. As she spoke, her voice became stronger. She talked of her sister and Victor's unstable relationship and how she'd talked Leslie into getting a restraining order, but not succeeding, and how eventually, none of it mattered because Leslie just took him back. "None of us have ever been able to influence my sister for very long."

"And Victor hit on you all along?"

"Yes, and, in the end, he started threatening me and"—she looked at the table—"he threatened my nephew."

"Lewis Boone, you mean?" I knew exactly whom she meant, but I wanted it clear for the recording.

"Yes. He was out of control."

"Can you tell me what day the actual incident that precipitated his night in the woods was?"

"It was a Thursday. I ran into him at a gas station, and he wanted me to go for a drive with him. I could tell he was high. I told him to get lost and to leave everyone in my family alone, but it just angered him. I drove away, went to the grocery store, and went home. I was in my kitchen unloading some groceries when I heard him pull up."

"Pulled up in what?"

"An old motorcycle. He followed me home. He came to the door and said he wanted to come in and that he wanted to talk about Leslie, that he was worried about her.

"I knew it was a bunch of crap, so I wouldn't let him in. I stepped out onto my porch and shut the door behind me, and he was getting more and more angry that I wouldn't let him in. He was saying that I'd been a bitch to him all along and that I should try to be nicer. I told him to leave or I'd call the cops, and then he said if I ever call the cops on him, he would"—tears sprang to her eyes—"he said he would hurt Lewis."

"Did he say in what way?" I asked.

"No, I didn't know what he meant exactly, but I knew it wasn't good, and I knew he was capable of it. But you can imagine how enraged I got. I asked him what he meant. 'What do you mean, *hurt* Lewis?' But he just smiled, that disgusting, meth-teeth grin. He knew he had me when it came to Lewis."

I could see the hate in her eyes, in spite of the ultimate outcome.

"'You could remedy that,' he said. 'All you need to do,' and he came closer to me and touched my cheek—" She wiped her face with the back of her hand as if she could still feel his touch. "'Is play nice for a change.' Then he grabbed me behind my head and tried to pull me in to kiss me, but out of instinct"—she fixed her eyes on the cinder-block walls—"I grabbed his wrist, twisted it, and turned him onto the ground."

I wanted to say, *good for you*, but I knew it wouldn't come across so well on camera. All I said was, "And?"

"And he was really pissed. He got up, brushed his pants off, and said I'd regret it. He started to head for his bike, and I was frantic, thinking about how Lewis would never be safe, how I knew there was no way I could prevent him from finding a way around him in this small town, and with my sister so unpredictable." She put the bridge of her nose between her thumb and forefinger and squeezed her eyes shut as if she had a headache.

"So what did you do?"

"Nothing." She looked up, her eyes wild. "I didn't do anything then, other than I told him if he ever lays a hand on Lewis, I would break every bone in his body. But—" She shook her head. "He, he just laughed. 'You do that,' he said, pointing at me, 'and I'll just turn it around to Lewis. You hear me'—he came back and pointed in my face—'you touch me again that way and it's Lewis's ass.'

"It took everything I had to not grab his arm and lay him flat. Then he turned and started to go for his motorcycle, but on his way, he stopped and walked over toward the storage shed on the other side of the driveway where Brady was leashed. I had no idea what he was doing until he got to him. I hadn't taken him off his chain yet since I'd gotten home from my errands. He walked right up to him and started kicking him, really hard, and stomping his boot down on him. He's such a sweet dog, he would never have expected it or fought back. He yelped loudly; Victor was really hurting him, he . . . " She shook her head, caught her breath, and swallowed hard.

"I was stunned, then enraged. I ran over there and side-kicked him in the head. It dazed him, then I did it again, a really hard one to the temple." She pointed to her own. "He fell over and just lay there. I realized that I had knocked him out. Then I started to panic, Brady was whimpering. He couldn't walk, so I took him off the leash and carried him into the house and put him in his bed."

"Then?"

"I ran back to check Victor's pulse. He was still out cold, but he had one. I lifted him up and put him in my truck."

"You lifted him?" I knew she was strong and Victor scrawny, but still.

She turned back to look me in my eyes. "Well, not at first. I had one of those plastic sleds by the shed, so I grabbed it, rolled him onto it, and slid him to my truck, but then I had to lift him. I was worried he might come to, so I grabbed my backpack from my truck. I knew I had duct tape in it because I had it in there so that I could bring it to the gym to tape some of my sparring bags that were starting to rip."

"And?"

"I taped his wrists and then, well, he, he was surprisingly light," she said softly, sadly. "All those drugs, I guess, and I was panicking and full of adrenaline and was able to use the back edge of the truck for leverage." She spoke louder again. "I didn't even know where the guy lived and I knew that when he came to, he'd take it out on Lewis, not to mention my . . ." She looked at me, then the camera, didn't finish what she was going to say, and I didn't push for it.

I knew she was going to say, *my mother*, but that she didn't want that piece of information out there. Her face looked deeply strained, and I wondered at that moment whether she was calculating it all: the statement, the trial, how it would affect her parents, how it would destroy her father.

"What did you do?"

"Once I had him in the pickup, I threw a tarp I use to cover hay over him and I did the only thing that came to my mind besides taking him to the ER, which I had no intention of doing." She crossed her arms before her chest stubbornly. "I needed to think and I needed no people around, so I took him to the place I knew best, to the place I grew up around—the park. I didn't really have a plan at first. I just knew that if I could get to the woods without anyone around, I could figure it out, deal with him on my terms, not his. I knew he was a coward, a total wimp, but I also knew he would hurt Lewis, just like my dog. I think"—she started crying—"that he might have already scared Lewis. I can't get Lewis to talk, but I know he's afraid of him."

"We can get some counseling for him if that's the case." I held out a box of tissue. She took several and nodded. "So, you drove to Glacier?"

"Yes, up the Inside Road, to the trailhead to McGee Meadow."

"And was Victor still out cold?"

"He was starting to come to, but still pretty out of it. I knew I needed to move fast, plus I wanted to get back to take Brady to the vet. On the way up, I had decided that I would teach him a lesson, that I would leave him alone in the woods to scare him while I took Brady in, and then I'd go back and get him and make it clear that if he ever went near any of my family members again, including Leslie, I would hunt him down, knock him out, and do it all over again."

"You thought of all this on the drive?"

"I did, it was the only thing I thought of. I didn't think about killing him, honestly, it didn't even cross my mind. I just knew the police weren't going to help and I had to take care of this guy myself—for Lewis's sake, for my entire family's sake."

"Did you have a gun then?"

"Yes. I'd run in and grabbed it. He had come to, so I made him go in front of me at gunpoint. He was still sort of out of it, but able to walk and I—" She was sitting up taller now, her shoulders straight and nearly proud as she spoke. Although she appeared almost frail when I came in, hunched into a ball on her chair, she seemed transformed—tall and strong with defined shoulders and biceps. In a strange way, she was opening like a flower as she told me her story—gaining strength from the relief of getting it off her chest. I could see that she would be more than capable of lifting a scrawny guy like Victor.

"You made him walk all the way out there?"

"I did. But he was stumbling a lot, so I ended up not going all the way to McGee as I initially planned and he was calling me a crazy bitch, which I guess I pretty much was, and a, a . . . cunt and every other name imaginable, and saying that I was going to pay for this, that Lewis would pay. My anger started to boil even more and I told him, 'No.'" She said firmly but in a whisper, "'It's you who's going to pay.'"

I felt a shiver go down my spine.

"And I was still thinking about Brady," she added. "But when I stopped by a tree and took off my pack, he lunged for a rock with both hands and tried to hit me in the head. I kicked him hard in his chest straight outward"—she pushed her heel firmly out showing me the Tai Kwon Do kick from her chair—"and he went backward and banged the back of his head hard against the tree. And with him being so unsteady, he went down easily and was out again. I propped him against the tree and taped him under his arms and around his hips while he was just limp. I was afraid if he got loose, he'd come for me, so I wrapped it layer after layer. I taped his mouth and then I ran back to the truck."

"On the trail?"

"No, through the brush, there and back."

"Were you thinking of footprints?"

"No, nothing like that. Honestly, I was crazed. I didn't have time to look for the trail, that's all. I just went. You have to understand—I was a mess. I thought my plan was good under the circumstances, but I was half-crazed. Out of my mind." Her tears had stopped and she had a faraway, dazed look in her eyes, her pupils large and pale.

"Where did you go?"

"I went home. I took Brady to the vet."

"Dr. Pritchard?"

She nodded, looked at me, confused that I knew that, but didn't ask how, just continued. "He was hurt worse than I thought. He was moving really badly by the time I got back, and then I was angry with myself for taking Victor into Glacier and wasting precious time. They took X-rays. The goddamned jerk fractured my dog's spine. And I'd heard rumors about what he and some other guy had done to that other dog earlier in the year. Fuck him, I thought." She crossed her arms stubbornly before her. "He could wait while I took care of this. I was thinking that I should just leave the piece of shit out there to rot anyway, but by the time I got home from the vet's, it's was already midnight. I checked the thermometer and it was surprisingly warm out, like fifty-six degrees. I was just so mad about Brady and so crazed about him threatening Lewis and I knew what I had done, tying him up like that, was beyond crazier than anything I'd ever done in my life and would now come with a load of consequences I couldn't even fathom. So the only thing I could figure to do was to stick with the insanity I'd begun, leave him out there to really show him I was serious."

"So in the morning?"

"I grabbed my gun again and my first-aid kit, thinking he'd be in tough shape. It was unusually warm out that week, but I grabbed a blanket in case, and I went out there."

"Do you know what time that was?"

Her eyes became watery and she nervously brushed her hair behind an ear. "When it finally got to be morning, I was a wreck and I kept walking around the house, rechecking for things I might need to take with me: the first-aid kit, a blanket, Advil, scissors to cut the tape with. I know." She looked at me. "I know how crazy I sound."

I didn't say anything at first, then went back to the time. "So you don't quite remember the time?"

"I think I remember it being about eleven or eleven thirty by the time I was actually on my way. Of course, I never went to sleep and planned to go earlier, but Dr. Pritchard was supposed to call me when he got in, and I didn't hear from him until around quarter to ten and I knew if I went to the park, I wouldn't have cell coverage. Then"—she sighed heavily—"Lewis showed up out of the blue. It was such a nightmare. He said he didn't want to go to school that day, and after Leslie dropped him off, he waited till she left, then rode his bike over. She had taken it with them so he could ride to my house after school, but I wasn't expecting him until around three forty-five. I spent some time convincing him that he needed to go back and drove him there with his bike and checked him in at the front desk. Then I went back home and grabbed the stuff. I remember pulling out, then pulling back in to get more bottled water. I don't know, I guess I had some kind of approach-avoidance seesaw going on in my head. I was afraid to go, afraid of what I'd find and how he'd be, that my plan wouldn't work, and mostly, still afraid he'd hurt Lewis or maybe Leslie really badly once I brought him back to town and he rested up. I'm guessing I was parking beside the McGee trailhead by noon or so."

I stayed quiet. I knew what was coming next was going to be the hard part, and I could hear her breathing quicken. I nodded to encourage her on.

"Then I walked out. I was so scared. When I got there, his head was hanging down, and I was afraid he had died. I checked his pulse and called his name, asked him if he was awake. I said his name several times, then decided to cut the tape, and in that split second, as I started to lower the gun so I could grab my pack and look for the scissors I'd brought, he grabbed for my wrist. I flinched, tried to back away, but he had ahold of my arm between his hands."

"His wrists still bound?"

"Yes." She nodded and mimed how his wrists were pressed together with the tape, but his hands free enough to grab her. "He, he"—she swallowed hard—"was stronger than I thought he'd be after being out there all night, and it freaked me out. I mean . . ." She cupped her palms around each side of her face. "A part of me really thought he'd be at my mercy, that he'd be thanking me for getting him out of there and giving him something to drink. I thought I'd have him right where I wanted him, scared and in my debt in a weird way. I twisted my arm"—she showed me the classic breakaway judo move—"and I broke free, and out of instinct again, I swung to his head, not that hard, but I had the gun in my hand still, although it had turned downward somehow in the struggle and I was holding it funny . . . I don't remember exactly. I've gone over it in my head millions of times, but, well, it went off and . . ." She looked down, her shoulders sagging—all the life gone out of her, the blossoming of strength over with the full confession.

"And he was shot?"

"He was bleeding." She placed her palm over the spot below her left rib. "It was an accident. It just went off."

"What did you do then?" I leaned in.

"I freaked out. I grabbed my pack and ran back to my truck and drove. Just drove until I got to about Coram and stopped and tried to gather my wits. But once I calmed down, I realized I couldn't leave him like that. All I could think was, oh my God, I've shot a man, I've *shot* someone. I could barely breathe." She squeezed her eyes tightly together as if she could shut out the memory. "I was hyperventilating." Her voice was dripping with the raw memory, dark and pained. "But I tried to calm myself down and eventually, eventually, I drove back. I knew I needed to get him to a hospital."

"You still had the gun?"

"In the car, but this time, I knew better than to bring it, so I left it under the seat. I grabbed my pack again with the first aid and I went back down the trail and when I started to get closer, I knew something was wrong. I could smell bear," she said, almost in a whisper. "And I could hear noises." She put her hands over her ears like a child as if she were still hearing them. "I couldn't hear Victor crying out; he must have already been gone." She shook her head and slammed her eyes shut again. "I froze where I was and tried to see. Between the trees, and I could make out the brownish-silver fur. He was grunting and pulling at him, his head bobbing up and down. Not violently, just steadily." She opened her eyes and added in a small voice, "I know this is going to sound messed up, but it . . . it looked almost, I don't know . . . natural, as if he was just eating berries off a bush, as if it was meant to be." She looked at me like I was a priest and would offer her absolution. Her eyes were large, searching, rimmed in pink from crying. In the span of the last two hours, she already looked five years older, and I was certain that the last two weeks had to have been utter hell, had to have shaved years from her life span. Her cheekbones were sharp and hollowed out and in spite of her strong build, her collarbones suddenly seemed to protrude. "I"—she shook her head slowly, tears flooding her eyes and streaming down her cheeks, down the line of her jaw—"I, I was too late. I had murdered a man."

I watched her shoulders rise and fall as she tried to calm her breathing. The room was cold and she began to shake, a small persistent tremor. The small cinder-walled room felt bare, ragged and unforgiving. I thought of the Inside Road, of the path to McGee Meadow, and the lone tree that she bound Victor to. I pictured Two Medicine Lake and its haunting sacred peaks. I saw Oldman Lake with its green water and stunted trees, peering upon my father and my demon phantoms. My cabin in West Glacier—a meek shelter among the vast wild—flashed into my mind. I thought of the summer attraction Glacier is, drawing and enfolding millions of tourists in its embrace. Hordes of people coming to see its endless beauty draped in golden-and-rose glory, to hike its trails, to witness its silver-sparkling waterfalls and its pastel-colored river rocks. Coming to see its wildlife as if it was only a zoo and nothing could go wrong. Finally, I thought of how out in this wild, Heather's mind had run feral, had reverberated around in untamed space with no boundaries, no anchor. I swallowed with effort, my throat dry. "What did you do with the motorcycle?"

"Oh, that." She glanced at the ceiling, then back, almost relieved to be asked another question. But she looked dazed, as if on autopilot. "When I got back from Dr. Pritchard's, I put it in my shed to hide. Then, when everything went from bad to totally inconceivable, I had to get rid of it, so I walked down to the river."

"You hid it down there?"

"It's in the water."

"And the type of gun?" Of course I already knew, but it was important to get her full confession.

"A Ruger. A Ruger Blackhawk. You apparently already know I got rid of it. Threw it in the Middle Fork on my way home." She stared at her tea, which she hadn't touched and had gotten cold by now. "Is there," she said hesitantly, "maybe some water?"

I got her some, then sat back down. "Our research indicates that you just recently acquired the gun from one of your students. Can you explain why?"

"Because"—she shook her head, her eyes watering—"after I had my suspicions about Lewis and with him harassing me, I thought I might need a little extra protection. I never figured I'd use it. One of my students, Martin Reilly, said another one of my students, Troy Hamlin, went to gun shows and collected them. I simply asked him if he'd like to trade out—Tai Kwon Do lessons for a gun. He offered me the Ruger."

I nodded.

"Okay," I sighed. "We're almost done. I'll need you to sign some forms before we get you somewhere where you can rest."

"I don't think there's much in the way of rest for me for a long time to come." She almost gave a timid smile but couldn't fully get there. The side of her lips attempted to curl, then fell right back down. She continued to shiver.

"It seems," I said, "that you've been wanting to get this off your chest. Why didn't you come to me earlier?"

She looked at me, her skin very pale and her expression intensely sad. She gave a small shrug. "I guess a small part of me was trying to convince myself, for my parents' sake, for Lewis's sake, that I could live with what I'd done. That if I remembered how bad Victor Lance was as a human being, that what I had done wasn't so horrible. But I know"— she held up her palm—"you don't have to say it. I know, he was still a human being, no matter how . . ." She didn't finish, just dropped her head.

I stood up. "Heather," I said, and she looked up, her face strained and ghostly. "He"—I looked into her haunted eyes and nodded once— "he really was despicable."

She stared at me for a moment, then bowed her head, her blond hair draping on each side of her face.

I stood still, watching her. I wanted to offer her some comforting gesture, to touch her shoulder or her cheek, but I resisted. All I had to offer her was what I'd already said: *He really was despicable.* "I'll be back with the paperwork," I said.

. . .

That night I didn't leave the county jail until about two in the morning. I got the tape and the capsaicin muscle spray from Monty and completed as much paperwork as I could. Monty had watched most of the confession through the two-way and didn't have much to say. When I walked in he let out a big sigh.

"The gun," I said. "You mentioned a Kevin Fuller?"

"Yeah, that gun's been traded more than . . ." He paused and looked down as if he realized it wasn't worth it to try for a metaphor. "Kevin Fuller," he began again, "traded the gun to a Troy Hamlin from Columbia Falls at the Fairgrounds one year ago for a riding lawn mower. At first he didn't remember who he traded it to, but when I mentioned that a riding mover would be somewhat more than the cost of the Ruger, he remembered that Hamlin had to write a check for the difference. And it turns out that Fuller's wife keeps check records for years. Mrs. Fuller had Troy Hamlin's name dug out of a file cabinet within twenty minutes for me."

"Good work," I managed.

"Ted," Monty said. "Joe isn't handling this so well."

I nodded.

"He's in the waiting area."

I walked out to it to see Joe sitting slumped in a chair, his head in his hands. When he heard me walk in, he looked up, his eyes bloodshot and his skin rough and red. "Joe," I whispered. He stared at me for a split second, then his face contorted and utterly unexpectedly, he lunged for me, grabbing my collar and pushing me against the wall. I wasn't expecting it and fell easily back with his strong shove, the back of my head slamming the cinder-brick wall.

"How could you?" His face was full of rage, his jaw set hard. "How could you do this to her?"

I didn't put up a fight. I'm quite a bit taller, not to mention younger, so it wouldn't have been hard to push him off, but I didn't. I stayed put, just held my hands up like I was surrendering, my back against the wall. I felt Joe's knuckles dig into the bottom of my neck. "I'm sorry," is all I said.

The anger stayed in his face, but I could feel that he started to release his grip just as Sheriff Walsh came in and grabbed Joe by the arms and pulled him away from me. Joe's shoulders stayed tense, and he ripped his arm away from Walsh, turned, and gave me a piercing look, then glared at Walsh as if to say, *Don't mess with me now.*

Walsh ended up asking Joe to go home for the night. "Joe," I heard him say after I'd gathered my things from one of the back offices and came back out to leave. He had put his hand on his shoulder. "There's nothing you can do. Go home to Elena."

"How am I going to tell Elena this?" he asked, his voice suddenly small.

That moment cut me to the bone. I knew I had to get out. I drove east of Kalispell to the Flathead River and parked in a lot on the west bank. I sat in my car and watched the ink-black water slide silently by. The cloud cover was dense, blocking any sign of the half-moon, and I was completely alone. No parked teens, no squatters camped in the trees by the shore as they sometimes did by this part of the river. Only two cars passed by on the road to my back as I sat and thought, their lights briefly skimming the water.

I thought about Shelly and how we came to this exact spot to make out a few times when we were dating. I thought of how she was still just a child, a girl really, when we got married, her full and rosy cheeks, her tea-length white dress, her hair up in a bun with baby's breath. But then, my own mother had married my father at an even younger age.

I thought of what it would have done to Ma or even my dad if Natalie or Kathryn had taken Leslie's messed-up road or done what Heather had done. It would have crushed them. But then again, although transformed forever, people move on. They strengthen their shells and forge ahead because there is no other good alternative. Just as the four of us did without my father.

· · ·

The next morning I called my mom and told her that I needed to go to Missoula for the suspect's initial appearance. I told her that when I returned, I'd take a few days to finish paperwork and would head back to Denver.

After providing my paperwork and testimony within forty-eight hours of Heather's arrest in Missoula at the courthouse, I saw Joe outside, sitting on a bench, his head bowed in his hands. I walked over and sat beside him, and he raised his head and looked at me with bloodshot eyes, then glanced away again. He looked exhausted, bone-tired, and I could tell it would be a long time before he would find rest.

"How are you holding up?" I asked.

His wiry frame looked even thinner. "Elena's in shock. As you'd expect. I'm afraid she might go into depression by the way she's acting already."

"I'm sorry to hear that. It's going to take time . . ." I almost said, *to understand*, then realized that comprehending would be impossible. "To figure out how to cope," I finished. "The attorney you've got, Roy Venery—he's excellent. And you know I will testify on her behalf. There are many mitigating circumstances when all facets are considered, especially the character of the victim and what he put her through. There's definitely an element of self-defense."

He didn't answer, just placed his elbows on his knees, and fixated on the sidewalk. The blue sky stretched endlessly away from us, living up to the Big Sky name. But the biting north wind whipped through the now half-naked trees, brushed the dead leaves off the gutters, coiling them and letting them settle briefly before the next gust. It seemed to me that winter, which had been nipping at my heels the entire stay, had finally taken over and solidified the surroundings.

"Joe," I said, "I don't mean to be disrespectful, sir, but, I mean, you guys are close, did you have any sense that—"

"No," he cut me off. "I had no idea. I was just plodding along in my own world. Thinking about Leslie and how everything she gets involved with turns bad in spite of her best intentions."

"Do you blame Leslie?"

He didn't answer for a long time. I thought he had decided not to respond, but then he sighed deeply. "For a lot of things," he said. "That's for certain. And she deserves the blame. But no, I can't"—he looked over his shoulder to the steps of the courthouse—"for this. But I do fault her for bringing that loser into Lewis's and Heather's lives. How he threatened Lewis." He shook his head. "Shit, I'd have taken him out to the woods myself. I wish I had. I'd take her place in a heartbeat."

"Are you going to talk to Leslie?"

"I can't think that far ahead right now."

"But Lewis, you need to be there for him."

Joe stared at the ground and wrapped his arms around himself.

"Listen," I said. "I know you're angry at me, and I would be too, but if it's any consolation, and I know it's not, I did think about doing nothing. About just letting the whole thing go unsolved, but you know, she couldn't have gone on that way. It was eatin' her up. She would've gone crazy. I could tell by the way she confessed. It was an enormous relief for her. She was dying to tell the truth; she would have eventually gone in on her own because that's the kind of person she is. And that confession will bode well for her in court."

Joe gave a small nod that he'd heard me but didn't respond.

I pulled the pearl-handled knife out of my pocket and held it in my palm. It actually looked shiny because I had bought some polish and worked on it. "This here . . ." I held my palm out.

Joe glanced at it.

"My father gave me this when I was about Lewis's age. I want to give it to you to give to him."

Joe turned and caught my eyes. His were watery, either from the cold or from tears, I couldn't tell.

"Please, take it." I lifted my hand a little higher.

"But your father gave that to you."

"It's time to pass it on. Please, I insist, give this to Lewis for me. But there's one catch."

Joe stared at me.

"You have to teach him how to use it safely and how to gut fish properly."

Joe slowly took the knife. He gripped it tightly, and I could see the tendons like a track of a large bird, fanning out to each knuckle. A web of strong veins crossed each tendon.

He simply nodded, and although his eyes showed nothing but ache, I knew he would not give up. Even amid Joe's family's tragedy, he would reach out to Lewis, possibly even to Leslie. I could see it in the strength of his grip that Joe understood that being alone, staying an island unto one's self, was not the answer.

. . .

When I returned to Glacier, Monty and I met at headquarters to clear out the office we had used. We gathered the files and put them in boxes, took down photos, erased drawings and lists we'd had on the whiteboard, and took down Monty's alibi chart. It wasn't as cluttered and messy as some cases, and I figured it was Monty's meticulousness that I could thank for that. I still needed to clean out my cabin, but figured I could do that later.

At the initial appearance in Missoula, bail was set by the federal judge since Heather's flight risk was low; her danger to the community practically nonexistent since she was a citizen and a productive member of the community; and she had no prior criminal record nor was she suspected of being involved in organized crime, a narcotics ring, or gang-related activity. Her probable-cause hearing wouldn't be for several months and her arraignment after that.

It was getting darker earlier each day, and as we packed up the office, a dim hue already surrounded us by five thirty. A soft rain pattered the roof, the building quiet. The type of day it was, no wind, a light rain, and gray skies, reminded me of Thanksgiving, and I thought of flying back up from Denver to spend it with Ma and Natalie, Luke, and the kids.

I had placed Monty's chart on the table for him, not knowing whether he'd want to keep it or not. It seemed odd to toss it, like I was throwing out someone's school project. I had my back to the table and was fitting a lid over a box of files, when I heard a rip. I turned around to see Monty tearing it down the center. "Won't need this anymore," he said.

"Guess not."

He tore it one more time and fit the pieces into the trash bin. "Well." He glanced around. "The place practically looks just like we found it."

I nodded.

"What do you think will happen to Joe and Elena?"

"They'll be okay," I offered.

"Yeah?" Monty eyed me. "Why do you think that?"

"They're strong, in spite of it all. I mean, obviously they're no cozy little family with what went wrong with Leslie and with Elena and Lou, and now . . ." We both knew I was referring to Heather. "I know it's tempting to ask where they went wrong. What monsters were swimming just below those surface waters all these years to create this." I held open my palms. "But it's just not that easy. Just not that black and white. Sometimes, there's no direct cause of anything."

Monty looked at me wide-eyed. After all that he knew about me and my history, I was surprised to see him look at me with an innocent anticipation, still waiting for me to lead the way. Still trusting me.

"I mean," I continued, unsure of what I wanted to say, "there's not always an answer, right? Sometimes trouble brews beneath no matter how hard you try, but it doesn't mean you quit trying."

Monty nodded, a rawness in his eyes shining through. I could see he was probably thinking of his wife and his situation, not just Joe's family. "Tell me," Monty said. "Did you think twice about it?"

"About what?"

"Arresting Heather?"

I looked at him for a long moment before answering. I could have said, *Hell no, of course not. The law's the law and in this job, you can't ever blur the line or you make a habit of it.* But I didn't. I let out a long breath. "Yeah, I did. But like I told Joe, she'd be in hell every day of her life if I hadn't."

"But she'll still be in hell, even in prison."

"I guess, but I'd like to think she'll at least feel like she's paying her debt."

"What debt? To Victor Lance? Away from her nephew, where she could actually do some good?"

"No, not a debt to Victor. To herself. To her conscience. Plus you can't ignore it, man. What she did . . ." I ran a hand though my hair and bit my lip. "What she did was, well, brutal—leaving someone in the park all night long? I know she was panicked and all, not thinking straight and stressed to the max. That she somehow just got pulled further and further into the craziness of the moment, but somehow, somewhere, something in her should have stopped her from tying him up out there." I thought again of how she had a strong animal instinct in her—of how, in many ways, she was probably like me. I thought of how nature continued to be predictably implacable. People hurting each other, killing one another, stray, aberrant behavior erupting out of nowhere—that atypical grizzly who normally would avoid people, suddenly lashing out, attacking, snapping. Stray behavior was inherent to the human condition too, and ultimately, I would always be fighting nature because human crime was a function of the natural. That was the job I had chosen.

"But he was never going to leave her family alone."

"I know, Monty, I know all the reasons. And truly, I feel like shit about it, but what can I say, we don't get to call the shots here. That's why we have laws. Kidnapping is kidnapping. We don't get to play vigilante in our society. You know this. That's a slippery slope we can't afford to get on. "

Monty looked to his feet, nodding that he did. "It's just such a waste."

I didn't say anything. I thought of beautiful, haunting Heather. Of how she made me feel shy, alive. Monty pushed his glasses up and took a long breath, then grabbed his satchel and began looking through it.

"Joe's getting her a great defense attorney." I sighed. "He's from Helena and I've heard he works wonders. It's not like there's no hope."

He nodded and gave me a half smile. "There's one more thing." He looked over his shoulder to the door. He reached over and shut it, then pulled a file out, and handed it out to me.

"What's this?"

"Just take it. It's yours to do what you want with."

"What is it?"

"He keeps everything. Records go back over twenty-five years."

I opened the file, saw a bunch of old, worn paper with typed text, crossed-out paragraphs, and handwriting in the margins.

"They're old press releases. I thought you might want to see them. If you look at the bottom, it has the name of the PR gal who submitted them to him."

I scanned down and saw a Margret Ostrem's name at the bottom with the title "PR Officer, Glacier National Park, September 24, 1987." It was obvious that she'd typed up the press release on the Oldman Lake incident and submitted it to Ford for review. And what was also obvious was that he'd crossed out large sections of it and, in his own writing, written the parts about careless camping habits, which were not in the original write-up. I felt every muscle in my body tense up, my fingers clenching the file like they might never open again. I forced myself to take a deep breath. I held it there for a second, then let it go, my body relaxing a little with it. My father's words came to me: *like those rings in the water that those fish make, we make them too and what we do reverberates way beyond what you can ever imagine.* "How much trouble," I asked, "are you going to get in for giving me this?"

"Depends on what you do with it. I don't think he remembers or knows that it even exists at this point. It was so long ago."

I stared at the old large type and the fading ink in the margins until it blurred.

"If it's just for you and your family for a little peace of mind, that's one thing," Monty said. "If you plan on writing up a piece for the local news, that's another."

I looked up at him in the dim light. He reached over and flicked on a switch, and in the sudden brightness, I felt something click inside me, like the slide of a lock opening on a car door. Something let go. My muscles relaxed even more. "There, now we can see." He nodded, pleased with himself, then glanced at my face, which must have had a strange expression. He smiled tentatively. "Look, I wouldn't give it to you if I wasn't prepared for either possibility."

I closed the manila folder and held it in both hands for a long moment. I was tempted to put it in my bag with my other work, take it just in case I needed it to show Sean or something. At the very least, to show Ma.

"Well." Monty looked around the room, "You up for a beer?"

I held out the file. "Here," I said. "You can put it back where it came from."

He didn't grab it. "You don't want it?"

I shook my head. "Seeing it once, that's enough. And you don't need the trouble."

"Really, I don't care about that."

"But I do. Come on, take it." I was still holding it out to him.

"But, you've got a review coming up. You might need it."

"It's not going to go down like that," I said. "It's going to be fine." This coming from a pessimist. I remained holding it out. I would continue this job. I would continue to fight nature. *That was the job I had chosen*. Ultimately, I would always be fighting Oldman Lake, fighting nature, in one way or another, and maybe that was exactly why I began this job in the first place, to insert some control into a harsh and beautiful world. "What's in this"—I dipped my chin to the file and held it up higher—"has been bothering me for more years than you can imagine. But now"—I nodded steadily, with certainty—"now it's time to let it go."

After a quiet moment, the rain steady and rhythmic on the roof, he reached out and grabbed it.

"And you know what it's also time for?"

"That beer?"

"An apology."

Monty furrowed his brow.

"To you." I lifted my chin to him. "I'm sorry for getting so bent out of shape over you and Ford. You're a good officer. Very capable, and I've appreciated your help."

"Thank you." He bowed his head.

"You ready for that beer now?" I said.

"Damn right I am." Monty smiled.

. . .

When I walked out to my car to go meet him, I saw on old beaten-up Ford Taurus sitting in the lot, which I recognized as Leslie's. Then I saw the glow of a cigarette and realized she was sitting alone. I went over and tapped on the window, which she had cracked to let the smoke out. When she saw me, she jumped, then opened the door and stepped out.

"I'm sorry. I didn't mean to startle you."

"It's okay," she said.

"Can I help you?"

"I just came by. I don't know, thought my dad might be here"—she gestured to the building to the dark windows of Joe's office—"but I can see that he's not." She threw the butt of her cigarette on the ground and toed it. "His car's not here either," she added with a wispy voice, like an afterthought.

"You check the house? I don't think he's been in at all since . . ."

"No." She looked down and scuffed the soles of her shoes into the pavement, still grinding the cigarette, then scratched the back of her neck. "I'm not really welcome there. At the house, I mean."

"Well, things are different now. You might be surprised." I let that settle and watched her fidget, shifting her weight from one foot to the other. "Where's Lewis?" I asked.

"At a friend's for the night. Good thing." She shrugged heavily. "Paul and I got into a fight. He said I'm whacked out, that he couldn't handle me, so he left. Said we were over."

I took a deep breath. "I see. Well, I'm sure once he calms down, he'll come back around."

She nervously glanced around the parking lot and wrapped her arms around her chest like a straitjacket. I thought of Heather hugging herself in the interrogation room and her father doing the same on the bench in Missoula. "How long have you been sitting here?" I gestured to the parking lot. It was dark now and only illuminated by the outside lights from headquarters. The lot we were in was next to the woods where the bear's cage was hidden by black trees—maybe a hundred yards away. I couldn't see it from where we stood.

"I don't know. A bit. It's, it's"—her large, dark eyes had a faraway look in them—"it's hard to be home right now without anyone there." She shuffled and began twisting her hair and looking around again, anything to avoid eye contact.

I didn't respond.

"What's, what's going to happen to my sister?"

"I'm not sure. Hopefully she'll get a mitigated sentence if not completely released."

"She'll have to go to jail?"

I nodded. "At least for a little while in the beginning, before her trial."

"No matter what?"

"Most likely." I didn't want to get into the details, that Heather could be bailed out and would end up spending seven or eight nerve-racking months before her sentencing, which probably could be mitigated from twenty, the federal guidelines under the felony murder rule stating that if you commit a felony like kidnapping or robbing a bank and accidentally kill someone in the process, it's still murder. "Like I said, she has a really good attorney."

Leslie's eyes filled with tears. She pulled out her pack of cigarettes, and her hand shook noticeably when she tried to pull one out. When she got it, she instantly dropped it. I leaned down to get it for her and handed it back. She tried to light it, but her hands quivered so badly she couldn't manage.

"Here," I offered. "Let me hold that." She placed the cigarette between her lips. I held the flame to it, then handed the lighter back to her.

"Well, I better go." She glanced at her car.

"Leslie." I reached out and put my hand on her elbow. I try not to make a habit of physically touching people that I've come across during investigations, but she looked so frail and lost—like she might fade away—and that if I just made contact, I might ground her at least momentarily while her sister was no longer around to do that for her. It seemed like a very small thing I could do for Joe and Heather.

She turned, still dazed, and met my eyes.

"I can give you the name of someone who can help with this sort of a loss. I mean, it's not death, but it is certainly a significant trauma."

She shrugged and tilted her head to the side and tried a small smile, but it fell away as quickly as it came, just as her sister's had. Both fragile smiles would later mesh into one and forever stay with me. She looked at the building her father worked in, then back at me. I gave a warm squeeze to her slight elbow and let go. She looked at the pavement, then got in her car and left. I watched her drive away, her red taillights disappearing as she rounded the corner.

24

SOME MIGHT CALL it closure. In fact, I'm sure my Missoula therapist might have called it that. But I tend to think of it as a type of conquering instead. Besides, I can't really bring myself to think that such a thing as closure exists, as if there's some button that you can push that will simply box and wrap trauma up and tuck it neatly away. Trust me, if there was, I'm sure I would have pushed it by now.

In fact, I don't know what to do with memories like mine. It feels wrong to forget, although there are certainly spans of time in which I try hard to do just that. Unfortunately, that kind of closure wasn't going to come my way, so I tried the trick performed in the movies: visiting the place. And that's where conquering comes to mind. Going back to Oldman Lake after all this time was an attempt to triumph over jumbled-up fears more than to reassemble memories so they could reside in a more peaceful place. I now knew I owed that much to myself—to the boy with the young hands.

Monty, believe it or not, said he'd go with me, which pleased me. And even though in the movies, it seems like a prerequisite that the protagonist goes it alone to the spot where the personal trauma occurred, there was no way in hell I was hiking by myself in bear country to Oldman Lake in the fall, or any season for that matter.

On a cloudy morning, two days before I was scheduled to leave for Denver (which I had stretched out as long as I could in order to stall getting back to undergo my psych evaluation), we packed all the necessities and headed out before sunrise and drove over to the Two

Medicine campsite, where I had been just days before. By the time we got there, the sky hung low and dark with a light drizzle, the aspen trees stood skeletal white without their leaves, and the peaks, although disappearing into the fog, hovered ominously around the lake. We hiked the six and a half miles, around the end of Two Medicine, over a ridge, through a valley where we crossed numerous dried-up stream-beds, and on and upward. I couldn't have pointed out the spot where the hikers found me unconscious if I had to, although Monty did ask for me to.

Monty and I barely spoke. He knew to be quiet and to let me have some space and honestly, it took every ounce of strength to keep putting one foot in front of the other and not turn back. I insisted on taking the lead. He had offered, but I knew with Monty behind me, he'd be the lo-comotive in my head, pushing me onward. If nothing else, it would have been too big of a knock to my ego to quit with him following me.

When we reached the higher elevation, we had to trudge through snow on the trail. Maybe it was my nerves, but I tired easily. As we got closer, I felt edgy enough to pause and take notice of the ghostly trees. *Yep, they're dead whitebark pines.*

"Everything okay?" Monty asked.

"Yeah, I'm good."

"Tired?"

"No, I'm good." I got my water out and took a sip.

"It's just a little farther."

I wiped my mouth and held out my hand for Monty to go ahead. He stepped in front of me without any comments, slogging forward on the wet snow. Patches of white surrounded us on the forest floor and the smell of wet pine filled my nose. We walked another quarter of a mile, came over a knoll, and there it was.

Its waters were as I remembered, a deep green, maybe a little grayer now in the dim light, but its size larger than I recalled. Its shape like a large teardrop, it sat in a basin, hemmed in by stunted pines and the tall snow-covered ridges leading up to Dawson and Ptimakan Passes. The shoreline was white from snow, and I was fairly relieved to know that it was too chilly for us to stay long. We had been hiking through intermittent drizzle—not cold enough for snow, but the air still felt raw, as if the rain could turn to sleet at any moment.

Monty and I found a log to sit on, had some snacks, and I appreciated the fact that he didn't keep glancing at me or checking me out for my reaction to the place. He treated it like any other hike, wiping the sweat off the back of his neck with a blue cowboy bandana he'd brought. He dug around in his pack for snacks and after he ate, tried to skip small, flat rocks over the dark water.

After a while, he announced, "I'm going to walk over there to explore. Just around a bit."

I nodded, a piece of apple in my mouth. I knew what he was doing—giving me space to contemplate. I sat and looked around at the trees surrounding me and saw the narrow trail, like a crooked scar, leading toward the campsite. I grabbed my pack, made sure my spray was on my belt loop, and slowly took the path.

There were only a few spaces for the backcountry permit camping, and I remembered clear-as-day which space we'd picked. *This one here, Dad. See, hardly any rocks and not too sloped.*

Good with me, he answered. *We'll set up the tent; then we'll make a fire. But first,* he said with the same smile he had when we saw the moose at Therriault Lake. *Let's sit down and just take it all in.*

I had rolled my eyes. Told him, *Uh, no, thanks*, in that too-cool way, *I'll just get started on the tent*. I began taking it out of the bag.

Suit yourself. He shrugged and got comfortable on the rock, twirled his mustache, and made a show of taking in the mountain air just to bug me. We both laughed.

I could see his smile now.

I spotted the boulder where he had sat looking out over the lake and up at the high ridge. I went and sat on it and did just as he said:

took it all in. Two small rings formed in the water from rising fish and slowly expanded. The trees were more numerous than I remembered, and I didn't know if that was a function of time or a faulty memory. I couldn't figure out where the bear had taken him, to which spot. The campsite seemed more closed in than I recalled, and I had to remind myself that grizzlies aren't really worried about small, stunted pine trees in their way when they barrel through an area.

I sat still, felt the cold air on my nose. I listened to the water, ever so faintly lapping on the pebbled shore, and spotted some small dark moving objects, which I figured were ducks splashing around on the opposite side of the lake. They moved in the shadows below the steep ridge to the north, which halfway down had a fringe of fluffy mist hanging stagnantly at its base like the trim at the bottom of Santa's hat.

I wasn't going to open the memory vault very far. Not now. It would be too much to let it all come flooding back while visiting the actual place. Instead, I breathed more calmly than I expected, felt the solid rock under the soles of my damp boots, and closed my eyes and pictured the bear in his cage, pent-up angst surrounding him and myself. I breathed deeply, focusing on keeping it slow and rhythmic, and pictured him finding his den. Truly, I was glad he was free.

After sitting for some time, only the one harrowing memory flashed out of nowhere at me again, the one that surprised me the most after being at Two Medicine Lake: *Give me your knife, Ted. Give me your knife.* I closed the door as quickly and fiercely as I could to that recollection—shut my eyes for a moment. There may have been something about a knife that had fueled my unease all these years, but with a calm certainty, I knew there was no candy bar, and I knew there was nothing my young hands or my father's adult hands could have done to change the outcome. When I opened my eyes, the place looked the same—as desolate and as raw as ever—and it had started to rain again. I put up my hood and listened to the drops make percussion sounds against the sides of the material.

No, I don't know what to do with memories like mine.

As much as I'd like to say it was peaceful, I can't say it was. I'll just say this: there are places so wild the ominous, natural cycle vibrates around you and you stand in awe of its lack of good or evil, its neutrality in spite of its unpredictability. Then there are certain human environments where people actually choose to be destructive and in some ways, it seems so much worse because of that choice.

I know I've told you several times that I'm not superstitious, but during my time in Glacier, I had secretly harbored the idea that there are places where events so terrible happen something in the fabric of the place alters. Perhaps just the atoms bounce off one another in an altered pattern, or maybe the event brands itself into the ether or the atmosphere in some mysterious way—like a red-hot iron on rawhide—so someone attuned to such vibrations will forever feel it upon entering. Perhaps it was just my solipsism making me think such foolish thoughts and really, for humans—it's simply a case of external reality matching whatever is going on internally. If you asked Monty, he might say something different about the place. But as sure as the quarter in my pocket (and I double-checked before we left to make sure it was there), in spite of my notions and superstitions, I was wrong. The place never changed after the night my father was lost to the wild. It just *is* as it *was*, as it will remain.

With the unforgiving and beautiful scenery surrounding me in close juxtaposition to Victor Lance's case, I realized that my father's fate was not at the hands of some evil nature god or some possessed grizzly bear. And nature certainly was not subject to my notions of justice. Out here, it was suddenly crystal clear that my attempt in my job to apply some measure of control to the wild was irrelevant. It was only relevant when people were involved because, in fact, the people Monty and I had investigated were much more destructive—by choice—than any grizzly simply surviving, even an erratic one. I felt relieved that the bear was loose now, not only because he seemed to be a metaphor for my need to let the bear inside of me go, as my Missoula therapist said years ago, but because the thought of someone like Tom Hess and Stimpy running free while the bear had been destroyed in the name of locking Heather up was too disturbing. At least, he was out where he belonged.

I took one more deep breath and looked for Monty. "You ready to go?" I yelled, hearing my voice echo. I could see him by the shore on the east side of the lake about fifty yards from me.

"Sure am," he called back over the water. "Man, as much as I love Glacier, this place is giving me the creeps." His fading echo, *eeps, eeps, eeps,* rang through the basin.

I smiled, grabbed my pack, and slung it over my shoulder to go meet him to make our way back. I looked at the campsite one more time and thought, *Let go of the grizzly.* I nodded to myself with satisfaction and turned to go, but before I started down the path, I checked—made sure of it once again for good measure—that my quarter was in my pocket.

ACKNOWLEDGMENTS

I DON'T KNOW A writer who doesn't understand that writing is a mixed bag of conflicting emotions: excitement, joy, pain, frustration, insecurity, euphoria . . . the list goes on. It's no different for me, and without the support of those around me, writing would be a much more difficult task. I owe heartfelt thanks to my family: my husband, Jamie, for his unwavering support and belief I could get the first novel published; to my father and mother, Robert and Jeanine Schimpff, for a life's worth of support; to my brothers, Eric and Clifford Schimpff, for their encouragement; to my stepdaughters, Caroline and Lexie, with their boundless energy and smiles; and to my son, Mathew, who, with big eyes, has asked me since he was four (he's a teen now and doesn't call me *Mommy* anymore), "Mommy, when are you going to publish one of those books you wrote?"

I am grateful beyond words to my agent, Nancy Yost, whose grace and professional savvy never fail to amaze me. And to the entire team at Atria, especially my editor, Sarah Durand, whose editorial instincts are spot-on; Sarah Branham, for her high level of expertise and generous help; assistants Daniella Wexler and Anne Badman; copy editor Toby Yuen; production editor Isolde Sauer; art director Jeanne Lee; and the sales, marketing, and publicity experts as well. It's been an amazing journey for me to witness such skill and dedication from all these talented people in making a beautiful book. I am also grateful to Lou Aronica for his help and advice early on. I owe special thanks for guidance on law enforcement matters to Frank Garner and Bill Dial and to those who I interviewed about Glacier National Park: Michael Jamison, Chuck Cameron, and Gary Moses.

As for my mentors, fellow writers, and draft readers: thank you, Dennis Foley, Kathy Dunnehoff, Leslie Budewitz, Marian Ellison, Barbara DuLac, Janie Fontaine. Thank you, Roxanne McHenry, for all the great ebook information and advice, and thank you to all the wonderful ladies of the Montana Women Writers group. Thank you also to the many booksellers and reps who work hard to bring these books to the shelves.

And last, but definitely not least, my brilliant friend, Suzanne Siegel, deserves more than I am able to ever express for her writing advice, limitless research assistance, infinite support, encouragement, wisdom, and tremendous friendship. I am certain that I would have been unable to come this far if it were not for her support.

I took many liberties with this story. Park Police officers are more present in urban national parks than in Glacier Park. Commissioned rangers handle most law enforcement issues in Glacier. In many places, where the story seemed to need it, I've taken liberties with facts (for example, the bear being caged in a compound near Glacier National Park headquarters is unlikely). Any mention of made-up businesses that resemble local businesses, actual businesses, or real landmarks is only done in an attempt to gain verisimilitude, and of course, all errors, deliberate or by mistake, are wholly mine.